A PLACE CALLED HOME

Born out of wedlock when her mother was only fourteen, Lucy Pocket has spent all her life with her disreputable grandmother, Eva. They are always in debt and resorting to theft in order to exist. Until her wealthy paternal grandfather buys her from Eva, determined to bring Lucy up to be a lady. When her grandfather dies, his despicable nephew cheats Lucy out of her inheritance, except for a run-down lodging house in Whitechapel, forcing Lucy to look after his three illegitimate children. Lucy is determined to make a life for herself, to search for her long-lost grandmother, creating the family she has always longed for.

A PLACE CALLED HOME

A PLACE CALLED HOME

by

Dilly Court

Magna Large Print Books
Long Preston, North Yorkshire,
BD23 4ND, England.

British Library Cataloguing in Publication Data.

Court, Dilly
A place called home.

A catalogue record of this book is available from the British Library

ISBN 978-0-7505-4165-7

First published in Great Britain in 2014 by Century

Published in Large Print 2015 by arrangement with Random House Group

Magna Large Print is an imprint of Library Magna Books Ltd.

Printed and bound in Great Britain by T.J. (International) Ltd., Cornwall, PL28 8RW

For my youngest grandson, Peter, who loves dinosaurs, and for the newest member of the family in New Zealand, Ashton Charles

Chapter One

Aldgate, London, 1861

The strange gentleman was there again, sitting in a brougham drawn by a sleek black gelding. The coachman sat as still as a dummy in a shop window, with his caped greatcoat pulled up to his chin and a striped woollen muffler covering the lower part of his face. He stared straight ahead, neither looking to left nor right.

Lucy Pocket shot a sideways glance at the man in the carriage, and was met with an unblinking stare. He had been in the same spot yesterday, and the day before. His eyes were a piercing blue, set wide apart beneath satanic-looking black brows, and he was clean-shaven, but his hair was long, reaching his shoulders in curls that gleamed like silver. She looked away quickly. There was a coat of arms in the lozenge on the carriage door, but heraldry was as unfamiliar to her as the languages spoken by foreign sailors from the ships that arrived daily at St Katharine docks. The man was obviously a toff, but the business which brought him to such a rough area as Nightingale Lane was anyone's guess. The romantic name of the road belied the fact that it was, and always had been, an area where the police worked in pairs, and ordinary people walked in fear.

Lucy quickened her pace, concealing the bundle

she carried beneath her ragged shawl as she headed towards Cat's Hole buildings, where she and her grandmother had been living for the past six months. They never stayed anywhere for long: they had to keep moving, but they had so far managed to steer clear of the law and the gangs who demanded protection money.

She sidled along the high brick wall which separated St Katharine docks from the London dock, glancing over her shoulder to make sure she was not being followed, but the carriage had gone, vanishing into thin air, or so it seemed. She tightened her grip on the bundle she concealed beneath her shawl and hurried on until she reached Burr Street and Cat's Hole, an aptly named building pinched between a tobacco warehouse and the King George pub. She was jostled by a large woman wearing a cloth cap, with a clay pipe firmly gripped between her teeth. 'Look where you're going, you stupid little cow.' The woman, who reeked of jigger gin, thrust open the pub door and a gust of warm air laden with tobacco smoke and the smell of unwashed bodies, stale beer and pickled onions slapped Lucy in the face. The noxious odours in the street were little better; the stench of the mud on the riverbank and night soil waiting for collection almost completely overpowered the rich aroma of molasses, tobacco and roasting coffee beans exuded in belches of steam from the manufactories and warehouses. Lucy sidestepped a soot-encrusted chimney sweep whose head was bent beneath the weight of his brush-filled sack as he cannoned along the road. She let herself into the building and closed the door.

The passageway was narrow, damp and dark. A shaft of light from a window at the top of the stairs helped her find her way to the first floor, and the back room where she laid her head at night. Ten feet square and bare of anything other than an iron bedstead, a deal table and two wooden chairs, it could not even with a stretch of imagination be called a home. Lucy tossed her bundle onto the table and looked round, playing the game: in her mind's eye she saw a comfortable living room furnished with chintz-covered armchairs, an inviting sofa and a rosewood table, on which stood a silver vase filled with red carnations. The clove scent of them filled her nostrils, momentarily blotting out the stink of the outside privy, which was used by all the occupants of Cat's Hole. There were pictures on the walls in her dream home. Sometimes she allowed herself the luxury of examining them individually, and they changed from day to day. On rare occasions, when she was dipping pockets in Trafalgar Square, she allowed herself time to visit the National Gallery and wander through its many halls, gazing at the great masters' works. She crossed the floor, her imaginary new boots barely sinking into the thick pile of the Chinese carpet, and her silk petticoats swishing beneath her merino gown. She drew back the wine-red velvet curtains, but the material seemed to dissolve at the touch of her fingers and the dream faded into reality; she was left holding a scrap of moth-eaten cotton. She looked down at her shabby boots, which were a size too small. The uppers had come away from the soles exposing her bare toes, and the heels were worn down to almost nothing. She lifted her skirt to reveal a red flannel petticoat that hung limp and mud-stained, ending well above her ankles, and she sighed.

'What's up, Lucy?'

Eva Pocket breezed into the room carrying a wicker basket which she placed on the table. She eyed her granddaughter with her head on one side. 'You was playing the game again, wasn't you?'

Lucy nodded, and her bottom lip trembled. 'Sorry, Granny. I know it's silly, but I can't help it.'

'Come here, my duck.' Eva held her arms outstretched and Lucy walked into her warm embrace. Cuddled up against Granny's generous bosom she felt like a child again, although at the age of ten, very nearly eleven, she considered herself to be a young woman. She had worked the streets since she was six and could sell matches or bootlaces with the best of them. She had toiled in a laundry and she had scrubbed floors, washed dishes and done all manner of jobs. She had even set herself up as a shoeshine, working outside Bishopsgate station, but she had been seen off by a group of boys who were plying the same trade. She was a grown-up now and able to take care of herself, but Granny's hugs were always welcome.

Eva released her, giving her a searching look. Nothing missed Granny's sharp eyes. 'Come on, love. Out with it.'

Lucy took off her shawl and laid it over the back of a chair. 'He was there again, Granny. That strange man was watching me, I'm sure of it.'

Eva discarded her faded blue bonnet and tossed her head so that her mass of curls floated about her pointed face like a cloud of spun gold. At forty-two she was still a handsome woman; not exactly beautiful, but her large, almond-shaped eyes brimmed with intelligence and their unusual shade of blue-green seemed to change with her mood. People said that Lucy looked just like her grandmother, but she could not see it herself. Eva turned away, unbuttoning her mantle. 'I'm sure it's just a coincidence, poppet. Maybe he's looking for someone, but it's not likely to be you or me. What would a gent want with a pair of guttersnipes like us?' Her merry laugh made the room seem bright and sunny and she spun round to tweak Lucy's curls, so like her own.

'Maybe he's looking for Ma,' Lucy murmured.

'Well he won't find that one here, now will he? Christelle is goodness knows where, singing her heart out and hoping to become the next star of the Paris Opera.'

'Is she very beautiful, Granny? I can't remember what she looks like.'

'You were only two when she took off with her fancy man, darling. She is a beauty, there's no two ways about it, and she has a lovely voice, but she has no sense when it comes to blokes. She never did, or you wouldn't have come into the world when she was only fourteen.'

'I won't let that happen to me,' Lucy said firmly. 'I'm going to make something of myself.'

'Of course you will, love.' Eva smiled and sat down at the table. 'I walked miles today and my dogs are barking. Anyway, that's my problem. How did you do?'

Lucy unwrapped her bundle. 'A few silk hankies and a wallet, but there's no money in it, Granny – just a few letters and some visiting cards.'

Eva examined it carefully. 'Peccary leather. This must have been expensive. Where did you get it?'

'A gent came out of a shop in Burlington Arcade and it fell out of his pocket.'

'Fell out?' Eva raised a delicate winged eyebrow.

'It did, honest. I wouldn't have the nerve to take it. Dipping for silk hankies is one thing, but lifting wallets is beyond me.'

'You could have given it back to him,' Eva said, frowning. 'He might have offered you a reward.'

'And he might have accused me of taking money from it, even though it was empty.'

Eva stared at the hankies with a practised eye. 'There's a couple of bob to be had for those, although old Pinch is getting meaner by the day, and more particular in what he's prepared to take.' She opened the wallet and took out a deckle-edged visiting card. 'I don't believe it. This belongs to Linus Daubenay, Esquire.'

'Do you know him, Granny?'

'He used to be one of the mashers who hung around the stage door when your ma was in the chorus. She was only thirteen, but she looked older, especially with all that greasepaint on her face.'

'Was he my father?' Lucy clasped her hand to her chest in an attempt to still her racing heart.

'My Christelle wouldn't have anything to do

with a man like that. She was flighty but she wasn't daft.'

'One day I'll find my dad, and then I'll know who I really am.'

'Sweetheart, you know who you are.' Eva reached out to clasp Lucy's hand. 'You're the best girl in the world.'

'But you won't talk about him. You must have known him, Granny.'

Eva frowned. 'He was a toff, that's all I'll say. He walked out one day, leaving my girl all alone in Peckham Rye, and you only a few weeks old.'

'Why did he go away? What happened to him?'

'He was killed in a duel, that's all I know. But he broke my girl's heart and set her on the path to ruin. I just wish I could have given you a better start in life.'

'You've given me everything, and I love you.' Lucy slipped her arm around her grandmother's shoulders.

Eva patted her hand. 'And I love you, sweetheart. But let's be practical: we need money and I had a bad day. I knocked on so many doors looking for any sort of work that my knuckles are raw.' She scanned Lucy's face, shaking her head. 'It's time we thought of a better way to earn our bread, and one that's on the right side of the law for a change.'

'You're tired and hungry, Granny.' Lucy bundled up the hankies. 'I'll take these to old Pinch, and I won't allow him to fob me off with a few pence.'

Eva turned her attention to the wallet, taking out folded slips of paper and opening them. Her expression brightened. 'You said there wasn't any money, but these are like cash in the bank.'

'I don't understand. What are they?'

'These are IOUs made out to Daubenay, and he's owed close to three hundred pounds.' She held up the slips of paper with a triumphant smile. 'Returning these to their rightful owner should entitle you to a generous reward.'

'Do you really think so?'

'I do indeed.'

'I'll go now, and I won't take no for an answer.'

'It'll be dark in an hour and I don't want you wandering the streets on your own. Take the wipes to old Pinch and get what you can and then we can eat. Tomorrow morning we'll go to Half Moon Street together.'

Next morning, Eva donned her widow's weeds complete with a heavily veiled bonnet. The fact that she was not a widow and had never been married did not deter her from wearing the outfit in order to gain sympathy from prospective employers, or from the unsuspecting public when circumstances forced her to beg for a few pennies in order to eat. Lucy had nothing to wear other than the frock she had on and it was quite unsuitable for the changeable April weather. The shawl she wrapped around her shoulders was lacy with moth holes, but her grandmother convinced her that this was all to the good.

'Demand to see Mr Daubenay in person,' Eva whispered as Lucy was about to knock on the door of the elegant Georgian terraced house in Half Moon Street. 'Don't be fobbed off by a servant. You'll do better without me, so I'll keep out of the way but I'm here if you need me.' She moved out of sight as a maid opened the door.

'No hawkers or traders and no didicois.' The girl was about to slam the door but Lucy leapt forward, leaning against it with all her might. There was a momentary trial of strength with both of them pushing, but Lucy had hunger and determination on her side and eventually the maid gave in. 'What is it you want?'

'I got something for Mr Daubenay and I must see him.'

'He's not at home.'

Eva stepped out of the shadows. 'Tell Mr Daubenay that we have something of vital importance to him.'

The maid stared at Eva's mourning clothes and her expression changed subtly. 'I'll go and see if he's in.' She closed the door.

'She'll be back,' Eva said smugly when Lucy turned to her with an anguished look. 'Our Mr Daubenay lives dangerously. He's a gambler and a womaniser.' She retreated as the door opened once again.

'He'll see you,' the maid said haughtily. 'Wipe your feet on the mat and follow me.' She glanced over her shoulder. 'And I got eyes in the back of my head, so don't swipe nothing on the way.'

Lucy obeyed her instructions without a word and followed her up two flights of carpeted stairs to a wide landing where bowls of potpourri filled the air with their delicate scent. The maid paused, squinting at her in a menacing fashion. 'You'd better not be gulling me, nipper. I got six brothers and five sisters at home and I know when I'm being hoodwinked. This is a respectable rooming house, just bear that in mind.'

'I don't know what you're talking about,' Lucy said primly.

'Street urchins have no place in Half Moon Street. If you try anything on with Mr Daubenay it'll be me what gets it in the neck for letting you in.' She rapped on the door and Lucy heard a faint command to enter. The maid admitted her with a disdainful curl of her lips. 'Remember what I said.'

Lucy marched past her, holding her head high. She had been tempted to answer back, but she was hungry and there was money to be had. She came to a halt, momentarily forgetting her mission as she looked round. It was almost like stepping into her dream, except that the furniture was leather-covered and there was a more masculine feel to the room.

Linus Daubenay stood with his back to a roaring fire. A portrait of him as a young man hung above the mantelshelf, but a life of excess and debauchery had left its mark, He was still handsome, but his face was pale and puffy and his brown eyes were bloodshot and underlined by dark smudges. 'Well?' he demanded. 'What do you want? Be quick, girl. I haven't got all day.'

Lucy bobbed a curtsey. 'You dropped your wallet in Burlington Arcade, guv. I saw it fall but by the time I picked it up you'd gone. I tried to follow you but I got caught up in the crowds and you'd disappeared.'

He held out his hand. 'Give it to me.' He snatched the wallet from her and opened it. 'If I discover anything to be missing…' His voice tailed off as he took out the slips of paper.

Lucy waited nervously while he examined them. 'There weren't no money in it, guv. I had to look inside so that I could return it to the rightful owner.'

'You're right,' he said, stretching his full lips into a smile. 'There were just these scraps of paper – completely worthless. Thank you, girl.' He put his hand in his pocket and took out a silver sixpence. 'Take this for your trouble.'

She shook her head. 'I ain't so green as I'm cabbage-looking, guv. I know what an IOU is, and they're worth more than a tanner.'

'Are you trying to extort money from me?'

'Call it what you like, but I know what their value is to you.'

His eyes narrowed. 'Call it a shilling and think yourself lucky I don't call a constable.'

Lucy looked him in the eye. 'I call that mean.'

'Do I know you?' He stared at her, frowning. 'Your face is familiar.'

'You knew my ma,' Lucy said recklessly. 'You might be me dad for all I know.'

He recoiled as if she had slapped his face. 'That's a preposterous lie. Who put that idea in your head?'

'She was a chorus girl and you was a masher. My granny told me so.'

'I daresay she was no better than she should be. I am not your father and I never met your mother or the woman you call your granny, so take the shilling and be off, unless you want me to have you arrested for picking my pocket.' He thrust the coin into her hand. 'I suspect that you're known to the police. You don't want to be hauled before the magistrate, do you?'

'My ma is called Christelle. You must remember her.'

'What if I do?' His casual tone belied the startled look in his eyes, but he recovered quickly. 'The name sounds familiar, although I can't recall her face any more than I can remember the other wantons who shared my bed. All of them were fully compensated for their favours.'

She knew she had touched a nerve and she pressed home her advantage. 'I'll accept the shilling, but what me and Granny need is work. Honest work with a proper wage.'

He stared at her open-mouthed and then he laughed. 'You were trying to extort money from me a moment ago. Now you want me to employ you and your aged grandmother.'

'Don't let her hear you calling her old. She's blacked a fishwife's eye for less.'

'Why should I help you? Give me a good reason for not turning you in and telling the police that you stole my wallet, which I suspect is the truth.'

'I think you was a bit fond of my ma. Why else would you remember her name?'

'Gentlemen don't consort with chorus girls, at least not on a permanent basis. I've no interest in you or your mother, but you have nerve. I acknowledge that. What's your name?'

'Lucy Pocket.'

'And where do you live, Lucy Pocket?'

'Here and there, guv. At the moment we're in Burr Street, near the Red Lion Brewery.'

'And your mother,' he said casually. 'Do you know where she is at present?'

'No, guv.'

His eyebrows shot together in a frown. 'Then I can't help you.' He took a half-crown from his pocket and tossed it at her. 'That's for your trouble. Now leave my house and don't come back. I don't want to see you again.'

Lucy drew herself up to her full height. 'The feeling's mutual, guv.' She left the room with as much dignity as she could muster.

'What happened in there?' Eva demanded anxiously. 'I was about to knock on the door and demand to know what he'd done with you. I never should have allowed you to do this on your own.' She flung her arms around Lucy and held her close.

'I'm perfectly all right, Granny.' Lucy extricated herself from her grandmother's arms, and taking the coins from her pocket she placed them in Eva's hand. 'Three shillings and sixpence. It ain't much for all the trouble we've gone to, but it's better than nothing.'

Eva tucked the money in the tops of her tightly laced stays. 'Well done, love.'

'He remembered Ma,' Lucy said slowly. 'I asked him if he was me dad, but he denied it.'

'You're a proper caution, Lucy Pocket.' Eva trilled with laughter. 'I've have given anything to see his face.'

'Let's go home, Granny. I don't feel comfortable here.'

'We're just as good as the likes of him,' Eva said,

linking arms. 'We'll treat ourselves to pie and mash and pretend we're rich.'

'The rent's due today, Granny.'

'Don't worry, my duck. I'll charm the rent collector. He'll give us another week's grace. You'll see.'

That night they slept huddled together in a shop doorway, which they had to share with a drunken old woman who wheezed and twitched in her sleep, and a small white mongrel with brown ears and a brown patch over one eye. The animal snuggled up to Lucy and she had not the heart to turn it out into the cold, even though it was mangy and running with fleas.

The rent collector had not been sympathetic. In fact he had demanded the back rent and refused to leave until Eva handed over the change from the money that Linus Daubenay had given Lucy. It was little enough and he had tried to snatch the silver locket that Eva always wore. It contained a lock of Christelle's hair intertwined with one of Lucy's baby curls, and Eva had resisted angrily. She had struck out with uncharacteristic violence and had chased the man along the landing, giving him a shove that sent him tumbling down the stairs. Lucy had held her breath, thinking he might have been killed, but the stream of invective which flowed from his lips indicated that he was alive, unhurt and extremely angry. Shortly afterwards the door of their room had been forced open by two burly men with cudgels, and they were not in the mood to be generous.

Lucy slept fitfully, waking occasionally and shifting position on the cold hard tiles, and every time she moved the dog opened its eyes and wagged its stumpy tail. It was getting light when she was awakened by the animal licking her face, and at first she could not remember where she was, and then it came to her that they were in the doorway of a tobacconist's shop in Upper East Smithfield. She shifted the old woman, who had collapsed against her shoulder and was unnaturally silent. The dog sniffed her and backed out into the street. Lucy touched the frail skin of the wrinkled cheek and felt it cold as ice. She gave her a gentle shake and the body collapsed into a heap. The person who had once lived and breathed now resembled nothing more than a pile of old clothes.

Stifling a cry of distress Lucy struggled to her feet. 'Granny, I think the old woman is dead.'

Chapter Two

Eva opened her eyes and yawned. 'What's the matter?' She looked round with the dazed expression of someone awakened from a deep sleep. Yawning, she stretched and pulled a face. 'Time was when I could sleep on a bed of nails, but not now.'

Lucy dragged her to her feet. 'She's dead, Granny. Stone cold dead.'

Eva was suddenly alert. She leaned over, placing her hand in front of the old woman's mouth and nose. 'She's not breathing and that's a fact.'

The dog whined and cringed, keeping close to Lucy. She bent down to pat its head. 'What should we do? We can't just abandon her here.'

Wide awake now, Eva glanced up and down the street. The traffic at this early hour was light. Men and women ambled with their heads down towards the docks and the warehouses where they worked. 'She's beyond our help,' Eva said, taking off the old woman's bonnet. She held it up, examining it carefully.

'What are you doing?' Lucy cried in horror. 'You can't steal a dead person's things.'

Eva gave her a direct look. 'She's departed this world but we're alive, and I want us to stay that way. She'll go to heaven or hell with or without her bonnet, but this will fetch a few pennies in the Rag Fair.' She unwound the dead woman's shawl. 'It's frayed and dirty but I'll get a penny for it. Take a look at her boots, Lucy. They might fit you.'

Lucy recoiled in horror. 'I'd rather walk barefoot, Granny.'

'Hold these.' Eva thrust the bonnet and shawl into Lucy's hands. She went down on her knees and unlaced the black boots. 'They'll do, but I'll have to get them off quick before she stiffens up.'

Lucy stood back, watching with a mixture of fascination and dismay. 'What are you going to do with her things?'

'Rosemary Lane is the place to unload this stuff. God alone knows why they renamed it Royal Mint Street, but to me it's still Rosemary Lane. Anyway, that's where we'll sell these duds.' She scrambled to her feet, tugging at the woman's red flannel petticoat. 'She won't need this to keep her warm where she's gone, and it'll buy us some breakfast.'

'This is all wrong, Granny,' Lucy protested. 'It's stealing.'

Eva snatched the bonnet and shawl from her and made a bundle of the clothes and boots. She straightened up, patting Lucy on the shoulder. 'If we don't make use of these things someone else will. Come along, don't loiter or we'll be spotted.'

'You can't just leave her here.'

'Walk on, love. I just seen a couple of bobbies on the other side of the road. They'll deal with the poor old soul. There ain't nothing they ain't seen, poor sods; they're always fishing corpses out of the Thames and the like.' She walked on briskly leaving Lucy no alternative but to follow her, with the dog ambling along at her side.

Eva strode on towards Glasshouse Street and within minutes they had reached the Rag Fair. Lucy knew it well as most of the garments she was wearing had been bought from the stalls that lined the street. She caught up with her grandmother and clutched her arm. 'What now?'

'We find a space somewhere. Leave the selling to me and get rid of that smelly cur.'

The dog looked up at Lucy with liquid brown eyes and a tentative wag of his tail. She gave it a reassuring smile, and a silent promise to share her food, if they managed to sell the soiled and shabby garments. Eva seemed to have no such worries and she held up the bonnet, calling out to passers-by to try it on for size. 'A finer and cheaper article of clothing you'll not get today. Threepence is all I'm asking for my dear mother's bonnet.'

A fat woman wearing a man's coat and a leather apron fingered the material. 'Is it silk?'

'Only the best,' Eva assured her.

'You ma wasn't wearing it when she passed on, was she?'

'Certainly not,' Eva said, frowning as if insulted by the question. 'What d'you take me for, missis?'

'Twopence,' the woman said, producing two pennies with a flourish. 'How much d'you want for the boots?'

Within minutes everything was sold. Eva turned to Lucy. 'Take off your petticoat.'

'But Granny, it's the only one I've got.'

'I've found a way to keep us from the gutter, so take it off. I'll take mine off too.' She pulled up her skirt and wriggled out of her calico petticoat. 'This is the way to make money,' she said, holding it up. 'Who'll buy a fine cambric petticoat, embroidered by one of the Queen's dressmakers?'

A gentleman wearing a bowler hat and a mustard yellow waistcoat stopped and stared at the garment. 'Are you sure it was the Queen's dressmaker who did the work?'

'Cross me heart and hope to die, sir.' Eva gave him a bewitching smile and he blinked as if dazzled by a sudden burst of sunlight.

'How much, my dear?'

'A special price to you, sir. Shall we say sixpence?'

He hesitated. 'That seems rather expensive. It is a little grimy.'

'It's nothing that a little lye soap and water

won't put right, sir. I'd say your lady would be delighted to own such an article of clothing.' She batted her eyelashes at him. 'I know I would.'

He dropped a silver sixpence into the outstretched hand. 'I'll take it.' He snatched the petticoat and walked away quickly, as if ashamed to be seen purchasing second-hand garments in the Rag Fair. 'That's not a present for his wife,' Eva said, chuckling. 'That'll be a sop to keep his bit of fluff happy.'

'How do you know that, Granny?'

'Let's just say that I've known a few gents like that one.' She jingled the coins in her pocket. 'We're in business, my pet.'

'But Granny, we haven't got anything left to sell.'

'Leave that to me. First things first.' Eva looked round, sniffing the air, and the dog lifted its head, eyeing her expectantly. 'Fried fish. I can smell it a mile off.'

'Fish, fried fish. Ha'penny fish. Fried fish.' The raucous repetitive sound echoed in Lucy's ear and she turned to see a young woman sashaying amongst the crowds with a tray of smoking hot fish clutched in her mittened hands. Lucy's stomach rumbled and she licked her lips. The dog nuzzled her hand and she stroked its head. 'I ain't forgot my promise, Peckham.'

'Peckham?' Eva turned to her with a startled look. 'What sort of name is that for a dog?'

'Peckham Rye, Granny. That's where you said I was born. It just came to me because he's an orphan too.'

'For one thing, you ain't no orphan, and for

another thing we got enough trouble looking after ourselves let alone a stray animal.'

'He's not very big and I'll share my food with him. Please don't send him away.'

Eva thrust a penny into her hand. 'Get two pieces of fish. I'm not sharing my grub with him.' She scowled at the dog. 'Peckham! Of all the stupid names to call a mangy creature like that.'

Lucy hurried over to the fish seller and handed her the penny. 'Two pieces, please.'

The woman wrapped the fish in newspaper. 'One penny, love.' She peered short-sightedly at Lucy. 'Do I know you, duck?'

'I don't think so, miss.'

'I never forget a face.' She leaned closer, squinting myopically, and reached out to touch Lucy's hair. 'You must be Eva Pocket's girl. You're the spitting image of her.'

'What's keeping you, Lucy?' Eva pushed her way through the milling crowds to join them. She came to a halt, staring at the fish seller in surprise. 'Is that really you, Pearl Sykes? I thought I recognised them dulcet tones.'

'Eva Pocket. I thought you was banged up in the Bridewell, picking oakum.'

'Cheeky mare. I thought you was in one of the dead houses along the riverbank.' Eva kissed Pearl's ruddy cheek and ruffled her already tousled mop of fiery red curls. 'It's good to see you, love.'

'And you, Eva.' Pearl grinned at Lucy. 'Your ma is a proper caution. We had some good times in the past, didn't we, Eva?'

'We certainly did.' Eva put her arm around

Lucy's shoulders. 'But this is my granddaughter, Lucy.'

Pearl's jaw dropped and her eyes widened in surprise. 'No! I thought this nipper must be Christelle.'

'You're a bit behind the times, my duck. Christelle is a woman now, but we don't see nothing of her,' Eva said grimly. 'Lucy's ma took off years ago with a bloke who promised to make her famous. For all I know she's singing in opera houses abroad or touring the music halls.'

'A penny, you said.' Lucy offered the coin, hoping to distract their attention from the painful subject of the mother she could not remember.

'I wouldn't dream of taking money off an old friend.' Pearl put two fingers in her mouth and whistled. 'Oy, Carlos. Take me tray, will you, love? There's only a couple of pieces left to sell.'

A mustachioed man dressed in the costume of a lion tamer strode towards them, hands outstretched. The billboards he was wearing bobbed up and down with each stride. 'I will buy them, querida mia. I am famished.' He snatched the fish with both hands and took a bite. 'Come to Astley's Amphitheatre tonight,' he bellowed with his mouth full. He swallowed and his eyes bulged. 'I got a bone stuck in my throat.' He coughed and spluttered as Pearl slapped him on the billboard. The noise attracted a crowd of curious onlookers. Carlos clutched his throat and dropped the remains of the fish, which was immediately pounced upon by Peckham.

'He's choking to death,' Pearl cried, looking round in desperation. 'Somebody help.'

Eva snatched a bread roll off the tray balanced on the head of a passing baker's boy. He protested loudly, demanding to be paid, but she ignored him and broke off a chunk, stuffing it in Carlos's open mouth. 'Chew and swallow,' she commanded.

By this time his face resembled a boiled beetroot and his eyes were watering. Lucy ran to a barrow where a vendor was selling ginger beer. She thrust a coin in his hand and ran back to Carlos with a brimming mug, spilling some of it in her haste. Eva forced another lump of bread into his mouth with instructions to 'Stop complaining and get on with it.' Carlos gulped and swallowed and the onlookers watched with growing interest. He coughed and spluttered and then a smile wreathed his face. He sighed with relief. 'I think it has gone.'

Lucy held the cup to his lips. 'This might help, mister.'

The crowd drifted off and Carlos drank the liquid in long thirsty gulps. 'Thank you,' he murmured hoarsely. 'I buy you a drink in the pub, ladies.'

'Now you're talking,' Pearl said, cuffing him gently round the ear. 'You scared us half to death, you silly old sod.'

He shrugged and returned the cup to the barrow. 'I lost me voice, so it needs lubricating with something stronger than that stuff.'

'Here, you can't make remarks like that.' The vendor glared at him beneath lowered eyebrows. 'I could sue you for libel, mate.'

Carlos walked off with a wave of his hand and

the billboards clanking against his thighs. 'Come, ladies. I am buying.' He glanced over his shoulder and winked at Pearl. 'The first drink only.'

Pearl grabbed Eva by the arm. 'C'mon, love. We got a lot of catching up to do.'

'Maybe later,' Eva said reluctantly. 'I got Lucy to think of, and we need to find lodgings. I can't face another night sleeping rough.'

'Just the one, Eva. For old times' sake.' Pearl started off after Carlos. 'The kid can wait outside.'

'We ought to be looking for a room, Granny,' Lucy said urgently.

Eva hesitated, looking from one to the other. She glanced down at Peckham, who was licking his lips and eyeing the parcel of rapidly cooling fish clutched in Lucy's hand. 'I'll have one drink and then I'll come,' she said hastily. 'You can wait outside and eat your dinner. Save a bit for me.' She allowed Pearl to march her off along the street. Lucy followed them with Peckham walking obediently to heel.

Smoky air billowed out of the pub as the doors opened to expel a drunken man and woman who staggered off crabwise along the street, leaning on each other and singing at the tops of their voices.

'Wait here and don't speak to no one,' Eva said sternly. 'I won't be long.'

Carlos unbuckled the billboards and propped them up against the wall. 'Look after these, querida,' he said, patting Lucy on the cheek. He leaned over, lowering his voice in a confidential whisper. 'I used to travel with Pablo Fanque's circus. I was one of the expert riders in his equestrian troupe, and I was almost as famous as Pablo himself, until a fall put paid to my career. Now, as you see, I am reduced to this.' He patted the billboards with a hearty sigh.

'Never mind the chit-chat,' Pearl said, grabbing him by the hand. 'We're wasting drinking time.'

They disappeared into the dark and noisy interior of the pub and the doors swung shut, leaving Lucy to guard the billboards and wait. Peckham nuzzled her hand and she stroked his head. 'You and me should stick together, cully.'

He wagged his tail and settled down at her feet. She ate her fish, throwing scraps for the dog to catch, which he did with amazing agility, gobbling them up with obvious enjoyment.

It was almost an hour before Eva emerged, bright-eyed and more cheerful than Lucy had seen her for some time. There was no sign of Pearl or Carlos. 'They've met up with some cronies,' Eva said airily. 'But Pearl's given me the address of her lodgings in Hairbrine Court. She said to mention her name to the landlady and we'd get a room with no trouble at all.'

'Is it far from here, Granny?'

Eva ruffled Lucy's curls with an affectionate smile. 'Not far, darling. Are you tired?'

'A little bit.'

'We'll go there right away and then I'll see about finding some duds to sell on the market tomorrow. It seems like an easy way to earn a few coppers, and I was never happy about you having to dip pockets for a living. That ain't the proper way to bring up a child.'

‘I’m nearly eleven, Granny. I’m almost a woman.’

‘So you are, but that makes it even more important for me to keep an eye on you. If I’d been stricter with your ma things might have turned out different.’ She grinned. ‘But then you come along and that was a blessing in disguise. You brought me a pocketful of love, as I always say.’ She chuckled and slipped her arm around Lucy’s shoulders. ‘Let’s go and find this lodging house.’

Hairbrine Court was a narrow canyon of near darkness, and even when the sun shone its rays barely reached the ground. Cheap lodging houses and semi-derelict workshops huddled so close together that it would have been possible to lean out of an upstairs window and shake hands with the person living opposite. Strings of washing festooned the street, hanging sooty and limp in air which was thick with the smell of overflowing privies and the sulphurous smoke from coal fires and factory chimneys. Ragged people moved in and out of the shadows like spectres from a nightmare world, and barefoot children scavenged in the gutters, vying with feral dogs and cats for scraps of rotting food. Lucy’s heart sank. It was worse than Cat’s Hole, and even Peckham seemed to have lost some of his exuberance. He hung back, hiding in the folds of Lucy’s skirts as Eva knocked on the door of number eight. They had to wait for several minutes before a woman opened it just wide enough to peer at them. ‘What d’ya want?’

Lucy took an involuntary step backwards. The

woman's voice was harsh, like the cackle of a witch, and her appearance did nothing to dispel that image. Her features were lean and mean and her calculating look seemed to strip them to the bone, totting up their worth inch by inch and ounce by ounce.

'My friend Pearl Sykes lodges with you, ma'am,' Eva said boldly. 'She said you might have a room vacant.'

'Who wants it?'

'I'm Mrs Pocket, a respectable widow working in the rag trade with my granddaughter Lucy. We're looking for lodgings close to Rosemary Lane.'

'Let's see the colour of your money. It's two bob a week for the room.' She glanced over Eva's shoulder. 'No dogs.'

Lucy was about to protest but Eva silenced her with a single look. 'I'd like to see it first, if you please.'

'Take it or leave it. I got plenty of people queuing up for my rooms. They're the best in Hairbrine Court. You won't get no better.'

Eva hesitated for a moment before putting her hand in her pocket. 'One week's rent in advance.'

The door opened wide and the woman beckoned them with a bony finger. 'Follow me. And definitely no dogs.'

Lucy followed with the greatest reluctance, leaving Peckham sitting disconsolately on the front step. The entrance hall was long and narrow, and even in the dim light she could see that the plaster was flaking off the walls, and the floorboards were worn and uneven. The smell inside was even worse than that in the street and it did not improve as they mounted the stairs, climbing to the top floor. Beneath the eaves the attic room was cold and draughty. Cobwebs festooned the ceiling and draped the tiny dormer window like ragged lace curtains.

'There's no fireplace,' Eva said crossly. 'How are we expected to boil a kettle?'

'You don't. That's the short answer.' The landlady stood arms akimbo, glaring at them. 'Take it or leave it. I got a–'

'A queue of people waiting to take the room,' Eva said, finishing the sentence for her with a curl of her lip. 'I didn't see them waiting outside, missis. This room ain't worth two bob a week, not without a fireplace and a decent bed.'

The landlady pointed to a couple of palliasses with the straw poking out through holes in the ticking. 'I never had no complaints afore, you stuck-up cow.'

'Watch your tongue,' Eva said coolly. 'I don't take lip from no one, missis whatever your name is.'

'It's Mrs Wicks. Are you taking the room or not?'

'What d'you think, Lucy?' Eva asked anxiously. 'Shall we give it a try?'

'I suppose it's better than sleeping rough,' Lucy whispered.

'I should damn well say it is.' Mrs Wicks slipped the coins into the pocket of her grubby apron. 'I'll take that as a yes, shall I?'

'Just for a week,' Eva said firmly. 'I don't want to disappoint Pearl.'

'Suit yourself. The privy is in the back yard and so is the pump. Hire of a towel is one penny. Doors locked at ten thirty prompt. No admittance afterwards and no gentlemen callers.' Mrs Wicks slammed out of the room.

'I've been in worse places,' Eva said with forced cheerfulness. 'It's not too bad and there's a pie shop on the corner. We'll be all right for supper tonight.'

'What about the dog? I can't leave him outside in the cold.'

'That one knows how to look after himself. He latched on to you with your big soft heart, didn't he?' Eva gave her a quick hug. 'I'm going out to find some goods to sell in the morning. You stay here and try to make it a bit more homely.'

'Can't I come with you? I don't like it here.'

'Not this time, duck.' Eva tugged playfully at one of Lucy's curls. 'I'm going to pay a visit to an old friend of mine. He's in the second-hand clothing business, in a manner of speaking. He'll give me a good deal.' She waltzed out of the room, closing the door behind her.

Lucy stood in the middle of the floor, staring round at the bare expanse of dusty floorboards and the worm-eaten wooden joists that supported the sloping ceiling. She closed her eyes and tried to summon up the will to play the game whereby she could turn the most dismal of lodgings into a palace, but this time she failed miserably. Without the benefit of a fire, and with no cleaning materials to hand, there was little she could do to improve their lot. She examined the palliasses for bed bugs, but they seemed to be reasonably clean and she gave them a good shake before laying them side by side. There were no blankets or pillows but she suspected that this was a deliberate ploy by Mrs Wicks in order to extract more money from her tenants. There was nothing she could do other than sit down and wait for her grandmother's return. Overcome with fatigue, she curled up on one of the palliasses and drifted off to sleep.

She was awakened by the sound of the door opening. The room was in almost complete darkness except for the flickering light of a candle.

'It's only me, love.' Pearl's voice was slurred with drink. 'Where's Eva?'

Lucy scrambled to her feet. 'I dunno, miss. She went out shortly after we arrived. I must have fallen asleep.'

Pearl held the candle higher. 'I can't believe the old trout put you up here.'

'It's not too bad,' Lucy said carefully.

'I may be a bit swipey, and my eyesight ain't what it was, but prisoners in jail get a bed to sleep on and a blanket. Come down to my room and wait for your grandma. I got a bit of a fire going and I'll make you a cup of cocoa.'

Lucy's teeth were chattering and she was chilled to the bone. Looking up, she could see starlight through gaps in the ceiling. 'Ta, Pearl. I'd like that.'

'And I bet you ain't had nothing to eat since that bit of fish.'

'It was very nice.'

'Come with me, nipper. Let's see if there's any bread left. The mice and rats have a habit of helping themselves when I'm not there.' She disappeared through the door, leaving the room in almost complete darkness. Lucy hurried after her; anything was better than being left alone in the eerie silence of the attic.

Pearl's room was on the floor below, and a waft of cheap cologne and cigarette smoke did not disguise the fishy smell that seemed to cling to everything, including Pearl. A coal fire burned in the grate and a kettle bubbled merrily on a trivet balanced over the flames. It was several degrees warmer than the attic and Pearl enjoyed the luxury of an iron bedstead, a table and two chairs. The bed was strewn with clothes and Lucy had to duck beneath a washing line hung with stockings. 'Take a pew,' Pearl said, pointing vaguely to a chair that was barely visible beneath a mass of damp washing. 'I got some cocoa somewhere, and there should be a crust of bread on the shelf, or at least there was this morning.' She ran her hand along the slat of wood nailed to the wall beside her bed. 'The little buggers have had it. Sorry, love, but you can have a hot drink.' She moved to the table and tossed a pile of newspapers on the floor, spilling an overflowing ashtray in her attempt to make a space. 'Can you see a cup anywhere, dear? I can't seem to find one, and there should be a lump of sugar somewhere.' She flopped down on the bed. 'I'm a bit tired. I have to get up at five to get to Billingsgate for the fish.' She leaned back and closed her eyes. 'Make yourself a cup of cocoa, dear. I might just snatch forty winks.' The words had barely left her lips when a loud snore shook her whole body.

Lucy looked round but she could not find a

cup, let alone the cocoa or the elusive packet of sugar. She took the kettle from the trivet and placed it on the hearthstone, making sure that there was nothing which might set the room on fire before she crept out onto the landing. The whole house seemed to be humming with noise. Footsteps on bare floorboards beat out a tattoo; raised voices, screams and cries of small children and babies echoed off the walls. Her first thought was for Peckham. She forgot her hunger and thirst in her concern for the animal who had touched her heart. She crept down the stairs to the entrance hall and opened the front door. Sitting on the step, shivering in the moonlight, the dog leapt to his feet and wagged his tail. She bent down and picked him up. 'You're frozen, you poor thing.' He licked her face and she closed the door carefully so as not to alert the fearsome Mrs Wicks. She carried him upstairs to the attic room and they curled up together on one of the palliasses. His small body was warm despite the fact that he had been locked out in the cold for several hours, and Lucy was comforted by the nearness of a living creature.

Daylight was streaming through the window when she opened her eyes. It took her a moment or two to remember that she was not in the room in Cat's Hole, and when Peckham stirred and yawned she sat up with a guilty start. It was only then that she realised they had been covered with a thick boat cloak and that her grandmother was lying on the palliasse at her side, snoring gently. She too had slept beneath a mound of clothes, all of which were apparently second hand, and smelled accordingly.

Eva stirred and opened her eyes. 'What time is it?'

'I dunno, Granny. The bailiffs took our clock.'

'We got work to do.' Eva raised herself on her elbow, shaking out her halo of guinea-gold curls. 'I could murder a cup of tea.' She reached beneath the palliasse and took out her purse. 'There's a stall on the corner of Brown Bear Alley. Get us something to eat too.'

'We haven't got any cups, Granny.'

'Yes, we have. I thought ahead and bought two tin mugs on my way home last evening.' Eva pointed to a paper bag lying by her bed. 'Your granny thinks of everything.'

'Where did you go last night?' Lucy took the purse, weighing it in her hand. 'You got more money than you had yesterday.'

'Don't ask, dear. Just go out like a good girl and get us something to eat and drink.'

With Peckham at her side, Lucy set off for Brown Bear Alley, and found the coffee stall set up and doing a brisk trade. She handed over the mugs and waited while the man filled them with tea, adding a dash of milk and a generous spoonful of sugar. Her stomach rumbled in anticipation. 'And two ham rolls, please,' she added, eyeing them hungrily. Peckham growled and she looked down at him, but he was standing with his ears cocked and his whole body alert, staring across the street. She followed his gaze and her heart lurched in her chest as she spotted the familiar lozenge and coat of arms on the side of the carriage, and the pale face of the old gentleman gazing out of the window.

Chapter Three

She turned her back on him, concentrating instead on the stall keeper. 'Have you got any scraps for me dog, mister?'

He glanced at Peckham, who seemed to know that he was on show and raised a paw. 'I might have a few scraps,' the man said, scraping bits of ham fat onto a crust of bread. 'Take that, but don't come back for more. I ain't a charity.'

'Ta, mister.' Lucy treated him to a smile. She looked down at the dog. 'Say thank you to the kind gent.'

Peckham obliged with a sharp bark and she tossed the food to him. He fell on it and gobbled it up. Lucy tucked the ham rolls into her pocket and picked up the mugs, but she could not resist a quick glance over her shoulder. The gentleman met her startled gaze with a steady look and she turned away, walking as fast as she could without spilling too much of the hot tea. She dodged into the maze of alleyways, which would be impossible for a carriage and pair to negotiate, but arriving back at the lodging house she could not shake off the feeling that she had been followed. The door was not locked and she let herself in. Peckham looked up at her expectantly and she had not the heart to shut him outside in the cold. She allowed him to follow her up the stairs, hoping that Mrs Wicks was otherwise occupied.

Eva was sitting up in bed, sorting through the pile of clothing. She looked up with a fond smile, holding her hand out for the mug, and gulped down the rapidly cooling tea. 'That was just what I needed, poppet. Your old granny can't take the drink like she used to.'

Lucy squatted on the palliasse. 'Where did you go last night, Granny? Who gave you all this stuff?'

'I told you, love. I got an old friend who can be very generous given the right amount of encouragement.' Eva tossed her head and laughed. 'And it took some persuading, but it was worth it. I got all these duds to sell today. We'll make a killing in Rosemary Lane. Who knows, we might even have enough cash to hire a stall and set up properly.'

Lucy offered her one of the ham rolls. 'You must be hungry. I'm starving.'

'Eat them both if you want,' Eva said, placing the mug on the floor and turning her attention back to the assortment of garments. 'I had a bit of supper with Abe, but the blue ruin was a mistake.'

'Why did you drink it then? And who is Abe?'

'He's just a bloke I've known since I was a girl not much older than you. He's helped me out in the past and he's come up trumps this time, as always.'

'But how did you pay him for all this?'

'Good God, child. Why all the questions? Just think yourself lucky to have a full belly. It doesn't matter how I got them, what's more important is that we sell them and make a fine profit. You won't have to dip pockets no more; I'll see to that.' Eva held her hand to her forehead, wincing. 'My head aches, so don't ask no more questions. Let's see if I got anything that will fit you.'

Lucy sat back, eating her roll and sharing some of it with Peckham, but she was worried nonetheless. Her grandmother rarely drank to excess, and she could only imagine what favours Granny had bestowed on the man she called Abe in order to procure such a wealth of saleable items. Lucy had learned early on that nothing in life was free, especially if you were poor and needy. She had witnessed hurried couplings in dark alleyways when prostitutes made themselves available for the price of a drink, or a meal for their numerous offspring. She had seen women selling their young daughters to men who were old enough and rich enough to know the difference between right and wrong. She knew of little boys who had been apprenticed to sweeps and sent up chimneys to clear the soot, many of them getting stuck and suffocating in the attempt, or at the very least suffering terrible burns and being scarred for life. Children as young as five or six picked over dust heaps, looking for anything that could be salvaged, and others were mudlarks, risking death by drowning on the banks of the River Thames as they searched for lost valuables. She also knew that, but for her grandmother, she might have been one of these; even worse, she might have been consigned to the workhouse.

Seemingly oblivious to everything other than the prospect of making money, Eva gave a cry of delight as she selected a frilly cotton lawn petticoat trimmed with broderie anglaise. 'This will fit you, poppet. Try it on for size.'

Lucy stood up reluctantly. 'You could get good money for that. It's too grand for me.'

'Nonsense, darling. I want you to have something pretty.' Eva tossed it to her. 'Put it on. You deserve to have something special.'

Peckham had been sitting beside Lucy but at that moment he sprang to his feet, growling and staring at the closed door.

'What's the matter with him?' Eva said crossly. 'You shouldn't have encouraged him, Lucy. That old hag will throw us out if she finds him up here.'

Lucy was about to defend her actions, but before she had a chance to argue the door flew open and a man stepped into the room. Her hand flew to her mouth and she uttered a cry of fright. 'It's him, Granny. The strange man in the carriage.'

Eva scrambled to her feet, sending clothes flying in all directions. Her face paled to ashen as she stared at him in disbelief. 'What are you doing here?' she demanded angrily. 'Have you been following my granddaughter?' She wrapped Lucy in a close embrace and the dog cowered at their feet, making low growling sounds deep in his throat.

'She's my granddaughter too.'

Lucy stiffened. 'What did he say, Granny?'

'Leave us alone,' Eva cried angrily. 'Get out of here.'

The gentleman took a step towards them, fixing his gaze on Lucy so that she was unable to look away. 'I am your grandfather, child. I don't even know your name, but you are my flesh and blood and I've been searching for you for a very long time.'

She opened her mouth to reply but Eva laid a finger on her lips. 'Let me handle this, Lucy.'

'Lucy.' The gentleman's stony countenance relaxed into a smile. 'That was your great-grandmother's name.'

'Is this true?' Lucy demanded. 'I want to know.'

'The child has spirit.' The gentleman took off his top hat to reveal a head of silver hair. His eyes were a similar shade, neither blue nor grey but the colour of the summer sky reflected on steel. 'My name is William Marriott and your father is my son.'

'Was,' Eva said quickly. 'The bastard who seduced my innocent child is dead and buried in a French cemetery.'

'Julius died in Paris as you well know, madam.'

'Served him right.' Eva released her hold on Lucy. 'Your son lured my little Christelle away with his fine words and fancy presents. He abandoned her and the child and God knows what would have happened to them if I hadn't come to their rescue.'

'I don't understand,' Lucy said slowly. 'If my pa was a toff, why was we left penniless?'

'A good question.' Eva fixed Marriott with a hard stare. 'If his father hadn't been such a toffee-nosed snob he might have helped the pair of them, instead of turning his back on his only son.'

Marriott shook his head. 'And I've lived to regret it, madam.'

'I found my little girl living in a hovel south of the river.' Eva slipped her arm around Lucy. 'This is her daughter, Sir William, but she'll have nothing to do with you.'

'I'm trying to make amends.' He held his hand out to Lucy. 'Come, child, I'm not an ogre. There's no need to look so scared.'

'I don't know you, guv.' Lucy bent down to pat Peckham, who seemed to sense her distress and growled again, baring his teeth.

He dropped his hand to his side. 'You speak like a street urchin and you dress like one too. Nevertheless, I can see a passing resemblance to my son and I'm prepared to accept you as my granddaughter.' He drew Eva aside. 'I won't mince words, madam. I came here today to offer you a considerable sum if you'll release Lucy to my care.'

'You want to take her away from me? You've got the cheek to offer to buy her? What for, I'd like to know? What sort of creature are you to want to take a child from her home?'

'Home?' He looked round, curling his lip. 'I've seen the slums where you've been living, and I'm well aware of the way you grub for money and that you send the child out thieving.' He glanced at the pile of clothes. 'I doubt whether any of this was come by honestly.'

'I never stole it, if that's what you're saying.'

He raised an arched eyebrow. 'There are other ways of procuring goods. You are still a handsome woman, Miss Pocket, and you know how to use your charms to good purpose.' He held up his hands in a gesture of appeasement. 'I'm not criticising you, madam. I've had you watched for some time, and from my own observations I know that you've struggled to survive. I'm offering you enough money to start again, but only if you allow your granddaughter to become my ward. I'll see that she's educated and brought up to be a lady. She'll take her place in society and have a future that you could never guarantee. What do you say?'

'I say that you can go to hell. Where was you when the baby was born? Where was you when her mother ran off? Where was you when this child had the measles and nearly died?'

'I should have done something sooner, but my dear wife was mortally ill and I could think of nothing else at the time. On her deathbed she begged me to find the child and make sure that she had a good start in life. After she died I had time to think about the opportunity I had missed by renouncing my only grandchild, and that's when I set out to find her.'

'My heart bleeds for you,' Eva said, curling her lip. 'Selfish to the last.'

'Selfish I might be, but this time I'm thinking only of the child. If you love her you'll do what is best for her. She is the only link I have with my dead son and I'm not giving up easily.'

'You're wasting your time. Go away and leave us alone.'

'You can't blame me for wanting to save my own flesh and blood from living a life of poverty and ignorance. What prospects has she got if she remains in your care, Miss Pocket?'

Lucy looked from one to the other, shaking her

head. 'Stop it, both of you. I ain't a bone to be fought over. The dog is better behaved than you two.'

There was a brief silence, broken by someone hammering on the door. It burst open and Mrs Wicks stood on the threshold, breathing heavily. 'No gentlemen callers. I told you that, missis.' She pointed a shaking finger at Peckham. 'And no bloody dogs neither. I dunno which is worse – men or dogs. Get out of here, all of you, and take that animal with you.'

'I paid a week's rent in advance, you old besom,' Eva said angrily. 'I ain't leaving unless you give it back.' She made a move towards Mrs Wicks, fisting her hands, but Sir William stepped in between them.

'There's no need for violence.' He turned to Mrs Wicks and she cowered beneath his stern gaze. 'I'd advise you to hold your tongue, madam. You will be recompensed for your trouble, but if you continue to harass us you won't get a penny piece.'

Mrs Wicks seemed to shrink into her black bombazine dress like a tortoise retreating into its shell. 'Very well, sir.' She shot a malevolent glance at Eva. 'I'll deal with you later.'

Sir William closed the door on her. 'Now, Miss Pocket, there's no need for us to be enemies. I'm sure we both have Lucy's best interests at heart.'

'I do, but I ain't so sure about you.'

He turned to Lucy with an attempt at a smile. 'Lucy, my dear child, I want you to come and live with me in Albemarle Street. You will want for nothing, and I'll do everything in my power to make up for the neglect you've suffered since birth.'

'Hold on, guv. I love my granny and I don't want to leave her. I don't know you and I don't want to be a lady. I ain't coming with you.'

'You heard her,' Eva said with a triumphant smile. 'Now sling your hook, Sir William. We've managed so far without you and we're just getting back on our feet.'

'You live from day to day, relying on pure chance to get you through. What will you do when you've run out of rubbish to sell? Will you send the child out thieving again?' He held up his hand as Eva opened her mouth to protest. 'I also know that you consorted with a man who is known to the Metropolitan Police as a fence for stolen goods. You were seen entering his premises in Clerkenwell last night and you left in the early hours of this morning, more than a little the worse for wear, with a large bundle slung over your shoulder. Do you want me to go on?'

Eva shook her head. 'Not in front of the child, sir.'

He put his hand in his pocket and produced a wallet, stuffed with notes. He took out three crisp white five pound notes and placed them in Eva's hand, closing her fingers over them. 'Fifteen pounds is more than you'll earn in a year.'

Eva made as if to throw the money in his face but she met his steady gaze and dropped her hand to her side. 'I can't sell her, not for ten times that amount.'

'And I won't go,' Lucy cried, clinging to her grandmother's arm. 'I won't leave my granny.'

Sir William regarded them with a hint of sympathy in his cool gaze. 'I understand, but your grandmother must do what is best for you, child.'

'She looks after me,' Lucy murmured. 'We're doing all right, guv.'

He focused his attention on Eva. 'What will happen to her when you aren't around to look after her? What future will she have if she remains in your care? Will she suffer a similar fate to that of her unfortunate mother? Will she fall for the first rogue who makes a play for her?' His expression changed subtly. 'I see that there is a strong bond between you, but if you love the child you'll do what is best for her.'

Eva's eyes filled with tears. 'He's right, Lucy. Much as I love you, I know in my heart that what he says is true. I can't give you anything other than the sort of life I've had to lead. I don't want that for you.'

Lucy threw her arms around her grandmother's slim waist. 'Don't send me away. I'll work harder and earn more pennies. I'll do anything if you'll just let me stay with you.'

'I'll make you an allowance, Miss Pocket,' Sir William said gruffly. 'You'll be able to rent rooms in a decent lodging house and live more comfortably than you do now.'

'No,' Lucy cried passionately. 'Don't let him do this to us, Granny.'

'Will I be able to visit her?' Eva said faintly.

He shook his head. 'It must be a complete break, ma'am. You have to understand that, and I want you to give me your promise that you won't try to contact Lucy.'

'That's cruel,' Lucy sobbed. 'You can't do this to me.'

'Have I your word that you will treat my granddaughter as if she were your own child?' Eva stroked Lucy's hair back from her forehead, dropping a kiss on her tumbled curls. 'Will you love her and care for her?'

'I'm not a demonstrative man, but I will do my utmost.'

'I hate to admit it, but he's right, Lucy.' Eva rocked her granddaughter in her arms as if she were a baby. 'You'll have everything that I can't give you, and you'll have a chance to better yourself.'

'But I don't want to go with him. I want to stay with you.'

'I will always love you, and it breaks my heart to let you go.' Eva raised a tear-stained face. 'I'm putting my trust in you, Sir William. If you make my girl unhappy I'll see that you suffer the torments of hell.'

'I don't want to be a lady.' Lucy broke away from her grandmother and dropped to the floor, wrapping her arms around the dog, 'We'll run away. Me and Peckham will disappear and you won't be able to find us.'

'You may keep the animal if it means so much to you,' Sir William said with an impatient edge in his voice. 'I have dogs at home. I daresay another won't make much difference.' He nodded in Eva's direction and smiled. 'You see, Miss Pocket, I am trying hard to make the child feel comfortable.'

'We're not going,' Lucy said firmly. 'Peckham and me are staying here, and that's final.'

She huddled in the corner of the carriage with Peckham curled up on her lap. Despite her protests and her earnest entreaties to be left with her grandmother, she had lost the battle and was now on her way to Albemarle Street. Sir William sat opposite her but made no attempt at conversation. She stared out of the window. At any other time she would have been thrilled to be travelling in such luxury, but in her present emotional state nothing registered in her brain other than the fact that every turn of the wheel and every hoofbeat took her further away from everything she knew, and the one person in the world she loved.

When the coachman reined in the horses outside the elegant five-storey house in Albemarle Street Lucy sat very still. If she did not move a muscle, maybe the strange man who purported to be her grandfather would get out of the carriage and leave her to return home. He had ignored her until now, but when a liveried footman opened the door and put the steps down Sir William gave her his full attention. 'You first,' he said abruptly.

The footman proffered his arm and Lucy thrust the dog into his startled embrace. 'Hang on to him. He might take fright and run away.' She leapt to the ground. 'Give him to me, mister. He don't like strangers.'

Sir William alighted from the vehicle and strode across the pavement to the front door, which opened as if by magic. Lucy followed him inside to the obvious surprise of the butler, whose eyebrows almost disappeared into his hairline.

'Miss Lucy has come to live with us, Bedwin.'

Sir William took off his top hat and gloves and handed them to the butler. 'Send Mrs Hodges to me. We'll be in the drawing room.'

'Yes, Sir William.' Bedwin shot a curious glance at Lucy and she stared back. Peckham wriggled in her arms and whimpered and when she put him down he ran to the front door, and turned his head to give her an expectant look.

'He wants to piddle, or he might want to sh–'

'Let him out, Bedwin,' Sir William said, cutting her off in full flow.

'Not out there.' Lucy ran to the door. 'He'll get lost.'

Sir William sighed heavily. 'Take him to the garden, Bedwin. Get someone to give the creature a bath before you let him back into the house.'

'Let me do it, guv,' Lucy said eagerly. 'He's my dog.'

'You'll do no such thing. We are going to start as we mean to go on. You have a lot to learn.' Sir William strode towards the staircase, motioning her to follow him.

Bedwin scooped Peckham up in his arms. 'Do as the master says, miss.'

'He's going upstairs. Is he going to bed?'

'The drawing room is on the first floor, miss.' Bedwin marched off with the dog tucked underneath his arm. Lucy hesitated; it was like playing the game, only this time it was real. Her feet sank into the thick pile of the carpet as she made her way up the wide staircase, and her fingers slid along the highly polished balustrade as if it were made of glass. The richly-papered walls were lined with gilt-framed oil paintings, mainly landscapes, but amongst them were portraits of prim-faced people wearing old-fashioned clothes. Their disdainful gaze seemed to follow her, and she took the remainder of the stairs two at a time.

The drawing room was furnished with more attention to style and elegance than comfort. The matching sofas were upholstered in gold damask and spindly chairs were set around equally fragile-looking tables, on which were silver-framed daguerreotypes and dainty porcelain figurines. Gold velvet curtains and swags framed the tall windows and the air was fragrant with the scent emanating from cut crystal vases filled with spring flowers. A fire blazed up the chimney even though it was relatively warm for the time of year. She stood in the doorway, gazing round in awe and feeling suddenly very small and in as much need of a bath as poor Peckham. She did not belong in a grand house like this and she was overwhelmed with a feeling of homesickness. Sir William stood with his back to the fire, staring at her with a frown wrinkling his brow. 'Mrs Hodges will look after you,' he said lamely. 'And we need to do something about those rags you're wearing.'

Lucy said nothing. He was talking at her rather than to her and she felt disorientated and strange, as if her body was present but her mind and heart were still in Hairbrine Court with Granny.

'Sit down, do.' Sir William's edgy voice sliced through her thoughts. Moving like an automaton she went to sit on the nearest chair. It was very hard and extremely slippery, and it took all her concentration to keep from sliding to the floor. Sir William paced the room, hands clasped behind his back. He glanced at her once or twice but she sat very still, waiting for him to speak. He came to a halt at the sound of someone knocking on the door. 'Enter.'

A woman, plainly dressed in black bombazine with a white lace cap on her head and a chatelaine hanging from her waist, glided into the room with a swish of starched petticoats. She folded her hands in front of her and bobbed a curtsey.

'Mrs Hodges, this is my granddaughter, Lucy Pocket. She will be living with us from now on and I want you to make up a room for her.'

If the housekeeper was shocked or surprised she was too self-disciplined to let it show. She flicked a glance in Lucy's direction. 'Very well, Sir William. I'll see to it at once.'

'And she'll need clothes,' Sir William said vaguely. 'She will require a whole new wardrobe, and I want you to advertise for a governess who is available to start immediately.'

'Yes, sir.'

'I'll leave you to select the woman you deem most capable, Mrs Hodges. I know little about such things.'

'I'll do my best, sir.'

Lucy was intent on their conversation and for a moment she lost concentration and found herself sliding onto the floor, where she landed in a heap at Mrs Hodges' feet. 'Sorry, missis.'

'Get up, child,' Mrs Hodges hissed. 'That's no way to behave.'

'I have business to attend to, Mrs Hodges,' Sir William said with an impatient edge to his voice. 'I'll leave Lucy in your capable hands.'

Mrs Hodges inclined her head. 'Of course, sir. Come along, Miss Lucy.' She seized her by the arm, dragging her to her feet. She sniffed and her nostrils dilated. 'It seems that we are in need of a bath.'

Lucy stared at her in surprise. 'You smell all right to me, missis.'

Mrs Hodges propelled her from the room, stopping outside to close the double doors. She turned on Lucy, her thin lips folded back to expose yellowed and stained teeth. Lucy tried not to stare, but she found herself wondering if the housekeeper chewed tobacco or perhaps she drank copious amounts of strong tea. She came back to the present with a start as Mrs Hodges pinched her arm. 'I suppose you think you're clever, but let me tell you that good manners cost nothing. You've got a lot to learn, you little guttersnipe.'

'You can't speak to me like that,' Lucy protested. 'That gent in there is my grandpa, or so he says. He wants me to grow up to be a lady.'

'And this is where we'll start.' Mrs Hodges grabbed her by the hand and marched her up to the fourth floor, pausing to catch her breath on each landing before continuing with what seemed to Lucy like climbing a mountain. 'This is the nursery suite,' Mrs Hodges said, flinging a door open. 'Master Julius spent his early years here with his nanny, who slept in the adjoining room.'

'If his nanny had that room I don't see why my granny can't come and stay here as well.'

'Don't you know anything, child?' Mrs Hodges snapped. 'A nanny looks after babies and small children. Your granny, I assume, is your maternal grandmother.'

'Maybe,' Lucy said doubtfully. She was not sure what that meant, but she did not want to admit her ignorance.

Mrs Hodges moved around the room, snatching Holland covers off the furniture. 'I'll send a maid up to light a fire and make up the bed. You're causing me a lot of extra work, young lady.' She cast a critical eye over Lucy, shaking her head and tut-tutting. 'A good scrub in hot water is what you need most, and your clothes are filthy and probably vermin-ridden. Take them off.'

'What?' Lucy wrapped her arms around her thin body. 'I can't take me clothes off. I'll catch me death of cold.'

'Don't be silly, child. Take everything off and wrap yourself in this.' Mrs Hodges stripped the coverlet from the bed and tossed it to Lucy. 'Undress now. Or do you want me to do it for you?'

Lucy could tell by the set of Mrs Hodges' jaw and the determined expression on her face that to argue would be useless, and she stripped off her clothes. The coverlet was cold against her warm skin and felt damp. She stood by the empty grate, shivering and biting back tears. Mrs Hodges bundled up her clothing with a look of distaste. 'Stay there and don't touch anything,' she said sternly. 'Someone will be with you shortly.'

'I want me dog,' Lucy said defiantly. 'The gent said I could keep him here.'

'Sir William is your grandfather. You don't refer to him as the gent. You address him as Grandpapa and you only speak when you are spoken to. You have much to learn, but I fear it will be an uphill task and nigh impossible.' Mrs Hodges flounced out of the room.

Lucy was left alone with the echoes of the past. The greyness of the sky outside was reflected in the clinically white walls. What little furniture there was remained covered with dustsheets that looked suspiciously like shrouds. It was as if all the colour had been drained from the room, leaving it austere and comfortless.

She sank down on the coir mat in front of the empty grate and huddled up in the coverlet, closing her eyes and attempting to play the game, but this time things were different. She was back in the attic room in Hairbrine Court waiting for Granny to come home from Rosemary Lane with enough money to buy supper and maybe breakfast next day. There would be cuddles and laughter, which made everything feel right, but the vision was growing misty. She could not hold onto her dream and it faded away. Tears oozed between her tightly shut eyelids despite her efforts to hold them back. She missed Granny more than she would have thought possible and the ache in her heart refused to go away. Sir William said he was her grandfather, but she knew instinctively that he had no affection for her. Mrs Hodges positively disliked her and Bedwin had treated her with barely concealed contempt. She would not stay here a moment longer than was necessary. She would find Peckham and they would run away.

She opened her eyes, struggling back from the

brink of sleep, and a cry of fright escaped her lips when she saw a spectral grey shape moving silently towards her.

Chapter Four

'What's up with you? Anyone would think you'd seen a ghost.' The housemaid set the coal scuttle down, groaning as she straightened up. 'Five flights of stairs I've had to climb with this bloody thing,' she grumbled. 'And when I've got the fire going I'm to fetch buckets of hot water for your bath.' She stared at Lucy with an impatient toss of her head. 'I dunno what you've got to cry about. It's me what's got the work to do.'

'I ain't crying,' Lucy said angrily. 'I never asked you to wait on me.'

'I shouldn't have to run round after the likes of you,' the girl said, dropping a bundle of kindling and a roll of newspaper onto the hearth. 'You'll have to shift yourself. I can't light the fire with you sitting there like a lump of cold porridge.'

Lucy scrambled to her feet with as much dignity as she could muster. 'I never asked to come here, and I'll be leaving as soon as I get me duds back. What has she done with 'em?'

'Mrs Hodges told Martha to wash them. She said they was probably running with fleas and lice.' She shot her a sideways glance. 'And I daresay your hair is full of nits.'

'I haven't got nits, and I don't have fleas and

lice neither.' She met the girl's scornful gaze with an unblinking stare. 'I dunno who you think you are, but you're supposed to be looking after me.'

'My name is Susan.'

'And you light fires. What else do you do?'

A flicker of something like respect lit Susan's green eyes for a moment, but then she slid her gaze away. 'I'm the tweeny.' She went down on her knees in front of the grate. 'That means I do all the jobs that no one else wants to do. I help Cook and I help the housemaids, but being a tweeny is one up from being a slavey.'

'What's a slavey?'

'Don't you know nothing? Martha is a slavey, which is another name for a scullery maid, because they're at everyone's beck and call. They do all the washing up and mopping floors and cleaning out bins and such. I started out that way.'

Lucy flopped down on a low chair close to the fireplace. 'I don't belong here. I want to go home.'

Susan paused with a twist of newspaper clutched in her grimy hand, staring at Lucy in amazement. 'Are you mad? You landed on your feet. I dunno what your home was like, but by the look of you it weren't much. You should think yourself lucky to be taken in by a rich toff. They're saying below stairs that you're his long lost granddaughter. Is that true?'

'I suppose so. It's what I was told.'

'Then you should make the most of it.' Susan arranged the paper and kindling and struck a vesta. Flames took hold and soon the fire was roaring up the chimney. She stood up, shaking the dust from her apron onto the hearth. 'I suppose I'd best start bringing up the hot water, Miss...' She put her head on one side, eyeing Lucy curiously. 'What's your name?'

'I'm Lucy Pocket and I'm ten, nearly eleven. How old are you, Susan?'

'I'm twelve, going on thirteen, if you must know.' Susan straightened her mobcap, which was on the large side and had fallen over one eye as she worked. 'Watch the fire, and don't let it go out or I'll be for it.' She stuck her mean little face close to Lucy's. 'And if I gets it in the neck I'll make you sorry you was born. I'll be back in a while.' She sauntered out of the room, leaving Lucy alone once again in the echoing silence of the fourth floor, with only the occasional hiss and spit of gas escaping from the coal for company. She curled up with her arms wrapped around her knees, glancing nervously into the dark corners of the room, but gradually as the warmth seeped into her chilled bones she began to relax and the shadows seemed less menacing. Mindful of Susan's threats, Lucy kept adding coal to the fire, nugget by nugget. She was wary of the young tweeny, and she was taking no chances. Life on the streets had taught her how to stand up for herself, but she knew nothing of this strange world, seemingly dominated by servants. Eventually the sound of footsteps heralded the arrival of Susan and another girl who, in answer to Lucy's question, said she was Martha the scullery maid.

'You shouldn't speak to us,' Susan said with a sly grin. 'You got to learn the ways of the gentry and treat us like dirt.'

'Why would I do that?' Lucy demanded.

'Because we're the lowest form of life.' Susan's cat-like eyes sparkled with malice. 'We aren't even supposed to look at you if you happen to come across us going about our work. We're supposed to be invisible.'

'Where do they keep the bath?' Martha asked plaintively. 'I ain't never been up here afore.'

'Look for it then, stupid.' Susan pointed to two doors on the far side of the nursery. 'Use your loaf, girl, and have a look.' She sighed and shook her head, leaning towards Lucy and lowering her voice. 'She's a bit soft in the head. They say her dad used to bang her head against the wall to stop her crying when she was a baby and it addled her brains. That's if she had any in the first place.' She glanced over her shoulder. 'Have you found it yet, Martha?'

'It's a bit dark in here, Sukey.' Martha's voice wavered and broke on a sob. 'Will you bring a candle? I'm afraid of bogeymen.'

Susan rolled her eyes and sighed, but she lit a candle and went to Martha's aid. 'You can't see for looking, you daft cow. What's that in the corner?'

'I can't see that far, Sukey.'

'You're blind as a bat, girl. You need specs. Give us a hand and let's get this done; then we can go downstairs and get a bite to eat. I'm bloody famished.'

Eventually, after several trips downstairs to fetch hot water, the zinc bath was filled and Lucy had to suffer the indignity of being bathed under the watchful eye of Mrs Hodges, who bustled into the room bringing a pile of clean towels. Susan was not the gentlest of souls, and she seemed to take pleasure in scrubbing Lucy from head to foot with unnecessary vigour. She was overly generous with the soap, and when Lucy complained that it stung her eyes Susan poured rapidly cooling water over her head, half drowning her.

The final insult was when Mrs Hodges raked a fine-toothed comb through Lucy's mop of curls. Her eyes watered but she was determined not to disgrace herself by crying. She eased the torment by imagining herself bathed in warm sunshine, floating on a fluffy pink cloud in a celestial blue sky.

'There, that's done.' Mrs Hodges rose to her feet. 'You'll have to wait for your clothes to dry Miss Lucy. Susan will bring you your luncheon when she's finished emptying the bathtub.'

'Can't I come downstairs, missis?' Lucy asked in desperation. She had seen the look that Susan gave her as she scooped the scummy water into a large enamel pitcher. 'I don't mind eating in the kitchen, and can I have my dog back, please.'

Mrs Hodges stared at her as if she had just sprouted two heads. 'No, you may not on both counts. I never heard of such a thing. You've got a lot to learn, Miss Lucy. You'll remain here until you're fit to be seen or until Sir William sends for you. Do you understand what I'm saying?'

'Yes, missis.'

'You address me as Mrs Hodges.' She rounded on Susan, who had barely stifled a chuckle. 'Get on with your work. I want that bath taken downstairs and scoured clean, and when you've done that you can make up Miss Lucy's bed.'

Lucy knew from the look on Susan's face that

she had made an enemy.

Susan said nothing when she eventually brought a tray of food to the nursery, but her tight-lipped silence held more menace than a tirade of words. Lucy thanked her politely, but the soup was cold and there was barely a slick of butter on the slices of bread. She found a spider floating in the water jug and there was a sprinkling of salt on the slice of apple pie instead of sugar. She sighed and fished the spider out of the water. She was too hungry to be fussy and the soup was tasty, although she suspected that it would have been even more delicious had it been hot. She was used to eating dry bread and the smear of butter was a treat in itself, as was the apple pie, even with the addition of salt. She cleared the plates and now that her belly was full she felt more optimistic, and began to formulate a plan. When her clothes were returned she would creep downstairs and look for Peckham, and when the house slept she would make her escape and go home. It was as simple as that.

But first she had to endure Susan's sly taunts while she made up the bed and attended to the fire. 'You won't last a week here,' was her parting shot. 'The master will see you for what you are, guttersnipe. You'll end up back where you belong and I'll say good riddance to bad rubbish.'

Lucy had bitten back a sharp retort, and she had so far managed to remain dry-eyed, but now her eyes were moist and she might have given way to tears had she not heard Mrs Hodges' stentorian tones and the softer replies of another woman. The door had barely closed on Susan when it opened again. Mrs Hodges breezed in, followed by a small lady who was carrying an overly large carpet bag.

'Miss Appleby has come to measure you for some new clothes,' Mrs Hodges announced with a finality that did not invite argument.

Miss Appleby smiled nervously. 'I took the liberty of bringing some garments that I had ready made, Mrs Hodges.' She opened the bag and took out a petticoat trimmed with lace, two pairs of drawers and a tartan merino dress. 'These were made for a child of ten who succumbed to scarlatina before the order was complete.'

Mrs Hodges recoiled, staring at the garments in horror. 'They should be incinerated, Miss Appleby. We don't want disease brought into the house.'

'No, no, Mrs Hodges. They were never worn by the poor girl. She sickened after the order was almost complete, but was too ill to have a final fitting.'

Lucy looked from one to the other. Neither of them had spoken directly to her and she was beginning to feel that she must be invisible.

'Stand up, Miss Lucy.' Mrs Hodges moved aside. 'Try them on for size.'

Lucy rose from her chair but she was reluctant to stand naked in front of strangers.

'It's all right, my dear,' Miss Appleby whispered. 'I'm used to seeing my clients in a state of undress.' She held up the petticoat, shielding Lucy from Mrs Hodges' critical gaze as she swopped the towel for the undergarment, and then she stood back, surveying her work with a satisfied smile. 'It's an excellent fit, Miss Lucy. And now for the unmentionables.' She handed her a pair of drawers.

Lucy put them on without argument. It was the thought of rescuing Peckham and setting off for home that made her compliant, and she stood very still while Miss Appleby slipped the frock over her head and did up the tiny pearl buttons at the back of the bodice. 'My dear, it could have been made for you,' she said happily. 'What do you think, Mrs Hodges?'

'Very fine, indeed.'

Lucy could tell by Mrs Hodges' tone that she considered the outfit far too good for a girl from the streets, but Miss Appleby was beaming with pride as she tied the scarlet silk sash around Lucy's waist. 'I've got your measurements now, Miss Lucy, and I'll work on the order as soon as I get home. Mrs Hodges has supplied me with a list of your needs.'

'Sir William wants only the best for his granddaughter,' Mrs Hodges said with barely disguised disapproval in her clipped tones.

'Yes, of course. I do understand.' Miss Appleby closed her bag with a snap of the lock. 'Nothing but the finest will do.'

Lucy waited until she was alone again, and when their footsteps died away she held out the skirts of her new frock and did a twirl. If only Granny could see her now. She tried to imagine her grandmother's expression when she walked into the attic room dressed like a young lady. The only problem now was to find her boots. They had been spirited away together with her clothes, and she would have to wait to put her plan in action. But she would walk barefoot back to Hairbrine Court if she could not find them. She glanced out of the window at the darkening skies, wishing that night would come quickly.

Supper was brought to her by Susan, who thumped the tray down on the table in the window and left without saying a word. Lucy did not bother to thank her this time. If Susan wanted her to behave like one of the toffs then that's what she would do. She ate ravenously. The food was delicious and like nothing she had ever tasted in her life. Feeling full and rather sleepy she settled in a chair by the fire, biding her time.

Martha sidled into the room to collect the tray. She glanced nervously at Lucy. 'Is it all right to take it, miss?'

Lucy nodded her head. 'What's going on downstairs?'

'I dunno what you mean, miss.'

'What are the servants doing now?'

'They're having their supper in the servants' hall as usual, miss.'

'And the master?'

'Lawks, I dunno, miss. How should I know what he's doing? I'm just a slavey sent to pick up your tray, and I'll get it in the neck if I don't hurry back.'

'I'm sorry. I didn't mean to hinder you.' Lucy eyed her warily. 'Do you know where they got me dog? He'll be scared without me.'

Martha hesitated in the doorway. 'He's with the

master's animals. They got a big kennel in the back yard. I daresay they'll eat your one for their supper.' She left the room, and Lucy could hear her giggling as she made her way towards the back stairs.

'That settles it,' Lucy muttered, jumping up from the chair. 'I'm leaving this drum and taking me dog. We're going home.' She hurried after Martha, following the sound of her as the slavey chattered to herself all the way down several flights of uncarpeted stairs to the servants' domain. Martha disappeared into the kitchen and Lucy dodged past the open doorway, heading towards the back of the house where she hoped to find Peckham. There were doors on either side of the long passageway and she became disorientated. She blundered by mistake into a room with a pungent smell that she recognised as boot polish, and sure enough there were shoes lined up in pairs awaiting the attention of the hall boy, but hers were not amongst them. She hesitated for a moment, peering out of the door to see if anyone was coming, and having satisfied herself that the servants were all fully occupied she snatched a pair of boots that must have belonged to one of the younger maidservants, but were now hers. She put them on and they fitted, more or less, but equally as well as the ones she had been wearing when she arrived. Soundly shod and filled with renewed energy she felt ready for anything.

She had to struggle in order to reach the top bolt on the back door, but eventually she managed to wrench it open and she stepped outside into almost complete darkness. The sound of barking led her to the brick-built kennels, and Peckham's white coat shone like a beacon as he jumped up and down, recognising her instantly. Sir William's dogs, a yellow Labrador and a bouncy cocker spaniel, kept a wary eye on the mongrel. What he lacked in size he made up for in spirit and it was clear that he had established his position in the pecking order. Lucy opened the gate and he leapt out, barking ecstatically and running round in circles of sheer delight. She scooped him up in her arms. 'Hush, now, you silly boy. Keep quiet until we're well away from here. We're going home.'

She had hoped to escape through the yard, but the gate was padlocked and the walls were too high to climb. The only way out was to go through the house and she retraced her steps, holding Peckham close. 'Please don't make a sound,' she whispered as she tiptoed through the maze of passageways, heading for the back stairs which would take her to the entrance hall. She had to dodge out of sight several times as servants hurried to and fro, but after several close encounters she emerged through the green baize door, and at the far end of the corridor she could see the hall lights blazing. The house above stairs was like a different country, far away from the stuffy heat of the kitchens and the seemingly endless toil of those who served their master. It was eerily quiet as she crept towards the pool of light where the passage opened out into the marble-tiled vestibule. She could see the front door and she broke into a run, but Peckham was suddenly alert and he wriggled free, leaping from her arms, barking frantically. She was about to remonstrate when someone caught her by the scruff of her neck. 'And just where do you think you're going, miss?'

She uttered a cry of fright and Peckham flew at Bedwin, sinking his teeth into the pinstripe material of the butler's trouser leg. Bedwin did not loosen his hold on Lucy as he hopped around on one leg, trying to shake the dog off, and a liveried footman appeared as if from nowhere. He tried to catch Peckham but the dog was too quick for him and avoided all attempts at capture.

'What in heaven's name is going on?' Sir William's angry voice echoed round the entrance hall. He marched down the wide staircase, glaring angrily at Bedwin. 'What's the meaning of this?'

Bedwin released Lucy. 'I caught her trying to leave the house, sir.' He turned to the footman, who was still running round in circles trying to grab Peckham. 'Stop that, James.'

Sir William descended slowly, coming to a halt by Lucy, who had dropped to her knees and was holding Peckham in a protective embrace. 'You shouldn't have locked him up with them big dogs,' she said angrily. 'He's only little and he was scared.'

James muttered something beneath his breath and received a reproving glance from his superior. 'Go about your duties, James,' Bedwin said icily. He turned to his master with an apologetic smile. 'I'm very sorry for the disturbance, Sir William. It won't happen again.'

'No, it won't,' Lucy said, finding her voice. 'You can't keep me locked up, mister. I ain't your long lost granddaughter, and even if I am, I don't want to live here. I want Granny.' She stifled a sob, burying her face in Peckham's furry coat. He smelled different now that he had been bathed, but his warm body was comforting and he belonged to her.

'Get up, child,' Sir William said impatiently. 'You're going nowhere. You were present when I made the arrangement with your grandmother, and she agreed that your needs would be best suited if you lived with me.'

She looked up, blinking back tears. 'I don't belong here. I want to go back to Hairbrine Court.'

Bedwin sucked air in through the gaps in his teeth, but he remained standing to attention, saying nothing.

'Go to your room, Lucy,' Sir William said firmly. 'Of course it will seem strange at first, but you will settle down in time. Tomorrow I will advertise for a governess and you will learn to be a young lady, as befits my son's child.'

Bedwin helped Lucy to her feet and she did not resist, but she held onto the dog as if her life depended upon it. 'I want me nana,' she muttered rebelliously.

'Your accent is dreadful and your grammar is appalling,' Sir William said coldly. 'But I am not a hard man. You may keep the dog with you, but you will be responsible for taking the creature for walks. James will accompany you to the park at all times, and if you make any attempt to run away the dog will be taken from you and destroyed. Do you understand what I'm saying?'

Lucy nodded wordlessly. The threat on Peckham's life was more frightening than anything they could do to her.

'Answer me, child. You are not a mute.'
'I understand, mister.'
'You will address me as Grandpapa.'
'Yes, Grandpapa.'
'That's better. James, take Miss Lucy to her room and lock the door.' Sir William held his hand up as Lucy opened her mouth to protest. 'You will remain so until I'm certain that you are ready to obey me.' He turned on his heel and ascended the stairs.

That night Lucy slept with Peckham curled up beside her. She was awakened next morning by the sound of the key turning in the lock. Peckham leapt off the bed and stood by the door, hackles raised. Susan burst in carrying a jug of warm water. 'Keep that bloody mongrel away from me,' she said, eyeing him nervously as she made her way to the wash stand. 'If he bites me I'll tell Mr Bedwin and he'll have him put down. I don't like dogs.'
Lucy sat up in bed. 'He doesn't seem to like you either, so it's tit for tat, ain't it?'
'You'll get your comeuppance, guttersnipe. The master will realise his mistake soon enough and then you'll be back on the streets where you belong.' Susan slopped the hot water into the wash bowl and thumped the jug down. 'Get up and get dressed. I ain't no lady's maid.'
'I don't want to be here,' Lucy said, holding her arms out to Peckham as he leapt back onto her bed. 'If you'll help me I could be out of here and away afore anyone realises what's happened.'
'I'd be dismissed without a character. I suppose

you'd like that, you little monster.' Susan made for the door. 'Looks like we're stuck with each other. I don't like it any more than you do.' She left the room, slamming the door behind her, and the key grated in the lock.

Outside the sun was shining with the promise of a fine day ahead. Lucy got up and went to look out of the window in an attempt to get her bearings. The street below was quiet and orderly by comparison with the hustle of the East End. A crossing sweeper was busy at work, clearing the straw and horse dung so that ladies could negotiate the streets without getting their skirts soiled, and gentlemen did not muddy their shiny shoes. Private carriages vied with hansom cabs and there was not a costermonger's barrow to be seen. Lucy had hoped that her grandmother might have had a change of heart. She searched the well-dressed crowds that thronged the pavements for a sign of her, but she was nowhere to be seen. It was hard to believe that Granny could have abandoned her, or that she had quite literally sold her for fifteen pounds. Surely she would regret her decision and return one day, saying it had all been a terrible mistake.

Lucy turned with a start as the door opened and Mrs Hodges marched in. 'Why aren't you dressed, child? Have you had a wash?'

'I had a bath yesterday, and it's only April. I'll catch me death of cold if I keep washing meself.'

'Stuff and nonsense. I never heard such silly talk. We keep clean in this household, Miss Lucy.' Mrs Hodges folded her arms across her bosom. 'If the water's cold it's your fault. Now wash your hands and face and clean your teeth. When you're done you'll get dressed and come downstairs for breakfast. Sir William has decided that you ought to join him in the dining room. Heaven help us all.'

Washed and dressed in the tartan frock that Miss Appleby had made for the child who succumbed to scarlatina, Lucy had to suffer while Mrs Hodges raked a comb through her hair. 'I never saw such a wild mop,' she said crossly. 'But at least it's clean and it will have to do.' She stood back, looking Lucy up and down with a critical eye. 'Come with me, but the dog stays here.'

'He'll be scared on his own,' Lucy protested.

Mrs Hodges grabbed her by the ear and propelled her out of the room, shutting the door before Peckham had a chance to follow them. 'Don't be silly,' she said sharply. 'And when you're in Sir William's company remember your manners. Speak only when spoken too and don't bolt your food.'

Lucy said nothing. It seemed best to say as little as possible when in the housekeeper's company, and she allowed herself to be led downstairs to the dining room. Mrs Hodges opened the door and thrust her in first, as if she feared that her charge might make a sudden dash for freedom.

'Will there be anything else, Sir William?' Mrs Hodges asked, giving Lucy a none too gentle push towards the vast dining table, which was laden with gleaming silver, crystal and fine bone china.

'That will be all for now, Mrs Hodges. My advertisement for a governess should appear in *The*

Times tomorrow, and I'm hoping to get a response quite soon. In the meantime, I suggest that you find something to occupy the child's hands. She should sew a sampler or whatever girls this age do to pass the time.'

Mrs Hodges did not look impressed. 'Very good, sir. I'll do my best.' She bobbed a curtsey and backed out of the room.

'Sit down, child,' Sir William said, waving his knife at her.

Bedwin stepped forward and pulled out a chair. Lucy perched on the edge, not knowing what to do next. Her grandfather was tucking into a plate of buttered eggs, bacon, kidneys and two fat sausages. He paused with the fork halfway to his lips. 'Aren't you hungry?'

She stared blankly at the array of silver cutlery set out in front of her.

She wondered if the servants would suddenly appear and fill the empty chairs set around the table, which would seat at least twenty people. 'Don't I have to wait for the others?' she whispered.

He stared at her, frowning. 'The others?'

'There's so many empty places. Do the servants come in when you've finished filling your face, Grandpapa?'

'Where did you learn that vulgar expression?' He dabbed his lips with a starched white napkin. 'No, don't bother to tell me. I should expect it, I suppose. You really do have a lot to learn, Lucy.' He speared a kidney on his fork and popped it into his mouth.

Lucy's stomach rumbled, but she sat very still

hoping that someone would bring her food on a tray, as had happened the previous evening. Bedwin picked up what she thought must be a teapot, although it was silver and very ornate. He hovered at her side. 'Would you like some hot chocolate, Miss Lucy?'

'Is that like cocoa?'

'Very similar, miss.'

'Then I will. I only gets cocoa when Granny's feeling flush.' She glanced up at Bedwin and saw his lips twitch. 'Is there any chance of a bit of toast or something? I'm bloody starving.'

'One helps oneself at the sideboard, miss,' he said in a low voice. 'Would you like me to assist you?'

'Yes, ta.' She stood up, knocking his elbow so that he spilled a little of the hot chocolate into the saucer.

Sir William clicked his tongue against his teeth. 'I'm afraid you'll have to treat her as if she were a savage brought back from the colonies, Bedwin. Miss Lucy has lived a completely different existence and will need to be instructed in everything. I fear it's going to be an uphill task.'

Bedwin went to the sideboard and lifted the lid of a silver breakfast dish. The aroma of fried bacon was too much for Lucy and she grabbed a couple of rashers. Bedwin shook his head. 'Use the serving spoons, miss,' he whispered. 'We don't use our fingers.'

Lucy was helping herself to buttered eggs when a sharp tap on the door made her jump and she dropped the spoon. 'I'll get a cloth and clean it up, Mr Bedwin,' she said apologetically.

Again he shook his head. 'The parlour maid will do that, miss.' He went to the door and opened it. 'What is it, Susan?'

'There's a gent to see the master, Mr Bedwin. I told him to come back later, but he won't take no for an answer.'

Chapter Five

'The master doesn't like being disturbed so early in the morning,' Bedwin said in a low voice. 'Tell whoever it is he will have to wait.' He guided Lucy back to her chair, and when she was seated he plucked the folded napkin from the table, shook it out with a flourish and laid it on her lap. He stepped away, but before he could resume his position the door flew open and a smartly dressed man burst into the room.

Sir William half rose from his chair. 'What do you mean by this intrusion, sir?'

Lucy turned her head to stare at the intruder. 'Blimey!' she said, staring at him in surprise. 'Does he owe you money too?'

'What are you talking about, Lucy?' Sir William demanded incredulously. 'Do you know this man?'

'Of course she doesn't know me, Uncle,' Linus said hastily. 'I don't know who this child is, but I've never seen her before in my life.'

Lucy leapt to her feet, stung by the injustice of this. 'You're a liar, mister. I found your wallet in

Burlington Arcade and returned it to you. You gave me a measly three and six.'

'It's a lie. Take no notice of her, Uncle.'

Sir William sat down slowly. 'Suddenly I've lost my appetite. Why do you always have that effect on me, Linus? What trouble are you in now?'

'I expect it's them bits of paper with IOU written on them,' Lucy said solemnly. 'They was worth a lot of money, judging by the look on his face when he saw they was still in the wallet, and I still reckon they were worth more than what he give me.'

Sir William sat back in his chair with a sigh. 'You've been at the gaming tables again. Don't you ever learn?'

'I could ask you the same, sir,' Linus said angrily. 'Your good works will bankrupt you one day. I suppose that's why you've taken this little street arab into your household. Did you know that her grandmother is a thief and a prostitute, and her daughter was no better? This is the child of Satan if you ask me.'

'This child of Satan as you call her is the daughter of my late son, your cousin Julius, and as such is heir to my fortune. As to her mother, no one seems to know her whereabouts, but I've bought off the grandmother. We won't be seeing her again, unless I'm very much mistaken.'

This was too much for Lucy and she dropped her knife and fork with a clatter. She sprang to her feet, facing her grandfather with her small hands fisted. 'Don't say bad things about my granny. She's done her best for me and I love her. I'd rather live in one attic room with her than stay in a big house with the likes of you. I've had about enough of you and your blooming toffee-nosed servants. I'm taking me dog and I'm going back where I belong.' She stormed out of the room without giving either of them a chance to respond, but when she reached the entrance hall she realised that leaving was easier said than done. Mrs Hodges, James the footman, Susan and a parlour maid were joined by Bedwin, who followed her from the dining room. He clapped his hands together. 'I have the matter in hand. All of you go about your business, except for Mrs Hodges. May I have a word with you, ma'am?'

She sidled up to him, keeping an eye on Lucy as if she expected her to vanish into thin air or float up to the ceiling like a hot air balloon. 'Yes, Mr Bedwin?'

'See that the child is kept to her room for the next few days. I suggest you allow her to keep the animal with her, but she's to have her meals brought to her. Sir William doesn't want a repeat of today's performance.'

Mrs Hodges shot an angry glance in Lucy's direction. 'The master will rue the day he brought that one in from the streets. In the gutter he found her and that's where she should have stayed. This is a respectable household.' She beckoned to Lucy. 'Upstairs, now. I shan't tell you twice.'

'I dunno why I'm copping it when that man Daubenay is to blame.' Lucy yelped as Mrs Hodges grabbed her by the arm, pinching the soft flesh above Lucy's elbow.

'Be silent, you little worm. I've had enough of you and your tantrums.'

'But it's not fair,' Lucy protested. 'That Mr Daubenay is a gambling man, I saw the IOUs with me own peepers. I bet he's on a losing streak, and he's come to touch his uncle for a loan, so why am I the wrong 'un and not him?'

Mrs Hodges swung her left arm, clouting Lucy round the head with a blow that made her ears ring. 'That's what you get for answering back and there's more where that came from. It's bread and water for you today, and you can sit in your room and think about what you've done.' Puffing and panting, Mrs Hodges clambered up the stairs, dragging Lucy by the arm with Peckham bounding along ahead of them. She opened the nursery door and gave Lucy a shove which sent her sprawling onto the bare floorboards. 'I don't want to hear a sound from you or that blooming mongrel, so keep him quiet.'

'He'll need to go outside to relieve hisself,' Lucy said defiantly.

'I'll send Martha up later. If it messes in the meantime, you'll clear it up yourself and scrub the floor on your hands and knees. You need discipline, my girl. Let's hope the master finds you a good governess who won't spare the rod.'

Lucy awakened on Monday morning to find Peckham lying on her feet, snoring gently. She had endured almost a week of incarceration in her room, and had suffered taunts and insults from Susan when she brought her food on a tray, and she had had to listen to Martha's moans when she had to empty the slops or take the dog out. The enforced idleness was torture, and to make it worse the sun had shone every day and spring was in the air. The nearest Lucy could get to freedom was to open the window, but it was barred and she had only a limited view of the people down below as they hurried about their daily business.

She yawned and stretched, disturbing Peckham who leapt to the floor, cocking his head on one side at the sound of the key turning in the lock. Lucy tumbled from the bed as the door opened, landing in a heap on the floor.

Mrs Hodges bustled into the room. 'Not dressed yet? You're a lazy little brat, but all that is about to change.' She picked up Lucy's tartan frock and tossed it at her. 'Your governess has arrived. Put your clothes on immediately.'

The words had barely left her lips when a formidable-looking woman of indeterminate age strode into the room, coming to a sudden halt and taking in the scene with a look of disapproval. She was dressed from head to toe in unrelenting grey which did nothing for her sallow complexion. Her hair, which was scraped back in an unflattering bun, was also grey and her eyes were the colour of snow that had turned to slush. 'Stand up straight when an adult enters the room, girl.'

'I'll leave you to get acquainted,' Mrs Hodges said with a grim smile. 'Ring the bell if you require anything, Miss Wantage.' She sailed out of the room with a triumphant look on her face.

Lucy had only just managed to put her frock on and was attempting to do up the pearl buttons, but she stopped and stood to attention. This woman was the sort who had to be obeyed, she decided, looking at the thin lips drawn into a tight line, and the cold grey eyes that reminded her of the fish lying on slabs in Billingsgate market.

'My name is Miss Wantage and I am your governess. Don't slouch and stop fidgeting. You should have been up and dressed hours ago. I can see I am going to have my work cut out with you.' She eyed Peckham with distaste. 'I don't like dogs. That animal should be kept outside in a kennel.'

Peckham growled deep in his throat and Lucy bent down to pick him up. 'Sir William says I can keep him with me.'

'We'll see about that.' Miss Wantage took off her cape and bonnet and laid them on a chair. She went round the room, examining everything in minute detail. 'This isn't how I like to organise my class room.' She flung up the sashes on both windows. 'Fresh air and exercise make a healthy body and a healthy mind. Put the animal on the floor and take a seat, Lucy. We'll start by finding out how much you know.'

There seemed little alternative but to obey the unsmiling stranger and Lucy sat down with Peckham curled up at her feet.

'Sit up straight or I'll have to tie you to a board. Poor posture cannot be allowed.' Miss Wantage opened the desk and took out a cane. She swished it through the air. 'Let this be a warning to you, Lucy Marriott.'

'Me name's Lucy Pocket.' She could not let this pass. 'I ain't a Marriott.'

'You are according to your grandfather and that's how you'll be addressed in future.' Miss

Wantage walked round the chair, prodding Lucy in the back. 'Head up, don't slouch. You will do exactly as I say. I don't put up with idleness, rudeness or disobedience. Do you understand?'

'Yes, miss.'

'Yes, Miss Wantage. Repeat after me.'

'Yes, Miss Wantage,' Lucy muttered. It seemed sensible to humour the grumpy old woman.

'Good. We have the basis of an understanding. Now stand up and recite the alphabet.'

Lucy managed to get through her letters without too many mistakes. She had learned to add and subtract at a young age, which Granny had said was important if you didn't want to be cheated in the market. Lucy had the satisfaction of seeing Miss Wantage look faintly disappointed by her new pupil's abilities, but she still managed to find fault with everything from Lucy's grammar to her posture, and in particular she remonstrated with her on her lack of manners and her appalling accent.

After a gruelling morning of lessons, Lucy had to walk round the nursery with a book balanced on her head for half an hour, which Miss Wantage said would improve her deportment. When luncheon arrived that proved to be another trial, only this time it was table manners, and Lucy failed miserably. The day was going badly, but then Miss Wantage decided that it was time for their constitutional, and she donned her bonnet and cape. 'Where is your bonnet, child?' she demanded. 'You cannot go out bareheaded.'

'I had one once, but the rats ate it.'

Miss Wantage uttered a shriek. 'Heavens, what

sort of family did you spring from?'

'Granny was good to me. I want to go back and live with her.'

'Don't be silly. You know that's out of the question. Your grandfather explained the circumstances of your birth and early life, and that is what I am being paid to eradicate.'

'I dunno what that means,' Lucy muttered. 'But I ain't got no bloody bonnet.'

Miss Wantage clutched her hand to her throat, rolling her eyes in horror. 'Such language in one so young!' She reached for the cane. 'Hold out your hand.'

'What for?'

'Because I say so. Hold out your hand now.'

Reluctantly, Lucy obeyed and was rewarded by six sharp blows across her palm. Tears sprang to her eyes but she bit her lip and tried hard not to cry even though the pain was almost unbearable.

'When we return from our walk you will write out one hundred times *I must not use bad language*. As for the bonnet, I will speak to Mrs Hodges. Something must be done about your wardrobe. My reputation is at stake here, and I cannot be seen with a charge who is not properly attired.'

'Can we take Peckham, miss?'

'May we take Peckham, Miss Wantage?'

Lucy repeated the sentence, but inwardly she was rebellious. She would escape from this prison one way or another. She just needed to find a way.

'Yes, Lucy. We will take the animal, but only if a collar and leash can be found.'

The sun was shining and narcissi nodded their creamy heads in a warm breeze as Lucy and Miss Wantage walked through Green Park. Peckham trotted along beside Lucy, behaving impeccably, as if he had been trained to walk at heel. Lucy raised her face to the sun, trying to forget the hideous straw bonnet that Mrs Hodges had found for her. It was wonderful to breathe fresh air after being imprisoned in the nursery for so long, but it would have been even better had Miss Wantage not been striding at her side like a wardress. They did a complete circuit of Green Park, and seeming to think they had not had sufficient exercise Miss Wantage took them into St James's Park, where they walked twice round the lake and then back through Green Park to Piccadilly. By this time even Peckham was showing signs of slowing down, but Miss Wantage it seemed could go on forever. When they arrived back in Albemarle Street she took off her lace mittens and bonnet. 'I was raised in Yorkshire,' she said with a slight curl of her lips that almost stretched her features into a smile, but not quite. 'I used to love walking on the moors. The parks in London cannot compare with the wildness and sheer beauty of the moorland.'

Lucy's feet ached, and although the borrowed boots had been replaced by a new pair she was certain she had blisters on both heels. Peckham sank down on the floor with a sigh and closed his eyes.

'This will be part of our daily routine from now on,' Miss Wantage said firmly. 'Mornings will be spent doing schoolwork and in the afternoon we will take our constitutional. Now you will sit at your desk and write out your lines. You will not get any tea unless they are neat and correct. After tea, assuming that you are allowed any, you will sit with a board strapped to your back to improve you posture, and this will remain in place until dinner, which will be taken in my presence and we will concentrate on table manners and etiquette. You are a street urchin at present, Lucy Marriott, but you will be a young lady by the time I have finished with you.'

Peckham raised his head and licked Lucy's hand.

The routine was relentless, as was Miss Wantage. Lucy was kept occupied from the moment she got up in the morning until she went to bed at night. She was hardly ever alone. Miss Wantage took her duties seriously, and if she left Lucy for even a few minutes the nursery door was locked, making a further attempt at escape impossible, but Lucy was still determined to find her grandmother and beg her to take her back. She could sell the clothes that Miss Appleby had made for her, and then Granny could return the money to Sir William.

When she was strapped to the backboard Lucy played the game, only this time she was with Granny in Rosemary Lane. She could smell the fried fish that Pearl was hawking round the market, and hear Carlos shouting the delights of Astley's Amphitheatre and Cremorne Gardens. Miss Wantage brought her abruptly back to the present by rapping the cane on her desk. 'Don't slouch, Lucy. You're the only child I've ever taught who could sit badly when strapped to a board. Sit up straight. Young ladies with round shoulders are not attractive.'

Lucy sat up straight and returned to the game: Miss Wantage had no authority in her make-believe world.

The days turned into weeks and Miss Wantage was firmly established in the household and deeply unpopular, if what Martha whispered in Lucy's ear was true. She had no reason to doubt the stories of how her governess had offended everyone from Bedwin and Mrs Hodges down to the parlour maids, and in particular Cook. Miss Wantage had her own ideas about diet and frequently sent dishes back to the kitchen if they were not to her liking. Lucy ate anything that was put before her. Having come close to starvation on many occasions she had a great respect for food and was not about to waste the smallest crumb. What she could not manage was given to Peckham, who was equally unfussy.

On a particularly hot day in the middle of June, Lucy was sitting by the open window trying to learn the poem that her governess had set for her. Miss Wantage had complained of a headache first thing that morning, which had gradually worsened to the extent that she had gone to lie down in her room adjacent to the nursery. The door had been left ajar so that she could keep an eye on Lucy, but her muffled groans had gradually subsided into slow breathing, punctuated by snuffly snores. Lucy waited until she was certain that her governess was asleep. She had planned her escape in her head countless times, and now she had her chance. It was the best present that anyone could have given her. No one in the house knew that it was her birthday, not even Sir William, whom she seldom saw.

Leaving the nursery did not present a problem. She picked up Peckham and made her way downstairs slowly, stopping to listen, and when satisfied that no one was coming she carried on until she reached the bend in the stairs above the entrance hall. She leaned over the balustrade and felt a gust of warm air. The front door was open and she could see James polishing the lion's head knocker. There did not seem to be anyone else about, but as she was about to descend further she heard the sound of a woman's voice and the deeper response from James.

Lucy's breath hitched in her throat. She knew that voice – she loved that voice. She raced downstairs, forgetting caution, and crossed the marble-tiled hall to push past the startled footman. He reached out and caught her by the arm but Peckham snapped at him and wriggled free from Lucy's grasp to stand his ground, snarling at James.

'Keep that brute under control, miss.' James thrust a small parcel into Lucy's hand. 'A person left this for you. Get that cur away from me, if you please.'

'Peckham, sit.' Lucy ripped the brown paper, revealing the silver locket that contained a lock of her mother's golden hair entwined with her own baby curl. There was no note, but it was the one thing of value that Granny had never sold or pawned, not even when they were in their most urgent need of funds. Lucy curled her fingers around the locket. 'Where did she go?' she gasped. 'That was my granny, where did she go?' She grabbed James by the hand, tugging him out onto the street. 'You must have seen which way she went.'

He shook his head. 'I don't know where she was headed, miss.'

Lucy looked up and down the street, but there was no sign of her grandmother. She ran to the corner of Albemarle Street and Piccadilly, but she could not see anyone who remotely resembled Eva Pocket. She retraced her steps, but as she was about to pass the house James stepped out onto the pavement, followed by Bedwin. The chase was over, and she was lifted off her feet and carried indoors with Peckham snapping at James's heels. 'Let me go,' Lucy sobbed. 'I must find her.'

'Where is Miss Wantage?' Bedwin demanded angrily. 'What is she thinking of, allowing the child to wander?'

James set Lucy back on her feet. 'It wasn't my fault, Mr Bedwin. I couldn't stop her, and that animal was trying to bite me.'

'He wasn't,' Lucy protested angrily. 'He was just protecting me. You let her go, you stupid man. You let my granny get away.'

Bedwin took her by the shoulders and shook her. 'That's enough of that talk, Miss Lucy. Where is your governess?'

'She's not well.'

'You should have remained in the nursery, Miss

Lucy. You know you're not allowed to go out on your own.'

'My granny was at the door. He let her go and now I've lost her again.'

A flicker of what might have been sympathy softened Bedwin's stony features, but only for a moment. 'It is for the best.'

'But it's my birthday and now she's gone forever.' The tears that Lucy had been holding back flowed down her cheeks and her small body was racked by sobs.

'Come with me, miss.' Bedwin led her along the corridor that led to the green baize door and down the stairs to a room near the kitchen. He opened the door and ushered her inside. 'This is my pantry, Miss Lucy. Sit down and compose yourself. I won't be long.' He left, returning minutes later with a steaming cup of chocolate. 'I always find this extremely comforting in times of stress.' He placed it on the table in front of Lucy and handed her a clean white handkerchief. 'Happy birthday, miss. Drink your chocolate, and then I'll take you back to the nursery.'

'It's all right, Mr Bedwin. I'm not a baby. I can find me own way, ta.'

He gave her a quizzical look.

'I mean,' she said, correcting herself, 'I can find my own way, thank you.'

'Very good, Miss Lucy. Have I your word of honour that you won't try to run away again?'

'I won't try to run away again today.'

His lips twisted into a wry smile. 'Finish your drink before you go, Miss Lucy. I'm a busy man so I'll have to trust you to keep your promise.' He left the room, closing the door behind him.

Lucy put her cup down and thrust her hand into the pocket where she had concealed her present. After a brief struggle with the clasp she hung it round her neck and tucked it out of sight under the bodice of her cotton print frock. She felt at once happy and sad. Granny had called at the house: she had been so close, and then she was gone. Her fingers traced the heart shape of the locket beneath the thin cotton of her bodice, and the precious metal was warm against her flesh. If only Granny had stayed for a moment longer she might have seen her, and if she could have spoken to her she might have persuaded her to take her home, wherever that was. She finished the chocolate and replaced the dainty cup on its matching saucer, but all the fine china in the world could not make up for the loss of the one person who truly loved her.

She left the pantry and made her way slowly to the staircase with Peckham at her side. She was tempted to run away again, but she had given her word to Bedwin and he had been kind to her. She would honour her promise today, but there was always tomorrow. She reached the entrance hall in time to see James opening the front door and she paused at the foot of the stairs, hoping that Granny might have changed her mind and come to take her home. Peckham stood alert with his brown ears cocked. He uttered a growl deep in his throat as Linus Daubenay strode into the vestibule, tossing his hat and cane at James. 'Where will I find my uncle?'

'I believe he's in the study, sir.'

Linus crossed the floor in long strides, coming to a halt beside Lucy.

'You should muzzle that cur,' he said, glaring at the dog.

Lucy knew better than to argue. She snatched Peckham up in her arms and started for the stairs, but Linus caught her by the sleeve. 'You may think you're clever, Miss Pocket, but you won't steal my inheritance, of that you may be certain. One way or another I'll make certain that you don't get the chance. Do you understand what I'm saying?'

She understood well enough, but she was not going to let him see that she was afraid. 'I never asked to come here, mister,' she said, returning his hard stare with a toss of her head. 'I don't want to stay and I don't want your inheritance, whatever that might be.'

He leaned over her, lowering his voice. 'And I'll make sure you don't get a penny of it, little girl. I'm going to tell my uncle just what sort of family you come from. Your mother is a whore and so is your grandmother. I should know, because I've had them both.'

'That's a wicked lie.' Lucy's voice broke on a sob. 'You're a bad man.'

'You don't know how bad I can be, but you're going to find out very soon.' His laughter echoed off the crystal chandeliers as he strode off in the direction of Sir William's study.

James hurried after him. 'Shall I announce you, sir?'

The front entrance was momentarily unguarded and Lucy forgot her promise to Bedwin.

She seized the moment to make her escape. She wrenched the heavy oak door open and with Peckham clutched in her arms, she ran.

Chapter Six

Lucy barged her way past startled pedestrians, and did not stop running until she reached Piccadilly Circus. By this time she was out of breath, and had a stitch in her side. She stopped and put the dog down, instructing him to sit and stay. He looked up at her with big brown eyes and nuzzled her hand as she bent over to ease the pain. The spasm passed and she took off her sash, looping it through Peckham's collar, using it as a makeshift lead. She continued at a slower pace, heading along Haymarket in the direction of the Strand. It was a long walk to Rosemary Lane, but she was determined to find her grandmother, and when she did they would never be parted again. Sir William could keep his money and his big house. She trudged onward, feeling the sun hot on her back and blisters forming on her heels, but she had been used to walking everywhere long before Miss Wantage had instituted the daily promenade in the park.

She was hot and she stopped to slake her thirst with water from the Buxton fountain in Parliament Square, cupping her hands and filling them so that Peckham could also drink. Feeling refreshed she went on her way, arriving late in the afternoon just as the stalls in Rosemary Lane were packing up for the day. She went from one end of the street to the other, asking if anyone had seen Eva Pocket, and although most people knew her, none of them had seen her recently. Lucy was not about to give up. It was not far to Hairbrine Court, and if Granny had moved on, Pearl might know where she had gone.

Mrs Wicks opened the door a crack. Her beady eye widened slightly as she took in Lucy's new clothes. 'What d'you want?'

'Does Eva Pocket still live here?'

'Who's asking?'

'You know me, Mrs Wicks. Miss Pocket is my granny.'

'She left weeks ago. Now clear off.'

Mrs Wicks was about to slam the door but Lucy was ready for her and she gave it a mighty shove. She stepped inside. 'I want to see Pearl and I'm not leaving until I've had a word with her.'

Caught off balance, Mrs Wicks staggered backwards, clutching at the newel post, which wobbled dangerously. 'You got no right to barge in, you cheeky little brat. I'll have the law on you.'

Peckham growled deep in his throat and crouched down, as if prepared to launch himself at her.

'Good dog,' Lucy murmured. 'On guard, boy.' She edged past Mrs Wicks, who seemed to be paralysed with fear. Peckham was relatively small, but with bared teeth and raised hackles he looked fierce. Mrs Wicks took one look at him and retreated to her domain at the back of the house.

Lucy took the stairs two at the time, coming to a halt outside Pearl's room. She hammered on the door. 'Pearl, it's me, Lucy Pocket. Let me in.'

After an agonising few moments she was beginning to think that she had missed her when the door opened to reveal Pearl, tousle-haired and sleepy-eyed, wearing nothing but her stays and a pair of drawers trimmed with lace. 'God almighty, where's the fire?' she demanded.

'It's me, Lucy. I'm looking for my nan.'

'Lucy, my pet. Come in and close the door.' Pearl reached for her wrap and shrugged it on. 'I was just having a lie-down, and I must have dropped off.'

Lucy summoned the dog with two short whistles and he came bounding up the stairs. She followed him inside and closed the door. 'Have you seen my nan, Pearl? I got to find her.'

Pearl moved to the table and searched amongst the clutter of beer bottles, newspapers and an overflowing ashtray. She found a packet of cigarettes, took one and scrabbled about until she found a match. Striking it on the tiled hearth she lit up with a sigh of satisfaction. Lucy watched, fascinated by Pearl's urgent need for a smoke, but she was growing impatient. 'Do you know where she is, Pearl?' she repeated anxiously.

'Can't say I do, love.' Pearl relaxed, regarding her through a haze of blue smoke. 'You look very smart. What's it like living with the toffs?'

'Horrible. I hate it there and I want to come home.'

'Well now, that's a bit difficult because I don't know where Eva is now. She was in a terrible state when she come back after leaving you with your granddad. I never thought to see Eva Pocket blubbing like a baby, but she was really upset. Then she packed her bags and took off, and I haven't seen her since.'

Lucy sank down on the nearest chair, but she leapt to her feet again having sat on one of Pearl's high-heeled boots. She put it on the floor and resumed her seat. 'What shall I do? I asked round the stalls in Rosemary Lane and no one knew where she was.'

Pearl sucked on her cigarette, inhaling deeply, and exhaled with a sigh. 'I really can't help. Can't you think of a place she might go?'

'She mentioned someone called Abe, and he gave her a bag of clothes to sell in the market, but I never met him.'

'I don't suppose you did, Lucy. He's not the sort of person a kid like you ought to mix with.'

'But Granny said he was an old friend.'

Pearl flicked ash into the empty grate. 'Do you know what a fence is? And I don't mean the wooden kind.'

'I ain't stupid,' Lucy said, forgetting Miss Wantage's rigorous attempts to correct her grammar. 'It's a person who deals in stolen goods.'

'Exactly. That's what Abe does, and more besides. If Eva's gone to live with him you'd be better off going back to the toff's house.'

Lucy responded to a nudge from the dog's nose, and automatically patted his head. 'I said I ain't going back there and that's the end of it. Tell me where to find this chap.'

Pearl took a last drag on her cigarette and

stubbed it out, adding to the pile of dog-ends in the ashtray. 'Tell you what, nipper. I ain't sending you into that den of thieves. You'd best stay here and let me go. If Eva's there I'll pass on the message and see what she says, although I can guess what it will be.'

'I want to be with her,' Lucy said stubbornly.

'I know, love. I understand, but your gran will do what's best for you.' Pearl reached for a stocking which was dangling precariously from the mantelshelf and pulled it on. Its twin was discovered on the far side of the bed, as was her petticoat and crumpled cotton gown. 'Tighten me laces, will you, love?' she said after a struggle with the strings of her stays. 'I ain't as slender as I was in the old days. It takes longer and longer to squeeze me into me frocks.'

Lucy tugged and pulled while Pearl held her breath and sucked in her tummy, and eventually, due to their combined efforts, they managed to get her waist down to the required size. 'I dunno,' Pearl said, gazing critically at her reflection in a mirror propped up on the chest of drawers. 'I don't have all this trouble first thing when I get dressed, and it ain't that I scoff lots of grub. It must be the beer I drink in the pub with Carlos what does it.' She tidied her hair and reached for a perky little straw hat trimmed with faded pink roses, which she secured with a vicious-looking hat pin. 'There, not bad, even if I say so meself.'

'You look splendid, Pearl,' Lucy said tactfully. She did not like to mention that Pearl's garments were grubby and smelled strongly of stale fish and tobacco smoke.

'Ta, love.' Pearl dropped a kiss on top of Lucy's head as she walked past. 'Stay here and lock the door. Don't let the wicked witch Wicks in, even if she threatens you with the law. That one wouldn't dare call a copper, so take no notice of her. I'll be back as soon as I can.'

With Pearl gone Lucy found herself with nothing to occupy her time. She locked the door, and stood looking round at the scene of utter chaos. After a moment's thought she decided that the least she could do in return for Pearl's kindness was to tidy the room. She opened the window to let out the smoke, but the stench from the outside privy and the foul smell of the riverbank at low tide made her change her mind, and she closed it again. It was hot and stuffy, but she worked diligently. Living with Granny had taught her to keep house in the most insalubrious places, and she soon had everything under control. Pearl's clothes, abandoned in heaps as if she had tossed them over her shoulder not caring where they landed, were folded neatly and put away. She emptied the ashtray onto a sheet of newspaper and bundled it up with the rest of the rubbish, placing it by the door ready to be disposed of later. Having done all she could, she lay down on the bed and curled up with the dog at her side.

She was awakened by the sound of Pearl's voice demanding to be let in, and she tumbled off the bed, still half asleep. It was dusk and the room was filled with shadows. 'Where've you been?' she demanded as Pearl breezed in, smelling strongly of gin and tobacco.

'Don't take that tone with me, kid,' Pearl said,

tossing her hat in the direction of the chest and missing. It fell to the floor, losing a petal from one of the silk roses. 'I've been searching for Eva in all the usual places. I visited every pub where she might have been, and no luck.'

'Did you find her friend Abe?'

'I did, and she weren't with him. Sorry, kid, but I did me best.' Pearl reached into her pocket. 'I got you a pie from the pub.' She produced a small grease-stained package and laid it on the table. 'It's got a bit squashed, but they're the best pies in the East End.' She sank down on a chair and began to unlace her boots. 'I got to get some sleep. I'm up at five to go and get me fish.'

Lucy snatched up the pie and peeled off the paper. Her stomach growled in anticipation and the delicious aroma made her mouth water. She had not eaten for hours and she was starving. She took a bite, tossing a piece of pastry to Peckham who gulped it down, wagging his tail furiously.

Pearl took off one of her boots, peering into the gloom as she dropped it on the floor. 'Where's everything gone?'

'I tidied up a bit,' Lucy said with her mouth full of pie. 'I thought it would be a nice surprise.'

'I won't be able to find a thing.' Pearl heaved off the other boot with a sigh of relief. 'It's all right, love. You did your best, but I liked things as they was. Anyway, I'm going to get me head down and you should too. You'd best come with me in the morning. I can't leave you here alone.'

Early next morning, Lucy accompanied Pearl to Billingsgate market to purchase the fish she would sell that day. They went on to the Three Tuns tavern, where Pearl had an arrangement with the landlady, who cooked the fish in return for her help in preparing the fish dinners for which the pub was famous. Peckham was not allowed indoors, but he sat patiently outside the front entrance while Lucy made herself useful in the kitchen.

The landlady was a motherly woman who insisted that no one could work properly on an empty stomach, and she provided a breakfast of bacon, eggs and sausages for all the staff on duty at the time. Lucy ate hers with relish, saving a sausage to give to Peckham later, and then it was back to the slimy business of clearing up after Pearl and the kitchen boy, who was learning to be a cook. The bones and skin went into the stockpot for fish soup, and the guts were tossed into the river, to be scavenged by a squabble of seagulls.

It was almost midday by the time they had completed their tasks and the fish was fried to golden perfection. They set off with Peckham trotting at Lucy's side. 'I always do well in Rosemary Lane,' Pearl said cheerfully. 'You never know, we might find someone who's seen Eva, or she might turn up in person.'

'I do hope so,' Lucy murmured breathlessly as she lengthened her stride in order to match Pearl's. 'But I'm not giving up. I'm never going back to that house in Albemarle Street. I'd rather end up in clink.'

'Don't you want to be a lady?' Pearl shot her a sideways glance. 'You got that pretty little frock and good boots; what more could a kid your age ask for?'

'Someone to love me like my granny does,' Lucy said with her bottom lip trembling. 'No one cared for me in that place, least of all Sir William.'

'But he's your grandfather, Lucy. He must care a bit or he wouldn't have gone to all that trouble to find you.'

'He only wants me because he's got no one else, apart from that horrid man Linus Daubenay. He scared me, and I ain't scared easily.'

Pearl threw back her head and laughed. 'You're a caution, Lucy Pocket. Come on, we'd best walk faster or the fish will be cold, and all my profits will fly out of the window.'

Lucy broke into a trot. Visions of pennies sprouting wings and flying up into the cloudless sky brought a smile to her lips. She was still in a dream when she realised that they had reached Rosemary Lane, and she had become separated from Pearl. Coming to a sudden halt she listened for the cries of 'Fish, fresh fish', but all she could hear was the babble of voices and the shouts of the vendors extolling the virtues of their wares. At first she was unworried and she strolled along the street, stopping to ask if anyone had seen Eva Pocket, but the answers were the same as before. Then she spotted Carlos, who was difficult to miss with his bright orange billboards and his waxed and curled moustache. She rushed up to him. 'Have you seen Pearl?'

He stared at her and his bushy black eyebrows shot up to his hairline. 'I thought you had left us for better things, little one.'

'I ran away,' Lucy said shortly. 'I was with Pearl just now, but I've lost her.'

'She's a difficult woman to lose,' Carlos said, chuckling. 'Follow your nose and you'll find her.'

'It's not funny. She's helping me to find my granny.'

His smile faded. 'Ah, yes, the lovely Eva. I haven't seen her for a long time.'

'You're no help,' Lucy said crossly. 'I must find Pearl.'

'You'll like as not find her in the pub,' Carlos called after her as she hurried off. She was angry with Carlos for laughing at her, and with Pearl for walking off without her, but most of all she was furious with herself for lapsing into a day-dream when she should have been concentrating on more important matters. She broke into a run, dodging in and out of the milling crowds who were on the hunt for a bargain, but just as she reached the pub she found her way barred by a tall, well-dressed gentleman. 'I thought I might find you here.'

She uttered a cry of fright and tried to sidestep him, but Linus Daubenay was too quick for her and he caught her by the arm, twisting it behind her back. 'I know Eva's haunts of old,' he said triumphantly. 'And when my uncle told me where he had eventually tracked you down, I knew exactly where to come.'

'Leave me alone. I won't go back there. You can't make me.' She looked round for her dog, but he was nowhere to be seen. It was the first time he had strayed from her side and now she had genuine need of him.

'Your grandfather has the police looking for you, but I've no intention of taking you to Albemarle Street,' Linus said casually.

'I won't go anywhere with you. Let me go or I'll scream and me friends will come and save me.' She caught sight of Peckham, who was romping with another mongrel. She whistled and he was suddenly alert. He came bounding up to them, wagging his tail.

'If that cur bites me I'll kill him,' Linus said through clenched teeth. 'Keep him quiet or it's the last you'll see of him.' He twisted her arm, making her yelp.

Peckham leapt at him and Linus kicked out with his foot.

'Don't hurt him,' Lucy cried. 'I'll do what you want.'

He propelled her past the public house and into the next street, where a carriage was waiting. 'Get in,' he said gruffly as the coachman leapt down to open the door.

'I'm not going anywhere with you.' Lucy sent a pleading look at the coachman but he turned his head away.

'Yes, you will,' Linus said firmly. 'I'm taking you to find your grandmother. That's what you want, isn't it?'

'Really?' Lucy stared at him, trying to decide whether he was telling the truth. 'You know where my granny is?'

'Of course. How else would I have known exactly where to find you?'

She decided that it was worth the risk. 'All right, but my dog comes with me.' For a moment she thought he was going to refuse, but he gave her a curt nod and she climbed into the carriage, followed by Peckham. He jumped onto her lap and she held him so close that she could feel his small heart beating nineteen to the dozen. The warmth of his body gave her courage and she sat very still, staring out of the window so that she did not have to look at Linus when he took his seat opposite her. He tapped the roof with his cane and the carriage moved forward, slowly at first and then picking up speed.

The city streets flashed past the windows, which at first was exciting as every hoofbeat was taking her closer to her grandmother, but the journey seemed to be taking a long time. Linus sat with his eyes closed, although Lucy did not think that he slept. She cleared her throat noisily in an attempt to attract his attention. 'Are you sure we're going the right way?'

He opened one eye. 'It's none of your business, so shut up.' He opened both eyes when Peckham growled deep in his throat. 'And keep that mongrel quiet or I'll pitch him out onto the road.'

Lucy subsided into silence, stroking the dog's head. It seemed strange that her grandmother had come this far, when they had always lived and worked in a small area of the East End. The manufactories and mills were giving way to flat and featureless open countryside: Lucy was beginning to panic. 'Where are you taking me? Granny wouldn't have come this far out of London.'

'Ask no questions, and you'll be told no lies,' Linus said smugly. 'That's what my nanny used to say to me.'

Lucy could see that she was not going to get an answer, but she was growing more suspicious with every passing minute. She considered the likelihood of being fatally injured if she were to open the carriage door and jump out, abandoning the idea almost instantly. A broken neck would not solve her problems. She settled back against the leather squabs. If she bided her time until they stopped somewhere she might be able to give Linus the slip and make her way back to London.

She awakened with a start, realising that she must have fallen asleep. The inside of the carriage was in semi-darkness, but only a short while ago it had been morning. She peered out of the window and saw that they were in what looked like the middle of a forest. When the coachman opened the door she knew for certain that they were a long way from the polluted atmosphere of the city: the air smelled fresh and clean, with just a hint of wood smoke and the rich, fruity aroma of damp soil.

Linus roused himself. 'This is your destination, Lucy Pocket.' He alighted from the carriage, leaving the coachman to assist Lucy. Peckham jumped to the ground and ran off into the trees, barking excitedly.

'Where are we?' Lucy asked anxiously. 'Where's my granny?'

'Why don't you go into the cottage and see if she's there?'

The grim smile on his face confirmed her suspicion that she had been tricked. There was a triumphant set to his shoulders as he strolled towards the open cottage door. 'Meg, where are you? What sort of welcome is this for your lord and master?'

Lucy turned to the coachman. 'Where are we, mister?'

'Epping Forest, miss. I wouldn't advise you to wander off on your own.' He climbed back onto the box, delving into the capacious pocket of his greatcoat and bringing out a pipe and a tobacco pouch. It was obvious to Lucy that he was not going to help her, no matter how much she pleaded.

'Don't just stand there, child.' Linus turned and beckoned to her. 'This is your new home.'

A young woman emerged from the cottage, brushing her mousy hair back from her forehead with a work-worn hand. Even at a distance of several feet Lucy could see the dark shadows beneath eyes which appeared too large for her pale face. She must, Lucy thought, have been beautiful once, but she looked as fragile as a winter rose, faded and dying from the cold. Linus slipped his arm around her shoulders and kissed her on the lips. Even to Lucy's inexperienced eyes it appeared to be a possessive gesture rather than an affectionate one. 'I've brought you a helper, my dear,' he said, pointing at Lucy, who stood motionless and undecided. 'This is Lucy Pocket. She'll be living with you from now on.'

'I can't look after another child, Linus. I have my hands full already.' Meg clutched her belly in a gesture that Lucy recognised, having seen it many times in women worn away to almost nothing by constant child-bearing.

'Lucy will help you with the children,' Linus said casually. 'You've got Bramwell to help with the chores, and Hester to keep you all fed. What more do you want, woman?'

'Have you come to stay this time, Linus?' Meg asked wearily. 'If so, you'd better come in, and bring the child with you.' She retraced her steps, dragging her feet as if every step was an effort.

Linus threw up his hands. 'Women! Who knows what goes on in their little minds?' He glared at Lucy. 'Get inside. I'm not telling you again.'

Reluctantly, and partly because it had started to rain, Lucy followed him into the cottage, and was immediately assailed by the delicious aroma of baking bread and something savoury that was bubbling away in a pot on the range. The kitchen was surprisingly large, with a beamed ceiling from which hung bunches of herbs and strings of onions. Ladder-back chairs with rush seats surrounded a pine table, which was littered with cooking utensils. A middle-aged woman, who Lucy assumed must be Hester, was up to her elbows in water at the stone sink. She gave Lucy a curious glance and then carried on with what she was doing. Meg hurried across the flagstone floor to pick up a small girl, who was sobbing and pointing at a little boy who had a wooden doll in his hand and was swinging it around his head.

'Bertie, you bad boy,' Meg said crossly. 'Give it back to Vicky. It's not your toy.'

Linus looked on with barely veiled impatience. 'Can't you stop her crying, Meg? Why is it that I come home to nothing but wailing infants?'

'It's not as if you had nothing to do with their

coming into the world, Master Linus.' Hester stopped what she was doing to glare at Linus.

Lucy could hardly believe that a servant would dare to speak to Linus in such a way. She fully expected him to berate her for her insolence, but he merely shrugged his shoulders.

'You're a religious woman, Nanny. I thought you would call it God's will that we've been so blessed.'

'Stop it, Linus. Don't tease Hester.' Meg took the doll from the boy and thrust it into the hands of her sobbing daughter. She picked her up and cradled her in her arms. 'There, there, dear. You have your dolly back, so all is well.'

'The children would be more blessed if they'd been born on the right side of the blanket,' Hester said gloomily. 'Your poor mother would die of shame if she knew how you'd turned out, Master Linus.'

'Well, as she's been dead for ten years it's not going to upset her now. I should have pensioned you off ages ago, but I kept you on out of the goodness of my heart.'

'You kept me on because I'm useful to you. I work for almost nothing, and do my best to look after Meg and the babies. It's a pity you don't do more for them.'

Lucy held her breath. She had seen Linus in a temper and she waited for him to erupt in anger. Meg seemed to share her concern and she stepped in between Linus and the irate Hester. 'That's enough, Hester. Don't let's spoil the short time that my husband is with us, my dear.' She set Vicky down on the floor and the little girl toddled over to her brother, waving her doll in triumph.

'Common-law, not legally wed,' Hester muttered, hobbling over to the range and opening the oven door. She closed it again. 'Another five minutes or so and the bread will be ready. I suppose you will want to eat in the dining room now that he's home?'

'Thank you, Hester. The master and I will take our meal together, but I think perhaps Lucy would be more comfortable if she ate in the kitchen with you and the children.' Meg turned to Lucy with a gentle smile. 'Bram will be in soon for his midday meal. He's a bit older than you, but I'm sure you'll be friends.'

'I'm Sir William's granddaughter,' Lucy said with dignity. 'And I've been brought here against my will.' She pointed at Linus. 'He told me that he was taking me to my granny, and he lied.'

Meg's blue eyes widened and her pretty mouth drooped at the corners. 'Is this true, Linus?'

He seized her by the arm. 'I think we need to talk in private.' He propelled her towards a door at the back of the room. 'Bring me a bottle of my good claret; better still, the child can make herself useful. She can wait on us, Nanny. Don't say that I never think of your aged bones.' His laughter echoed round the kitchen as he left, taking Meg with him.

'Well now. Here's a pretty kettle of fish.' Hester looked Lucy up and down as if calculating the cost of her outfit. 'I think I can guess the reason why you're here, Lucy Pocket. I didn't know Sir William had a granddaughter.'

'Well, he does, and it's me,' Lucy said angrily. 'I

don't want to be here any more than I wanted to live in that big house in Mayfair. I've run away once and I can do it again.'

At the sound of her raised voice both children started to bawl and Hester rushed over to them. 'Now look what you've done. You've upset my little darlings.'

Lucy ran to the door and wrenched it open. She raced outside and found herself caught in a heavy shower. Blinded by the rain she cannoned into someone with such force that they were both knocked off their feet.

Chapter Seven

Lucy found herself lying in a puddle winded and gasping for breath, with Peckham licking her face.

'Look where you're going, nipper.' A boy scrambled to his feet and stood looking down at her with a puzzled expression on his freckled face. 'Who are you?' He held out his hand and helped her up, ignoring the dog's threatening growls. 'Good dog,' he said firmly. 'I mean her no harm.'

'It was your fault,' Lucy gasped. 'I was just walking out of the door.'

'You were racing as if the devil himself was on your heels.' He pulled her into the porch. 'I'm soaked to the skin and now you are too. What's your name?'

She shook free from his grasp. 'Let me pass. You can't keep me here.'

'Go on then,' he said with a wave of his hand. 'Run if you must, but you won't find your way through the forest. You'll be lost and you'll never find your way out.'

Lucy glanced at the coachman, who had taken shelter in the log store, but he was staring into space, smoking his pipe, oblivious to anything that was going on around him. 'I ain't afraid of nothing,' she said crossly. 'Tell me which path to take and I'll be off.'

He ran his hand through his wet hair, brushing it back from his forehead. His eyes sparkled as if he was about to burst out laughing at any moment, and his generous lips curved in a grin. 'You're a spunky little thing, but you still haven't told me your name, or what you're doing here.'

Lucy shivered. Her clothes were wet and she was close to tears, but she was not going to let herself down in front of a stranger. 'I'm Lucy Pocket.'

'Bramwell Southwood, commonly known as Bram,' he said, shaking her hand. 'I'm Meg's brother, but you're a bit of a puzzle. I suppose he brought you here, because we don't get visitors in the normal run of things.' He jerked his head in the direction of the carriage. 'It was a bad day when Meg took up with Daubenay. I hope you're not his kid.'

'Indeed I'm not,' Lucy said indignantly. 'He kidnapped me and he's going to leave me here.' The words tumbled from her lips. She had not meant to tell this strange boy so much and she watched him closely, trying to judge his reaction. Would he help her? Or would he think she was lying?

He opened his mouth to reply, but was cut short by the sudden appearance of Hester. She caught Lucy by the scruff of the neck. 'I can see you're going to be a pest,' she said, sighing. 'Haven't I got enough on my hands without having a runaway child to look after?' She propelled Lucy into the kitchen, followed by Bram and the dog.

'I'm not a runaway,' Lucy protested. 'I've been kidnapped. I just told this boy so but I don't think he believed me.'

Hester let her go, shaking her head. 'You're wet through.' She turned to Bram. 'And you're leaving muddy footprints on my clean floor. I don't know what the world is coming to.'

Bram shrugged his shoulders, looking down at Hester from his superior height. Despite everything Lucy was impressed. At a guess she put his age at fourteen, or maybe fifteen, but he was tall and broad-shouldered, making him seem much older. Despite her reservations she found herself drawn to him. He looked like someone she might be able to trust, and she liked the way his hazel eyes twinkled. He bent down to drop a kiss on Hester's lined cheek. 'Don't blame me, Hester my darling.' His expression darkened. 'Linus is the one to blame for us being stuck in the middle of nowhere, and it seems he brought the kid here against her will.'

Hester gave Lucy a searching look. 'Is this true, child?' She frowned thoughtfully. 'It would account for the fact that she doesn't seem to have any luggage.'

'I was trying to find my granny. Sir William paid her to give me up, but I know she didn't want to lose me. We was always close.'

'Who is Sir William?' Bram asked curiously. 'None of this makes sense.'

'Sir William Marriott says he's my grandfather.'

Hester stared at her, frowning. 'Then you must be Julius's daughter. That would make Linus your second cousin, or something like that. How come I've never heard of you until this day?'

Lucy shrugged her shoulders. 'Don't ask me. I didn't know who my pa was until a short while ago. Ma ran off when I was two and I've always lived with my nan. That is until Sir William turned up and spoiled things. He wants me to grow up to be a lady.'

'And you're in line to inherit his fortune,' Hester mused. 'No wonder Linus wants to get rid of you.'

'You understand.' Lucy's voice broke on a sob. 'I think he wants to kill me.'

'What nonsense is this?'

The sound of Meg's voice made them turn with a guilty start. Hester moved swiftly to the range and lifted the lid from the bubbling pot. 'I'll serve up now, shall I?'

'Where is the claret? The child was supposed to bring it.' Meg fixed her gaze on Lucy. 'You're wet.' She glanced at her brother. 'And so are you, Bram. What's going on? Can't I have a quiet meal with my husband without all this fuss?'

'Common-law,' Hester muttered beneath her breath. She lifted the pan from the hob. 'Sit the little ones in their seats, Meg,' she added, jerking her head in the direction of Bertie and Vicky, who had found a common interest in trying to catch Peckham, who so far had managed to dodge their clutching fingers. 'Bram will fetch the wine and I'll serve the stew. Let's hope it's good enough for Master Linus. He was always a fussy eater.'

Lucy's first reaction was to save Peckham from being mauled by two lively little children, but it was obvious that he could take care of himself, and she helped Hester by slicing the bread and spreading it with butter. She would eat first, she decided, and make her getaway when Linus had gone. There must be a well-trodden path leading out of the forest and she intended to find it.

Darkness had fallen with surprising speed considering the fact that it was early summer, but the foliage of the ancient oaks, beeches, silver birch and hornbeam formed a dense canopy, excluding all but the smallest glimpses of sky. Lucy had been walking for hours: she was exhausted and even Peckham, despite his usual boundless energy, was exhibiting signs of fatigue. The dried leaves crunched underfoot and twigs snapped, sending eerie echoes resonating through the forest. There were other sounds that made the hairs on the back of Lucy's neck stand on end, sounds that were unfamiliar to a city child. Slithering noises in the undergrowth were followed by snorts and snuffles which were chillingly human. Wings flapped in the branches overhead, and nocturnal animals were beginning to wake up and move about. This was their territory and not hers. She sank down against the thick bole of a pollarded oak, with Peckham snuggling up at her side. The thundering of hooves on the hard-packed forest floor was too close for comfort. Visions of a headless horseman galloping through the trees flashed before her eyes, and she screamed in terror, covering her face with her hands.

Then, in the distance she heard someone calling her name. She held her breath, thinking that once again it was her active imagination playing tricks on her.

'Lucy? Where are you?' Bram's voice was loud and clear.

'Here,' Lucy shouted. 'I'm here.'

Peckham joined in, yapping joyfully as if he realised that help was at hand.

Moments later Lucy could see the beam of a lantern bobbing about between the trees, and then Bram emerged from the darkness. He knelt at her side. 'Are you hurt?'

'No. I was tired and I couldn't find the path.'

'What did I tell you?' he said triumphantly. He lifted her to her feet. 'Next time perhaps you'll listen to what I tell you.'

'Yes, Bram. Is it far to walk from here?'

He chuckled. 'Not far, kid. You must have been going round in circles all this time.'

'I think a headless horseman gallops through this forest. I heard hoofbeats.'

'Deer,' Bram said, taking her by the hand. 'It'll be deer. The forest is full of them.'

'Has Linus gone back to London?'

'Yes. He never stays long, unless he's being dunned for money, and then we can't get rid of him. Meg never complains, but she's besotted with him. God alone knows why. I hate the bloke.'

'Did he know I'd run away? Was he cross?'

Bram squeezed her fingers. 'I think he was pleased. Meg wanted him to look for you, but he said you'd run away so you had to take your chances. Then he upped and left. I daresay he's headed back to London and the gaming tables. He thinks I don't know what he gets up to, but I got a good idea, and he's a wrong 'un.'

'He said he'd do for me.' Lucy stifled a yawn. 'I think he meant it.'

'If that's what he wants he made a mistake bringing you to the forest. You've got Meg, Hester and me to look after you, nipper.'

'And Peckham,' Lucy said tiredly.

'We'll all look after both of you, so don't worry.'

'Maybe you could help me find my granny.'

'That too.' Bram slowed down, pointing to a thin stream of light just visible through the trees. 'There's the cottage. You see how close to home you were?'

'It's not my home, but I'm glad you found me. Ta, Bram.'

Lucy dragged her feet as she walked and was overwhelmed by the reception she received in the cottage kitchen. Meg embraced her with tears in her eyes, and Hester fussed over her like a mother hen. She sent Bram outside to lock up the animals while she helped Lucy to undress. 'But this is all I got,' Lucy protested. 'I left everything in Grandfather's house.'

'Sir William will be worried.' Meg pulled up a chair and sank down on the hard wooden seat, her face pale with fatigue. 'I told Linus he had to tell his uncle that you are safe.'

'And pigs might fly,' Hester said sharply. 'You know he won't do that, Meg. Why do you choose to think the best of him?'

'You wouldn't understand. You still see him as a small child, but I love the man he has become, faults and all.'

Lucy shivered despite the fact that it was a warm summer evening and the fire in the range made it even warmer. 'He's a bad man, miss. He wants me dead so that he can inherit.'

Meg's eyes flashed angrily. 'That's a wicked thing to say, Lucy. Linus brought you here so that we could look after you while he searches for your grandmother. He said that Sir William was wrong to take you away from her.'

'He's lying,' Lucy said stubbornly.

'You're completely and utterly wrong.' Meg rose slowly to her feet. 'I'll make allowances for you because you're very young and you're tired out, but I won't let you say nasty things about the man who's done his best to make you happy.'

Lucy looked to Hester for support, but she shrugged her shoulders. 'I'm just a servant,' she muttered. 'Although servants get a wage and I don't, so I'm little more than a slave.' She bundled up Lucy's soiled dress. 'You'd best put her to bed, Meg. The child is falling asleep on her feet.'

Meg held out her hand. 'Come with me, Lucy. You can sleep in the children's room, but I've only just got them off, so please don't make a noise.' She led the way through the kitchen, along a narrow passage and up a steep flight of stairs to the first floor. The children's room was at the back of the building, beneath the eaves. Lying top to tail in a narrow cot, their rosy cheeks and tumbled baby curls gave them the appearance of sleeping angels, but Peckham gave them a wide berth and leapt onto the bed nearest the wall.

'I sometimes sleep in here with them,' Meg whispered, handing Lucy a nightgown she had taken from her own room. 'This will be too large, but we'll sort something out tomorrow. It's a pity Linus didn't think to bring your clothes, but gentlemen rarely consider such things.' She leaned over to kiss Lucy on the cheek. 'Goodnight, dear. Sleep well.' She left the room, closing the door softly.

Next morning, having been awakened early by Bertie and Vicky bouncing on her bed, with Peckham seeking refuge beneath the covers, Lucy had little option but to get up and take the children downstairs. They arrived in the kitchen to find Hester up to her elbows in flour as she kneaded bread dough. She dusted her hands off and seized Bertie, who was about to follow Peckham out into the yard. She closed the door, ignoring Bertie's howls of protest, and set him down on the floor. 'They're a handful,' she said with a wry smile. 'I love them dearly, but I'm getting too old to run round after little ones, and with another on the-way it's going to be very hard work indeed.' She picked up the dough and slammed it down onto the table top, sending up a cloud of flour. 'You could make yourself useful in that direction, my girl.'

Lucy kept a wary eye on Vicky, who was attempting to climb onto a chair. 'I don't know nothing about kids, but them two would try the patience of a saint.'

'Your grammar is appalling,' Hester said, sniffing. 'But I don't suppose that matters if you're prepared to help keep an eye on the little ones. Meg sees to most of their needs, but she's delicate and ought to rest. Maybe you were sent here for a purpose after all.'

'I want to find my granny. I can't stay here, miss.'

Hester placed the dough in a bowl and covered it with a damp cloth. 'All in good time, Lucy. I want you to promise not to pester Meg with such talk. First things first, and you need something to wear. That pretty tartan frock is all but ruined. I've washed it and hung it out to dry, but in the meantime we'll tie a pinny round your waist and hitch the nightgown up so that you don't trip over the hem.' She wiped her hands on her apron and reached up to snatch a clean one off the drying rack. 'Come here, and I'll fix it for you.' Somewhat reluctantly, Lucy stood very still while Hester tied the strings. 'There, that's better.' She surveyed her work with a satisfied nod. 'We'll have to get you some new clothes, but the market in Epping isn't until Monday week, so you'll have to wear your tattered frock until Meg and Bram go there to sell our eggs and any milk we have to spare.'

'I know about markets,' Lucy said eagerly. Here at last was something with which she was more than familiar. 'Me and Granny sold clothes at the

Rag Fair.'

'Then you'll know what to look out for. Maybe some of the stallholders travel as far as London. You might even meet someone who knows your grandmother.' Hester had to raise her voice in order to make herself heard over the sound of the two small children's demands for food. She lifted a saucepan from a hay box and set it on the table. 'Porridge,' she said tersely. 'Serve the little ones first and then help yourself, Lucy. Bram's already had his, and Meg has hers in bed. That's if she's feeling up to eating.'

Lucy found some bowls on the pine dresser and she gave the children their food before serving herself. She took a seat at the table. 'I'm Lucy,' she said, giving them an encouraging smile. 'I think we must be related in some way, but I'm not sure how. Anyway, you two are going to be good for me, aren't you?'

Bertie spooned porridge into his mouth. 'No.'

'Don't worry,' Hester said hastily. 'He's going through that naughty stage. It's "No" to everything with Master Albert Southwood.'

Lucy met Bertie's defiant gaze with a casual shrug of her shoulders. 'If that's the way he wants it.' She turned her attention to Vicky, who had spilled most of her porridge down her front. 'You seem to have difficulty finding your mouth, little 'un. We'll have to get Peckham to clear up the mess on the floor, and if you're good we'll go outside and throw sticks for him.'

'Me too,' Bertie said eagerly.

Lucy glanced over her shoulder. 'Would you like to play with the dog?'

Bertie opened his mouth as if to make his usual response and then closed it. He nodded vigorously.

'What do you say?' Lucy asked, trying hard not to giggle.

He hung his head. 'Yes.'

'Yes, what?'

'Yes, please, Lucy.'

She smiled. 'Good boy.'

'I couldn't have done better myself,' Hester said with a nod of approval. 'I'll just take the tray to Meg...' She broke off as the door opened and Meg wandered into the kitchen with her hair tied up in rags and a shawl draped over her nightgown.

'It's very quiet in here,' she said, gazing at her children in surprise. 'I came to give them their breakfast.'

'We have a born nursemaid in Lucy.' Hester placed Meg's breakfast on the table. 'Sit down and eat, my dear. Lucy can take the little ones outside as she promised.'

'But they're not dressed for outdoors,' Meg protested. 'They'll catch cold.'

'It's warm and sunny. They don't need coddling. Fresh air and good food is what youngsters need, and the freedom to run round and enjoy themselves. Have your breakfast in peace for once, Meg, and let Lucy look after them.'

Lucy rose to her feet, lifted Vicky in her arms and held her hand out to Bertie. He ignored the friendly overture with a toss of his head and raced outside into the yard. Lucy followed more slowly with Vicky, and Peckham walked sedately at her side.

Bram was mucking out the stall where the donkey was stabled at night. He stopped, leaning on his broom as the small procession crossed the yard. 'What's all this? How did you persuade Meg to let them come outside?'

'I didn't. It was Hester.'

He balanced the broom against the wall and strode over to them, picking Bertie up and swinging him round. 'So you've decided to stay, have you, Lucy?'

'Only until Monday week. Hester said you'd take me to market to get some new clothes, and I might find a stallholder who knows Granny and can give me an idea where she might be now.'

'I wouldn't pin too much hope on that, nipper. But there's no harm in asking, and we might just be lucky.'

'You will help me, won't you, Bram?'

'Yes, but only if you promise you won't wander off into the forest on your own again. You might not be so lucky next time.'

'I promise.'

'Throw sticks for doggie,' Bertie said, tugging at Lucy's skirt.

Bram ruffled his hair. 'Don't be a pest, Bertie.'

Lucy bent down and picked up a sliver of bark from the log pile. She gave it to Bertie. 'Throw it for him and see if he'll fetch it.'

'He'll wear you out and the dog,' Bram said, laughing. 'I'd best get back to work or I won't get through my chores.'

'Maybe I can help a bit. I daresay these two have naps.'

'Tire them out and then they might fall asleep,

if you're lucky. It's no wonder my sister is exhausted.' Bram's expression darkened. 'I hate Daubenay. He's the one who brought her to this, but she won't hear a word against him.'

'I'm sorry. I know how you feel. He's a wicked man and she deserves better.'

Lucy hurried away to rescue Vicky, who had fallen over and was lying on the ground sobbing. It was, she thought, going to be a long day, and judging by the boundless energy displayed by Bertie she knew who was going to flag first, and it wasn't Peckham.

She had some respite later when both children were put to bed for an afternoon nap. Meg was in the small room at the back of the house which served as a parlour and dining room when Linus was at home. She was sitting by the window in order to take advantage of the sunlight, and had her workbox on a small table at her side. She stopped sewing and looked up with a welcoming smile. 'I thought you might like to help me,' she said eagerly. 'I have two shirts to finish before we go to town, and I'm a bit behindhand. Do you know how to sew a straight seam, Lucy?'

Lucy went to sit beside her, pulling up a stool. She shook her head. 'Not really. I was supposed to be embroidering a sampler but I didn't get very far with it.'

'Can you do backstitch?'

'That's the only stitch I know.'

'That's wonderful.' Meg put her sewing aside and reached for another pile of fine white cambric. 'I've already tacked the seam. You just have to work along it in backstitch, keeping it neat and straight and using small stitches. Do you think you could do that?'

'I can try, but I'm not very good.'

'Let's see what you can do.'

Lucy tried hard, but she kept pricking her finger and her stitches were anything but even. 'I can't do it,' she said in desperation.

'It comes with practice.' Meg took the material from her and examined it closely. 'I'm afraid I'll have to unpick this, but thank you for trying.'

'Why do you have to sew shirts? Don't he give you enough to live on?'

Meg looked up, startled. 'My goodness, you are direct. No, I'm afraid Linus has a great deal of expense in London. He gives me what he can afford.'

Lucy thought of the IOUs, and the vast amount that Linus had won and lost at the gaming tables. She decided that there were some things that even a grown-up person did not need to know. 'I'm sorry,' she murmured, staring at her unsuccessful attempt at a fine seam.

Meg folded the material. 'You tried, my dear. That's the most important thing. Why don't you go outside and see if you can help Bram?'

'Ta, miss.' Forgetting everything that Miss Wantage had attempted to instil in her, Lucy leapt to her feet and bounded out of the room.

She found Bram tending the vegetable bed in the small patch of kitchen garden. He stopped hoeing. 'It's too hot to keep this up,' he said, wiping a trickle of sweat from his brow. 'I'm going for a swim.'

'A swim in the forest?'

Bram threw back his head and laughed. 'No, silly. Come on, I'll show you.' He threw down the hoe and strode off in the direction of the trees. Lucy was reluctant at first; the memory of being lost and frightened had kept her from making a further attempt to escape, but Bram knew his away around and she trusted him. She ran after him, catching him up just as he entered the cool green shade of the forest.

They walked along barely discernible paths with Lucy clutching Bram's hand. He seemed to sense her fear and diverted her attention by pointing out and naming the different trees. Squirrels leapt from branch to branch overhead, and Peckham raced on ahead causing small animals to dash for safety in the hollow trunks of fallen trees. Sunbeams filtered through the thick canopy of leaves, casting golden shadows on the carpet of dead leaves and beech mast. Lucy was entranced. This was a different world, unlike any other she had created in the game, and with Bram at her side she felt happy and carefree.

Then, quite suddenly, they were in a clearing and sunlight sparkled on the still surface of a large pond. Patches of wild iris made vivid splashes of yellow amongst the tall reeds, and on the margins of the water spikes of feathery white bogbean poked their heads up through a spread of olive-green leaves. 'It's fairyland,' Lucy whispered. 'I never seen nothing like it, Bram.'

He pulled his shirt over his head and dropped it on the ground. 'Can you swim?'

'No. I was taught never to go too near the water's edge. They pull corpses out of the

Thames every day.'

'You can sit on the bank and dip your feet in,' he said, chuckling. 'I'm going for a swim.' He dropped his trousers and waded into the water, and to Lucy's consternation Peckham leapt in after him, and soon their heads were bobbing about side by side, sending ripples across the surface of the pond. She did not know whether to laugh or cry for help, but after a few anxious moments she began to relax. Bram was obviously a strong swimmer, as was Peckham, but after a while the dog obviously decided that enough was enough and was heading for the bank. He scrambled to safety and shook himself all over Lucy, who jumped aside too late to miss the worst of it. Her freshly laundered tartan frock was spattered with mud and Hester would be cross. Lucy shrugged and sighed. Grown-ups were difficult to please at the best of times.

'Take your boots off and have a paddle,' Bram called out breathlessly as he swam towards her.

She backed away. 'No, ta. Don't think I will.'

He reached the shallows, and finding his footing emerged from the water with sunlight caressing his bronzed torso. He stretched, shaking droplets from his wet hair, and raised his arms above his head. Lucy stared at him in wonder. She knew that she ought to look away, but he was a picture of youth and physical perfection. She had seen bare-arsed street urchins, and the shrivelled members of old men pissing in the street, but Bram's nakedness was a thing of beauty. He might have stepped out of an old master's painting she had once seen in the National Gallery, but he was a living, breathing example of male perfection. The feelings he aroused in her were as thrilling as they were alien. She felt the blood rush to her cheeks and she forced herself to look away.

'Oy!' he shouted, breaking the spell. 'Throw my shirt to me, there's a good kid.'

On the way home and that evening she found she could not look at him without blushing, and she was sure that everyone noticed her embarrassment at supper that evening although no one said anything, least of all Bram, who seemed oblivious to everything other than the planned outing to Epping market. 'It's my one chance to see a bit of the world,' he said, spearing a boiled potato on his fork. 'We might be lucky and find someone who knows your granny, Lucy.'

She nodded, staring down at her plate. 'I do hope so.' But the thought of leaving them had lost some of its appeal.

Despite her eagerness to find her grandmother, Lucy settled into life in the cottage as if she had been born to it. For the first time in her life she was part of a loving family. Meg did everything she could to make her feel welcome and Hester was kind in her brusque, no-nonsense way. The children followed her everywhere, clamouring for her attention, and she responded with genuine affection, but Bram was her idol. He taught her the ways of the forest and showed her how to milk the goat, and where to look for the eggs in the hen coop. Every day brought a fresh wonder to a child brought up in the brick and concrete world of the inner city. Lucy was in a constant state of wonder, learning something new each day, and Bram was an excellent instructor. He made her laugh and he teased her mercilessly, but it was good-natured banter and she took it in her stride. If she had not been so desperate to find Eva she might have been happy to stay in the cottage forever.

The days flew by and everything was prepared for the trip to town, but on Monday morning Meg was suffering from a bout of sickness and did not feel well enough to travel to Epping. Hester had to stay at home and look after the children, which left Bram and Lucy to take the eggs, milk and butter to market and deliver the shirts to the tailor. Bram sat on the driving seat and Lucy huddled in the back of the cart with instructions to keep the milk churn upright if the cart wheels hit a particularly deep rut. Peckham stood up all the way, his ears flapping in the breeze as he leaned his head over the side of the cart.

It took over an hour to reach the market place, having stopped briefly at the tailor's cottage, but they arrived without mishap and Bram set about selling the produce from the back of the cart. 'I can do this on my own,' he said cheerfully. 'We've got all morning, so there's no hurry.' He put his hand in his pocket and took out a penny, pressing it into Lucy's palm. 'There's a woman who sells toffee from a stall over yonder. Buy some for yourself and don't forget to bring some back for me.'

She gave him a shy smile. 'Ta, Bram. I won't be long.'

'Take your time,' he said airily. 'If I sell the lot

I'll treat you to a ham roll and a cup of tea. I'm well in with the girl who works on that particular stall.'

Somehow that news did not please Lucy and she hurried off trying not to hate the wretched female who had caught Bram's eye. She walked round the market place with Peckham trotting dutifully at her side, stopping to make enquiries of any likely-looking traders who might have come across Eva Pocket during their travels, but all her efforts were in vain. She was downhearted and even the purchase of two pokes of toffee failed to raise her spirits. It seemed that her grandmother did not want to be found, and presenting her with the locket had been her way of saying goodbye forever. Head down, Lucy made her way back to the cart. It seemed as though she would spend the rest of her days a virtual prisoner, and even though she could think of no better place to live, she knew she would not rest until she had found her grandmother. Lost in her thoughts, she did not see the familiar lozenge on the side of the carriage, and as she was about to walk past the door opened and Sir William stepped out. 'Get in,' he said angrily. 'You've led us all a pretty dance.' He grabbed her by the arm, sending the toffees flying in all directions.

Chapter Eight

Albemarle Street, London, 1871

Lucy sat behind the desk in her grandfather's study. The pile of ledgers and sheaves of bills from tradesmen did not tell a particularly happy story. The chair she was sitting on had once seemed to her like a throne from which Sir William ruled his domain, but now he was dead, and she was no longer a frightened ten-year-old crying for her granny. It was her twenty-first birthday, but there would be no party to celebrate the event, and she doubted if there would be many presents to open. She fingered the silver locket, which always hung round her neck, wondering if Granny was thinking about her on her special day. All her efforts to trace Eva Pocket had come to nothing, and Lucy's own mother had proved just as elusive. The pain of being abandoned had gradually faded over the years, but it had never completely gone away.

Lucy and her grandfather had come to an uneasy truce, and Miss Wantage had eventually mellowed to such an extent that Lucy had been sorry to say goodbye when her governess left for Yorkshire to take care of an aged parent. Bedwin was older and slower, but he still ruled supreme in the servants' hall with Mrs Hodges as his second in command. Arch-enemy Susan had been dismissed for what had been described as 'lewd behaviour' soon after Lucy returned from her brief sojourn in Essex. Martha had also left, having been a bit too free with her favours and found herself in the family way at fourteen. Sir William had put pressure on James, the alleged father, who had married Martha, albeit reluctantly, and was now the proud father of three small children with another due at any moment. With her tormentors gone Lucy had gradually settled down to her new life.

She glanced at the longcase clock, which she had always disliked. It stood against a wall at the side of the desk, and when she was younger she had been convinced that it glared at her from its great height and at any moment might pounce and trap her in its coffin-like body. She knew now that it had been her fertile imagination running away with her, but even so her antipathy towards the clock persisted. It would, she decided, be the first thing to go to the auction house, and she would replace it with a pretty little ormolu timepiece which would stand on the mantelshelf. In any case, there were more important matters to think about than childhood fantasies. She had stopped playing the game long ago and now she was taking on the grown-up world. Mr Goldspink, her grandfather's solicitor, would arrive as the clock chimed the hour. He had visited several times towards the end of Sir William's long illness and had always been on time, never a minute early, nor a minute late.

At the first stroke there was a knock on the door and Bedwin hobbled into the study, but Mr

Goldspink rushed past him, clutching a leather document case in his hand. 'No need to announce me, my man. Good morning, Miss Marriott.' He came to a halt in front of the desk, turning his head to glower at Bedwin. 'What is it? Have you something to say?'

Bedwin looked mildly surprised, like an aged tortoise that had just awakened from hibernation. 'No, sir. Will there be anything else, Miss Lucy?'

'Thank you, Bedwin,' Lucy said hurriedly. 'That will be all for now, unless Mr Goldspink would care for some refreshment.'

'No, no, I'm happy to get down to business, Miss Marriott.'

Bedwin bowed stiffly, his aged bones creaking audibly as he left the room.

'Please be seated, Mr Goldspink.' Lucy struggled to keep a straight face. The name Yorick Goldspink had always made her want to laugh, and his appearance did not help. His beaky nose and button-black eyes put her in mind of a small bird, and he was inclined to flap and flutter when asked a question he could not immediately answer. She had visions of him pecking food from his plate at dinner and sleeping with his head tucked beneath his arm at night. He was speaking in his chirruping high-pitched voice, and she had to exercise rigid self-control to keep from smiling as he rambled on, quoting past cases in the court of chancery. In the end she had to stop him.

'I'm sorry to interrupt, Mr Goldspink, but what has this got to do with my grandfather's affairs? He told me that he was leaving everything to me.'

He came to a sudden halt, staring at her as if he

had forgotten her presence. He put his head on one side. 'I have Sir William's will here. You may read it at your leisure.'

'Can you just tell me what it says?'

He sat down and opened the leather case. 'He left everything to you, including the estate in Essex and this property.'

'I've never seen the country house, Mr Goldspink. My grandfather closed it up when my grandmother died, and as far as I know he never went there again.'

'That's true, but in the circumstances you may wish to sell the house, although there is a considerable income from the farms on the estate and I'd advise you to think carefully before disposing of any assets. There is also this property and what is left of Sir William's fortune, which is sadly depleted. Your grandfather made some ill-judged investments and he donated generously to various charities.' He produced the will and laid it on the desk in front of her.

'I see,' Lucy said slowly. 'So I'm a comparatively rich woman.'

His lips moved soundlessly for a moment, as if he was working himself up to burst into song. 'You would be, but I'm sorry to say that a certain person has come forward to challenge the will.'

'Would that be Mr Daubenay by any chance?' A cold shiver ran down her spine. She had seen very little of Linus over the past few years, and then only fleetingly at social occasions where their paths happened to cross, or when he had paid his annual visit to Albemarle Street on Sir William's birthday. Linus was not one to give up easily, especially where money was concerned.

Mr Goldspink bobbed his head several times: an annoying habit that grated even more than usual on Lucy's already stretched nerves. 'Yes, I'm sorry to say it is he.'

'But surely Grandfather's will made it clear that he wanted me to inherit?'

'There's no easy way to put this, Miss Marriott. Mr Daubenay's solicitor has put forward the case that your parents were unmarried and you are not the legitimate heir.'

'But that's not true, Mr Goldspink.'

'Mr Daubenay has a certified copy of your parents' marriage certificate, Miss Marriott. Unfortunately it proves that your parents were not legally wed until after you were born. I'm afraid that does make things rather difficult when it comes to inheritance.'

'You mean that I'm a bastard.'

Mr Goldspink's round cheeks flushed scarlet. 'I'd hesitate to call it that in front of a lady, but legally he has a case, and he's determined to follow it through.'

'Will I have anything, Mr Goldspink?'

'The court of chancery can take years and costs a great deal of money. I cite the case of Mr William Jennens, sometimes referred to as the miser of Acton, whose will was found in his pocket unsigned when he died suddenly in 1798. His feuding relatives went to court, and the case is still unresolved, which should be a lesson to us all. With your permission I would like to approach Mr Daubenay to see if we can come to a mutually acceptable agreement.'

Dazed by this wordy explanation, Lucy knew she must take his advice. 'What do you suggest?'

'That Mr Daubenay should have the country estate together with this property, leaving you with the house in Whitechapel.'

Lucy stared at him, mystified. 'I don't know of any house in Whitechapel.'

'It belonged to your late grandmother and was leased to a merchant who only recently went bankrupt. Unfortunately the house in Leman Street has been badly neglected, but I've inspected it and there is nothing that is beyond repair. However, it is situated in what I would call an insalubrious area.'

'I see.' Lucy stared at her hands tightly clasped on the tooled-leather surface of the desk. 'I spent my early years in the East End and the thought of returning there doesn't scare me, but how do I stand financially, Mr Goldspink?'

'We won't know until matters are settled.' He rose to his feet. 'I did warn Sir William that he ought to be more prudent, but he chose to ignore my advice. I'll do what I can, Miss Marriott. You'll be hearing from me again in the very near future.'

Lucy stood up. 'What should I do in the meantime?'

'Continue as you are. There are sufficient funds to pay the servants up to the end of the quarter, although you will have to be careful with your expenditure.'

'I'm not an extravagant person, Mr Goldspink.'

'I'm sure you'll manage very well.' He picked up his document case. 'Good day, Miss Marriott.

I'll see myself out.'

Lucy sat for a long time after he had left, wondering what to do for the best. She had grown used to a life of leisure with servants at her beck and call, although she had refused to have a lady's maid, preferring to look after herself. She had been educated in all things required of a young woman who was destined to marry well, but none of this would help her to earn her own living. She had come from nothing, but to return to a life of poverty would not be easy. And then there was Piers. She conjured up a vision of his suavely handsome face, dark and brooding but saved from being saturnine by the twinkle in his velvet-brown eyes. Piers Northam had been her grandfather's choice, and at first Lucy had resisted angrily. She was not going to allow anyone to rush her into a marriage of convenience, but somehow Piers had won her over. His undeniable charm, good looks and elegant manners had overcome her prejudice, and they were all but engaged. The announcement would have been made today, on her twenty-first birthday, but Sir William's sudden decline and demise had made it necessary to cancel the planned celebrations.

Lucy stood up and walked over to the window, gazing abstractedly at the street below. She saw Mr Goldspink scurrying towards Piccadilly, waving frantically to attract the attention of a cabby. Even from above he presented a comic figure, but the news he had just broken was anything but funny. She would have liked to have time to think things over but a brougham, drawn by a pair of bays, pulled up at the kerb. Lucy watched with mixed feelings as Piers alighted, followed by his sister Theodora. She wondered how he would react when he learned that his future wife had almost nothing to bring to the marriage. There was only one way to find out. She went downstairs to greet them, saving Bedwin the painful process of negotiating the stairs for a second time that morning.

Theodora spotted her first. 'Lucy, darling, how well you look, you poor thing. You've had such a dreary time recently.'

'Dora,' Piers said sharply. 'Lucy is in mourning for her grandfather.'

Lucy was suddenly conscious of the severity of her black silk gown and a glimpse of her reflection in one of the tall, gilt-framed mirrors was enough to convince her that she was not looking her best. She had confined her hair in a chignon at the back of her head, but tendrils had escaped and were curling wildly around her face in a frivolous manner quite unsuited to deep mourning. Her normally pink cheeks were pale and there were faint bruise-like smudges underlining her eyes. She managed a smile. 'It's lovely to see you both.' She turned to Bedwin, who was standing very still, clutching Piers's top hat and cane with a puzzled expression on his lined features, as if he had forgotten why he had taken them. 'Tea and cake in the drawing room, please, Bedwin.' She turned to Piers. 'Or would you prefer Madeira or a glass of sherry?'

'Tea will suit me very well.' He proffered his arm. 'How are you keeping, my dear? It's been a trying time for you.'

Dora danced on ahead of them. 'It's such a pity that your party was cancelled, Lucy. Anyway, we came to wish you well on your birthday, and Piers has a present for you.'

'Have you, Piers?' Lucy allowed him to take her arm as they followed Theodora up the sweeping staircase. 'A present for me? I'd almost forgotten that it was my birthday.'

'It was going to be a surprise, but my wretched little sister has spoiled the moment,' Piers said with an indulgent smile.

Dora reached the landing and leaned over the balustrade, pulling a face at her brother. 'Someone has to cheer poor Lucy up, and it might as well be me, since you're determined to be a grouch.' She tossed her head and strutted off towards the drawing room with Lucy and Piers not far behind.

Lucy slipped into the role of hostess, which had been drummed into her by Miss Wantage, who had believed firmly that good manners were of the utmost importance, followed by excellent deportment and the ability to maintain a ladylike appearance even in the direst of circumstances. 'Do sit down,' Lucy said, perching on the edge of a sofa upholstered in pale green watered silk. She had only been allowed in the drawing room on Sundays when she was younger, and then she had to sit on one of the less valuable antiques.

Dora sank down on a chair by the fire, sending a meaningful glance at her brother. 'Go on, Piers. What are you waiting for?'

'Will you please stop nagging me, Dora? You drive a fellow mad.' Piers sat beside Lucy, taking her hand in his. 'I was going to do this at the party, my darling, and I certainly didn't want to propose to you in front of my wretched sister, but she insisted on accompanying me today.'

Lucy's heart missed a beat, leaving her breathless. This was not the most romantic setting for a proposal, especially with Dora sitting on the edge of her seat with her hands clasped and a look of expectation on her face. But she had to stop Piers before it was too late. 'Not now, Piers. There's something I must tell you.'

His startled expression might have been amusing at any other time, but it was followed by an impatient frown. 'Can't it wait, Lucy? I think you know what I was about to say.'

'It's only fair to tell you that I'm about to lose everything, Piers. My grandfather's solicitor left just before you arrived, and the news he gave me was not good.'

Dora clapped her mittened hands to her mouth. 'Oh dear!'

'Precisely,' Lucy said grimly. 'There's no easy way to say this, but my grandfather's finances were shaky when he passed away.'

'But he must have left you something, darling.' Piers held her hands, his expression neutral.

'He left me this house, together with the estate in Essex.'

A smile softened Piers's handsome features, and he raised her hand to his lips. 'But that still leaves you a wealthy woman. This house must be worth a small fortune.'

'I agree, but my father's cousin, Linus Daubenay is contesting the will.'

Piers frowned, releasing her hand. 'On what

grounds, may I ask?'

'Yes, do tell,' Dora said eagerly. 'It sounds like the plot of a penny dreadful, not that I read such rubbish.'

Lucy glanced at their expectant faces and braced herself for their reaction when she told them the truth of her birth. She took a deep breath. 'Apparently I was born out of wedlock. My parents didn't marry until after I came into the world. I'm sorry, Piers, I know this makes a difference.'

He stared at her as if seeing her for the first time, saying nothing.

'Surely not,' Dora cried anxiously. 'It doesn't affect the way you feel about each other, does it?'

Piers rose to his feet, pacing the room with his hands clasped tightly behind his back. 'Not to me, but it might to others. If it became common knowledge I'm afraid it would have an adverse effect on my parliamentary career.'

'But you haven't been elected yet.' Dora stood up, wringing her hands. 'This is so unfair. It's not Lucy's fault.'

'I quite understand that it wouldn't look good if the truth came out, and I wouldn't want to hold you back.' Lucy's voice shook despite her effort to control the feeling of disappointment that threatened to overcome her. She had been abandoned as a child and she could see it happening all over again.

Piers came to a halt in front of her. 'I need to think about this, Lucy. For one thing I was counting on your help in establishing myself as a prospective candidate in the next election. I can trace my family tree back to William the Conqueror, but funds are a little low at the moment. You do understand, don't you?'

Dora caught him by the arm. 'That sounds awful, Piers. Are you saying that you were going to marry her for her money?'

'No,' he said angrily. 'Of course not, although I have to admit it was a factor. I thought I'd found the perfect bride, a woman I loved who was also financially independent. I never pretended to be a rich man, Lucy. I didn't deceive you.'

She rose slowly to her feet and even then she had to tilt her head back in order to look him in the eye. 'I think we're even on that score, Piers.'

He flushed and looked away, clearing his throat. 'I'm sorry, but you must understand...'

Dora enveloped Lucy in a hug. 'You're a beast, Piers Northam,' she said angrily. 'How could you do this to my dear friend?'

'Don't be so dramatic. Lucy knows that I admire her greatly. This decision has nothing to do with my feelings for her.'

Lucy withdrew gently from her friend's sympathetic embrace. 'I don't think any the worse of you for being honest, Piers, but perhaps we were never meant for each other in the first place. You know my background; I never made a secret of my origins.'

'Except for one small detail,' he said bitterly.

'That's so unfair.' Dora faced him angrily. 'I think you've forgotten something, haven't you, Piers?'

'I don't know what you mean.'

A bubble of hysterical laughter threatened to overwhelm Lucy, but she managed to control it by taking a deep breath. She had never seen Piers at a loss, and she experienced a wave of sympathy for the man she had thought she loved. Suddenly she saw him for what he was, vain, self-centred and utterly selfish. 'Don't tease him, Dora. I think I know what my present was to have been, and I would have had to return it anyway.'

'It's a family heirloom,' Piers said, clutching his hand to his breast pocket. 'It has to be given to the prospective bride of the eldest son.'

Dora picked up a cushion and threw it at him. 'Balderdash, Piers. You talk as if we're an old aristocratic family. If we came over with William the Conqueror our ancestors were probably foot soldiers. Great-grandfather Northam made his money as an overseer on a sugar plantation in Jamaica. Slavery was the basis of the family fortune, most of which has been frittered away. We've nothing to crow about, and I'm ashamed of you for treating Lucy this way.'

'It's all right, Dora.' Lucy could see that her friend was close to tears and she forced her lips into a smile. 'Piers has to think about his career, and I would be the last person who would want to hold him to a vague promise of marriage.' She fixed him with a steady gaze. 'I was besotted, but now I see you for what you are. I wouldn't marry you now even if you begged me on bended knee. I think you'd better go.'

'Yes, Piers,' Dora said tearfully. 'We must leave now, but I hope Lucy has it in her heart to believe that I am her true friend.'

Lucy turned to her with a misty smile. 'We will always be the best of friends, Dora.'

'I'm sorry, Lucy.' Piers left the room without looking back and Dora hurried after him.

The door closed on them and Lucy realised this was the end of a dream, but it was not hers. She had been a reluctant participant in her grandfather's desire to make her a suitable wife for a man of good family and even better prospects. She had grown fond of the irascible old man, but she was glad that he had not lived to see his ambitions for her shattered. She decided to do nothing until Linus made the first move.

She did not have to wait long. Two days later a letter arrived from a solicitor with an office in Lincoln's Inn. Lucy was in the morning parlour mulling over its contents when Mr Goldspink turned up in a state of considerable agitation. 'As I feared,' he said breathlessly. 'Mr Daubenay had nothing to lose and everything to gain by pursuing his claim, and even if we could produce a strong argument in defence we would find ourselves caught up in the legal system, which might very well bankrupt you as well as Mr Daubenay.'

Lucy placed the solicitor's letter on the table, smoothing out the folds as she studied the elegant copperplate writing. 'What do you suggest, Mr Goldspink?' For once she had no desire to laugh at his eccentricities.

'Perhaps we can come to a compromise,' he said slowly. 'I would suggest that you consider moving to the house in Whitechapel. According to a bequest by your paternal grandmother the property should pass to the eldest grandchild on the death of her spouse, which quite clearly is you. She left a small annuity which accompanies the bequest. It will hardly be enough for you to live on, but at least you will be free from debt.'

'But what about the estate in Essex and this house?'

'The estate will be Mr Daubenay's concern, not yours.'

'And Linus will have this house and what is left of my grandfather's fortune.'

'From what I know of that gentleman he will go through it within a year.' He angled his head, giving her a questioning look. 'Have I your permission to put this to Mr Daubenay's solicitor?'

Lucy nodded slowly. 'Yes, Mr Goldspink. Please do whatever you think is necessary.'

'A wise decision, if I may say so.' He picked up the letter and folded it carefully, slipping it inside his document case. 'I'll take care of the legalities, but might I suggest that you go to Leman Street and inspect the property?' He put his hand in his pocket and took out a bunch of keys, laying them on the table in front of Lucy. 'All this will take a little while, which gives you time to have the house made habitable.'

'Thank you, I'm sure that's sound advice. I'll go there today.'

'It is a rough area, Miss Marriott. Best not to go on your own.'

'I grew up in a just such a place, Mr Goldspink.' This time she could not hide a smile.'

'But you were a child then,' he said, looking pointedly at her silk mourning gown, trimmed with braid and cut to the latest fashion. 'You are a young lady now.'

His words echoed in Lucy's head as she was about to climb into the carriage. She had originally intended to visit the house on her own, but now she was having second thoughts. She hesitated. 'I want to call at Mr Northam's house in Jermyn Street first, Tapper. Then we'll go on to Leman Street.'

The coachman leaned over to tip his hat. 'Very good, Miss Marriott.' She picked up her skirts and allowed Franklin, the footman who had replaced James, to assist her into the carriage. He put up the steps and closed the door, standing back as Tapper cracked the whip over the horses' ears. She wondered vaguely if Linus would keep the servants on. It would be a shame to dismiss people who had given years of service to the family, but she knew that Linus had little or no conscience. She had often wondered what had become of Meg, his sweet-natured common-law wife, and their children. Bertie and Vicky would be almost grown up now and the baby Meg had been expecting must be nine, getting on for ten. Then there was Bram. He was the one she had missed the most. The short time she had spent with them in their woodland cottage had left her with happy memories, but it had come to a sudden end when her grandfather snatched her from the market place. She had written a long letter to Bram, explaining why she had left so abruptly, but she had no way of knowing whether it reached its destination. All her efforts to persuade her grandfather to allow her to visit Meg and her family had come to nothing, and she knew it was useless to ask Linus to pass on a message.

Even now, in her dreams she could see Bram as

he emerged from the silky green depths of Strawberry Hill pond, his naked body bronzed and gleaming in a shaft of sunlight as he shook the water from his hair. The image still had the power to bring a blush to her cheek. She wondered what sort of man he had become, but it was unlikely they would ever meet again.

She sighed, turning her attention back to the present. She hoped that Piers would not be at home, as it was Dora she wanted to see. Having enjoyed a sheltered upbringing and rarely seeing anything of the world outside Mayfair and the delights of Oxford Street, Dora would be the ideal companion to take to Leman Street, and she would consider it an adventure. For once, Lucy was glad that she had roamed the streets of the East End as a child. Whitechapel held no terrors for a girl who had lived in Cat's Hole Buildings and Hairbrine Court.

Piers was not at home, but Dora was unaffectedly delighted to see Lucy and only too pleased to have an excuse to leave the house. 'Mama wanted me to be there when her boring friends came to luncheon; she likes to show me off as if I were a prize cow at a country fair. She's quite desperate to see me married to a rich man, especially since Piers has failed to come up to scratch.' She clapped her hand over her mouth with a nervous giggle. 'I'm sorry, Lucy. I didn't mean it to come out like that. I am so tactless sometimes.'

'Yes,' Lucy agreed. 'You are, but I still love you, and I'm still fond of Piers in spite of the fact that he was marrying me for my money.'

‘No, don’t think that,’ Dora said anxiously. ‘He really does care for you, Lucy. It’s just that the family are putting such pressure on him to marry well. He was very upset when we left you the other day. I hope you weren’t too devastated.’

‘Not at all. It was Grandfather’s wish that I married well, but I don’t think we would have suited. I want to marry for love.’ Lucy turned her head away to look out of the window. ‘I’m quite excited at the thought of being the sole owner of a property, even if it is in Leman...’ She broke off, blinking hard before taking a second look. ‘It’s – no, it can’t be.’

‘What is it?’ Dora demanded. ‘What have you seen?’

Chapter Nine

‘I thought it was someone I once knew,’ Lucy said dazedly. ‘But I must have been mistaken.’ The woman had looked exactly like Hester Gant even though ten years had passed since Lucy had last seen her, but their acquaintance had been brief and it seemed unlikely that Hester would be in this part of London.

‘I’m always getting people muddled up,’ Dora said cheerfully. ‘Anyway, what were you about to say?’

‘I was going to say that the house in Leman Street is in a bad state, according to Mr Gold-spink, and it’s a rough area. Are you sure you want to come with me?'

'Most certainly. It would be much more exciting than a boring lunch with Mama's stuffy friends.'

'My carriage is outside.'

'I wouldn't miss this for the world.' Dora leapt to her feet, her cheeks flushed with excitement. 'I'll ring for Dobson and tell her to fetch my bonnet and shawl.'

Leman Street was crowded with horse-drawn vehicles of every sort from hansom cabs to brewer's drays, all vying for position with coster-monger's barrows and carts laden with night soil. Shabbily dressed pedestrians milled around, risking their lives by weaving in and out of the traffic or barging into each other on the pavements as they hurried towards their destinations. Beggars sat in doorways and street arabs worked in gangs, picking the pockets of the unwary. Older boys and girls, who were less quick on their feet, waylaid passers-by demanding money, and when this failed they resorted to violence, snatching purses or dragging their victims into narrow alleyways and robbing them of their valuables.

Once a prosperous area inhabited by silk weavers and merchants, the wide street was now lined with cheap lodging houses, pubs, brothels, pawnbrokers and shops selling second-hand goods. The side streets and alleyways were knee-deep in filth and even less salubrious, housing opium dens and illegal gambling clubs. Lucy was only too familiar with this area, but Dora was shocked into silence. She sat with her handkerchief clutched to her nose as the noxious smells flooded the carriage,

'We're here,' Lucy said, stepping down onto the pavement, assisted by Franklin. She stared up at the Georgian façade of Pilgrim House. Soot-blackened and sadly neglected, it had obviously seen better days. It had once been the home of a wealthy merchant, but had fallen into disrepair and had latterly been used as a doss house.

'Are you sure this is the right place?' Dora removed her hanky for a moment, but replaced it hurriedly and sank back against the leather squabs. 'Do you think it's safe to leave the carriage?'

'You can sit there while I investigate, or you can come inside,' Lucy said, smiling.

'I – I think I'll come with you.' Dora looked round nervously as Franklin helped her to alight. 'Open the door quickly. I don't like the look of those boys loitering across the street.'

With a cursory glance at the group of half-starved, ragged children with stick-thin arms and legs, Lucy decided that they were unlikely to be a threat. She marched purposefully up the steps and unlocked the door, but as she stepped inside the oak-panelled entrance hall her nostrils were assailed by a variety of odours, none of them pleasant. Dora hurried in after her and stood looking round at the scuffed skirting boards and the crumbling plaster cornices with a look of horror on her face. Cobwebs festooned the ceiling and rubbish was piled up in front of a door which Lucy assumed must lead to the basement area.

'You can't mean to live here,' Theodora wailed.

'It's awful, Lucy. It's a slum.'

'I've seen worse and I've lived in equally bad conditions,' Lucy said stoutly. 'It's amazing what a little soap and water and a lot of hard work will accomplish.' She opened the door to her right and found herself in a generous-sized room, with two windows overlooking the street, and a neo-classical burr-oak fireplace which had also seen better days, but could be brought back to its former glory with the application of beeswax and elbow grease. The grate was filled with cinders and ash spilled onto the hearth. Old newspapers littered the floorboards, which might once have been polished to a mirror sheen but were now splintered and ingrained with dirt. The windowpanes were thick with grime, both inside and out, and the wallpaper was peeling.

'If this is the drawing room I hate to think what the rest of the house is like,' Dora murmured, eyeing a mouse hole in the skirting board.

'There's only one way to find out. I'm going to explore.' Lucy left the room and went to investigate further, but Dora's fears proved well founded. There was another reception room of a similar size and shape on the ground floor, and two smaller rooms, one of which had shelves built into the alcoves on either side of the chimney breast, and could have been used as a study. The other room overlooked the back yard, and might have been used as a sewing room or a morning parlour in days gone by. Below stairs the basement kitchen was as it must have been when the house was built in the mid-eighteenth century, with an open fire over which a blackened kettle dangled from a chimney crane. A thin layer of soot lay like a mourning veil on the pine table and dresser, and the larder and store rooms were cluttered with empty bottles, flour sacks and traces left by the resident vermin.

Dora could hardly conceal her disgust as she picked up her skirts and tiptoed through the detritus on the flagstone floor. 'This place is a nightmare. I shudder to think what Piers would say if he thought you had to live in this wreck of a house.'

'It's no longer anything to do with him,' Lucy said calmly. 'He made that very clear, and I don't blame him. I'm free now to do as I please.'

'Can we go now?'

'I'm not leaving until I've seen everything, but you can sit in the carriage if you don't want to look round any more. Franklin will look after you.'

Dora shuddered visibly. 'It's worse outside than in here. I'll come with you.'

There were four upper storeys with rooms of varying sizes, the smallest being in the attics, where palliasses and flock-filled mattresses had been abandoned as if the occupants had only recently risen: the indentations left by sleeping bodies still visible. The larger rooms on lower floors were equally crowded with bedsteads and the occasional wooden chair. The smell of unwashed bodies and urine hung in the air like a damp cloud, with dust and city smut carpeting the bare boards.

'It's disgusting,' Dora said faintly. 'Please think again. There must be another way.'

'It's much larger than I imagined.' Lucy looked round with a critical eye. 'But it will have to do.' She turned to her friend with a tremulous smile. 'I've no choice, Dora. It's this or the streets, and I know which I prefer.'

'You can't mean that. Surely Linus wouldn't be so cruel as to force you out of your home to live in poverty amongst the criminal classes?'

'That's exactly what he wants. Linus tried to get rid of me once before and failed. This time he's succeeded, but I won't allow him to beat me. I'll make the best of this situation and be damned to him.'

'Lucy! What would your grandfather say if he could hear you talking like that?'

'He'd be proud of me.' Lucy made her way downstairs to the ground floor. 'That's enough for now. The whole house needs to be cleaned from the attics to the basement before I move in, and I'll have a new range installed in the kitchen, and a proper sink with running water.'

Dora hurried after her. 'You're not going to cook for yourself, are you?'

'I don't know yet. I might have to learn.'

'I think you've lost your senses. You mustn't do this.'

'I haven't much choice, Dora. Mr Goldspink advised against taking the case to the court of chancery and I think he's right. I'll just have to make the best of things.'

Lucy arrived back in Albemarle Street with a great deal on her mind. The annuity from her paternal grandmother would be sufficient to live on, providing she was not extravagant, but there were no monies for the renovation needed to make the house in Leman Street habitable. The size of the property had surprised her, but she had already decided that the only solution to her financial problems would be to take in boarders. The main problem as far as she could see was that it would be difficult to find respectable citizens who wanted to live in such a rough area.

Bedwin opened the front door. 'Mr Daubenay is waiting for you in the morning parlour, Miss Lucy. He insisted on staying even though I told him I didn't know when you would return.'

Lucy sensed his agitation and she gave him an encouraging smile. 'It's all right, Bedwin, I'll see him.'

She entered the room to find Linus standing with his back to the fireplace. 'Well?' she said coldly. 'What do you want?'

'That's not a very friendly greeting, Lucy.'

'What do you expect? You've got your own way at last, so what else is there?'

'I thought we might come to an amicable arrangement, thus avoiding court costs, which would be considerable.'

She was puzzled by this sudden and unexpected show of thoughtfulness, and although she had no intention of going to court, she had no intention of putting his mind at rest on that score. 'Go on.'

'You have no hope of winning; I daresay your man Goldspink told you that.'

She shrugged her shoulders, saying nothing.

'I'm offering you fifty guineas if you'll quit this house as soon as possible, and allow the due process of the law to take place without challenging the case.'

Lucy's first instinct was to refuse, but fifty guineas was a handsome sum and would help make her new home habitable. 'Why this change of heart, Linus?'

'Make that fifty-five guineas,' he said hastily. 'I'm a generous man.'

She had only to look at him to know that he was hiding something. 'What is it you're not telling me?'

For the first time since she had known him, Linus appeared at a loss for words. He took a quick turn around the room, coming to a halt by the window, staring out as if looking for inspiration. After a brief pause he turned slowly to face her. 'I'll make it sixty guineas if you will take in Hester Gant and the children.'

'I don't understand.'

'The Gant woman is trying to force my hand. She wants me to acknowledge the little bastards and bring them up as my own.'

Lucy sat down suddenly as her legs gave way beneath her. This was low talk, even for Linus Daubenay. 'But they're your flesh and blood.'

'Born out of wedlock, so you'll have something in common with them.'

'I don't have to put up with insults, Linus. This is my house for the time being at least, so I'm asking you to leave.'

He held up his hand. 'I take that back. What I meant to say was that you spent some time with Meg, and you are no stranger to the children. I want you to look after them for me.'

'I still don't understand. What does Meg say about this?'

'She died some weeks ago.'

'I'm so sorry. She was such a sweet and gentle lady.'

'I treated her well enough. I supported her and asked very little in return,' he said sulkily. 'But now I am saddled with her brats.'

Lucy rose to her feet. 'I won't listen to this any longer. You're going to take my inheritance from me, which might not make you rich, but I'm sure you could afford to bring up your own children.'

'I'm engaged to be married. My fiancée knows nothing of my past.'

'So you don't think this lady would be too pleased if she discovered you had fathered three illegitimate children?'

'Four, actually. Meg died giving birth to the last one and it didn't survive.'

'You're a callous brute. Meg was a good woman, who deserved better than you,' Lucy's voice broke with emotion. 'Those poor motherless children.'

'I might have expected such a mawkish response from you, but all to the good. You wouldn't stand by and see your cousins sent to the workhouse, would you?'

'You are an evil man, Linus.'

'I'll give you sixty guineas and that will be the end of my involvement with the little bastards. You will take full responsibility for them.'

Lucy was struck by a sudden thought. 'But what about Bram? Surely he won't stand by and see his sister's children treated in such a callous manner?'

'The boy joined the army six years ago. According to Gant his regiment, the 7th Hussars, was in India until a year ago. I've no idea where he is now or even if he survived the rigours of a posting to such a harsh environment, but he's not my concern and I really don't care what's happened to him.'

Lucy gave him a long, pitying look. 'You have no heart, Linus. I always thought so, and now I know I was right.'

He shrugged his shoulders. 'Spare me the sermon. Will you take them or do I put them in the workhouse? It's a simple question.'

'Of course I'll look after them. They're my flesh and blood.'

'And sixty guineas is a small fortune. Think yourself lucky, my girl. I could have had you thrown out of Albemarle Street with nothing and nowhere to go.'

'I think my grandmother must have known what sort of fellow you would turn out to be, which is why she left her house to the child she had never set eyes on.'

'Much good it will do you. Property in the East End is worth nothing. You'll end up taking in thieves and vagabonds, drunks and prostitutes. By this time next year you'll be running a brothel.'

'Think what you like, but I promise you that won't happen. Your children will be safe with me and I won't let anything or anyone harm them.'

'To be perfectly honest, I don't care what happens to them.' Linus produced a leather wallet from his breast pocket and counted out crisp five pound notes. 'Thirteen,' he said, grinning. 'An unlucky number.' He tossed the money onto the table. 'The court hearing is next week. It will go my way and when it does I'll give you two days' grace; after that I want you out of this house taking your personal possessions and nothing else.'

'What about Hester and the children?'

He took a slip of paper from his wallet and handed it to her. 'They are in temporary lodgings in Dorset Street, Spitalfields. Taking into consideration your early upbringing, you should feel at home in that sort of area.' He picked up his top hat, gloves and cane. 'I'll bid you good day. Or should I say farewell?'

'Goodbye, Linus. I hope we never meet again.'

'The feeling is mutual.' He was about to walk past her, but he stopped, leaning over her with a grim expression twisting his handsome features into an ugly mask. 'I'm a dangerous man to cross. Remember that, Lucy Pocket. I call you that because you're not a Marriott by birth.' He left the room, allowing the door to close of its own accord. The sound echoed throughout the silent house.

No matter how shocked she was by Linus's cavalier treatment of his own children, Lucy was determined to make a home for her young cousins. Suddenly the move to Whitechapel did not seem such a daunting prospect, despite the obvious disadvantages, and the first thing she did was to mobilise the underservants in Albemarle Street. The next day she set off in the carriage with two housemaids and a plentiful supply of carbolic soap, soda crystals and chloride of lime to disinfect the drains. Mops and broomsticks stuck out of the windows like the prickles on a hedgehog, and buckets were crammed with dusters, cleaning cloths and scrubbing brushes. It was not a comfortable journey, but as soon as they arrived Lucy engaged Tapper's services to help them unload while Franklin was sent to purchase coal, kindling and matches so that a fire could be lit and water heated in a large cauldron, which Cook had reluctantly allowed Lucy to borrow with strict instructions to return it at the end of the day.

By noon Lucy was beginning to realise that they were hopelessly understaffed, and the two housemaids were flagging. She sent Franklin out to buy hot pies and baked potatoes from street vendors, but they needed more help and she was struck with a sudden idea. She summoned Tapper, who had been clearing some of the crates and empty beer bottles from the back yard, and gave him instructions to drive her to Dorset Street.

Linus had not exaggerated when he had described the place where Hester and the children had been forced to reside. Having insisted that Tapper must wait at the corner of Dorset Street and Commercial Street, Lucy wrapped her shawl around her head and set off, walking briskly and ignoring the taunts from slatternly women who hung around in doorways soliciting for trade. Their barefoot, filthy children played in the street, which was knee-deep in straw, horse dung and rotten vegetable matter that clogged the gutters and polluted the atmosphere. Flies feasted on corpses of dead rats and birds, half eaten by feral cats, but suddenly she was ten years old again and unafraid. She was used to this sort of life – Granny had taught her how to look after herself, and, if all else failed, when to take flight. She held her head high and made for the address that Linus had scribbled on a scrap of paper torn from his pocket book.

An old woman was attempting to sweep dust onto the pavement but was hampered by a gang of urchins who had decided that she made a good target and were throwing stones at her. Lucy caught one of them by the ear. 'Leave her alone, you little brute. How would you feel if someone threw pebbles at your granny?'

'She is me gran,' the boy snarled. 'Lemme go, you stuck-up tart.'

Lucy released him with a smart cuff round the ear which made him yelp with pain. 'That's for nothing. See what you get for something.' The expression came back to her from childhood, when she had tried Granny's patience too far. She marched up to the woman, who was leaning on her broom, watching with her mouth open. 'Are you all right, missis?'

'He had that coming, the little bugger. I'll swing for him one day.' She shook her fist at the boy, who ran off to join his mates, cocking a snook and shouting obscenities.

'I'm looking for Miss Gant,' Lucy said hastily. 'Do you know where I might find her?'

The old woman put her head on one side, a calculating look in her eyes. 'How much is it worth?'

Lucy put her hand in her pocket and took out

a penny, but the woman shook her head. Lucy offered her tuppence and her informant snatched it. 'Back room, basement.'

Inside the building Lucy had to step over objects scattered on the floor, taking care not to get her heels caught in the many gaps where the floorboards had rotted away. She pressed herself against the damp wall to avoid being mown down by a burly man who rushed out of a doorway doing up his trousers. He stumbled off, muttering beneath his breath. She moved on, feeling her way along the walls of the dark corridor until she found the basement door. Stone steps led down to what was in reality a large cellar with only a grille above eye level to allow in just enough light to make out huddled shapes on the floor. Stepping over inert bodies and clutching her hanky to her nose in an attempt to escape the disgusting stench of human excreta and overflowing drains, Lucy heard the sound of a child crying. 'Hester,' she called as loudly as she dared. 'Hester, where are you?'

'Who's that?' A faint voice answered her from the depths of the darkness.

'Hester, it's Lucy Pocket. I've come to help you.'

A bedraggled figure emerged from the gloom. 'Lucy?'

'Linus sent me.' Lucy reached out and caught Hester by the sleeve as she started to back away. 'Don't be frightened. I've come to take you and the children away from this dreadful place.'

Another figure appeared at Hester's side. 'Who are you? Is this a trick?' The boy's voice cracked on a suspicious note.

'Bertie, is that really you?' Lucy gazed at him in amazement. The small child she remembered had grown tall and slim and was on the verge of manhood. 'You won't remember me,' she added hastily. 'Your father brought me to your cottage in the forest many years ago. You were only little then.'

'I'm fourteen. I'm the man of the house, or I would be if we still had a proper home.' He held his hand out to two girls who were lurking in the shadows. 'I take care of my sisters.'

Hester moved closer to Lucy, staring at her suspiciously. 'I remember you, but you were just a child in those days. Why would that brute send you here to taunt us? Hasn't he done us enough harm already?'

'Linus is no friend of mine,' Lucy said, glancing nervously over her shoulder as one of the other denizens of the cellar rose from his patch of straw and lumbered towards them. 'Let's get out of here.' She held her hand out to Hester. 'I'm here to help you.'

'So you say, but you're a lady,' Hester said doubtfully. 'What would a lady want with the likes of us?'

'I trust her,' Bertie said suddenly. 'Anything is better than this, Hester.' He beckoned to his sisters. 'Let's get out of this stinking pit.'

Lucy led the way, hoping that Hester would see sense and follow them. The atmosphere in the cellar had changed subtly; shadowy figures had risen from their beds and were advancing on them like wolves surrounding their prey. She knew only too well that desperate people like these needed little excuse to set about a stranger and strip them naked, robbing them of everything. Racing up the steps, she did not stop until she reached the street. She came to a halt, taking deep breaths of air that was far from country fresh, but anything was better than the stench in the cellar. Bertie led his sisters from the house with Hester stumbling after them. They blinked, screwing up their faces, blinded by the daylight.

'How long have you been underground?' Lucy asked gently. 'Why did you stay there, Hester?'

'Where else would we go, miss?' Hester avoided meeting Lucy's eyes. 'He left us penniless and with nowhere to turn for help. I went to his house and begged him to look after the children, but he laughed in my face.'

'I tried to find work,' Bertie said sulkily. 'But they called me country boy and sent me packing.'

'I tried too,' Vicky murmured. 'But a man caught hold of me and dragged me into an alley. He put his hand up my skirt and I screamed.'

Bertie turned on her angrily. 'Lucky for you that I was following close behind or you might have ended up in the river. I told you to stay with Hester but you wouldn't listen.'

'This isn't getting us anywhere,' Lucy said firmly. She glanced at the younger girl and smiled. 'What's your name? We haven't met before.'

The child bobbed a curtsey. 'Maggie, miss. I was called after Ma.' Her blue eyes filled with tears. 'She died and went to heaven.'

'I know, and I'm very sorry for your loss.' Lucy patted Hester on the shoulder, seeing the older woman was also close to tears. 'My carriage is waiting at the end of the road. I'm going to take you somewhere safe.'

Hester moved closer to her, lowering her voice. 'He said he'd kill me if I pestered him for money, although God knows how he thought I was going to care for the children. He's an unnatural father and he's capable of anything.'

'You won't see him again,' Lucy said firmly. 'And that's a promise.'

Franklin and Tapper were too well schooled to allow their feelings to show, but Lucy could feel disapproval and distrust emanating from them in waves as she helped the children into the carriage. Hester followed with her head bowed as if ashamed of her dirty and dishevelled state.

When they reached the house Lucy sent Franklin out to purchase more food. She filled the stone sink with hot water from the simmering cauldron, and gave Hester a towel and soap, leaving her to supervise the children while they had a wash. She refilled the pot with water and hung it over the flames. It would take some time to heat up, but cleaning the house came a poor second to looking after her charges.

Franklin arrived with more pies and baked potatoes and the children fell on the food, swallowing huge mouthfuls as if they were afraid it might be snatched away from them. While they were busy eating Lucy took the opportunity to explain how she came to be in her present situation. She tried not to make Linus out to be too much of a villain, telling the children that their father wanted them to be well cared for, and keeping the fact that he wanted nothing further to do with them to herself. She suspected that Hester already knew, and Bertie gave her a sceptical glance, saying nothing. The boy, she thought, was older than his years.

'So you see,' she concluded with an attempt at an encouraging smile, 'I need your help to make this house into a home.'

'You want us to work for you,' Bertie said angrily. 'You were rich and had servants and you think we'll do their job for nothing.'

'Bertie!' Hester glared at him, shaking her head. 'That's uncalled for. Miss Lucy is trying to help us.'

'It's just Lucy. I'm not Miss Lucy any more, and never really was.' Lucy faced Bertie, knowing that only the truth would do. 'I was a child of the streets before my grandfather found me, but the best time I ever had was in the forest with you and Bram.'

'Bram's gone to be a soldier,' Vicky said eagerly. 'He's ever so brave.'

Maggie's eyes filled with tears. 'But he won't know where to find us when he comes home. He'll go to the cottage and there'll be strangers living there.'

Hester rose from the table and started clearing away the plates. 'If he comes home,' she said in a low voice.

Lucy saw Vicky's lips tremble and Bertie turned his head away. She stood up. 'You aren't servants. This is your home and it will be what we make it, so let's go and choose your rooms. You girls can share, if you like, but I'm sure Bertie would like somewhere that he could call his own.' She smiled as she saw their faces light up.

Bertie leapt to his feet. 'Do you mean that?'

'You may have first pick,' Lucy said firmly. 'You too, Hester. I'm sure you want a say in where you're to sleep tonight.'

'Are you sure about this, Lucy?' Hester asked in a low voice as she followed Lucy from the kitchen. 'What will we do if you decide to sell up?'

'That won't happen. This will be our home from now on. It's where I grew up until I was forcibly separated from Granny, but I've never given up hope of finding her, Hester. Circumstances forced me to stop searching for her, but now I'm going to start again in earnest.'

She was about to mount the stairs when there was a commotion outside. Someone was hammering on the front door.

'Police. Open up.'

Chapter Ten

A burly constable stood on the doorstep. His face was red with exertion and beads of sweat stood out on his forehead. 'I'm looking for two young criminals, miss. They was seen running this way.' He glanced over Lucy's shoulder, glaring at Vicky and Maggie, who were huddled together at the foot of the stairs. 'Do they belong to you, miss?'

'Indeed they do, officer.' Lucy faced him squarely. 'They are my wards.' Out of the corner of her eye she caught a flicker of something moving in the area at the bottom of the steps which led to the tradesmen's entrance. 'If I find any criminals lurking round here I'll inform the police immediately,' she added, stepping back into the hall and preparing to close the door.

'Very well, miss. But I warn you, the youngsters might look like butter wouldn't melt in their mouths but they're vicious little brats.' He held up a finger wrapped in a grubby handkerchief. 'One of them bit me. They're worse than rabid dogs. Good day to you, miss. Bear in mind what I said.'

Lucy waited until he was out of sight before turning her attention to the shadowy area below ground level. Peering up at her between the iron steps she could see two pale faces. 'Wait there. I'm coming down.' She turned to speak to Hester, who was hovering behind her with a worried frown. 'It's all right; just some youngsters who've run foul of the law. I'll sort it out, so why don't you take the children upstairs and have a look at the rooms. I'll be with you in a minute.'

'All right, but I won't let them loose until you've agreed their choices. If I know Bertie he'll pick the biggest bedroom for himself.' Hester went to join the children, shooing them up the staircase.

Lucy made her way carefully down the slippery steps to the area outside the kitchen. 'Come here,' she said, beckoning to the children who were clinging to each other as if terrified to let go. When neither of them moved she walked slowly towards them, her shoes crunching on empty snail shells and small mounds of moss that had grown between the cracks in the tiles. 'I won't hurt you,' she added, holding out her hand.

The elder of the two, a ragged boy, peered at her suspiciously. 'Go away.' The peaked cap he was wearing was at least two sizes too large and it half obscured his grimy face, but Lucy could feel the fear emanating from his small body.

She came to a halt. 'No, I won't go away. Tell me what you've done wrong and I'll try to help you. If you don't speak up I'll have to send for the constable.'

Reluctantly the boy emerged from his hiding place, dragging a small and equally ragged girl. Her dirty face was streaked with tears and a livid bruise threatened to turn into a black eye.

'What's your name?' Lucy squatted down so that they were on the same level. 'I can't begin to help if I don't know who you are.'

'Sidney,' the boy said through clenched teeth. 'Sid Smith, and she's me sister, Essie.'

'Sid and Essie,' Lucy repeated softly. 'What did you do to make the police chase you?'

Fresh tears spurted from Essie's brown eyes, running freely down her pale cheeks. 'I bit 'is finger.'

'And the copper blacked her eye,' Sid said angrily.

'That's awful.' Lucy reached out to Essie but the child backed away and hid behind her brother. 'Why did you bite the policeman, Essie?'

Sid put his arm around his sister's thin shoulders. 'He nabbed her as we was making off, miss. I dipped a cove's pocket but I never saw the copper until it was too late.'

'I see.' It was a situation all too familiar to Lucy. She had had many narrow escapes in the past. 'So you ran away.'

'I lifted a pocket watch, but I dropped it when I heard the copper shout and we took to our heels. It were all for nothing.'

'Where do you live? I'll see that you get home safely.'

Essie huddled up to her brother and Sid's expression hardened. 'We ain't going back to the workhouse, miss. I'd sooner we drownded ourselves than go back there.'

'You ran away from the workhouse?'

'Sharp, ain't yer?' Sid met her gaze with a defiant lift of his chin. 'We're going now, and you ain't gonna stop us.'

'I won't try,' Lucy said, straightening up and brushing the creases from her skirt. 'But there's a tasty meat pie in the kitchen. You might like to have something to eat before you go on your way.'

Sid tightened his hold on Essie. 'We can look after ourselves.'

She moved to open the kitchen door. 'So you don't want the pie. It's a pity to let it go to waste.'

Essie opened her mouth and let out a wail. 'I'm hungry.'

'Suit yourselves. You can come in or go on your way. It doesn't bother me.' Lucy stepped inside and waited.

Moments later Sid marched into the kitchen with Essie close on his heels. 'Where's the grub, miss?'

Lucy watched them gobble up the pie, followed

by two slices of bread and butter. 'Tomorrow I'll bring jam,' she said cheerfully. 'And I'll get Cook to bake a cake.' She made a fresh pot of tea and filled two cups. 'I suppose you ought to have milk, but there isn't enough. Tomorrow I'll make sure we have plenty of everything.'

'I'd rather have beer, if you don't mind, miss,' Sid said, wrinkling his snub nose. 'They never let us have it in the workhouse, but our dad used to give it to us every night. He said it was good for growing nippers.'

'Did he now? Well, you won't be getting it here either.' Lucy looked up as Hester clattered down the stairs, stopping at the bottom to stare at the two dirty little creatures seated at the table.

'What on earth are you doing, Lucy? Surely you can't be thinking of taking them in?'

'No, of course not,' Lucy said casually. 'Sid is eager to go back to the streets. He plans to jump in the river if things don't work out.'

Hester raised an eyebrow. 'Well, I daresay one street arab less won't make much difference.'

'I heard that,' Sid muttered, cramming the last morsel of bread and butter into his mouth. 'Don't worry, lady. We'll be off as soon as Essie's finished eating.'

'We'll see about that,' Lucy said, frowning thoughtfully. 'There's plenty of room here. I don't see why you can't stay until we can find you a more permanent home.'

'Be careful, Lucy.' Hester drew her aside. 'Next thing you know we'll have all the waifs and strays in Whitechapel knocking on the door.'

'I know what it's like to live on the streets, and

I wouldn't wish it on my worst enemy.'

Hester shrugged her shoulders. 'Be it on your own head, that's all I can say. Anyway, the children have chosen their rooms and the girls want to share. I managed to persuade Bertie to have a smaller one than he wanted, and young Mary has given them brooms and dusters and set them to work cleaning.'

'I can sweep floors,' Essie lisped. 'I can do all sorts of things.'

Sid pushed his cup away. 'We ain't skivvying for nobody. I can take care of me sister.' He slid off the chair, tugging at Essie's sleeve. 'C'mon, we're going. Ta for the eats, miss.'

Essie clutched the table top with both hands. 'I don't want to go, Sid. I want to stay here. I don't want to sleep in a doorway again.'

Lucy put her arms around the little girl and gave her a hug. 'I know what that's like, Essie. You will have a nice warm bed tonight, and you can stay here as long as you like.'

Hester threw up her hands. 'Think about it, Lucy. How are you going to support two more nippers? The money Linus gave you won't last forever. What will you do when it runs out?'

Lucy turned to face her. 'I'm not letting these poor mites roam the streets. They escaped from the workhouse, and only the most heartless person would force them to return to that sort of life. I'll manage somehow, but they're staying here with us.'

Sid drew himself up to his full height. 'What if I don't want to, miss?'

'You can come and go as you please,' Lucy said

calmly. 'You can walk away now, but I'm offering you a place to sleep and food in your belly.'

'What would we have to do in return?' Sid demanded suspiciously.

'You'd have to stop dipping pockets and keep out of trouble. You could help with the chores because I can't afford to pay servants, but we'll all take our turn.'

'Even you, miss?'

'Even me.'

'And you'll have a bath tonight before I let you climb into a nice clean bed.' Hester stood arms akimbo. 'Miss Lucy might be easy-going but I expect children to behave properly and respect their elders.'

Essie wrapped her small arms around Lucy's waist. 'I love you. I'll be a good girl.'

Lucy returned the hug. 'I'm sure you will, Essie.' She gave Sid a searching look. 'Is it still the river for you?'

A slow grin spread across his gamin features. 'Maybe not today, miss. I might wait and see what the cake turns out like.'

Lucy returned to Albemarle Street that evening, exhausted but happy in the knowledge that the house in Leman Street was almost habitable. The top floor rooms had not been touched and there was plenty of cleaning left to do, but the kitchen and the bedrooms they intended to use were reasonably liveable. She had left Hester in charge with enough food and fuel to last until the next day, and Sid and Essie had settled into a room adjacent to the one Lucy had chosen for herself.

All that was needed now was to raid the linen cupboard and send bedding to the house in Leman Street. Tapper could take it before he stabled the horse and carriage.

Mary and Dot, the two housemaids who had worked so hard all day, had fallen asleep during the ride home, but Lucy's head was filled with plans for the future. She would take in boarders, and Bertie was old enough to find work outside the home. Vicky and Maggie could help in the house and continue their education at the nearest board school. Linus for all his faults had been born a gentleman, and his offspring deserved better than to end up as menial workers.

She arrived home to find the house in an uproar. Bedwin greeted her with an unusual display of emotion. 'Thank goodness you're back, Miss Lucy.'

'Whatever is the matter, Bedwin?' Lucy was distracted momentarily by Peckham, who came to greet her, hobbling along as fast as his rheumatics would allow, but his welcome was as enthusiastic as ever. He nudged her hand, looking up at her with adoring eyes, and she bent down to make a fuss of him.

'Mr Daubenay has been here,' Bedwin said urgently. 'He insisted on going through all Sir William's papers, and the man who accompanied him went round making notes of all the valuable items in the house.'

Lucy straightened up. She was shocked, but unsurprised. 'He probably thinks I'll make off with the family silver,' she said with a wry smile.

'Mr Daubenay has dismissed us all, Miss Lucy.

We only have until the end of the week to find employment elsewhere.' His aged knees buckled and he sank down on a spindly hall chair which creaked beneath his weight.

'Don't upset yourself, Bedwin. I'm sure something can be arranged.'

He dashed tears from his wrinkled cheek with a hand that shook visibly. 'Who would take on a man of my age? I've served this family since I was a boy.'

'I need someone like you to help me in my new venture, Bedwin. I've just come from Leman Street and it would benefit me greatly to have a man about the house.'

He raised his head to give her a searching look. 'I don't want charity, Miss Lucy.'

'You would be doing me a kindness. I intend to take in lodgers and I'll need someone like you to keep order.'

Bedwin rose shakily to his feet. 'I won't let you down.'

'I know you won't. I suppose I should speak to Mrs Hodges next. Will you send her to me in the drawing room, please?'

Bedwin treated her to one of his rare smiles. 'I daresay a tray of tea would be welcome, Miss Lucy.'

'It would indeed. You're a mind reader, Bedwin.'

The interview with Mrs Hodges was fraught. She was understandably distressed by the sudden turn of events and dismayed at the prospect of having to give notice to Cook and the remaining servants.

'I can pay everyone until the end of the month,' Lucy said, remembering Mr Goldspink's words. It was a reckless decision, but she could not in all conscience allow people who had served her grandfather faithfully to be cast off without a penny. She would be left with her grandmother's annuity and the money from Linus.

The tea and a slice of Cook's seed cake was more than welcome. Lucy sent a message to the kitchen praising Cook's culinary efforts, adding a request for a chocolate cake which she intended to take to Leman Street, fulfilling her promise to Essie. She sighed. She had never pictured herself in the role of guardian, but Bertie, Vicky and Maggie were her flesh and blood, and she had been pitched headlong into the unlikely position of head of their small family, with Sid and Essie thrown in for good measure.

She rose from the sofa and crossed the room to the escritoire set between two windows overlooking the street. She was about to begin writing references when Bedwin knocked and entered the room, closely followed by a tall young man wearing the uniform of a hussar.

'I'm sorry, Miss Lucy,' Bedwin said breathlessly. 'The young man refused to wait downstairs.'

'It's all right, Bedwin. I'll handle this.'

Bedwin shot a wary glance at the newcomer. 'Call if you need me, Miss Lucy. I won't be far away.' He backed out of the room, leaving the door slightly ajar.

Lucy stared at the young officer and for a blinding moment he was bathed in sunlight, naked and as beautiful as Michelangelo's statue of David.

'Bram?' she murmured. 'Is it really you?'

His angry expression softened for a moment but a hint of a smile was quickly replaced by a frown. He took off his cap and tucked it under his arm. 'I've just come from Half Moon Street. Linus told me where to find you.'

She took a step towards him, holding out her hand, but dropped it to her side again as a cold shiver ran down her spine. 'What did he say to make you so angry?'

Bram did not answer immediately. He cast his eye round, taking in the elegant furnishings and expensive silk wall covering. The room had a voice of its own and it spoke of old money, time-less elegance and good taste. He dragged his gaze back to look her in the eyes. 'So this is what you ran away from. It explains why you left me in the market place.'

'I didn't run away,' Lucy said crossly.

'I searched for you for hours, questioning all the stallholders and anyone who might have seen you, but you'd vanished into thin air. Meg was distraught when I returned home without you. We thought you'd been kidnapped.'

'I was taken against my will. My grandfather had had his spies out searching for me and he was there waiting in his carriage. I had no choice but to go with him, Bram. I was a child. I wrote to you explaining what had happened.'

'I didn't receive anything from you.'

'What else was I supposed to do? I was a virtual prisoner and I couldn't ask Linus for help.'

He shrugged his shoulders. 'You're grown up now, but you still take the easy way out. Linus told me what you did.'

Aghast, she stared at him in disbelief. 'I don't know what he said, but I can't believe you took his side against me. You know him better than I do.'

'He said you persuaded your grandfather to cut him out of his will, and that he had to take you to court to claim what was rightfully his.'

She sank down on the nearest chair. 'That's not how it was at all. Grandfather left everything to me, but Linus discovered that my parents didn't marry until after I was born. I'm not the legal heir.'

'But you were named in the will.'

'Linus threatened to take the case to the court of chancery if I stood out against him. Grandfather's solicitor advised me to move to a property in Leman Street left to me by the grandmother I never knew. I'm in the process of doing that now.'

'He said that you demanded money to take care of Meg's children. You almost bankrupted him.'

'He offered me money to take them off his hands. I would have done it for nothing, but I'm virtually penniless. I only agreed to his terms so that I could give your nephew and nieces a decent home.' A wave of anger swept over her as she met his steely gaze. 'And where were you in all this? I see that you've got a commission; I suppose that was his doing too. He wanted you out of the way.'

Bram sat down beside her, his angry expression softening. 'He bought it to please Meg. She didn't want me to end up as a woodsman beholden to Linus for everything. My sister was a fool when it came to men, but she was a saint as far as I was concerned.'

'Where were you when she needed you most?'

'I was stationed at Aldershot, but I didn't know anything about it until too late.' His voice cracked and he turned his head away. 'I had a letter from Linus telling me my sister had died, and that he was making suitable arrangements for the children.'

'I'm sorry if I misjudged you, but you should have known better than to believe anything Linus said. He's abandoned his family and wants nothing more to do with them. It would upset his plans to marry an heiress if she discovered the truth.'

'I hope he rots in hell. Meg deserved better.'

Lucy felt his pain. Her instinct was to give him a hug, but they were no longer children. Instead, she picked up the plate of cake and offered it to him. 'Forget Linus, Bram. I'll do my best for the children.'

'I'm sorry for what I said earlier.' He took a piece of cake and bit into it. 'I'm famished. Would you mind if I finished up what's left?'

She handed him the plate. 'Of course not. There's plenty more in the kitchen.'

'I haven't eaten since breakfast, and my lodgings are less than perfect. The landlady couldn't boil an egg, let alone cook a decent meal.'

Lucy laughed and the tension between them was broken. 'I'll ring for a fresh pot of tea.' She stood up and went to tug the embroidered bell pull at the side of the fireplace. 'I'll tell Bedwin to lay another place for dinner.'

'If you're sure,' Bram said doubtfully. 'Linus told me you're engaged to be married. I don't want to make things awkward for you.'

'It was never an official engagement and the gentleman in question backed down when he discovered that I wasn't an heiress.' She tempered her words with a wry smile.

'You look wonderful. I don't know what I was expecting, but I was surprised to see that you'd grown up to be such a fashionable young lady, and a very pretty one too.'

'I suppose I must look different after ten years, but then so do you.' She returned to sit on the sofa, keeping a safe space between them. Grandfather, she thought, would turn in his grave if he could see her entertaining a young man without a chaperone. She shot him a sideways glance and saw that he was smiling.

'You were all arms and legs topped with a mass of coppery curls that shone like new pennies in the sunlight.'

'Bram! I didn't know you were so poetic.'

'I'm not, but that's how I saw you then, and I never forgot you.'

'Nor I you,' she said shyly.

'What I remembered most about you were your eyes; they change colour with your moods. That hasn't changed a bit.'

She smiled. 'And what colour are they now?'

'As blue as the sky on an English spring day. I never forgot you, Lucy.'

'I would have been happy to stay in the forest with you and Meg and the little ones, but it wasn't to be. My grandfather saw to that.'

'He made you into a fine lady.'

'He might have given me a good education, but I'm still the same person I was when he found me. In a way Linus has set me free.'

Bram stared at her, a frown creasing his brow. 'I don't understand.'

'I'm going back to the East End where I belong, and I'm going to search for Granny and give her the home she deserves. Maybe I'll find my mother too. Who knows?'

'You always were a determined little thing. I remember when you tried to find your way out of Epping Forest and I had to rescue you. I was out of my mind with worry when you disappeared from the market place. I wanted to go to the police, but Meg insisted that we waited until Linus paid us a visit. She said he would know what to do.'

'Linus knew that Grandfather had found me, but for some reason he chose not to tell you and Meg that I was safe.'

'That's another reason for me to hate the man. Anyway, I've found you now, and I'm sorry that I believed what Linus said. I'm truly grateful to you for taking the young ones in.'

'I can't wait to see their faces when you walk in the door tomorrow.'

'I was thinking of going there this evening.'

She had a vision of him walking into the chaos of Leman Street, and being horrified by the conditions in which his nephew and nieces were living. She laid her hand on his sleeve. 'Stay and have dinner with me. I'll take you to see the children first thing in the morning.'

He nodded his head. 'I'd like that.'

'We'll give them a wonderful surprise, and to be honest we could do with another pair of hands. The old house is in a terrible state and we've only just begun to make it habitable.'

'Are you sure about this, Lucy? You're very young to have taken on such a burden. The children should be my responsibility, not yours. I won't be able to help until I sell my commission. I made up my mind to leave the army when I heard that Meg had died. I knew the children needed me.'

'Don't you want to follow your career?'

He grinned. 'I'm not officer class. They tolerate me and I've proved myself in battle, but it's not how I want to spend the rest of my life.'

'It seems to me that we're both wolves in sheep's clothing,' Lucy said, chuckling. She turned her head as Bedwin entered the room. 'Another pot of tea, please. And tell Cook that Lieutenant Southwood will be staying for dinner.'

Next morning Bram arrived in Albemarle Street just as Lucy was supervising the loading of boxes into the carriage. She hurried to meet him. 'You're nice and early. There's such a lot to do.'

He took a box from her and tossed it into the carriage. 'Is that the last?'

She hesitated. 'Have you had breakfast?'

'I thought we might stop on the way to buy what we need. I've a month's pay in my pocket so I'm feeling flush.'

'I'll just get my reticule and we'll be off.'

Bram helped her to alight from the carriage outside the house in Leman Street. 'This is worse than I anticipated,' he said warily. 'What possessed your grandmother to purchase a house in this godforsaken place?'

Lucy stepped to the ground. 'I think the ancestor who built it was a wealthy merchant, and this was a more prosperous area then. It was entailed to her to save it from becoming the property of her husband, and she left it to her eldest grandchild, which happens to be me. I think I'm very lucky to own such a place.'

Bram took her firmly by the arm and led her to the relative safety of the front step. He rapped on the knocker. 'I'm not sure I agree with you.'

Before she could argue the door opened and Hester's welcoming smile faded into a look of disbelief. 'Bram?'

He stepped over the threshold and wrapped his arms around her. 'Hester, my darling. It's so good to see you again.'

She extricated herself, laughing and crying at the same time. 'You devil. Why didn't you let us know you were coming?'

'I had to find you first,' he said, giving her another hug. 'Where are the young 'uns?'

Lucy followed Bram inside. She was about to close the door when another carriage drew up. Her heart sank as she recognised the coachman who leapt down to open the door.

Chapter Eleven

Piers emerged from the carriage and helped Dora to alight. She gathered up her skirts and stepped cautiously over the detritus on the pavement with an expression of disgust. 'I don't know how you can consider living here,' she said as she hurried up the steps to greet Lucy.

Piers followed her, issuing a curt instruction to the coachman to walk the horses and return in half an hour. He entered the house, coming to a sudden halt when he spotted Bram. 'Won't you introduce us?' he demanded in a tone that was anything but friendly.

'Of course,' Lucy said hastily. 'Lieutenant Bramwell Southwood.' She turned to Bram with an apologetic smile. 'These are my friends Piers Northam, and his sister Theodora.'

Bram clicked his heels together and bowed from the waist. 'How do you do?'

Dora bobbed a curtsey, treating him to a dazzling smile. 'How do you do, Lieutenant?'

Lucy drew her aside. 'Why did you bring your brother here today? You know how things are between us.'

'He insisted on coming,' Dora said vaguely, but her attention was fixed on Bram.

Piers seemed equally disconcerted. 'I thought I knew all Lucy's acquaintances,' he said suspiciously. 'How do you two know each other?'

'It's a long story,' Lucy said vaguely. 'But we're related in a roundabout way.'

'If that's true I'm surprised that the lieutenant countenances this move.' Piers took in his surroundings with a disapproving shake of his head. 'This area is totally unsuitable and the house appears to be near derelict.'

She bridled angrily. 'What I do is none of your concern, Piers. You made it perfectly clear that there was no future for us, and you've no right to question my decisions now.'

Bram moved to her side, eyeing Piers with an uncompromising scowl. 'Is this the fellow who let you down, Lucy?'

'What has it got to do with you?' Piers stood his ground. 'What is your part in this calamitous state of affairs?'

'Stop it, both of you.' Lucy thrust herself between them. 'This is my house and I'll ask you to behave yourselves.' She faced Piers with a determined lift of her chin. 'I'm happy to remain as friends, if only for Dora's sake, but don't you dare tell me what I should or shouldn't do.'

He ran his finger round the inside of his stiff collar, and a flush stained his cheeks. 'I am your friend, and I don't want to see you taken in by a man in uniform.'

'I came here to see my nieces and nephew,' Bram said coldly. 'Think what you like, sir, but leave Lucy alone. She's made her feelings perfectly clear.'

Piers looked as though he was about to explode, but at that moment the baize door at the far end of the entrance hall flew open and Bertie raced towards them, closely followed by his sisters. They hurled themselves at Bram and their cries of delight echoed throughout the old house. Lucy's eyes were moist as she witnessed their show of affection for him.

'Perhaps we shouldn't have come,' Dora murmured apologetically. 'I'm sorry, Lucy. I thought perhaps it might help if Piers saw for himself how you've been placed by that villain who stole your inheritance.'

'I'm determined to make the best of things,' Lucy said firmly.

'You'll be murdered in your bed if you remain here.' Piers made an attempt at a smile, but he was clearly uncomfortable with the situation. 'I came here today to offer you my help. I have a good solicitor and you should seek his advice.'

Lucy shook her head. 'Thank you, but I've taken advice from Mr Goldspink. I'm satisfied that this is the best course to take.'

'You need someone to stand up for you, my dear.' He lowered his voice. 'This isn't a fight that a woman could win without the support of a strong man.'

'Hold on.' Bram looked up, glaring at Piers over the children's heads. 'Lucy isn't alone, and most important of all she knows her own mind. She doesn't need you to tell her what to do.'

'I suppose you're putting yourself forward for the position of adviser and protector, are you?'

Bertie broke away from his uncle, facing up to Piers like a bare-knuckle fighter. 'Leave Bram be. He's a soldier and he could beat you hands down.'

Bram grinned, hugging Vicky and Maggie, who

were clinging to him as if they would never let go. 'Thanks, Bertie, but I can handle this. Why don't you take your sisters downstairs? I'll join you in a minute.'

'I'm not leaving you,' Bertie said stoutly. 'Lucy needs us.'

'I'm more than capable of standing up for myself.' Lucy's smile faded as she turned to give Piers a steady look. 'I'm grateful to you for your concern, but I've made my decision, just as you made yours to break off our engagement.' She held up her hand as he opened his mouth to protest. 'I know it was unofficial, but I think you were right. We wouldn't have suited.'

'Perhaps I was too hasty,' Piers said, casting a sideways glance in Bram's direction. 'I've had time to think it over since then.'

'It wasn't to be. But Dora and I are still friends.'

'I did so want you for a sister-in-law.' Dora dabbed her eyes on a lace-trimmed handkerchief. 'I'm so disappointed, and it's all your fault, Piers.'

'Don't be a baby,' he said impatiently. 'I don't think there's any more I can accomplish here. We'll wait for the carriage to return and then we'll be on our way.'

Lucy held her hand out to the children. 'Why don't you go outside and help Franklin bring in the things we brought from Albemarle Street. Cook sent cake and all manner of treats for you.'

Bertie made for the door. 'Give us a hand, Bram.' He opened it and a gust of foul air wafted in from the street.

Vicky tugged at her uncle's coat sleeve. 'Come on.'

'Yes, please help us,' Maggie added, gazing up at Bram with adoring eyes.

He laughed and ruffled her hair. 'All right, and then you can show me round the house. That's if Lucy doesn't mind.'

'Go ahead,' she said, smiling.

'Well, really. You'd think the fellow owned the place,' Piers muttered as Bram ushered the children outside.

Lucy had a sudden desire to giggle, but she managed to keep a straight face. 'Don't look so disapproving. The children only recently lost their mother. It's wonderful to see them happy again.'

'Of course it is,' Dora said firmly. 'We've just come at a bad time, but we'll call again when you're more settled. Won't we, Piers?'

He nodded reluctantly. 'I don't like leaving you here, Lucy. You're worth better than this.'

'I'm no stranger to this part of London or this way of life,' Lucy said calmly. 'I'm not the young lady you thought I was. It's a thin veneer, and beneath it I'm still the girl who used to pick pockets when we were desperate for food. I wouldn't have been the meek and mild wife you wanted, Piers. I'm my mother's daughter and I don't pretend to be anything else.' She stood aside as Bram re-entered the house, hefting a large box in his arms, closely followed by the children and Franklin, who was staggering beneath a pile of bedding.

'The carriage has returned, Piers,' Dora said urgently. 'We should leave now.' She gave Lucy a hug. 'I'll see you soon, and if you need anything you just have to ask.'

Lucy saw them to the door and stood for a

moment, watching them climb into their carriage. Piers did not look back and for some reason that hurt. Not so long ago she had imagined herself to be in love with him, and despite her brave words he still inhabited a small place in her heart. They had shared happy times: riding in the park, dancing the night away at society balls, trips to the theatre and extravagant dinner parties in elegant houses. She had been a lady then, or so she had believed. Now she was not so sure.

'Are you all right, Lucy?'

She spun round to see Bram standing behind her. She forced her lips into a smile. 'Indeed I am. This is the beginning of my new life, and I'm glad you're here to share it with me.'

He took her hand in his. 'Were you in love with him?'

'I thought I was, but I realise now that I was mistaken.'

'Are you sure? He obviously has deep feelings for you or he wouldn't have come here and made such a fuss.'

She squeezed his fingers. 'That's just his way. Piers likes to be in control and I've slipped through the net. He'll get over it and find an heiress who can help him in his career. He'll forget all about me.'

'Bram.' Bertie thrust the baize door open and beckoned frantically. 'Come and get some cake before the girls eat it all, and then I want to show you my room. I've got one all to myself.'

Lucy and Bram exchanged amused glances, and she slipped her hand through the crook of his arm. 'This is what matters,' she said softly.

'Looking after family is what's really important.'
He laid his hand on hers. 'I'll do anything I can to help you find yours, Lucy. That's a promise.'

Bram left his temporary lodgings and to the delight of the children and Hester he moved into one of the many spare rooms in Lucy's house, which she said was to be kept solely for him. He had a few days' leave remaining and he put all his energy into helping to make the house more habitable. With Bertie's help he put up curtain poles and mended broken windows; between them they cleared the back yard and cleaned the privy, making it less of a health hazard. Hester and Lucy worked tirelessly in the house, aided by Mary and Dot. Franklin and Tapper brought more cleaning materials, cooking pots and crockery from the house in Albemarle Street, but Lucy insisted on taking only the things that Linus would not miss. She did not want to be accused of taking what was rightfully his.

At the end of the week she said her goodbyes to the servants, most of whom had found positions in households elsewhere, although some of the younger ones were going home to their parents until they found new jobs. Bedwin moved into a small room on the ground floor in Leman Street, which Lucy had taken pains to make comfortable for him. His few personal possessions had been brought from Albemarle Street, including the threadbare armchair from the servants' hall in which he had spent many evenings sitting by the fire while he waited to be summoned above stairs by the jangling of a bell. Lucy did not think Linus would be interested in the fate of a saggy, tapestry-covered piece of furniture in much need of renovation, and she resolved to have it reupholstered when funds allowed.

Peckham had already taken up residence and was now a firm favourite with Vicky and Maggie. He had assumed the role of ratcatcher in chief, and by the end of the first week he had killed several large rodents and the rest had apparently fled. The mice retired behind the skirting boards and Bram came home one afternoon with a suspicious bulge in his jacket pocket. Vicky pounced on him, demanding to know if it was the present he had promised, and both she and Maggie uttered cries of delight when a tiny ginger head popped up, followed by the fluffy body of a kitten. Bram handed him gently to Vicky. 'He's very young, just old enough to leave his mother, so you must look after him and make sure he has plenty to eat. You'll have to house-train him and keep him free from fleas.'

'We will,' Vicky cried ecstatically. She turned to Lucy with a persuasive smile. 'May we keep him, Lucy? Please?'

'Of course,' Lucy said, laughing as the kitten scrambled up Vicky's arm to nuzzle her cheek. 'And when he's fully grown I'm sure he'll be a good mouser.'

Bram leaned over and brushed Lucy's cheek with a kiss. 'Thank you.'

'What for?'

'Thank you for being a wonderful woman and giving us a home. It was a good day for us when Linus brought you to the cottage in the forest.'

Hester looked up from stirring a pan of stew on the newly fitted range. 'It was so, Bram. I don't know what we'd have done if Lucy hadn't come to our rescue. I think we'd have ended up in the workhouse.'

'Stop,' Lucy cried, clapping her hands to her flaming cheeks. 'You're making me blush.'

'It's time I did something for you.' Bram smiled down at her. 'Get your bonnet and shawl. I've been doing a bit of detective work and I think I've found someone who might be able to help you in your search for your grandmother.'

'Really? Who?'

'You told me about the people you knew as a child, and your description of Carlos stuck in my mind. I found him in a pub near the old rag market, and he'll be there still with a bit of luck. If we're quick we might catch him.'

Carlos was seated in the ingle nook with a pint of porter on the table in front of him, and judging by the rosiness of his cheeks it was not his first drink that day. Lucy spotted him through a haze of tobacco smoke and made her way between the crowded tables. 'Carlos, is it really you?'

He was considerably plumper than she remembered, and his black hair was now streaked with silver, as was his moustache, which had lost none of its bushiness. He stared up at her with a blank expression. 'I'm sorry, miss. Do I know you?'

She sat down opposite him. 'I'm Lucy Pocket. I'm Eva's granddaughter.'

'Eva Pocket.' He smiled tipsily. 'Now who could forget that woman?' He narrowed his eyes, peering at her short-sightedly. 'You're grown up, but I do recall a little girl with a mass of golden curls and a cheeky face. Is it really you?'

She smiled and leaned over to pat his hand as it rested on the table top. 'Yes, I'm Lucy, and I'm searching for my nan. Have you seen her recently?' She hardly dared to breathe, watching him closely as his slow mental processes mulled over the possible answers.

He was still thinking when Bram made his way towards them carrying two tankards, which he placed on the table. 'Is this your man, Lucy?'

'Who are you?' Carlos demanded, coming back to life with a start. 'I don't remember you, cully.'

'This is my friend Bram,' Lucy said hastily.

Carlos narrowed his eyes, taking in Bram's uniform. 'You're a hussar,' he muttered. 'Good at horsemanship, are you, mate?'

'I can ride well enough. Can I get you a drink?'

'Now that's uncommon civil of you. I was trained by the great Pablo Fanque; you'll have heard of him, of course. In my youth I was in his circus troupe.'

Bram nodded. 'I know he was a great horseman, but I never saw him perform.'

'He's been dead these ten years, but he's still a circus legend.' Carlos took a swig of his drink. 'Anyway, ta for asking. I'll have a pint of porter and a meat pie. Haven't eaten since breakfast.'

'My pleasure, sir.' Bram left them and returned to the bar.

'Is he your man, Lucy? Fine fellow, that.'

'He's just a friend, Carlos. He's helping me to look for my grandmother. Have you seen her recently?' Lucy tried to sound unconcerned but her heart was racing.

'Saw her with Abe some time ago. Can't say when exactly. Memory's going, Lucy. Old age is catching up with me. You wouldn't think that once I was a top act at Astley's.' He took another sip of his drink. 'That was before Lord George Sanger bought it, of course. That was a sad day for me, but all those memories are fading into nothing.'

'I'm sorry to hear that,' Lucy said softly. 'But you might be able to help me find Eva. Do you know the whereabouts of her friend Abe? Perhaps he can help me?'

'Abe,' Carlos mused, staring into space. 'He died some months back. Found in a pool of blood with a knife through the heart. Daresay he deserved it, the old devil. He'll be stoking the fires of hell for eternity.'

Lucy stared at him in horror. 'Do they know who did it?'

Carlos shook his head. 'He weren't a popular fellow. There's many who will be happy to see the back of him.' He finished his drink, wiping his mouth on his sleeve. 'Where's that young man of yours? I'm starving.' He took a small comb from his pocket and ran it through his moustache, finishing off the procedure by licking his fingers and twirling the ends into sharp points. 'Ah, I see him coming. Just in time too. I was about to perish from hunger.'

Bram wended his way back to them with another pint mug and a pie on a tin plate. 'There you are, sir. Eat and enjoy.' He sat down beside Lucy. 'Any luck?'

She shook her head. 'I'm afraid not.' She pushed the tankard towards Carlos. 'I'm not keen on beer. You have it, Carlos, and if you should see Eva Pocket, please tell her that Lucy is looking for her. She'll find me at Pilgrim House, Leman Street.'

Carlos nodded, rendered speechless as he stuffed pie into his mouth, washing it down with gulps of ale.

Bram downed his drink. 'Shall we go, Lucy?' He pushed back his chair and stood up.

'Yes, there's no point in staying now.' Struggling against an overwhelming feeling of disappointment, she rose to her feet and was about to walk away when Carlos caught her by the sleeve. 'Pearl might know,' he said thickly. 'She's still around.'

'Thank you, Carlos. I'd almost forgotten Pearl.' Lucy leaned over and kissed his whiskery cheek before hurrying after Bram. She caught him up on the pavement outside. 'Hairbrine Court,' she said breathlessly.

He stared at her as if she had gone mad. 'What?'

'Hairbrine Court. It's where Pearl had lodgings. She was Granny's friend and she might know something.'

'Then that's where we'll go. Is it far?'

'No. It's quite near.'

The door opened a crack and Lucy could just make out an eye and a mop of untidy brown hair. 'Who's there?'

'I'm looking for Pearl Sykes. I believe she lodges here,' Lucy said boldly.

'Never heard of her.' The door was about to close but Bram put his foot over the threshold.

'She did live here ten years ago,' Lucy insisted.

The door opened to reveal a young, slatternly woman. A small child clung to her dirty skirts and she had a baby hitched over her shoulder like a small sack of washing. 'Ten years?' The words came out on a bark of laughter. 'I was just a nipper then. How d'you expect me to remember that far back?'

'You lived here ten years ago?' Lucy put her foot on the top step.

'What's it got to do with you?' The baby began to wail and the woman jiggled it up and down as if she were shaking a bottle of medicine.

'Does Mrs Wicks still own the property?' Lucy eyed her hopefully.

The toddler took her thumb from her mouth and began to hiccup. 'Shut up, Nellie.'

The irate woman was about to slam the door but Bram was too quick for her and he crossed the threshold. 'We're only asking for information, ma'am,' he said, doffing his cap. 'It's a family matter and very important to the young lady.'

The woman gazed up at him and her hand flew to her hair in an attempt to pat it into place. 'Well, sir, if you put it like that, then yes,' she said, simpering and fluttering her pale eyelashes. 'I was born and raised here. Ma runs a respectable lodging house.'

Lucy stepped inside. 'Then you must be Mrs Wicks's daughter.'

'Who's asking?'

'Lucy Pocket. And you are Mrs…?'

'Miss Molly Wicks. Not that it's any of your business.'

'May I see your mother? She's bound to remember Pearl, and she might be able to tell me where to find her.'

Molly Wicks looked from one to the other, her expression changing subtly when she gazed at Bram and her pale cheeks flushed a delicate pink. 'Well, if it's so important I suppose Ma won't mind the intrusion. Follow me.' Hitching the baby over her shoulder and dragging Nellie by the hand, she set off along the passage towards Mrs Wicks's rooms at the back of the building. Lucy wrinkled her nose. The stench of the outside privy and the smell of boiled cabbage, rotten fish, soot and smoke took her back to the fateful day when Sir William came to claim her. The light was poor in the passageway but Lucy could just make out the peeling wallpaper, which hung like broken blisters from the walls. Jagged cracks ran from ceiling to floor and the exposed brickwork was blackened with mould. It was a wonder, she thought, that the house was still standing. She had to jump a gap in the floorboards, and a lump of plaster fell from the ceiling, narrowly missing Bram's head.

'This is more dangerous than the Khyber Pass,' he whispered, chuckling.

Molly opened a door at the far end of the hallway. 'Ma, you've got visitors.' She stood aside. 'She's a bit deaf so you'll have to shout.' She thrust the baby into Lucy's arms. 'Hold him for a minute, will you? I got to go for a piss or I'll wet me drawers.' She shoved the small child into the room. 'Stay there, Nellie, and don't snivel. You know it makes Granny cross.' She pushed past

Bram and Lucy, heading towards the door which led into the back yard.

Lucy held the baby at arm's length. 'He's sodden,' she whispered. 'And he stinks.'

'Who's there?' A quavering voice emanated from the depths of an armchair by the empty grate. 'Is that you, Moll?'

Bram pulled a face. 'You'd best deal with this, Lucy. I don't want to scare the old girl.'

'If it's the Mrs Wicks I remember, the devil himself wouldn't frighten her.'

'Who's that talking? I ain't deaf, despite what she says. Come close where I can see you.'

The baby began to whimper, working himself up into a full-blown howl. Despite his soggy clothing and the strong odour, Lucy held him close as she approached the chair. 'I don't suppose you remember me, Mrs Wicks. I'm Lucy Pocket.'

Hooded eyes stared from a face that was wrinkled and brown like a walnut. 'Can't say I do. If it's money you want, you're out of luck. I ain't got none.'

'It's not like that, Mrs Wicks. I'm looking for someone who used to lodge with you. Pearl Sykes, do you remember her?'

'I ain't senile, young woman. Of course I remember her, the slut. I had to keep a close watch on that one or she'd have had men in her room all hours of the day and night. Smoked like a chimney, she did. It's a wonder she didn't burn me house down.'

Lucy rocked the baby in an attempt to stop him crying. 'Does she still live here?'

'What are you doing with young Arthur?

Where's Moll? I want me dinner.'

'She popped outside for a moment, Mrs Wicks. She'll be back directly.'

'I'm a prisoner in me own home.' Mrs Wicks leaned forward, lowering her voice. 'She's trying to kill me. Poisons me food. I have to feed it to the cat first to make sure I won't die in agony. Where is that girl?'

Lucy was growing desperate. 'Do you know where I can find Pearl?'

'Last I heard of her she was living over the broomstick with the landlord of that pub she used to work at. His wife died and Pearl was in his bed afore the coffin left the house, or so I heard.' Mrs Wicks pursed her lips. 'I'm not one to gossip.'

'Thank you, Mrs Wicks.' Lucy turned to Bram with a gasp of relief. 'I know that place. I went there once with Pearl and it's not far from here.' She cuddled the baby but he refused to be comforted.

'The poor little bugger's hungry too,' Mrs Wicks said gloomily. 'Molly's took to the drink since her man up and left. I told her not to get in bed with a married man, but she wouldn't listen. She's a wild 'un, and no better than she should be, even if she is me own flesh and blood. That baby suckles more gin than it does milk.'

Lucy stared down at the baby's red face and gaping mouth, and experienced a surge of pity for the neglected infant. She looked up at Bram but he shook his head.

'Don't even think about it, Lucy. You've got enough to do with my family, let alone those two orphans you took in. You can't look after all the waifs and strays in London.'

She was about to protest when Molly burst into the room, snatching the baby from Lucy's arms. 'He ain't no waif, mister. Keep your hands off me child, Miss Hoity-toity.'

Lucy glanced ruefully at the damp patch on her bodice. 'I think he needs changing and he's ready for his feed,' she said mildly. 'He's a fine boy, Molly.'

'And he's mine.' Molly clutched the child to her bosom, smothering his cries. 'If you've got what you wanted you'd best get out. You're upsetting Ma.'

'She's trying to poison me,' Mrs Wicks said gloomily. 'One day the police will come and find me stretched out on the floor, dead as a doornail.'

'Shut up, Ma.' Molly unbuttoned her blouse and put the baby to her breast. 'That shut the little sod up. Now get out, both of you.'

Bram put his hand in his pocket and brought out a florin, which he pressed into her outstretched palm. 'That's for your trouble, ma'am.'

She gave him a broken-toothed smile. 'You're a toff, captain.'

'Spend it on food,' he said sternly. 'It's for all of you, including your ma.'

Lucy made a move towards the door. 'We must go now, but thank you for the information.'

Mrs Wicks whistled through a gap in her teeth. 'She's come up in the world. I do remember her now. Skinny little thing she were, dressed in rags and dirty as a sweep's boy. Don't come here putting on airs and graces, miss. Get off with you both.'

Lucy hurried from the room and did not stop until she was outside. Bram caught her up, stopping briefly to put his cap on. 'Where now, Lucy?'

Chapter Twelve

The new landlord of the Old Three Tuns was tight-lipped when asked questions about the former tenants. He said he had been in residence for two years and the affairs of his predecessor were nothing to do with him. The potman was more forthcoming, and although he did not know Pearl's address he said she had parted from her lover and the last he had heard of her she was working in a pub in Limehouse.

After supper that evening, Lucy and Bram sat at the kitchen table, talking over the events of the day. Peckham lay sleeping on a rug by the range, his aged limbs twitching occasionally and his teeth bared, as if he were chasing rats in his dreams. Hester had retired to her room, having cooked a hearty stew with suet dumplings, followed by spotted dick and custard. Sid and Essie had gobbled their food like hungry hounds, earning a rebuke from Hester and a warning from Bram that they would suffer bellyache if they did not slow down. Lucy had watched indulgently; it made her happy to see the improvement in them, even though they had been with her for less than a week. Their pinched faces had plumped out and there was colour in their cheeks. Most important of all they had lost their hunted look, and did not jump and hide beneath the table at every knock on the door.

Sid had formed an attachment to Bertie, following him around with dog-like devotion, and Vicky had taken Essie under her wing, bossing her about in a good-natured way, which Essie seemed to enjoy. Maggie clung to Hester, and Lucy suspected that she had suffered the most after losing her mother. It was something with which she could empathise entirely.

'So what next?' Bram reached across the table to hold Lucy's hand. 'You know that I have to return to the barracks in two days' time. I wish I could stay longer.'

She smiled and squeezed his fingers. 'It's been wonderful having you here to help me over this difficult time, but I understand. You're a soldier and you have to do your duty.'

'Not for much longer if I have my way. I've had enough of army life, and it's rumoured that the buying and selling of commissions is about to end. I need to find a buyer quickly, or it'll be too late.'

'But what will you do then? And won't Linus want his money back? I find it hard to believe that he bought it for you out of the kindness of his heart. I'm not even sure that he has one.'

'He did it to get rid of me because I was growing up and becoming a serious threat. I was sick of the way he treated my sister, and he knew it.'

'But why go to those lengths, Bram? It must have cost him a fortune.'

'He knew I wouldn't enlist in the normal run of

things, and I suppose he hoped that as a cavalry officer I stood a good chance of being killed in action. He'd get his money back then because my commission could be sold on.'

'I knew he was a hateful man, but that is so calculating and cruel.'

'Well, it didn't work. I survived my time in India, and now my regiment is back home, I can sell up without disgracing the family name.' He grinned. 'Such as it is.'

'You'll always have a home here with us, but how will you earn your living?'

He removed his hand, running it through his thick mop of sun-streaked hair. 'I haven't decided yet. Maybe I'll get Carlos to coach me so that I can follow in his footsteps and become a trick rider at Sanger's Amphitheatre.'

'Are you serious?'

'I can think of worse ways to earn a living, but I'm a resourceful chap. I'll think of something.' He gave her a searching look. 'But what about you, Lucy? Are you going to be content letting out rooms and looking after other people's children?'

'I haven't thought very far ahead, but for now I have to make enough to pay the bills, and I'm determined to find Granny and my mother too, if at all possible. I can't say that I remember her, although I have a vague picture of her in my mind. I need to be sure that she's all right and not in some foreign country, alone and starving on the streets.'

'I'll do what I can to help you, Lucy. Tomorrow we'll go to Limehouse and try every tavern until we find your friend Pearl.' Bram pushed his chair back, stood up and stretched. 'But now I think it's time I took you back to Albemarle Street. This is your last night in your old home.'

'It's out of my hands now.' Lucy rose from her chair, moving slowly so that she did not disturb Peckham. 'I'm quite looking forward to living here now that we're getting things straight, although there's still a lot to do.'

'I'll go outside and try to find a cab.' Bram hesitated in the doorway, turning to give her a steady look. 'You must promise me you won't go out alone at night, Lucy.'

She smiled, plucking her bonnet and shawl from the rack of pegs on the wall. 'You mustn't worry about me. When I was a child I used to flit in and out of the shadows like a small ghost. I never came to any harm then, and I won't now.'

'You're not a kid any more,' he said, frowning. 'There are ruffians lurking in those same shadows who would do you harm. You need to be careful.'

'And I will.' She fastened her bonnet, tying the bow beneath her chin at a jaunty angle. It was on the tip of her tongue to scold him, but his concern for her safety gave her a warm feeling inside. They had known each other briefly as children, but he had always had a special place in her heart. They had been reunited only to be parted again, but she knew she would miss him terribly when he returned to his regiment.

The house in Albemarle Street seemed to have gone into mourning. A dim light shone through the two windows on either side of the main entrance, but the rest of the building was in darkness.

A series of sharp showers had left the window-panes scarred with raindrops, trickling slowly like tears to pool on the sills, and the atmosphere indoors was hardly more cheerful. Mrs Hodges bustled to greet her with her usual briskness, but her eyes were reddened and her mouth pulled down at the corners. 'This is a sad day for all of us, Miss Lucy.'

'Yes, indeed it is, Mrs Hodges. I'm very sorry to have to say goodbye to you and the rest of the servants.'

'I remember the first day you arrived. You tried so hard to get away, and now you have your chance. You're free to live your life as you please.'

'I grew to love it here, Mrs Hodges.' Lucy held out her hand. 'I hope you find happiness in your new position. You've been a faithful servant and my grandfather relied on you entirely, as have I.'

Mrs Hodges bobbed a curtsey. 'It's kind of you to say so, Miss Lucy.' She cleared her throat. 'Perhaps you would say a few words to the remaining servants before you leave in the morning. Most of them have found positions, and Franklin has agreed to stay on, as has Tapper, although I think they might live to regret their decisions.'

'I hope not,' Lucy said fervently. 'I'll go to my room now, so goodnight, Mrs Hodges.'

'Breakfast will be served in the dining room, as usual,' Mrs Hodges said firmly. 'We won't allow our standards to slip on our last day.'

'No, of course not. And if ever you need a reference you have only to write to me at Pilgrim House, and I'll be happy to oblige.' Lucy walked slowly towards the staircase, and suddenly she was a child again. Echoes from the past filled her head as she mounted the stairs. Her grandfather's voice boomed in her ear and she could hear the mocking tones of her tormentors, Susan and Martha. She walked slowly and purposefully up to the fourth floor and the old nursery suite. Opening the door she went inside and stood in the darkness with only the faintest glow from the street lamps to reveal the shrouded shapes of the furniture. She could hear Miss Wantage's sharp tones and the swish of the wooden ruler as it came down on her outstretched hand, again and again. She clenched her fist, experiencing real pain as well as the ache in her heart for a lost childhood. She left the room, closing the door on her memories.

She went down two flights of stairs to her room and found a fire burning brightly in the grate. This was a small act of kindness that touched her to the core. Mrs Hodges had seen to it that her last night in the old house was warm and comfortable. The woman who had seemed like an ogre to a frightened ten-year-old was human after all. Life in Albemarle Street had been constrained by rigid rules and even more rigid attention to etiquette, but there had been security and her future had been mapped out for her. She undressed and climbed into bed, pulling the coverlet up to her chin. Tomorrow would be the start of a journey into the unknown. She would be Lucy Pocket from now on. Young Lucy Marriott would remain as a shadow of the past in the shrouded schoolroom.

Breakfast was a silent meal. Lucy sat in state at the

head of the vast table attempting to do justice to the kedgeree, which Cook had prepared specially, knowing that it was one of her favourites. With Bedwin safely ensconced in Pilgrim House it was left to Dorcas, the under parlour maid, to wait on table. She looked nervous and about to burst into tears at any moment. After a few mouthfuls Lucy had to admit defeat, although it grieved her to leave such a delicious plateful of food. She would regret it later when faced with a simple meal of bread and cheese or a bowl of vegetable broth, but her throat felt swollen and it was difficult to swallow. She rose from the table, thanking Dorcas and shaking her hand. 'I hope you find another position soon.'

'Thank you, Miss Lucy.' Dorcas curtsied. 'Shall I clear away now?'

'No.' The sound of a man's voice made them both jump. 'You may fetch a pot of fresh coffee and some toast.'

Lucy turned slowly to see Linus about to take a seat in the chair she had just vacated. 'You're early, aren't you?' she said coldly. 'You simply couldn't wait to throw me out of my home.'

He picked up her discarded table napkin and made a show of spreading it across his lap. 'Go on, girl, don't stand there like a waxwork.' He dismissed Dorcas with a wave of his hand, and the maid scuttled out of the room.

'I see you've lost none of your charm.' Lucy headed for the door. 'Good luck, Linus. I hope you get everything that's coming to you.'

He bared his teeth in a humourless smile. 'Oh, I will, my dear. I'll live life to the full. And how are you getting on with your adopted family? I imagine you must have taken Bramwell into the fold as well. That won't please your fiancé.'

Lucy glared at him. 'I have no fiancé, as I'm sure you must know by now. Piers decided that we weren't suited after all, and I agree.'

'I suppose you prefer the more earthy charms of a certain young hussar. I regret my generosity in purchasing his commission, but then I'm a good-hearted fellow.'

'He's survived the rigours of serving in India, no thanks to you. It will be a good day when he quits the army.'

Linus was suddenly alert. 'He's selling up?'

'I – I don't know what his intentions are.'

He leapt to his feet. 'You're lying.' He moved towards her, grabbing her by the throat. 'Take this message to Bramwell. I know that the buying and selling of commissions is likely to end before the year is out.' He released her with a bark of laughter. 'You might think I'm a fool, Lucy Pocket, but I keep abreast of current affairs, particularly when it concerns me. I want my money back, every last penny. Tell him that, and inform him that unless he repays me in full I will announce to the world in general that his sister was a whore, and that her children are bastards in the true sense of the word. Do you understand?'

Lucy knew she must warn Bram that a careless slip of the tongue had alerted Linus to his plans, but she kept putting off the moment. It was not until later that morning when they were in a hansom cab on their way to Limehouse that she managed to pluck up the courage to admit her faux pas. She stared straight ahead, not daring to look at him. 'I've done something awful,' she said, clasping her hands tightly in her lap. 'I didn't mean to tell him, but it just came out.'

'What are you talking about? It can't be that bad, surely?'

'It is, Bram. Linus made me so angry that I didn't realise what I was saying until it was too late.' She shot him a sideways glance. 'I told him that you were going to sell your commission.'

'I can guess the rest.'

'I'm so sorry. The moment the words left my lips I knew I'd made a terrible mistake.'

'He would have found out sooner or later,' Bram said after a brief pause. 'These things have a habit of coming to light.'

'I am truly sorry.'

'What's done is done.'

'But you don't know what he said.'

'I can guess, and it wouldn't have been pleasant. I imagine he made dire threats which he would carry out unless the money was returned to him in full. Am I right?'

'He threatened to blacken Meg's name and put it about that the children are illegitimate. He has no shame.'

'It's only what I would have expected from someone like him. It will give me pleasure to throw the money in his face. I want nothing that came from him.'

Lucy breathed a sigh of relief. 'I know you're right, but it hardly seems fair.'

'You mustn't worry about me. To quote Hester,

water finds its own level. I'll do exactly that when I'm a free man.' He leaned over and kissed her on the cheek. 'I intend to find work so that I can contribute towards the children's upkeep. They're my responsibility, not yours.'

'They're my family too, Bram. Their grandmother was my father's aunt.'

'We'll agree to share the little darlings, shall we?' he said, laughing.

They shook hands and any tension that Lucy had felt vanished like morning mist, but as she looked out at the unfamiliar streets she had a feeling of foreboding. 'I don't know this part of London,' she murmured. 'But I can smell the mud on the foreshore so we must be nearing Limehouse.'

Bram lifted his cane and tapped the cab roof. The window flipped open and the cabby peered down at them. 'Yes, guv?'

'Is this Limehouse?'

'It is. Where d'you want me to drop you off?'

'The nearest pub.'

'Right you are, guv.' The cabby reined in his horse. 'This ain't a good area. Are you sure about this?'

Lucy could see that they had stopped outside a rough-looking tavern sited between a warehouse and a pawnshop. If she had thought that the area round the London docks was run down and filled with doubtful characters, this place was ten times worse. Despite the fact that it was a sunny day very little light filtered through the miasma of smoke and industrial pollution. The air was filled with noise from the docks and the sounds of the river as well as a cacophony of voices, all of them raised and speaking in a dozen or more different languages. Buckets of night soil remained uncollected on the pavements and the road was ankle-deep in horse dung, straw and rubbish tossed carelessly from upstairs windows.

Bram helped her to alight. 'Wait here, cabby. We'll move on to the next one if the person we're seeking doesn't work here.'

'Good luck, guv. You'll need it.'

The atmosphere in the taproom was thick with smoke and alcohol fumes. Bram took one look inside and insisted that Lucy waited in the doorway while he made enquiries at the bar. She had to fend off several whisky-soaked propositions before Bram eventually threaded his way back through the crowd. 'No luck here.' He ushered her outside. 'Perhaps I should have come on my own. This isn't the place for you.'

'If Pearl is working near here I need to speak to her.'

'Get back in the cab.' Bram practically threw her up onto the seat, leaping after her as the cabby flicked the whip and the horse lurched forward. 'I hope to God we find her soon.'

The pubs nearest to the docks were even rougher and more crowded. Bram refused to take Lucy inside, insisting that she remained in the cab under the watchful eye of its driver. Eventually, after many such unsuccessful attempts to find Pearl, they had almost given up hope of finding her. Bram had given the cabby instructions to take them back to Whitechapel, but as they drove along Narrow Street Lucy spotted a woman who looked familiar. There was something about the way she walked that reminded her forcibly of Pearl, and she thumped on the roof, ordering the cabby to stop. Without giving Bram a chance to argue she climbed down to the pavement. 'Wait. Please wait.'

The woman came to a halt, glancing nervously over her shoulder. 'What d'you want?'

The resemblance had been fleeting and Pearl would be ten years older than this gaudily dressed woman with wild black hair and rouged lips. 'I'm sorry,' Lucy said breathlessly. 'I thought you were someone I once knew.'

'What's a lady like you doing round here?' The woman looked her up and down as if calculating the cost of Lucy's clothes.

She had deliberately worn her plainest gown of grey poplin, such as a governess might wear, but even so there was no denying the cut and quality of her outfit and she realised that she must present an odd figure. 'I'm looking for a friend,' she said breathlessly. 'Pearl Sykes. I don't suppose you know her?'

'Pearl Sykes. Never heard of her. Take my advice, dear, and go home. If your friend lives in a place like this you don't want to know her. She's past hope, like me.' The woman was about to walk away when Lucy caught her by the arm.

'If she's fallen on hard times where might I find her? She used to work in a pub somewhere in Limehouse, but we've tried almost all of them and no one remembers her.'

The woman stared at her. 'What's it worth?'

Lucy opened her reticule and took out sixpence, pressing it into her hand. 'Any information would help.'

'That all you got?'

Lucy was about to give her more when Bram arrived at her side. 'What tale has she spun you, Lucy?'

The woman sidled up to Bram with a provocative wiggle of her hips. 'D'you want me to tell your fortune, mister? Send the little girl home and Froniga will find you a woman who'll know how to pleasure a brave soldier.'

'Thank you for the offer, but I'm spoken for.' Bram held his hand out to Lucy. 'Come on, the cabby's getting impatient.'

Froniga turned to Lucy. 'If your friend is down on her luck she'll either be in the workhouse or a bawdy house. Take your pick.'

'I was hoping she might have news of my grandmother,' Lucy said tearfully. 'It's Granny I want to find and Pearl was her friend.'

'Come away, Lucy. You won't get anything here,' Bram said impatiently.

'That's all you know, mister.' Froniga tossed her head and her gold earrings flashed in the sunlight. 'My granny was Romany and I got second sight.'

'Then you might be able to help me.' Lucy was not about to give up. She had come this far and somehow she had a feeling that this strange person held the secret. 'Eva Pocket,' she whispered. 'My granny is Eva Pocket and I haven't seen her for ten years.'

'I'd need something of hers to hold and take me to her.'

Lucy slipped the chain over her head and dropped the locket into Froniga's outstretched hand. 'She used to wear this all the time but she gave it to me for my eleventh birthday.'

Froniga closed her fingers over it, closed her eyes and stood swaying slightly on the balls of her feet.

'This is nonsense,' Bram said angrily. 'She's gulling you, Lucy.'

Froniga either chose to ignore him or she was in a state where she heard nothing but the voices in her head. 'I see Eva Pocket. She's in a bad place.'

'Where is she?' Lucy's voice rose to a high pitch. 'Tell me, Froniga. Please tell me.'

'It's dark and I can't make out exactly where it is, but I could take you there.'

'This has gone far enough.' Bram dragged Lucy aside. 'Don't listen to her. She's just after money.'

Froniga blinked as if waking from a sound sleep, focusing her eyes on Bram with a downward curl of her lips. She pointed a shaking finger at him. 'You shouldn't have interfered. Now she's lost again.'

'How could you, Bram?' Lucy's lips trembled. 'I was so close to Granny that I could almost feel her presence.'

'The gypsy woman has cast a spell on you. We need to get away from this place.' He grabbed her by the hand. 'Get in the cab, please.'

'What are you afraid of, mister?' Froniga snapped her fingers at him. 'You just want to keep her to yourself, but she is a free spirit. She won't be tied to any one man unless he wins her heart and her mind.'

Lucy snatched her hand free, turning her back on Bram. 'How will I find my grandmother,

Froniga? Tell me, please.'

'The moment has passed. I can't help you now.' Froniga dropped the locket into Lucy's hand and walked off, her ample hips swaying.

Lucy ran after her. 'No, please. I must know more.'

Froniga slowed her pace. 'The Waterman's Arms. It's not far from here. I go there every day about this time. Come tomorrow, but come alone.' She hurried off, leaving Lucy staring after her.

Bram approached slowly. 'I'm sorry. I know how much finding Eva means to you, but I don't trust that woman.'

'She's all I have to go on.'

He helped her into the cab. 'I wish I could stay longer, but you know I have to leave in the morning.'

She nodded dully, realising how much she would miss him. 'I'm sorry.'

'But I'll put all my efforts into selling my commission. The sooner I'm a free man the better, and I'll repay every penny to Linus, even if it leaves me with nothing.'

Lucy gave him an encouraging smile. 'I know exactly how you feel.'

When they reached Leman Street Lucy was dismayed to see the Northams' carriage waiting outside. It had started to rain and their coachman was huddled in his caped greatcoat. Lucy called to him as she climbed down from the cab. 'Have you been waiting long?'

He tipped his hat. 'A good while, miss.'

Her heart sank as she knocked on the door and waited for a response. Tired and saddened by their lack of success in finding her grandmother, the last thing Lucy felt she needed at this moment was a confrontation with Piers.

Bedwin opened the door and she could tell by his expression that he too was at the end of his patience. 'That man is here again, Miss Lucy,' he muttered as he took her shawl and bonnet. 'I told him that I didn't know when you'd be back, but he insisted on waiting for you. He's in the front parlour.'

'Thank you, Bedwin. I'll deal with this.' Lucy entered the room prepared for battle.

Chapter Thirteen

'Why are you here?' Lucy was too overwrought to hide her feelings behind a mask of good manners.

Piers rose swiftly from a chair by the empty grate. 'I had to see you again. My last visit didn't go as I had planned.'

'I thought we'd decided that there was no future for us, Piers.'

'I still have feelings for you. I've tried to overcome them, but it seems that you have me bewitched.'

'That's nonsense. You wanted a rich wife and I'm poor. It's as simple as that.'

'Nothing is ever that straightforward when it comes to human emotions. I can't get you out of my mind, although heaven knows I've tried.'

'You just want what you can't have.'

'That's unkind, Lucy. Mightn't we put all this behind us and begin again?'

'Are you proposing marriage, or had you something else in mind?'

His shocked expression seemed genuine and for a moment he seemed lost for words, but he recovered quickly. 'That's an outrageous suggestion and one that doesn't merit an answer.'

'But I'm still virtually penniless and the circumstances of my birth haven't changed.'

'That doesn't matter. I see it all clearly now.' Piers took her hands in his, his eyes alight with enthusiasm. 'I plan to stand as candidate for this constituency, and having a home here would be to my advantage. Even if they were aware of the situation, the fact that your parents weren't married would mean little to my prospective constituents.'

She stared at him, unable to believe her ears. 'Let me get this clear, Piers. Are you saying that in order to get yourself elected you would be willing to marry me and live in this house?'

'Of course I want to marry you. We were about to get engaged, if you remember. But I couldn't see a way of balancing my career prospects and my personal life. Now I can.'

Lucy snatched her hands away. 'And now you plan to make me part of your election campaign?'

'Of course,' he said enthusiastically. 'You've created a home for poor orphans. What better adjunct for a parliamentary candidate than a wife who does good works? We might even allude to your early years spent growing up in the East End, although of course it would have to be adapted a little.'

'You are incredible.' Lucy gazed at him in disbelief. 'Does Dora know of your plans?'

'Not in their entirety, but she loves you and she'll be thrilled to know that we're officially engaged...' He broke off, glaring at Bram who had burst into the room without knocking.

'You've agreed to marry him?' Bram roared. 'After the way he's treated you?'

'What's it to you?' Piers advanced on Bram, fists clenched at his sides.

Lucy stepped in between them, fending them off with her hands. 'I haven't agreed to anything.'

'But he just said you're engaged,' Bram said, scowling.

'And we are.' Piers put his hand in his pocket and took out the ring. 'I had planned to announce our engagement at Lucy's twenty-first birthday party, but circumstances worked against us. Hold out your hand, my dear.'

Lucy backed away, shaking her head. 'You're mad, Piers. If you think that I'd marry you now, you're very much mistaken.'

'You'd better leave.' Bram took a step towards him, but Piers stood his ground.

'I don't take orders from you. Come outside and we'll settle this like gentlemen.'

Bram threw back his head and laughed. 'We're in Whitechapel. Brawling is an everyday occurrence and if I didn't thrash you, someone else would take over just for the fun of it.'

'Piers, I want you to leave now,' Lucy said firmly. 'We are not engaged and never will be. I'm sorry, but that's how it is.'

He snatched up his top hat and cane. 'Dora will be very upset when she hears how you've thrown my generous offer back in my face.'

'Dora is my friend and I hope she always will be. Go home and find someone else to support your political ambitions.' Lucy held the door open.

'This isn't over.' Piers stormed out of the room.

Lucy heard him snap at Bedwin, telling him to get out of his way, followed by the slamming of the front door. She sank down on the nearest chair. 'I don't know what possessed him,' she said tiredly. 'He's not always like that, or I wouldn't have imagined myself to be in love with him.'

Bram stood by the window, his back to her as he looked out on the street. 'I'm almost sorry for the fellow.'

'Sorry for him? Why? He jilted me and now he's come creeping back because he needs a wife to help him in his election campaign.'

'He's gone.' Bram turned to her with a wry smile. 'Despite the fact that I dislike the chap intensely, I think he has genuine feelings for you, and who could blame him?'

'Is that an unsubtle way of paying me a compliment, Bram?'

'You deserve better than this,' he said, looking round the shabby room. 'You've been brought up to a different way of life.'

'It wasn't my choosing, Bram. I'm still a street arab at heart.'

He laughed and took a seat opposite her, stretching out his long legs. 'So you say, but I remember you as a child, and even then I knew that you were different from us. You were touched by a little bit of magic that set you apart from ordinary mortals, and that was before your grandfather took you permanently under his wing.'

'You're talking nonsense, Bram.' Struggling against a sudden feeling of exhaustion, she raised herself from the chair. 'I must see how the children are doing and rescue poor Hester. She had them all day and she'll be worn out.'

He jumped to his feet. 'You're right. And I need to have a chat with young Bertie and make him realise that he'll be the man of the house while I'm away.'

'Don't let Bedwin hear you say that. He thinks he's my guardian angel and I don't want to disappoint him.'

The children cried when they saw Bram off next day, and Lucy shed a tear in private, although she made an effort to appear cheerful for the sake of the others. Sid and Essie were similarly affected even though they had only known Bram for a short time, and Peckham lay on his blanket with his head between his paws, looking sorrowful. Hester waved him off with a show of cheerfulness that did not fool anyone, and Bedwin made a pot of tea, lacing each cup with a tot of the brandy he had liberated from the cellars in Albemarle Street.

But there was no time to wallow in self-pity and Lucy set everyone a task in the seemingly never-ending work of refurbishing of the house. They took the remaining rooms one at a time, sweeping, mopping and polishing until every inch was scoured clean. Bertie had secured a job in the local bakery, which relieved him of his domestic duties to some extent, but in his spare time he helped Bedwin to restore the peeling paintwork.

Lucy waited for a couple of days, making certain that things were running smoothly in Bram's absence. She was surprised to find how much she missed his company, and how much he had done to create order out of chaos. He had the gift of command without being overbearing or making others resentful. She worked tirelessly, but her determination to find Eva had not waned, and on the third morning after Bram's departure she set off for Limehouse, using some of her dwindling resources to pay for a cab.

The Waterman's Arms was relatively quiet, with only a few old men seated at tables with their pint pots in front of them and clay pipes clenched in their teeth. The barman eyed her suspiciously. 'What can I do for you, miss?'

'I'm looking for a woman called Froniga. She said I might find her here.'

'I know her,' he said, nodding. 'You'd do best to steer clear of didicois, miss.'

'Nevertheless I want to speak to her. Is she likely to come in this morning?'

'Can't say for certain, but if she's really got second sight she should know that you're here.' He winked and grinned. 'You can wait if you want, but this ain't no place for a young lady.'

Lucy sighed inwardly. She had worn her shabbiest gown and borrowed an old shawl and bonnet from Hester, but it seemed to have made no difference. 'I'll have a glass of lemonade, if you please.' She placed a penny on the counter.

He poured her drink, placing it on the counter in front of her. 'I think you'd best take it in the back parlour. We'll be busy soon and you'll find it a bit crowded, if you get my meaning.'

'Yes. Thank you.' She picked up the glass and followed him through a door at the back of the bar, and along a dark corridor to a room at the far end. The reek of stale beer and tobacco smoke made her catch her breath, but she thanked the barman and took a seat by the fireplace. The hearth was littered with broken clay pipes and ashes tumbled from the grate. Dust covered the wooden settles and the table tops were sticky with spilled beer. Housekeeping was obviously not a priority. She settled down to wait.

She had almost given up and was thinking of leaving when the door opened and Froniga swept into the room, making it seem even smaller. Her colourful costume was in sharp contrast to the dingy surroundings and her loud voice shattered the stillness like cockcrow at dawn. 'I knew you'd be here,' she said triumphantly. 'You've come to ask my help in finding your granny.'

Lucy rose to her feet. 'Her name is Eva Pocket.'

'Names don't mean much in the twilight world, my duck.'

'What do you mean?'

'It's a place where those who've lost everything find oblivion.'

'I still don't understand. Do you know where I can find my grandmother, or not?'

'No, but I think I've found your friend Pearl. Come with me.' Froniga left the room in a swirl of grubby red flannel petticoats, leaving a waft of strange and exotic perfume in her wake. Lucy hurried after her.

The men in the bar stood aside to let them pass with expressions varying from overt hostility to fear. A foreign seaman made the sign of a cross on his chest and others turned away, as if the mere sight of the gypsy woman would cast a spell on them. When they reached the street Lucy kept close, afraid of losing Froniga in the dark alleyways and courts. It was eerily quiet, and the men and women who stumbled out of the taverns and opium dens were hollow-eyed and gaunt. 'This is a terrible place,' Lucy whispered. 'Surely we won't find Pearl here?'

Froniga put her finger to her lips, saying nothing as she parted a filthy, ragged curtain which separated the outside world from the place where the desperate came to seek escape. Lucy clutched her hand to her nose as the stench hit her with the force of a slap in the face. The foetid air was thick and smoke-filled, and a single paraffin lamp set on a low table was the only form of lighting. Inert figures were sprawled on the floor with opium pipes clutched in their hands. Lucy tugged at Froniga's sleeve. 'There must be some mistake. Pearl would never sink to this.'

'Who have you brought to me, gypsy woman?' A haggard crone rose from a stool behind the table, eyeing Lucy critically. 'She looks too young and fresh to want my services.'

'We're looking for a woman called Pearl Sykes,' Froniga said tersely. 'Is she here?'

'She's broke, so take her and good riddance.'

'Where is she?'

The woman took a clay pipe from her mouth and pointed it into the gloomy interior. 'Over there.'

Froniga stepped over a body prostrate on the bare boards, and beckoned to Lucy. She made her way round the shapeless mound, treading carefully. It was impossible to tell whether it was male or female, alive or dead, but she did not look closely enough to see. As her eyes grew accustomed to the darkness Lucy could make out more bodies, some lying as if dead to the world, and others in a semi-comatose state. Damp oozed from the walls, leaving trails of green slime, and fungus sprouted like ghostly fingers from the cracked brickwork. The smell was suffocating and she covered her mouth and nose with her hand. This place was a living hell, and although she wanted desperately to find Pearl, a small part of her hoped that it was a stranger who lay drugged and unconscious in the dark alcove.

'Pearl Sykes.' Froniga went down on her knees, dragging the unconscious woman to a sitting position. 'Pearl.' She slapped her face and the sound ricocheted off the walls and ceiling. 'Wake up.'

Lucy leaned closer. 'Pearl, it's Lucy.'

'Is this the one?' Froniga asked brusquely. 'Is this your friend?'

Pearl's head lolled to one side and although her face was thinner and streaked with dirt, her hair matted and filthy, Lucy would have known her anywhere. This was a mere shadow of the plump, lively woman who had sold fish in the market, but it was definitely Pearl. She nodded. 'Yes, it is.'

'Give us a hand then.' Froniga heaved Pearl to her feet and somehow, between the two of them, they managed to get her out of the building. Looping her arms around their shoulders they marched her as far as Narrow Street. 'What will you do with her?' Froniga asked curiously. 'It's not likely you'll get much sense out of her in this state.'

'She was good to me when I was a child,' Lucy said stoutly. 'The least I can do is look after her until she's well again.'

'It won't be easy. She depends on the stuff and she'll do anything to get it.'

'I can't abandon her, and she might know what happened to Granny.'

'Her brains will be addled by now.' Froniga allowed Pearl to slide to the ground as she stepped into the road to hail a hackney carriage, but it drove past them. 'You won't see me again. I have to leave London for the sake of me health.'

'Are you ill?'

Froniga gave her a pitying smile. 'No, but I need to disappear for a while, if you get my meaning.'

'But where will you go?'

'My family used to travel with Charter's circus, although they're all dead and gone now. I'm Madame Froniga, the Romany fortune teller, when I choose to join them, and where better to hide than in a travelling show?'

Lucy was impressed. 'I've never seen a circus or a travelling fair.'

'They're in Essex at the moment. The last I heard they were in Chelmsford. That's where I'm going now.'

'I'm sorry you're leaving, and I'm truly grateful for your help.' Lucy took her purse from her pocket and opened it, but there was only enough to pay her cab fare home. She felt obliged to show her appreciation even though Froniga had not asked for money. 'I'm sorry. I haven't got enough to pay you for your trouble.'

'Call it a favour. One day I might need your help.' Froniga was about to turn away when a shaft of sunlight pierced the clouds, catching Lucy's silver locket in its beam. Froniga reached out to touch it, closing her eyes. 'Your grandmother is trying to tell me something. I feel her heart beating as strongly as my own.'

Lucy's breath hitched in her throat. 'Where is she? I have to know.'

'She's far away from here, but I can't see her clearly.'

'Can you tell me more?'

'She's fading away, but I'm certain that you'll find her very soon. Now I must go.' Froniga hailed another cab and this time it slowed down and came to a halt.

Lucy would have liked to question her further but getting Pearl into the cab was her main concern and they dragged her to her feet, manhandling her into the vehicle. Lucy climbed in after her, but when she turned to thank Froniga she had disappeared into the milling crowd of dockworkers.

Pearl was given a room on the top floor where, for her own safety, she was locked in day and night. Lucy would not have known how to handle her, but Hester had previous experience of such a case in one of the houses where she had worked in her youth. She had been an under parlour maid but had often been called upon to help the nurse who was hired to look after the eldest son: a young man who had fallen into bad company and become addicted to laudanum and opium. Hester did everything for Pearl, refusing to allow anyone into the room, including Lucy. It was frustrating, as she was desperate to question her, but Hester stood firm and Lucy was forced to bide her time.

She saw nothing of Piers, but Dora was now a regular visitor to Leman Street. She had overcome her dislike of the neighbourhood, and her fear of being set upon the moment she stepped from her carriage.

'You've done wonders,' she said, gazing round the front parlour, which had benefited from a fresh coat of paint, a pair of curtains made from material bought in Petticoat Lane, and a slightly faded rug purchased from the pawnbroker further along the street. The furniture, also second hand, together with other day to day necessities, had taken a sizeable chunk out of the sum that Linus had given Lucy for the support of his children.

'To tell you the truth all this has left me a bit short of money,' Lucy admitted, pouring tea from the chipped but otherwise perfectly usable china teapot, another purchase from the market. 'I must find some respectable lodgers who can be relied upon to pay their way and supplement my income.'

'I suppose you could advertise in the newspapers,' Dora said doubtfully. 'But anybody could reply, and it might prove difficult to check their references.'

'I know. I've thought about nothing else. Even though Bertie has a job he doesn't earn very much, and I think that I ought to seek a position somewhere, but I don't know what I could do.'

'I'd love to help you, but I've spent all my dress allowance.' Dora stared into her teacup, frowning. 'If only you'd married Piers, you would at least have had a roof over your head.'

Lucy smiled ruefully. 'I can't imagine Piers adopting my cousins, let alone Sid and Essie. Then there's Hester, not to mention Bedwin, who's too old and frail to find another position. How would they manage without me?'

'And you've taken on Pearl.' Dora shook her head. 'You've created a home for waifs and strays, and now you have to find a way to support them all. I don't envy you your task, Lucy.'

'Pearl is recovering slowly, and Carlos visits her at least once a week. They cheer each other up, according to Hester. I'm only allowed to see Pearl briefly, but I'm told that she's showing signs of recovery.'

'But Pearl doesn't know where you might find Eva.'

Lucy bowed her head. 'She hasn't seen her for years. It seems that my grandmother has vanished into thin air.'

'Like a conjuror's trick.' Dora sipped her tea. 'I'm sorry, Lucy. I know it's no joke, but perhaps you ought to stop thinking about her and concentrate on looking after yourself.' She placed her cup and saucer on the table. 'I know you don't want to hear this, but Piers still loves you. You only have to say the word and he'll come running. He's never got over you.'

'But I don't love him,' Lucy said softly. 'I'm sorry, Dora. I know he's your brother and you're fond of him, but I can't forget how he let me down when I needed him most.'

'He knows he made a mistake, and he's genuinely sorry.'

'Maybe, but I like being independent, even though I've very little money. I'll find a way to make things better for all of us, you'll see.'

'What about Bramwell? Does he support his nephew and nieces?'

'He gave me what he could, and promised more when he received his pay. I trust Bram and I know he'll do his best for us.'

Dora glanced out of the window. 'My carriage has arrived. I have to go, but I'll come again next week. Or perhaps you'd like to come shopping with me? It would be fun to go out together again.'

'I can't afford to spend money on fripperies. It's not like the old days; you and I live in different worlds now.' Lucy stood up to embrace her friend as she prepared to leave. 'Don't worry about me, and please don't repeat any of this to Piers. I don't want him to get the wrong impression. There really is no hope for us.'

'I won't say a word, but I wish you'd reconsider.'

'There's no chance of that.' Lucy saw her to the door and watched her climb into the carriage, assisted by the footman. The coachman drove off, taking Dora back to the world of wealth and privilege, leaving Lucy to wonder how she was going to feed her family after paying for the urgent repairs to the roof. She returned to the parlour and set about writing an advertisement for a respectable lodger, but although it seemed like a logical step she was wary. With young and vulnerable children to care for and only a boy and a frail old man to protect them, the thought of having complete strangers living in the place she called home was daunting.

She was still sitting there, chewing the end of her pencil, when the door opened and Pearl walked into the room. Lucy leapt to her feet. 'What are you doing out of bed? You should be resting.'

Pearl sank down in the nearest chair. 'I'm a bit weak on me pins, but I'm not an invalid.'

'Hester was supposed to be looking after you.'

Pearl grinned. 'She forgot to lock the door, if that's what you mean. She remembered she had bread in the oven and she was off like a shot.'

'How are you feeling?' Lucy asked nervously.

'I'm not going to rush out to the nearest opium den, if that's what you're thinking. I promise you I'm done with that stuff forever.'

'I'm so glad, if only for your sake, Pearl.'

'I dunno why you went to all the trouble of saving me, but I am grateful. I was a poor wretch and now I've got to prove you were right. I won't let you down, Lucy.'

'It was Froniga who found you, and it was only by chance that I met her. I was looking for you because I thought you might know what happened to my grandmother.'

Pearl shook her head. 'I wish I did. The last I

saw of Eva she was with Abe.'

'He was murdered. I heard that he was stabbed to death.'

'Was he now? That doesn't surprise me. He was a bad lot.'

'You don't think that she could have done it, do you?'

'Not Eva. You ought to know her better than that. If she'd fallen out with him she would have up and left. She might have bashed him over the head with a frying pan, but she wouldn't have stuck a knife in his heart.' Pearl took a pack of Passing Cloud cigarettes from her pocket and struck a match, inhaling deeply. 'A present from Carlos,' she said, exhaling with a satisfied sigh. 'A girl's got to have some vices.'

Lucy smiled indulgently. It was good to see Pearl almost back to her old self. 'Tell me about Granny and Abe. I never knew him.'

'She kept you away from him and his crooked deals, but I think she really cared for the old sod in her own way, although Eva wasn't the faithful type. I'm sorry, Lucy, but it's the truth.'

'Froniga said she could see Granny, but then she faded away. Do you think she really has got second sight?'

'She found me, didn't she?'

'Yes, that's true, but she's gone away and now I'll never know if she was telling the truth or not. I'm beginning to think I'll never find Granny or Ma.'

'Maybe they don't want to be found. Have you thought of that? As far as Eva is concerned you're a grand lady. She wouldn't want to spoil your life by turning up on your doorstep.'

Lucy eyed her thoughtfully. 'But if she knew the truth she would come home, wouldn't she?'

'She might. It all depends on how she's situated now.' Pearl took another drag on her cigarette, exhaling through her nostrils. 'If you get my meaning. She might have found another fancy man.'

Picking up her pencil, Lucy chose to ignore this last remark. 'I'm going to finish off this advertisement and put it in the tobacconist's window. We'll take in lodgers and you're going to help me.'

'Glad to be of service,' Pearl said, chuckling. 'What are my duties?' She wriggled suggestively in her chair.

'I've got a plan. I can't tell you yet, but you'll find out soon enough.'

Chapter Fourteen

Hopeful applicants queued outside the door. Bedwin was given the task of letting them in one at a time, dismissing those who looked too disreputable or were drunk. Hester ushered the prospective lodgers into the parlour, where they were interviewed by Lucy and Pearl. In the end they selected the three who were the least likely to cause trouble, all of whom were in employment. One of them, a balding middle-aged man wearing a shabby suit with leather elbow patches and down-at-heel shoes, worked as a clerk in one of the nearby shipping offices. He introduced himself as Gilbert Harker, admitting reluctantly when questioned about his reasons for needing a room that his wife had run off with the tally man. He could not afford to pay the rent on the home they had shared for twenty years, and his grown-up children had shown no inclination to take him in.

The second successful applicant was a shiny-faced boy whose crop of curly fair hair made him look even younger than his sixteen years. Cyril Aitken told them he was an orphan raised in the Foundling Hospital, and was apprenticed to a locksmith with a premises in Dock Street. Lucy would have given him a room for nothing, but Pearl intervened and they agreed to let him have one of the smallest attic rooms at a greatly reduced rent. Cyril's brown eyes shone with gratitude and he promised to do odd jobs around the house in order to make up the difference. Lucy could have hugged him, but she managed to control the urge and merely smiled and welcomed him into her home.

The last person they saw was Leonard Rossman, a Jewish immigrant who worked for a master tailor in Leman Street. His sad story of love and loss in his homeland made Lucy want to cry and even Pearl, who had heard many such hard-luck stories, had to wipe away a tear. Ever practical, Lucy went to the kitchen to make a pot of tea. She cut a thick slice from Hester's seed cake and put it on a plate. 'The poor man needs building up,' she said when Hester protested.

Hester regarded her with overt disapproval. 'We're supposed to be making money out of the lodgers. You won't pay the bills by treating them to afternoon tea.'

'They're all guests as far as I'm concerned. You'll love them all when you get to know them,' Lucy said, smiling. 'Leonard has promised to make curtains for us, and young Cyril is going to do odd jobs. We'll soon have an army of workers helping us to make this old house habitable. You'll see.'

'All I see is bankruptcy looming.' Hester snatched up the remains of the cake and placed it in the larder.

The lodgers moved in and the children took instantly to Cyril, who was not much older than Bertie, and soon the pair of them were firm friends. Leonard and Gilbert worked long hours, spending much of their free time in their respective rooms. They ate dinner with the family and earned Hester's approval by complimenting her on her cooking. Leonard made curtains for the dining room and brought home off-cuts of gentlemen's suiting, fashioning them into waistcoats for Bertie and Cyril. Not to be outdone, Cyril took out the night soil each morning, swept the back yard and hefted buckets of water into the house. Indoor plumbing was a luxury that Lucy could not afford, and bath night involved the lengthy and back-breaking task of fetching water from the pump, heating it in pans on the range, and tipping it into the zinc tub which was placed in front of the fire. The youngest children were first, followed by the women. Bertie decided that he was now a man and opted to accompany Cyril to Nevill's public baths in Aldgate, where Leonard and Gilbert also did their ablutions.

The rent money from the lodgers was a great help, but the roof still leaked when it rained, and although the main rooms were made habitable there was still much that needed doing. Lucy was torn between the desire to find work, which would boost their meagre income, and the desperate need to find her grandmother or at least to discover her fate. It was almost impossible to know where to start her search, and Pearl had nothing to add. It seemed that Eva Pocket had vanished into thin air, leaving not a trace.

One May morning, Lucy rose early and went to market to purchase the best of the day's produce at the cheapest price possible. She arrived back at the house at the same time as the postman, and he handed her an envelope. 'Fine morning, miss.' He tipped his cap, mounted his bicycle and pedalled off at considerable speed.

She unlocked the door and let herself into the house, almost bumping into Leonard, who had a slice of toast in one hand and his battered bowler hat in the other. He smiled and nodded, swallowing a mouthful of breakfast and mumbling a greeting. Lucy stood aside to let him pass, but before she could close the door the pounding of footsteps on the stairs alerted her to the fact that, as usual, Cyril was late for work. He shot past her, grinning and tipping his cap, and was followed by Leonard moving at a much more sedate pace.

'Good morning, Miss Pocket. It's a lovely day.'

He doffed his hat.

'Yes, indeed it is, Mr Rossman.' She closed the door after him, and went downstairs to the kitchen.

Bertie had just finished his breakfast and was scraping the last of the porridge from his bowl, receiving a frown from Hester, who was toasting a slice of bread in front of the fire. 'You'll take the pattern from the plate if you keep that up, young man.'

'It's too good to leave any,' Bertie said, unabashed.

Hester glanced at Lucy. 'You're up and about early.'

'It's such a lovely morning I thought I'd go to market first thing.' She put the basket on the table. 'Hurry up, Bertie. You'll be late for work.'

He licked his spoon and replaced it with a clatter. 'I'm off.' He leapt to his feet and snatched up his cap from its peg, ramming it on his head. 'Old man Mould is a stickler for punctuality and a blooming slave driver. I'd be better off in the army, like Bram.'

'You're too young to even think about it,' Lucy said severely, but noting his crestfallen expression she moderated her tone. 'And we rely on you, Bertie, dear. What would we do without the man of the house?'

He gave her a suspicious look. 'You've got Cyril and the old men. You don't need me.'

She wrapped her arms around him. 'Of course we do. You're family, Bertie. The others are commercial gentlemen who pay for their lodgings. They help us to settle the bills, but you're still my best boy.' She kissed him on the cheek before giving him a gentle push towards the door. 'Now go, before you get into trouble with your boss.'

He backed out of the kitchen, blowing her a kiss.

'You spoil him,' Hester said, fanning the toast to extinguish the flames as it caught light. 'A spell in the army would do him good. We don't want him growing up like his father.'

Lucy was horrified. 'He's nothing like Linus. He's a good, kind boy and he takes after his mother.'

'You're right, of course.' Hester scraped the burnt bits off the bread. 'But he's easily influenced. Who knows what trouble he'll get into with that young Cyril?'

'Don't say things like that.' Lucy picked up the envelope and studied it. 'My goodness. It's for me. I quite thought it must be for Leonard or Gilbert.' She shot a sideways glance at Hester, smiling. 'Don't look so worried. I try to keep it formal when I address them personally, but we all live under the same roof.'

Hester scraped butter onto her toast and took a bite. 'In my opinion men have to be kept in their place or they get out of hand. Linus is a good example. If Meg hadn't been such a sweet-natured creature she would never have allowed him to take advantage of her.'

'Most men aren't like that. Linus is the meanest, most despicable person I've ever met.' Lucy opened the envelope and took out a single sheet of paper. 'It's a poster.' She held it up. 'Charter's circus. That's where Froniga was headed.'

'Why would she send you such a thing?' Hester squinted short-sightedly at the large print. 'I think I need spectacles.'

'It says that they're performing in a village near Chelmsford.' The print danced before Lucy's eyes and she could almost feel the Romany woman's presence. 'It's a message from her, that's what it is. She knows something, Hester. She wants me to go to her.'

'Stuff and nonsense. She's playing games with you.'

'No. She wouldn't do that. I trust her.' Lucy looked round as the door opened and Pearl breezed into the room. 'I've had a message from Froniga. Look.' She thrust the poster under her nose.

'It's just a flier for a circus, love. Nothing more.'

'That's what I think.' Hester nodded vigorously. 'I'm going to get those nippers out of bed and set them to work. Talk some sense into her, Pearl.' She stalked out of the kitchen, slamming the door behind her.

'I have to go,' Lucy said eagerly. 'Can't you see that she's trying to tell me something?'

Pearl went to the table and picked up the teapot. She hesitated, gazing at Lucy and shaking her head. 'Not really. I know she led you to me, but that doesn't mean she can find someone who's been missing for a long time. Eva could be in Timbuktu for all we know.'

Lucy giggled. 'I don't think so, but I have to do this. I don't care what Hester says, I'm going to see Froniga and hear what she has to say. It might be my only chance to find Granny. I can't ignore this, Pearl. You must see that.'

Pearl filled a cup and added a dash of milk. 'I understand, but I think you might be heading for a serious disappointment.'

'Even so, it's something I must do. I know I can trust you and Hester to look after the children, and the lodgers.'

'Of course you can.' Pearl fumbled in her pocket for her cigarettes. 'We'll be fine, but don't stay away too long.'

Lucy breathed a sigh of relief. 'I promise to come home as soon as possible, and hopefully I'll bring Granny with me.'

It was still light when the train pulled into Chelmsford station. Lucy was too excited to feel tired after the journey. She made enquiries at the ticket office and was told that she might catch the carter who had just collected supplies for the circus people, and was about to leave. She raced outside and managed to attract the driver's attention just as he was about to urge his old nag into action. He was unwilling at first, but when she offered him a silver florin he changed his mind and allowed her to climb up beside him. 'I ain't a stage coach,' he grumbled. 'But I suppose it won't hurt to oblige a young lady.'

She settled down at his side, holding onto her bonnet as the breeze tugged at the ribbons. The sun was plummeting towards the horizon, leaving bruise-like streaks of purple and crimson to mar the perfection of a duck-egg blue sky. The air was fresh and sweet-smelling, quite different to the fug and smoke of London. The stench of the factories, putrid river mud and overflowing sewers had been swapped for the scent of blossom on the May trees and the heady aroma of freshly tilled soil. From the vantage point of the driver's seat she could see over the top of the hedgerows. Neatly ploughed fields pierced by green spears of sprouting crops spread like a patchwork quilt, with stands of trees hazy with new growth.

As dusk fell it was the relative quiet of the countryside that struck her most forcibly. The only sounds were the clip-clop of the horse's hooves, the rumble of cartwheels and a chorus of birdsong. Used as she was to the hectic hustle and bustle of the crowded city streets, and the constant babel of voices, the deserted country lane was a world apart and it seemed to stretch into infinity. Her companion said nothing. He chewed tobacco, spitting a stream of brown juice onto the road at regular intervals.

Then, just as it was growing dark, Lucy saw the glow of naphtha flares against the indigo sky. 'Is that the circus?' she asked excitedly.

'What else would it be?'

She subsided into silence, craning her neck to catch sight of the first signs of habitation since they left the town. The fiery glow grew brighter and more intense as they drew closer, and silhouetted against the night sky she could see the dome of the big top. It was surrounded by booths, caravans and much smaller tents. The savoury smells of cooking over camp fires mingled with the fragrance of wood smoke, and suddenly the air was filled with sound. The carter drew his horse to a halt and climbed down to the ground, tossing the reins to a small child who had allowed his curiosity to get the better of him and had come out to investigate. A young woman appeared suddenly, gesticulating and shouting at the small boy, but her angry expression melted into a smile of welcome when she saw the carter. She looped her arm around his shoulders and led him away, leaving Lucy to alight unaided.

Clutching her small valise in her hand, she hitched up her skirts and clambered from the seat with as much dignity as she could muster. She turned to speak to the boy, and found herself surrounded by small people, the tallest of them no higher than her hip. They had emerged from the deep shadows, and in the flickering firelight it was almost impossible to tell whether they were welcoming her or whether they were a threat. Lucy looked round, searching for a friendly face. 'Froniga,' she cried in desperation when no one spoke. 'I've come to see Froniga.'

A ripple of conversation, no louder than the murmur of the wind in the trees, was cut short by the sudden appearance of a tall man dressed in a scarlet coat. He carried a horsewhip in his hand, but despite his outlandish appearance he was smiling. 'You must be Lucy Pocket, the equestrienne we've heard so much about.'

Lucy stared at him aghast. 'I – I think there's been a mistake, sir.'

'You are modesty personified, Miss Pocket.' One of the dwarfs stepped forward. 'Obadiah Starr.' He bowed from the waist. 'Welcome to Charter's circus.'

'That's my line, Obadiah.' The man in scarlet

held out his hand. 'It's a pleasure to make your acquaintance, Miss Pocket. I am Montague Charter, owner and ringmaster of this grand circus.'

'Don't let your pa hear you say that, Monty.' Obadiah grabbed the whip from him and cracked it above his head, receiving a round of applause from his troupe.

Monty snatched it back. 'Only I am allowed to do that, as you well know, Obadiah.' He proffered his arm to Lucy, who was dumbstruck by the sudden turn of events. She thought she must be dreaming, but pinching the back of her hand hurt, confirming the fact that she was wide awake. There must be a logical explanation, but for the moment it eluded her. She slipped her hand through the crook of his arm and he led her through the gap between the caravans, accompanied by a burst of applause from the tiny onlookers. He came to a halt outside one of the tents. 'Froniga, where are you? Hasn't your crystal ball informed you of your friend's arrival?'

Lucy stifled a sigh of relief. Obviously there was a misunderstanding, but Froniga would soon set this man straight. The tent flap parted and Froniga emerged, blinking sleepily. 'Lucy? You've come.' She smiled and enveloped her in a warm embrace. 'Come inside and rest. You must be tired after your journey.' She turned to Monty. 'I'll look after her. She can share my accommodation until we've sorted something out for her.'

'You must join us for supper. Father will want to meet our new star.' Monty clicked his heels together and raised his hand in a mock salute. 'Half an hour, Froniga. Don't be late.' He walked off with a swagger in his step.

Froniga slipped her arm around Lucy's waist. 'That young man is too big for his boots.' She lifted the flap and ushered Lucy into the tent. 'This is my home while we're camped here.'

It was warm inside and the smell of crushed grass and damp canvas almost overpowered the scent of patchouli favoured by Froniga. Brightly coloured cushions were strewn on a palliasse and clothes spilled out of an open suitcase, covering what remained of the floor space. 'What's going on?' Lucy demanded. 'You couldn't have known for certain that I'd come in response to the poster you sent me.'

'I've got second sight, haven't I? Anyway, I knew you'd do anything to find your grandmother.'

'Even so, I don't understand why you told these people that I was looking for a job with the circus. Such a thing never crossed my mind.'

'You need somewhere to stay, and this seemed the ideal solution. I didn't think you'd have enough money to pay for lodgings in the town.'

'I wasn't planning on a long stay.' Lucy stared at her, frowning. 'Where is she, Froniga?'

'I do know where she is, but it's not straightforward, and it's going to take time.' She slumped down on the cushions, sitting cross-legged. 'If you're here with me I can help you, but it's best to keep it to ourselves. That's why I told Monty that you were an excellent horsewoman.'

'But I'm no equestrienne.'

'You can ride, can't you?'

'Of course, but I only rode in London and that was mostly in the park. I've never done tricks on horseback. I wouldn't know how.'

'Calm yourself, my dear. You'll only have to sit on the animal and go round the ring a few times, looking pretty. No one will expect you to ride bareback.'

'This is madness, Froniga.' Lucy moved a few garments and sat down beside her. 'Grandfather took me to Astley's Amphitheatre when I was a child and I saw the horsemen perform. I can't do anything like that. You must tell them it was a mistake.'

'So you don't care about Eva now?'

'Of course I do. It's not fair to say that.'

Froniga leaned closer. 'The circus will be here for several weeks, giving you a chance to do what is best for her.'

'What do you mean? Why are you being so mysterious? Where is she?'

Froniga reached for a bottle of wine that had been cooling in a bucket of water, and poured a small amount into a chipped enamel mug, passing it to Lucy. 'Have a drink, my duck. What I have to say might come as a bit of a shock.'

'Tell me what you know.'

'Eva Pocket is doing time in Chelmsford prison.'

Lucy stared at her in disbelief. 'No. That can't be true.'

Froniga nodded vigorously. 'I wouldn't lie to you about something like this.'

'But how do you know?'

'I heard the gossip when I was working the London markets, but I didn't want to tell you until I was certain. When I heard that Charter's circus had set up here I thought I could do us both a favour by coming to Essex. I dunno why, but I was touched by your story, Lucy, my duck. I suppose it's because I got no family of my own and you was struggling so hard to keep yours together.' Froniga took another mouthful of wine, wiping her lips on the back of her hand.

Stunned, Lucy shook her head. 'It must be a terrible mistake.'

'She was done for theft. The police must have had a tip-off and they found stolen property when they searched her lodgings.'

'She must have been desperate.'

'If anyone was to blame it was Abe. I knew the old bugger and he was the lowest of the low. There wasn't anything that he wouldn't stoop to, but those I spoke to said she wouldn't hear a word against him. Anyway, he must have gone too far in the end, and as far as I can gather she walked out on him, but he wouldn't leave her alone. I reckon he planted the stuff on her.'

'Why didn't you tell me all this when I saw you at the Waterman's Arms?'

'What was the point, my duck? I could have been wrong, and I had to find out if it was true.'

The wine had gone straight to Lucy's head and the awful news had hit her like a physical blow. She rubbed her hand across her eyes. 'I knew he was her friend, but that's all.'

'They were lovers off and on for years. Eva must have known deep down that Abe was bad through and through, but I suppose she couldn't resist the danger and excitement of being involved with a man like him.'

'I knew he'd been murdered.' Lucy stared at

her wide-eyed. 'You don't think...'

'Don't worry, my duck. It wasn't Eva who did for him, although she had reason enough.' Froniga laid her hand on Lucy's shoulder. 'He got what was coming to him, but it happened after your grandma was put away, so she's above suspicion for that at least.'

'How do you know all this?'

'Word of mouth. Eva was well known amongst the market traders where I used to do my stint. They're a tight-knit community and they look out for one another.'

Lucy took another sip of the cold wine. It was sour and not to her taste, but it quietened the ball of tension knotting her belly. 'If Granny was in trouble why didn't she come to me?'

Froniga gave her a pitying look. 'She wouldn't want to ruin your chances. She wanted you to have a wonderful life.'

'If only I'd known about this sooner I might have been able to help. I must see her, Froniga. I'll do anything I can to get her released from prison.'

'First things first, Lucy. It will take money to hire a mouthpiece, and unless you've come with a pocketful of the reddies you won't get very far.' Froniga poured herself a drink and downed it in one. 'That's why I lied about you being an equestrienne. Monty has his faults but he's not mean. He pays well, but he expects value for money.'

'He'll soon find out I'm a fraud.'

'I'd lay bets you can sit a horse with the best of 'em.'

'I suppose so.'

'You just have to convince the boss that you

know what you're doing, and we have a few weeks before the grand parade in Chelmsford, so you'll have time to rehearse.' Froniga scrambled to her feet. 'Let's have another drink, and then we'll go and face Monty's father. He's the head of the circus, no matter what his son thinks. That young man needs taking down a peg or two.'

Lucy held out her mug. 'I'll do anything I can to help Granny.'

'Drink up. It'll give you courage. And just remember, these circus people keep to themselves. They don't normally welcome strangers into their midst, but you'll be all right. Just flutter your eyelashes at young Monty, and as long as you don't fall off the horse on the first day you'll be fine.' She raised her cup. 'We'll drink to getting Eva out of jail.'

Bertram Charter was sitting on the grass outside his caravan in a high-backed and ornately carved chair that resembled a throne. White-haired, with a drooping moustache and a neatly trimmed beard, Bertram was a man in his eighties, although his upright stance, tanned skin and clear eyes made him seem years younger. He looked Lucy up and down. 'So this is our new act, Monty. She looks the part, but can she ride?'

'We'll find that out tomorrow, Father.' Monty pulled up a chair for Froniga and another one for Lucy. 'Take a seat, ladies.' He clapped his hands and a young woman emerged from the caravan. 'We'll eat now, Stella.'

She shot a sideways glance in Lucy's direction, retreated into the van and reappeared seconds later with a pile of dishes and a ladle. Walking slowly down the steps she made her way to the camp fire and removed the large, soot-blackened saucepan from the embers, placing it on a flat stone. She served the men first and came to Lucy last, handing her a bowl of steaming rabbit stew. 'I hope it chokes you,' she said in a low voice.

At first Lucy thought she must have misheard, but the spiteful downturn of Stella's pretty mouth and the angry flash of her violet blue eyes was enough to convince Lucy that she had made an enemy. 'Thank you,' she said politely. 'It smells delicious.'

'Watch out it ain't poisoned,' Stella whispered, tossing her head. Her lustrous dark hair framed the perfect oval of her face and her large eyes were fringed with impossibly long lashes. Lucy cast an anxious glance in Froniga's direction, but she was tucking into her meal with evident enjoyment, as were Monty and his father.

'Stella is a wonderful cook,' Bertram said proudly. 'She took pity on us when my dear wife died and she prepares our meals. I've never tasted the equal to her rabbit stew. Sit down and eat with us, poppet.'

Lucy almost choked on a mouthful of the delicious, herb-scented stew. The term of endearment, more usually applied to a child, seemed grossly inappropriate. Stella was undoubtedly a beauty, but there was nothing childlike in her attitude: she was very much a woman, and one who was best avoided, Lucy thought, eyeing her warily.

Stella dropped the ladle into the pot, turning to Bertram with an angelic smile. 'Thank you, boss, but I've already eaten. I promised Dario that I'd rehearse our act this evening.'

Bertram threw back his head and laughed. 'So that's what he calls it, does he? I was young once and hot blooded.'

Stella sashayed over to him and kissed him on the cheek. 'You're a bad man.' She twirled away, swishing her skirts as she walked past Monty. 'It's just a rehearsal.'

'Of course it is,' Monty said, pinching her cheek. 'Enjoy yourself.'

Stella strolled past Lucy. The smile painted on her lips did not reach her eyes. 'He's mine,' she whispered. 'Accidents happen, so be warned.'

Chapter Fifteen

'Don't take any notice of that girl,' Froniga said airily as they made their way back to her tent. 'Stella's parents were killed in an accident when the high wire snapped. Bertram took her in and brought her up as his own. It's obvious that he's spoiled her, and she plays up to him. That young woman gets away with murder.' Opening the flap she went inside and sorted out a blanket and a couple of cushions for Lucy. 'Try to get some sleep, you've got a busy day tomorrow.' Froniga sank down on her bed with a sigh. 'I'm not as young as I was. One day I'll have a feather bed all to myself.'

'Goodnight, and thank you for everything,

Froniga.' Despite her attempts to make herself comfortable, the ground was hard and Lucy could feel the damp rising through the hard-packed earth. She tried to forget Stella but her harsh words kept repeating themselves in her mind.

'What's the matter?' Froniga demanded. 'You're tossing and turning as if you've got bellyache. Are you worrying about tomorrow?'

'I am, but it's not that. I can't think why Stella would take such a dislike to me when we've only just met. What did I do wrong?'

'You're young and you're much prettier than she is.'

'That's nonsense. She's beautiful and I'm just ordinary.'

'You might think so, but others see you differently.' Froniga stretched out on her bed of cushions. 'Stella Smith has her eye on Monty and she sees you as a threat.'

'That's nonsense, Froniga. I've only just met him and he's not the sort of man to make my heart beat any faster.'

'But he likes you, Lucy. I don't need my crystal ball to tell me that.' Froniga raised herself, resting on her elbow.

Lucy turned her head away to hide her blushes. 'He hardly spoke to me.'

'That doesn't matter, my duck. He looked and he liked what he saw. You wouldn't have been invited to the high table if he hadn't taken to you, and Stella knows that. She's a minx, that one. Keep away from her and you'll be fine.'

'I just want to see Granny and tell her that I'll

do everything I can to secure her release.'

'Convince Monty that you're good enough to join the show and then we can plan our visit to the jail.'

'The sooner the better,' Lucy said sleepily. 'I can't wait to see her again.'

She slept badly, plagued by disturbing dreams, and awakened with a start, blinking in the sunlight as someone opened the tent flap. 'Froniga,' she murmured, shielding her eyes with her hand, but it was Stella who tossed a bundle of clothes into the tent.

'That's your costume. Put it on and come to the big top. Monty's there now and he doesn't like to be kept waiting.'

Froniga snapped into a sitting position. 'What's going on?' she demanded sleepily. 'What time is it?'

'Time you were up, old woman.' Stella walked off, leaving the tent flap to fall back into place, where it hung moving idly in the gentle breeze.

Froniga reached for a small leather case and opened it to reveal a brass carriage clock. 'It's only seven o'clock,' she said crossly. 'I'm going back to sleep.'

'No, please stay awake.' Lucy scrambled to her feet, holding up a ridiculous pink velvet riding habit trimmed with gold frogging. 'Does she expect me to wear this?'

'It's the sort of thing they wear in the circus ring. You'd better try it on for size.' Froniga reached for her tobacco pouch and clay pipe, watching Lucy as she struggled into the costume.

‘I’ll need some help with the lacing,’ Lucy gasped. ‘I doubt if I’ll be able to breathe in this, let alone sit on a horse.’

Froniga put her pipe aside and stood up. ‘I’m a fortune teller not a lady’s maid, but I’ll have a go.’ She seized the strings of Lucy’s corset and tugged hard.

Feeling more than a little ridiculous, and very glad that Bertie and the others were not here to see her in such a rig-out, Lucy made her way to the big top. She had to dodge a man who was juggling with flaming torches, and when she took what she thought was a short cut between two large caravans she ran into a troupe of tumblers. The human pyramid collapsed, but the performers sprang lightly to the ground, the smallest of them ending up with a series of somersaults. Lucy stopped to apologise and found herself clapping their expertise. ‘I was heading for the big top,’ she said lamely.

A child appeared from a nearby tent and took her by the hand. ‘I’ll show you the way.’ It was only when she spoke that Lucy realised her guide was a grown woman.

‘Thank you,’ she murmured. ‘I’m Lucy.’

The young woman looked up at her with an impish smile. ‘I know who you are. News travels fast round here. I’m Jenny.’

Lucy looked down at the tiny hand and saw with something of a shock that Jenny was wearing a wedding ring. She recovered quickly, not wanting to offend the small person. ‘I’d better hurry. I don’t want to be late on my first day.’ Realising the implication of what she had just said, she felt herself blushing. 'I – I'm sorry. I didn't mean that we weren't walking fast enough…' She broke off, too embarrassed to continue.

'It's all right, my dear,' Jenny said, trilling with laughter. 'I'm a midget and so is my husband Obadiah, and our two little ones, Johnnie and Jim. We're used to being looked at, and laughed at too. We're circus folk and we entertain people.'

'You look too young to have babies.'

'I'm twenty-three and my elder boy is four.' Jenny came to a halt as they arrived outside the big top. 'There it is. Good luck, girl.'

'Thank you.' Lucy entered the vast tent with her head held high and her heart thudding within the confines of her tightly laced stays. Monty came striding towards her and to her dismay she could see Bertram seated in the front row. Above them a scantily dressed man was negotiating a tightrope, balancing himself with a long pole clutched in his hands. What was even more disturbing was the sight of a young man leading a large black horse which pranced and snorted, pawing the ground as if eager to be off on a long gallop.

Monty followed her anxious glance with a wry smile. 'Imperator is a bit lively this morning. Let's see how you handle him, Lucy.'

Almost before she knew what was happening he tossed her up onto the side saddle. The youth handed her the reins, backing away as Imperator began to move. The horse seemed to be dancing or marching to music that only he could hear, and at a command from Monty he raised himself on his hind legs, almost unseating Lucy. She managed to hold on and allowed him to trot around the ring, coming to a halt in front of Bertram, and as if knowing he was at the end of his brief performance, Imperator took a bow. Lucy had seen such feats at Astley's but it was the first time she had ridden such a well-trained animal.

Bertram leaned forward. He was silent for a moment, eyeing her up and down, and then he began to clap. 'Well done. You are unfamiliar with your mount, but you have a good seat.' He turned to his son. 'She'll do, Monty. I'll leave it to you to work out a routine, but remember you only have a few weeks before the grand parade.'

'Yes, Father. I'm well aware of that. We'll be ready.' Monty stepped forward. 'Well done, Lucy.' His smile and the sincerity in his voice went a long way to soothing her shattered nerves. How she had managed to remain in the saddle was something of a puzzle, for she was shaking inwardly, and she was afraid her legs might buckle under her if she tried to stand. However, Monty seemed impressed by her abilities, and he swung her to the ground as if they had just finished a performance and were about to take a bow.

'Thank you, but I'm quite capable of mounting and dismounting on my own,' she said stiffly.

'You won't have a mounting block in the ring, so I'll help you to dismount. It goes with the act.'

'We perform together?'

'Yes, in the second half we do. You have your own spot in the first half. Are you worried that I'll steal the limelight from you?'

'No, that's not the case at all. But I would like to know exactly what is expected of me. You seem to think that I have a crystal ball like Froniga.'

Bertram rose from his seat. 'You sound like an old married couple and you've only just met. You must sort it out between you, but I'm going to have my breakfast. I hope Stella hasn't burned the bacon. She was in one of her moods this morning, Monty. I think she was hoping to be your new partner, so you'd best make your peace with her, my boy. My digestion won't stand up to ruined food.' He walked off across the ring, pausing to talk to the tightrope artiste, who completed his performance by sliding down a rope and taking a bow in front of an imaginary audience.

Lucy shot a questioning look at Monty. 'I think you owe me an apology.'

He raised his eyebrows. 'What for?'

'You should have warned me that Imperator would go straight into his routine. I might have been thrown.'

'If you'd been unseated you wouldn't have been the woman I'm looking for. You stayed on and that's all that matters. I can see you have possibilities.'

'Your father seems to think that Stella wanted the job. No wonder she resents me.'

'Resents you?' His look of surprise seemed genuine, and he shook his head. 'Stella can ride and she's fearless, but she's impatient and the horses don't give their best. On the other hand she can do anything with reptiles. Stella is our snake woman.'

'Snakes?' Lucy stared at him in horror. 'She performs with snakes?'

He chuckled. 'Don't let her know you're scared of reptiles. Stella has a mischievous sense of humour. I'll say no more, but beware.'

'I think you ought to tell me exactly what's expected of me in the show.' Lucy glanced down at her costume. 'This isn't the most comfortable outfit when it comes to sitting on a horse.'

'I suppose you'd like to wear riding breeches, like a man.'

'Why not? I rode astride once when I was a child, much to Miss Wantage's horror.'

'Miss Wantage?'

'She was my governess.' The words came out before she had time to think and she could tell by Monty's startled expression that she had made a mistake. 'I mean, she was governess to the young mistress. I was her maid.'

'Do maidservants usually learn to ride?'

'I lived on a farm before I went into service,' Lucy said, improvising wildly. 'I used to ride bareback.' Once again she had allowed her tongue to run away with her. She could tell by his thoughtful expression that this had given him an idea for the show, but it was too late, the damage was done. She faced him with a defiant look. 'Perhaps we'd better go through the routine.'

At the end of the session Lucy was stiff and sore, but she was not going to admit this to anyone, least of all Monty. He seemed satisfied with her performance, but she had the feeling that he was being over-generous with his praise. Anyone who could sit a horse could have done what he asked, and she left the ring wondering why he had agreed to include her in his act. She stepped outside into the sunshine and was confronted by

Stella with a large python draped around her shoulders. Lucy's initial reaction was to back away, but she knew instinctively that this was exactly what Stella wanted. She managed to stand her ground, forcing herself to remain calm. 'Good morning, Stella.'

'I can see that you've been put through your paces,' Stella said coldly. 'Monty is a hard taskmaster. You'll have to be good or you'll be out on your ear, my girl.'

'He seemed satisfied.' Lucy kept a wary eye on the snake. It moved its head in her direction and it was all she could do not to panic. She forced her lips into a smile. 'I can't wait to see your act.'

Stella's eyes widened. 'You like snakes?'

'Who could dislike such a fine animal?'

'Would you like to hold him?' Stella took a step towards her, pinning Lucy against the guy ropes supporting the big top. 'I'm sure he likes you.'

'I – I like him too, but I'm not used to handling reptiles. I might hurt him.'

Stella made as if to lift the large creature from her shoulders. 'He's used to being handled and he loves women.'

Lucy's heart was hammering against her tightly corseted ribcage and she was finding it hard to breathe. If Stella moved a step closer she was certain she would faint from sheer terror.

'Stop teasing Lucy.' A small voice piped up close to Lucy's elbow.

Stella jumped visibly, peering through a loop of the snake's sinuous body. 'Jenny Starr. How many times have I told you not to creep up on people?'

'You wouldn't have took no notice if a brass

band had come up behind you.' Jenny held her hand up to Lucy. 'Ignore the serpent.' She led her away, waiting until they were out of earshot. 'The snake's harmless enough,' she said with a wry smile. 'It's the other one you need to watch.'

Lucy took several deep breaths, and when her pulses stopped racing she leaned over to drop a kiss on the top of Jenny's dark curls. 'Thank you so much. I was really scared.'

'As I said, the snake's not the dangerous one. If Stella takes a dislike to someone they'd better watch out, and if that particular person happens to catch Monty's eye they'd better be very careful.'

'Thank you for the warning.' Lucy fell into step beside her, walking slowly so that she did not outpace the small woman.

'I got some liniment that might help,' Jenny said, grinning. 'You'll be sore for days but it'll wear off eventually.'

'Thank you again.' Lucy managed a tight little smile. 'I haven't ridden for some time.'

'I daresay you're more used to travelling in a carriage. You ain't like the rest of us, Lucy. It's as plain as the nose on your face.'

'What makes you say that?' Lucy asked, startled.

'Why, my dear, it's quite obvious that you was brought up to be a lady.'

'No, you're mistaken, Jenny. I'm no better than anyone here.'

'That's as maybe, but Monty spotted it and so did the boss. You'll have a job to make the circus folk think otherwise.' Jenny stopped as they reached her caravan. 'Wait here and I'll fetch the embrocation.' She skipped nimbly up the steps, returning moments later. 'Rub this on the affected parts and you'll feel the benefit almost immediately. My old granny used to swear by it.'

'I'm in your debt, Jenny. If there's anything I can do in return, just say.'

'Lor' love you, duck. We're like a family and we look after our own.'

'Even Stella?' Lucy murmured, suppressing a giggle.

Jenny laughed and winked. 'I'm saying nothing.'

'But it will go against me if others think I don't fit in,' Lucy said anxiously. 'I'm no different from any of you here, and that's the truth.'

'Maybe and maybe not, but take my advice and don't get too friendly with Monty. Stella's not the only jealous woman in the circus.'

'What do you mean? Is every female besotted with him?'

'Not me, that's for certain. But you ought to watch out for Tallulah, the tattooed lady, and Ilsa has a soft spot for Monty, although she has to keep it from her old man, Johann. He's billed as the strongest man in the world and he'd break a man's neck if he caught him making eyes at his wife.'

Lucy gulped and swallowed. 'I thought the animals were the dangerous ones, but it seems I was mistaken.'

Jenny laughed and patted her hand. 'Animals can be tamed.' She clutched her hands to her breast. 'It's the beast within that causes the trouble.' She turned her head at the sound of childish voices and her face lit up. 'That's my boys. I'd best go and relieve my mum; she's getting on a bit and they're a real handful.' She hurried off, leaving Lucy to make her way back to Froniga's tent. She was stiff and sore and Stella's open enmity had shaken her more than she cared to admit, but she must not lose sight of her reason for being here in the first place. As she limped through the maze of caravans and tents, she caught sight of Tallulah and tried hard not to stare at the tattoos which covered every visible part of her body, including her face. Lucy murmured a greeting and hurried on, smiling and nodding to the curious circus folk, some of whom responded in a friendly fashion while others turned away or pretended not to see her.

She slowed down when she came to where a male and a female lion were confined behind steel bars, and she was consumed with pity for the caged beasts. Their lacklustre coats were matched by their dull eyes and dejected poses, and she wished that she could set them free in their native land. But these poor beasts would die in captivity, as would the tiger in the neighbouring van, and the two elephants which were shackled and tethered to steel posts driven into the ground. The animals were obviously well fed and their physical needs cared for, but Lucy remembered only too well what it had felt like when she was first taken to her grandfather's house in Albemarle Street. She too had been like a wild thing snatched from the life she had known and robbed of her freedom. She walked on at a slower pace.

She found Froniga seated on the ground in front

of a camp fire, stirring the contents of a soot-blackened pot. 'That smells good,' Lucy said appreciatively.

Froniga looked up and smiled. 'You've been gone a long time. I was beginning to think you'd cut and run.'

'Monty made me ride Imperator,' Lucy said, rubbing her sore backside with a rueful grin. 'I managed to stay on, but he didn't ask me to do anything that was too difficult. I think he was being kind as it was my first day.'

Froniga gave her a searching look. 'That doesn't sound like Monty. He must have a plan in mind for you.'

'I don't know how I'd manage if I had to leave before I've seen my grandmother. It's not easy to find work when you're not trained for anything useful. I can't even cook, although I can scrub floors with the best of them.'

'You'll be all right, my duck. You've done well if you've got Monty and the boss on your side. Their word is law round here.'

Lucy's stomach rumbled and she realised that she was very hungry. She leaned over the pot, inhaling the savoury aroma of the stew. 'That smells tasty,' she said appreciatively.

'I can cook when I put my mind to it.' Froniga dipped the ladle in the pot and sipped. 'That's good, even if I say so myself.' She glanced at the brown glass bottle clutched in Lucy's hand. 'What have you got there?'

'Jenny gave me this liniment. She must have noticed that I was a bit stiff after all that exercise.'

Froniga put her head on one side. 'There's

something other than a sore bum that's worrying you. You can't fool a Romany.'

Lucy sank down on the grass beside her. 'I'm not sure this will work, Froniga. I managed to stay in the saddle, but, as I said, Monty was going easy on me.'

'I told you he likes you. Make the most of it.'

'It's not him I'm worried about. It's Stella.'

Froniga eyed her with a twinkle in her dark eyes and a smile on her lips. 'Did I forget to mention the snake?'

'You knew?'

'Of course I did, but pythons aren't poisonous, and this one isn't big enough to crush the life out of you. It might be different when it's fully grown.'

'It's huge.'

'And will be even bigger in time, but we won't be here that long.' Froniga reached for her tobacco pouch and clay pipe. 'The carter was here again this morning and I paid him to take a message to the prison, requesting permission to visit Eva Pocket on Sunday, after the grand parade.'

Lucy threw her arms around her. 'You're wonderful. I don't know what I'd do without you.'

'Mind my pipe. It's the last one I've got.' Froniga's sharp tone was belied by the warmth of her smile.

Rehearsals for the opening show went on all day and well into the evenings for the next three weeks. Lucy had to learn the routine she was to do solo as well as her part when she worked with Monty. He was an excellent horseman, fearless and in total command of his mount, treating the high-spirited animal with patience and surprising gentleness. Lucy was constantly surprised by the changes in Monty's moods. Sometimes he was autocratic and domineering, verging on the unreasonable, and at other times he was encouraging, giving praise where and when it was due. He made her laugh and at times he made her want to cry. She was too proud to shed a tear in front of him, even when she was humiliated by her failure to achieve the exacting standards he set for both her and himself, but eventually she became more confident and the difficult routines became easier. The aching limbs and sore buttocks that plagued her in the beginning lessened, and she was able to conquer her nerves when performing in the ring, although she preferred not to think about how she would feel when she had a real audience watching her.

The day of the grand parade dawned fine and warm, and the air of anticipation seemed to have affected everyone, including the animals. It was early morning when the cavalcade set off for town. Lucy rode Imperator and Froniga travelled in the van with Johann and Ilsa. Monty had chosen Lucy to ride beside him as he led the parade and she knew that Stella would make her suffer for enjoying such a privilege, but she did not care. It was not the appreciation of the crowds lining the streets cheering and waving that made her stomach churn with excitement, it was the thought of being reunited with her grandmother.

When the parade came to an end they stopped on common land on the outskirts of the town in order to rest the animals before making the return journey to the camp. Lucy and Froniga took the opportunity to slip away, and set off for the prison, hitching a lift with the carter, who had brought his family to enjoy the spectacle. It was a noisy ride as the children were overexcited and one of the younger ones was sick over the side of the cart. His mother patted him on his back, mopped him up and told him off for eating the sweets that the performers had tossed into the crowd as an added incentive to buy tickets for the show.

The carter drew up outside the prison, and his wife informed the eldest boy that this was where he would end up if he didn't behave himself. Lucy and Froniga climbed down to the pavement, thanked the carter and waved to the children as the vehicle lumbered off.

Lucy looked up at the fortress-like exterior of the county jail and her heart sank. 'What will I do if she doesn't want to see me?'

Chapter Sixteen

A grim-faced warder led them through a maze of corridors, using a huge bunch of keys to unlock doors and locking them immediately after they had passed through. In the dim light with the cold striking up through the flagstone floor, Lucy felt as though they were being taken deep into the underworld where all hope was lost and souls writhed in torment. Muffled sobs and moans were accompanied by pleas for help, and the smell of unwashed bodies mingled with the foul odour from the slop buckets. She covered her mouth and nose with her hand, stifling a rising feeling of panic as a sudden urge to leave this dreadful place made her want to run away.

Seeming to sense her growing distress, Froniga slipped her arm around Lucy's shoulders. 'Think of Eva,' she whispered. 'She's had to endure this for years.'

The warder came to an abrupt halt, turned and gave her a withering look. 'This is paradise compared to some places I've worked.' He selected a key and unlocked the cell door. 'Five minutes is all I can give you.' He thrust it open and stood aside to allow them to enter.

Lucy stepped over the threshold and was immediately accosted by a skeletally thin woman with lank grey hair and a wild expression contorting her features. 'Get me out of here, and I'll make you a rich woman.'

Froniga pushed her away. 'Sit down, Mother. We can't help you.'

The woman collapsed onto the floor, burying her head in her hands as she started to wail. Lucy patted her on the shoulder. 'I'm sorry, but I can't do anything for you.'

'Eva Pocket.' Froniga stepped in front of Lucy, fending off two more of the inmates who made a grab at her. 'Eva, where are you?'

The cell was in semi-darkness, and for a moment Lucy thought that the warder must have brought them to the wrong place, but as her eyes grew accustomed to the gloom she saw a shadowy shape in the far corner. The woman was crouched on her haunches, peering at them through a wild mass of tangled curls. Slowly, Lucy made her way towards her, holding out her hand. 'Granny? Is that you?'

'Granny, is that you?' One of the women took up the cry in mocking tones and the others joined in. The deafening chorus rose in a crescendo, ceasing as suddenly as it had begun when the object of their derision rose to her feet.

'Shut up.' Eva Pocket raised herself with difficulty and hobbled towards her granddaughter, peering at her in disbelief. 'Lucy?'

The voice was hoarse but Lucy had heard it often enough in her dreams. The ragged, shapeless figure could not have looked more unlike the lively, attractive grandmother she remembered, but when she looked into her eyes Lucy knew that she had found her. She flung her arms around Eva, regardless of the lice-ridden condition of the pathetically thin creature, a mere shadow of her former self. 'Granny, I've found you at last.'

'Keep away,' Froniga snapped as one of the women slunk up to Lucy, fingering the material of her riding habit.

The woman seemed to shrink inside her prison gown and she retreated, cowed and whimpering like a beaten animal.

Lucy turned to Froniga, a tremulous smile on her lips. 'We've found her. This is my granny.'

'How long are you in for, Eva?' Froniga demanded brusquely.

'Don't speak to her like that.' Lucy tightened her hold on her grandmother's frail body. 'Can't you see she's ill?'

'I don't know how much longer I've got to serve,' Eva said with touching dignity. 'Time doesn't count for much in here. I hardly know if it's night or day.'

'We must get you out of here.' Lucy clutched her hand, raising it to her cheek. 'I've wanted to find you for years, but I didn't know where to start. Why didn't you let me know you were in trouble? I could have helped.'

'You're a lady now,' Eva said, turning away. 'Go back to your life and leave me here where I belong.'

'No. Don't talk like that.' Lucy grabbed her by the shoulders, twisting her round so that they were face to face. 'I won't listen to such nonsense. I'll get you out of here if it's the last thing I do.'

Eva subsided, leaning her head wearily against Lucy's shoulder. 'I'm a lost cause, my duck. You're even more beautiful now that you're a grown woman.' She fingered the velvet costume, the garish pink softened by the dim light. 'You're doing well for yourself, I can tell.'

Froniga tapped Lucy on the shoulder. 'I can hear the guard's flat feet. I think our time is up.'

'I can't leave her in this terrible place.' Lucy clutched her grandmother's hand. It was happening all over again. She was ten years old facing separation from the person she loved most in the whole world. 'I won't abandon her here.'

'You must, but only for now,' Froniga said in a low voice. 'We'll appeal against her sentence, and we'll find a lawyer to speak up for her.'

Eva snatched her hand free. 'It won't do no

good, gypsy woman. Your sort can foretell the future so you must know there's no chance of me getting off. Unless by some miracle you find a pot of gold at the end of the rainbow and use it to bribe the beak.'

'There must be a way,' Lucy cried in desperation. 'I've found you, Granny. I'm not giving up now.'

The sound of the key grating in the lock was followed by the grinding of the hinges as the door opened and the warder stepped into the cell. 'Get back,' he warned, raising his truncheon as two of the women moved towards him. 'Time's up, ladies.'

'I will return,' Lucy whispered as she kissed Eva on the cheek. 'I won't let you down, Granny.'

'Get her out of here. This ain't no place for a girl like my Lucy.' Eva motioned to Froniga. 'She mustn't come back to this hell.' She turned her face to the wall, standing resolutely stiff and silent.

'Time's up,' the warder repeated in an ominous tone.

Froniga grabbed Lucy by the shoulders, propelling her towards the open door. 'We're leaving, mister. Don't get in a stew.' She gave Lucy a shove, sending her stumbling into the corridor to the obvious amusement of the women prisoners. They clustered round the door cackling and thumping on it as the warder locked them in.

Outside the prison walls, Lucy shielded her eyes from the brilliance of the sunshine. The air was clean and sweet-smelling in comparison with the stench inside the jail, and a cool breeze fanned her hot cheeks. 'I can't believe how horrible that place is,' she said, shuddering. 'I don't know how she's managed to survive in such conditions.'

Froniga shook out her skirts. 'I feel as if I'm running with fleas and lice. Anyway, we'd best starting walking or they'll have left without us and it's a long way to the camp.' She marched off without waiting to see if Lucy was following. 'Come on. You won't do her any good standing outside the bloody jail. We've got to find a way to get Eva out of there.'

With one last glance up at the forbidding walls, Lucy hurried after her. 'I'll secure her release,' she said breathlessly when she caught up with Froniga. 'I'll save every penny I earn so that I can hire a good solicitor.'

The parade had been a great success, so Monty announced when they arrived back at camp. They could expect bumper crowds at the first performance and he hoped that people would come from miles around to see the wonders of Charter's circus. That evening there was an impromptu party in the big top where everyone contributed food and Bertram supplied a barrel of beer and a keg of cider. Lucy was not feeling very sociable, but Froniga persuaded her to attend. 'People will think you're stuck up if you don't go,' she said firmly. 'You can't help Eva by worrying and making yourself miserable. You need this job and so do I, so we'll both go and look as though we're enjoying ourselves.'

'Why did you join the circus, Froniga?' Lucy slipped off her costume and stepped into a clean cotton print gown. 'I thought Romany people always travelled together.'

'I married a gadjo,' Froniga said calmly. 'My husband was not of our culture and by marrying him I disgraced my family. They wanted nothing more to do with me.'

'But that's so sad. Where is he now?'

'He died.'

'I'm sorry.' Lucy was lost for words. She wanted to know more, but only if Froniga was willing to confide in her.

'I chose not to return to my people. I couldn't forgive them for the way they treated us, and I made a life for myself working the fairgrounds and setting up my stall in market places.'

'Don't you miss your family?'

'They turned their backs on me and I can't forget that. I choose my friends, and I chose to help you. Now put your hair up and let's join the party.'

They entered the arena together and Froniga went off to join Ilsa and Johann, leaving Lucy standing by the trestle table where Dario had been left in charge of the drinks. He picked up a tin mug, waving it in front of her face. 'What is your pleasure, pretty lady? Do you like the beer or the cider?'

'Cider, please.' Lucy managed a smile, although she was feeling far from happy. The dire conditions of the prison and her grandmother's suffering had etched a picture in her mind that was almost impossible to erase.

Dario filled the mug and handed it to her. 'You

like to take a walk with me?'

She shook her head. 'Not at the moment, thank you. I'm rather tired after the parade.'

'Ah, yes. The parade was good, no?'

'It went well, I think.' She was about to edge away when she saw Stella bearing down on them. Her expression was not encouraging.

Dario threw up his hands, grinning absurdly. 'Here is the love of my life: my beautiful assistant, who also charms snakes.'

Lucy took an involuntary step backwards. 'I must go and find M–' She broke off. 'I mean, I see Jenny and Obadiah. I must speak to them.'

'Don't hurry away on my account,' Stella said, baring her lips in what looked more like a snarl than a smile. 'You two seem to be getting along splendidly.' She reached past Lucy to slip her hand into Dario's pocket. Taking out a hip flask she unscrewed the cap and took a long drink. 'Brandy is so much nicer than cider or beer.'

Dario snatched it from her. 'I keep it for medicinal purposes only. Strong drink and knife throwing do not go together, and tomorrow is our opening night. We both need to keep a clear head, tesoro mio.'

'Don't tell me what to do, Dario.' Stella's dark eyes narrowed. 'Play with your little friend. I'm going to find Monty.' She shot a sideways glance at Lucy. 'Unless you have designs on him too, you Jezebel.'

'I don't know what you're talking about,' Lucy said coldly. 'I was on my way to talk to Jenny.' She walked off before Stella had a chance to respond. 'That woman is impossible,' she muttered beneath her breath.

'What's this? Talking to yourself? You know what they say about people who do that.'

She came to a halt, turning her head to meet Monty's amused gaze. 'I'm not mad, I'm angry.'

He took her hand and linked it through the crook of his arm. 'Tell me all about it.'

'You're laughing at me.'

'Not at all. I overheard what Stella said to you, but you mustn't take any notice of what she says. Beneath it all she's a decent person, if a little temperamental, as are many performers. She'll come round.'

'I just want her to leave me alone, and I don't like snakes. They scare me.'

A flicker of sympathy lit his eyes and he smiled. 'Don't worry. The animals are kept under lock and key when they aren't performing. We have very strict rules about that.'

'Yes, I suppose so.'

'Come and sit down. You've had a busy day.' He led her to the seating area at the edge of the ring. 'Where did you and Froniga go when the parade ended?'

'We went to the common like everyone else.'

'That's not entirely true, is it?'

'How do you know?'

'It's my business to know everything that goes on around here. These are my people and what concerns them also concerns me.'

'But I'm not...' She slumped down on one of the chairs set around the ringside.

He sat down beside her. 'You're not one of us? Is that what you were going to say?'

'No. Well, yes. Maybe.'

'I knew from the moment I set eyes on you that you weren't a performer, but I guessed that you must be desperate to find work.'

'Why did you take me on, then?'

'Maybe I was curious to discover why a well brought up young lady would run away to join a travelling circus. You don't look as if you were half starved, or beaten by a wicked stepfather. Or are you escaping an arranged marriage? I'm curious.'

His whimsical smile brought an unwilling response and she chuckled. 'None of those.'

'Then why did you come here, and how do you know Froniga?'

'It's a long story.'

He leaned back in his seat. 'And we've got all night if necessary. You're a bit of a mystery woman, Lucy Pocket, and you still haven't told me where you went after the parade.'

She was tempted to confide in him, but she was reluctant to reveal her past history to a man who until recently had been a stranger, and to admit that her grandmother was a convicted criminal might make things even more difficult. If she lost her job she would never be able to raise the money for a lawyer. 'Froniga had an errand to do in town and I went with her,' she said vaguely. 'It was nothing very interesting.'

'And that's all you're going to tell me?'

She shrugged her shoulders. 'That's all there is to it, sir.'

'Have I offended you in some way, Lucy?' He stared at her, twin furrows deepening on his brow. 'Why the sudden formality? We're partners in the ring, and you saw fit to call me by my Christian name during rehearsals.'

She rose to her feet. 'I'm sorry, Monty. I am a bit tired, after all. If you don't mind I think I'll turn in. It has been a long day.' She walked off, resisting the temptation to glance over her shoulder.

The party was in full swing and the sound of laughter reverberated off the canvas dome of the big top, echoing into the night. Lucy left with the sound ringing in her ears, but she was not in a mood to celebrate. She was tired, but she doubted whether she would be able to sleep, even though Jenny had found her a straw-filled palliasse and a clean blanket. The full moon shone down on the camp site and diamond-bright stars twinkled in a black velvet sky. She opened the tent flap and went inside. Moonlight shone through the canvas, making it unnecessary to light the paraffin lamp, and she stepped out of her dress, unlaced her stays and was about to pull back the blanket when it moved. She leapt back, uttering a loud scream as the snake uncoiled and reared its head.

She ran, stumbling over grassy tussocks, but her cries for help were drowned by the noise in the big top. Forgetting that she was only wearing a thin cotton shift, she rushed inside, colliding with Tallulah. 'Good God, what's happened to you?' Tallulah took off her shawl and wrapped it around Lucy's trembling body.

'S-snake.' The word tumbled from her lips as she struggled for breath.

When she opened her eyes she was lying on her bed with Froniga kneeling at her side. She struggled to sit up but was restrained with a firm hand. 'You're all right now, Lucy.'

'The snake?' She shivered convulsively. 'It was here in my bed.'

Tallulah's large frame filled the entrance to the tent. 'Don't worry, my pet. It's back in its crate. You caused quite a sensation running into the marquee in your shift.'

Lucy groaned and subsided against the cushions. 'Oh no. I don't remember anything except that horrible creature raising its great head.'

'Now, now,' Froniga said soothingly. 'It's all over. Stella collected the animal, and as Tallulah said, it's locked up safe and sound.'

'She did it,' Lucy muttered. 'Stella put it here on purpose.'

'Maybe she did,' Tallulah said, chuckling. 'I wouldn't put anything past that one, but if I was you I'd say nothing.'

Froniga helped Lucy to sit up. 'Have a sip of this,' she said, holding a glass of water to her lips. 'Tallulah's right. Everyone knows that Stella was responsible, although she swears she doesn't know how the beast escaped, let alone how it found its way into our tent.'

'I've made a fool of myself.' Lucy sipped the water. 'Thank you, Froniga. I'm all right now, I just feel embarrassed. Did everyone see me?'

'I don't know why you're worrying, my pet,' Tallulah said with her throaty laugh. 'I wear a more skimpy costume than that when I'm in the ring, and the tightrope walkers wear even less.

We're show folk; we don't shock easily. Anyone would think you was a little princess the way you talk.'

Froniga scrambled to her feet. 'Thanks, Tallulah. But I think she needs a rest now. It'll all be forgotten in the morning.'

'Yes, they'll all have sore heads and seeing you in your shimmy will have faded from their memories.' Tallulah backed out of the tent, still chuckling.

Lucy held her head in her hands. 'Did Monty see me like that?'

'He couldn't help it, my duck. You were screaming your head off and then you fainted. It was a grand entrance.'

'It's not funny. I've played right into Stella's hands.'

'Don't worry about it, Lucy. I saw Monty take her to one side. He's no fool, and he knows how to handle her. I've heard they was close once, if you get my meaning.'

'They were lovers?'

Froniga shrugged her shoulders. 'I never mentioned the word love. I doubt if Stella has ever loved anyone other than herself. Just be careful and keep out of her way as much as possible.'

Lucy leaned back on her cushions, overcome with exhaustion. 'I'll do that, but if she pushes me too far I'll forget that Grandfather brought me up to be a lady. I learned how to stand up for myself when I was a nipper.'

'Go to sleep and forget her. You'll need to be fresh for the first show tomorrow, and you'll probably be the only one with a clear head.' Froniga doused the lamp and lay down on her bed, fully dressed. Within moments she was snoring loudly.

There were obviously some sore heads next morning, but by the early afternoon when the audience had packed the seats all the performers were at their positions ready to give their best. Monty looked every inch the dashing ringmaster in his black hunting coat and riding breeches when he introduced the first act, aided by Arturo, the white-faced clown, Pepe the character clown in his tattered clothes and battered hat, and Leon the auguste, who played the joker in the ring but in real life was an ill-tempered drunk who beat his wife and children, and was regularly threatened with dismissal.

Lucy watched their antics and found herself laughing as heartily as the audience even though she had seen it all before during rehearsals. The shining faces of the children reminded her of those she had left at home. Hester and Pearl would look after them, of course, and they had Bedwin to keep them in order, but she missed them all more than she could say. She had only been away for three weeks but it seemed like years since she left London, and even though she loved the country she knew at heart she would always remain a city girl. The grimy buildings and the crowded streets were still home to her, and she missed the noise and bustle of the metropolis. Her need to secure her grandmother's release was even more pressing now, and she realised that it would take a long time to save enough from her wages to fund a lawyer. Perhaps she had been over-optimistic, but the pay packet she had received earlier that day would only just cover her living expenses. She turned with a start as someone tapped her on the shoulder.

'You're on next,' Froniga said urgently.

The time had come, and within minutes she would have to prove to Monty and Bertram that she could hold the audience's attention. She hurried outside to mount Imperator and waited for her cue. The well-trained horse behaved impeccably, carrying her through the act like the seasoned trouper he was, and Lucy began to relax. She rode out of the ring to deafening applause, cheers and whistles of appreciation.

Monty was waiting for her outside the marquee and he lifted her from the saddle. 'Well done.'

'I did it,' she cried exultantly.

'You certainly did.' Monty smiled and strode back into the big top to introduce the next act.

Dazed and hardly able to believe that everything had gone well, Lucy led Imperator to where Joe was waiting to groom and take care of him. She was making her way to the ringside to wait for the second half of her performance when Stella appeared as if from nowhere. 'You think you're very clever, don't you?'

'Leave me alone.' Lucy walked on but Stella caught her by the wrist, digging her long fingernails into Lucy's flesh.

'If you've got any sense you'll pack up and go before something bad happens to you.'

Lucy came to a halt, turning to face her. 'What do you mean by that?'

'Accidents happen.' Stella moved closer, her

eyes narrowed and filled with malice. 'Monty was mine long before you put in an appearance and he'll be mine again when you're gone.'

'I'm not going anywhere,' Lucy said evenly. 'And I'm not interested in Monty. You can have him for all I care.'

'You set your cap at him from the first, and he's fool enough to be taken in by your simpering, little girl innocence. Leave him alone or you'll suffer for it.'

Lucy wrenched her arm free, rubbing her wrist where tiny spots of scarlet blood bore witness to the pressure of Stella's sharp fingernails. 'I'm not afraid of you. Believe what you like, but I'm telling you the truth.' Lucy marched off, head held high, but for all her show of bravado she knew that Stella meant every word she said.

The routine with Monty went reasonably well, but Lucy had been more upset by her encounter with Stella than she had realised and she missed one of her cues. Monty covered her mistake with the expertise of many years' experience, but that did not prevent him from reprimanding her severely when they left the ring. Stella was waiting outside with Dario as they prepared to make their entrance and it was obvious by the smirk on her face that she had overheard Monty's heated remarks. Lucy's chagrin was complete. She apologised for her mistake, but even though he made light of it, she could tell that Monty was disappointed. She was angry with herself for allowing Stella's spiteful warnings to affect her performance. It would not happen again, she thought, as she hurried back to her tent.

Next morning Monty made her go through their routine again and again, until he was satisfied that there would be no more mistakes. Lucy was tempted to tell him why she had lost concentration, but she knew he would confront Stella, who would put on her innocent face, smile sweetly and deny everything. Stella, Lucy decided, was a consummate actress and needed to be handled even more carefully.

'That was excellent,' Monty said as they rode out into the sunshine. 'Last night's errors were probably due to nerves. You'll do better today.'

'I'll do my best.' Lucy controlled Imperator with difficulty as he became agitated and caracoled, moving to the left and then the right and almost unseating her. 'Something's upset him,' she said, leaning forward to stroke the animal's silky neck. 'Good boy, Imperator.' Then suddenly, out of the corner of her eye, she saw a plume of flames shooting into the air. 'Pedro shouldn't be practising so close to the big top, should he?'

Monty peered into the shadows. 'He knows better than that. Hey, Pedro. Pedro Sanchez, what the hell are you doing?' He was about to dismount when another burst of flame caused Imperator to rear on his hind legs, unseating Lucy. She was thrown to the ground, landing with a loud thud and a cry of pain.

Chapter Seventeen

'I'm afraid it's broken.' Johann ran his fingers gently along Lucy's left arm, causing her to wince. 'I'll have to set it, Liebling. It will hurt.'

Monty grasped Lucy's right hand, his brows drawn together in a worried frown. 'Hold onto me. It will be over in seconds. Johann is an expert bone-setter.'

Froniga pushed him aside, holding a cup to Lucy's lips. 'Let her drink some of this first. It will ease the pain.'

'What is it?' Lucy demanded anxiously.

'Laudanum and water,' Froniga said, raising Lucy's head with her free hand. 'Drink up and don't argue.'

Lucy drank the mixture and lay back against the cushions on her bed. 'It was Stella,' she murmured. 'She did it.'

Monty and Johann exchanged puzzled glances.

'A fever must have set in,' Johann said, shaking his head. 'Hold tight, Liebling. It will be over in a moment.' He took her arm in a firm grip and pulled. Ignoring Lucy's scream, he patted her on the shoulder. 'There. It is done. Now I will make a splint and you will keep it on until the bones knit together.'

Monty released Lucy's hand and sat back on his haunches. 'I suppose this rules her out of the show.'

'For a few weeks, certainly.' Johann reached for the strips of bandage that Froniga had torn from an old sheet provided by Jenny, and with the aid of some strips of wood hastily cut to size by Barney, the labourer who did all the odd jobs for the circus performers, Johann made a passable splint. 'That should do, although a doctor could do better.'

Monty slapped him on the back. 'I doubt it. Well done, Johann.' He leaned closer, gazing at Lucy with a worried frown. 'How do you feel now?'

'Don't ask stupid questions, Monty,' Froniga said crossly. 'How would you feel if you'd just had your bone set by a man with hands like hams?'

'I've done my best.' Johann struggled to his feet. He had to bend his head and shoulders and even then he grazed the roof of the tent.

Lucy peered up at him through a haze of laudanum and saw a genial giant who had stepped straight from the pages of a children's storybook. 'I'm grateful to you, Johann.'

'It was nothing.' He bowed and backed out of the tent.

'How is she?' Ilsa's anxious voice floated in from outside, but Johann's response was lost as they walked away. Lucy felt as if she were floating on a fluffy pink cloud, far above the great dome of the big top.

'You must rest, Lucy.'

Monty's voice pierced her consciousness and she struggled to raise her head. 'I'm sure I'll be able to ride tomorrow. I can manage with one hand.'

'You'll do nothing of the sort. I'll perform as I

did before you joined us, so you mustn't fret. As soon as you're feeling stronger we'll see what you can do.'

Froniga made a shooing motion with her hands. 'Out, please. Let the girl sleep and she'll heal all the quicker.'

Monty rose to his feet, beckoning to Froniga, and they went outside. Lucy strained her ears to hear what was being said.

'I've spoken to Pedro.' Monty's voice carried on the breeze. 'But he was nowhere near the big top. He checked his equipment and one of the torches was missing, and the bottle of spirit.'

'It was deliberate then,' Froniga's reply was equally clear.

'It looks that way, and I won't stop until I discover the culprit.'

'But you have an idea who it was?'

'I do.'

'And you'll put a stop to it?'

'Nothing like this will happen again. I promise you that, Froniga.'

Had they really said all that? Or was it the laudanum talking? Lucy lay back and allowed the drug to take full effect.

When she opened her eyes it was growing dark. Her head was still muzzy from the effects of the laudanum, and at first she could not remember what had happened and why she was in bed. But as she moved the pain in her arm brought it all back to her and she groaned.

'It's a pity it wasn't your neck.'

The voice was all too familiar, and Lucy was

suddenly wide awake. 'It was you, I know it was,' she said hoarsely. 'You tried to kill me, Stella.'

'You have no proof.'

'Monty knows it was you.'

'I convinced him otherwise. Like all men, he's a fool, and I can twist him round my little finger.'

'I hope you're satisfied,' Lucy said angrily. 'I won't be able to ride for a week or two.'

'There's only one star of this show and it's me. If you've got any sense you'll go back to London or wherever you came from. This was your second warning. There won't be another, and next time I'll make certain it's final.' Stella rose swiftly to her feet and left the tent as silently as she had entered.

Lucy made an attempt to rise but the pain was too great and she sank back against the cushions. She took a sip of the medicine that Froniga had left for her and closed her eyes, drifting into a light sleep.

It was some time before Froniga appeared, having finished her stint of fortune telling in a stuffy little tent close to the entrance of the encampment. She regarded Lucy with a worried frown. 'How are you, my duck?'

'It's sore, but I can put up with the pain. But Stella came here and made dire threats. I think she's mad, Froniga. I really do.'

'That woman has a nerve. I'll tell Monty if she's bothering you.'

'I don't think that would help. She said she can make men do anything she wants and I believe her.'

'I'll make you some supper and give you another dose of laudanum. You'll feel better in the morning, and I'll keep Stella away from you, so stop worrying.'

Lucy dragged herself to a sitting position. 'I've been thinking while I've been lying here.'

Froniga chuckled. 'That's a bad sign. It's never a good thing to try to think when you're under the influence of laudanum.'

'I was trying to work out how I'm going to raise the money for a lawyer. I don't suppose they'll pay me while I'm laid up.'

'Probably not.' Froniga peered in the crock where they kept their food. I'm afraid it will have to be bread and cheese.'

'I'm not very hungry.'

'You must keep your strength up.'

'I don't know why I didn't think of him before, but I need to see Mr Goldspink, Grandfather's solicitor.'

'There's still the small question of money, my duck. And you won't be earning anything for a good while yet.'

'Mr Goldspink might be able to get me an advance on the annuity left to me by my grandmother. Or perhaps I could take out a mortgage on the property in Leman Street. I simply can't leave Granny to rot in that dreadful place. I must go to London as soon as possible.'

'I'd come with you, but I can't afford to lose my pitch here.'

'Of course not. I wouldn't expect it of you.'

'What will you tell Monty?'

Lucy shook her head. 'I don't know, but I'll think of something. I'm too tired now, but I'll speak to him first thing.'

The early morning sun pierced the rainclouds, creating deep shadows and contrasting pools of light between the gaily painted caravans. The scent of wood smoke from recently lit camp fires mingled with the appetising aroma of frying bacon, but Lucy was not hungry. 'You're running away?' Monty said, frowning.

'I'm not afraid of Stella, if that's what you mean.'

'She swears she had nothing to do with the unfortunate incident.'

'And you believe her?'

'I've known Stella for a long time. She's impetuous and has a fiery temper, but you're accusing her of attempted murder. That's a different matter altogether.'

'I didn't come here to argue with you, Monty. As I can't ride for a while I thought I'd take the opportunity of visiting my family.'

He leaned against the side of his caravan, folding his arms. 'You led me to believe you were an orphan, and had been in service since you were a child.'

'I didn't think you'd take me on if I told you everything.'

'What are you afraid of, Lucy? Why can't you tell me the truth?'

'Do you mind if I sit down? I'm still feeling a bit groggy.'

'Wait there; I'll fetch something for you to sit on.' He bounded up the steps, disappeared into the van and reappeared carrying a wooden stool. 'Are you all right? Perhaps you ought to go back to your tent.'

'I'm fine now.' She perched on the stool.

'Do you feel like telling me why you're leaving us?'

'I'm not leaving, Monty. I'll be back when my business in London is completed.'

'Business?'

'I might have misled you slightly.'

'In what way?'

'For a start, I was never in service.' She had been evading the issue but she realised that she must tell him the truth or lose his trust completely. She took a deep breath and launched into a brief account of her early childhood on the streets of the East End, and how her life that changed when her grandfather took her under his wing.

Monty listened intently. 'You must have missed your grandmother very much.'

'I cried myself to sleep every night for months and I tried to run away, but I was caught and taken back to Albemarle Street. In the beginning I must have given my grandfather a lot of heartache, but we became reconciled as I grew up. I was to inherit everything until Linus contested the will.'

'Linus?'

'My father's cousin.' Lucy wrapped her arms around her body, shivering at the memory of their last meeting. 'He's a hateful person. He took a common-law wife and when she died he wanted nothing more to do with their three children. I'm taking care of my young cousins and glad to do it. They're better off without him.'

'He cheated you out of your inheritance and then saddled you with his bastards?'

'He discovered that my parents didn't wed until after I was born, and that made him the legal heir. He plans to marry and the children are an embarrassment.'

'Wasn't there anyone you could turn to?'

'I was about to get engaged, but...'

'Let me guess. Your fiancé jilted you when he discovered your lack of fortune.'

'He's destined for public office and can't afford a scandal.'

'I'd say you've had a lucky escape.'

'That's as maybe, but it's not why I left London,' Lucy said hastily. 'I wanted to find my grandmother and give her a proper home. I met Froniga by chance and she said she could help me find Granny. The rest you know.'

'Not quite. You haven't told me why you're rushing back to London.'

'You asked me where we went after the parade.' Lucy stared down at her tightly clasped hands, unable to look him in the eye. 'My grandmother is a prisoner in Chelmsford jail. We had permission to visit her, and I can't even begin to describe how awful it was. Whatever she did in the past she doesn't deserve such a harsh punishment.'

'So what do you hope to achieve in London?'

'I'm going to see Mr Goldspink, my grandfather's solicitor, in the hope that he can help, and I want to make sure that the children are all right. Hester is getting on in years and Bedwin is quite ancient. Pearl is a recovering drug addict, but she's an old friend and she's in need of help too. They're coping with five young ones and three lodgers. It was a lot to ask of anybody and none of them are exactly young.'

'You're full of surprises, Lucy Pocket. I always knew you were different, and a story like that confirms it.'

'You understand now why I must go to London.'

'I'd go with you if I wasn't needed here, but I'll take you to the station and make sure you travel first class.'

'I'd like to go today, if possible.'

'There's only one condition.'

'What's that?'

'You must promise to return to us.'

'I promise.' She managed a wobbly smile. 'I can't allow Stella to get the better of me. I'll have to come back if only to prove that I'm not afraid of her.'

'Stella won't harm you again. You have my word on that.'

Hester was at first amazed and then shocked to see Lucy standing on the doorstep. 'What's happened to you, love?' she said, staring at the injured arm. 'Come in out of the rain.'

Lucy stepped inside, shaking the raindrops off her straw bonnet, which she feared was already ruined. She put her valise down with a sigh of relief. 'I fell off a horse and broke my arm.'

'Fell off a horse?' Hester stared at her in dismay. 'What was you doing on a horse?' She went to the foot of the stairs. 'Bedwin? Where are you?' She waited for a moment and when there was no reply she turned to Lucy, shaking her head. 'You need to take off those wet things before you catch your death of cold.'

Lucy did as she was told, trying not to giggle. With Hester clucking round her like a mother hen it was like old times and she knew she had come home. She handed her the sodden bonnet and shawl. 'Is everything all right? How are the children? Are you coping with everything, Hester?'

'We're all fine. Never mind the questions, come downstairs to the kitchen and I'll make you a nice cup of tea. When did you last eat? You look a bit peaky, girl.' She bustled off in the direction of the basement stairs. 'Bedwin, Pearl, where are you? Put the kettle on. Lucy's come home.'

Lucy hesitated for a moment, looking round the wainscoted entrance hall with a sudden rush of affection. The panelling shone from the application of beeswax and elbow grease, as did the floorboards. In her mind's eye she could see the girls on their hands and knees with Hester cracking a metaphorical whip, although she knew that they needed little encouragement as both Vicky and Maggie took pride in their new home. The scent of lavender polish filled the air and the delicious aroma of baking bread wafted up from the kitchen. She followed Hester down the stairs but had barely reached the last step when Vicky rushed to embrace her, closely followed by Maggie. 'You're back,' Vicky cried ecstatically. 'We thought you'd deserted us.'

'No, we didn't,' Maggie said firmly. 'I always knowed she'd come home.'

'What've you done to your arm?' Vicky demanded. 'Mind you don't hurt her, Maggie.

You're such a clumsy kid.'

Her sister's big blue eyes brimmed with tears. 'I didn't hurt you, did I, Lucy?'

'No. I'd soon tell you if you did,' Lucy said, smiling. She ruffled Maggie's golden curls. 'It's good to see you both. I've missed you.' She glanced round the room. 'Where are Essie and Sid?'

Vicky dragged her towards the table. 'Sit down, and I'll tell you.'

Bedwin stepped forward and pulled up a chair. 'Stop pestering her, girls. You make my head spin with all your chatter.'

'Thank you, Bedwin.' Lucy sank down on the seat, overcome with exhaustion. 'It's lovely to be home, but where are the others? I suppose Bertie must be at work.'

'Of course he is.' Hester filled the teapot and set it down on the table. 'Vicky, fetch the cake from the larder, and Maggie, leave Lucy alone. Can't you see she's tired and in pain?' She turned to Bedwin. 'Best go to the pharmacy and get some laudanum. She looks as though she might need a drop or two.'

'No, I'm all right, really I am. I want to keep a clear head,' Lucy said hastily. 'A cup of tea and a slice of cake will set me up nicely.' She sat back in the chair. 'You still haven't told me where Sid and Essie are. It's not like them to be so quiet. And where is Pearl? She hasn't gone back to her old ways, has she?'

'Pearl has got herself a little job at the vicarage of all places,' Hester said, spooning tea into the pot. 'The vicar is a widower and he needed someone to cook his dinner. Although I think he'll get fed up with fried fish before too long, because that's all she can do.'

Vicky put the cake on the table, leaving Hester to cut a slice. She edged her sister out of the way and sat next to Lucy. 'Your friend, Miss Theodora, found a home for Essie and Sid.'

'She did what?' Lucy looked to Hester for an explanation. 'Is this true?'

'Miss Theodora came here to see you, and when she found out where you'd gone she was most concerned.' Hester filled a cup with tea and passed it to Lucy before attacking the seed cake. 'She was still here when the police brought Sid home. He'd been wagging school and was caught pinching fruit from a barrow.'

'Oh dear,' Lucy said faintly. 'I thought he'd learned his lesson.'

Hester sliced the cake. 'I suppose you want some too?' she said, pointing the knife at Vicky and Maggie, who were watching her and licking their lips in anticipation.

They nodded enthusiastically and she gave them each a piece, saving the largest slice for Lucy. 'That boy is a limb of Satan. He'd have been up before the beak if Miss Theodora hadn't taken his part. She spoke so prettily to the copper that he let Sid off with a caution, providing Miss Theodora vouched for him.'

'Good heavens,' Lucy said, swallowing a mouthful of hot tea. 'I didn't know Dora was so public-spirited.'

'Not only that, but she came back the next day having found a place for both nippers with a childless couple who wanted a bright boy to work as a stable lad. They were prepared to take Essie in as well and send her to school.' Hester sat down, stirring sugar into her tea. 'There are some good people about, if you know where to find them.'

'I'm amazed. I didn't think Dora was interested in anything other than clothes and parties. When did all this happen?'

'Last week.' Hester sipped her tea with a satisfied sigh. 'Sit down, Mr Bedwin. Take the weight off your feet.'

He shook his head. 'I've got the brass door furniture to polish, Hester. Those commercial travellers have greasy fingers and it soon tarnishes.' He turned to Lucy with an apologetic smile. 'You'll excuse me, Miss Lucy. But may I say it's good to have you home. You've been missed.'

She gave him a tired smile. 'Thank you, Bedwin. I've missed all of you.'

He moved slowly and she could almost hear his bones creaking as he mounted the stairs.

Vicky licked her fingers, having already demolished the cake. 'I think Miss Theodora likes Bram. That's why she put herself out for the young 'uns.'

'Bram was here?' Lucy looked from one to the other.

'The 7th Hussars are stationed at Hounslow,' Hester said proudly. 'He had leave of absence to visit us and Miss Dora happened to be here. I think she was impressed, poor dear.'

'Why do you say that?' Lucy asked curiously. 'Did Bram say something to upset her?'

'No, of course not: he was his usual charming self. But he's a fine figure of a man and he looks dashing in uniform. It was obvious that she was smitten from the moment she set eyes on him, although I don't think he felt the same.'

'I see.' Lucy tried not to look too pleased. Not that she would blame Bram if he had fallen for Dora's brand of helpless femininity and pretty face, but he deserved a wife who could equal him in every way. He would tire easily of someone like her scatterbrained friend.

'Why are you smiling like that?' Vicky eyed her suspiciously. 'What's funny?'

'Absolutely nothing. I'm just happy to be home, and I'll thank Dora when I see her, but I want to be sure that the home she found for Sid and Essie is a good one.'

'She took them to see the people first,' Maggie volunteered. 'Essie said she liked the lady and the gentleman, and Sid wanted to work in the stables.'

'I wouldn't have let them go if I hadn't thought it right,' Hester said hastily. 'And Bram went to see the people too. He said they were a decent couple and they'd promised that both nippers would finish their education.'

'Well, if he thinks they're all right it must be so.' Lucy frowned. 'I'll pay a call on Dora as soon as I've seen Mr Goldspink, which is part of the reason why I left the circus.'

'Tell us about it,' Maggie pleaded. 'I never see'd a circus.'

'Then I must take you to see a show,' Lucy said, smiling. 'I never thought I'd be an equestrienne riding in the sawdust ring, but I've done it and done it quite well, so Monty said.'

'Who's Monty?' Vicky's eyes shone with interest. 'Have you got a gentleman friend, Lucy? Bram will be so jealous.'

'Don't talk nonsense, child,' Hester said sharply. 'You two can talk to Lucy later, but she's tired after her long journey and her arm must be painful. She needs to rest, so you can finish up your chores and chat after dinner.'

'Oh, no.' Vicky rose from the table, pouting. 'Do we have to dust the commercial gents' rooms? We did them yesterday.'

'And you'll do them tomorrow and the next day. Nice clean bedrooms is what we offer and they must be spotless, or I'll want to know the reason why. Off you go.' Hester waited until the girls were out of earshot. She leaned across the table. 'So why are you here, Lucy? And why do you need to see a solicitor? What's going on?'

Chapter Eighteen

Yorick Goldspink's chambers were at the top of a seedy building in Pickett Street, off the Strand, which, although it was close to the Inns of Court, was even closer to the rookeries surrounding Clare market. Cheap lodging houses packed together in the dismal courts and narrow alleyways were home to the poor and dispossessed as well as criminals who could melt into their surroundings and evade capture. Lucy had put on her oldest clothes and her ruined straw hat in an attempt to merge with the shabbily dressed people who thronged the streets. She walked purposefully, head held high to show she was not afraid of the gangs of feral children who loitered on street corners, or the beggars importuning passers-by from the dank doorways.

Even so, she heaved a sigh of relief when she entered the premises, closing the door on the outside world, although the interior of the building was not particularly welcoming. A strong smell of carbolic acid, stale tobacco and soot hung in a damp miasma, and the sound of raised voices assaulted her ears. Directly in front of her was a flight of uncarpeted stairs, and to the left a long corridor wandered off into darkness. She was wondering where she might find Mr Goldspink when she spotted a wooden sign nailed to the wall with the names of the occupants scrawled on it in chalk. *Top Floor, Y. Goldspink.* She mounted the stairs, taking care not to touch the handrail, which was covered in a thick film of grime and grease. It was a steep climb, and even through closed doors she could hear the chatter of disembodied voices with the occasional burst of laughter.

When she reached the top floor she paused for a moment to catch her breath. It was hot and stuffy beneath the eaves and the only light came from a roof window, covered in a haze of soot and a lacy mesh of bird droppings. She knocked on the door and entered without waiting for an answer.

Yorick Goldspink was seated behind a desk littered with papers, dirty crockery and empty wine glasses. A small dormer window allowed in only a modicum of daylight, and a paraffin lamp close to his right elbow emitted a yellowish glow and a strong smell of burning oil. He looked up, and for a moment his expression was blank, and then his bird-like features froze in an expression of astonishment. 'Miss Marriott?'

'Due to the change in my circumstances I'm using the name Pocket now, Mr Goldspink.' Lucy made her way carefully across the bare boards, which were littered with papers, some of them rolled into scrolls and tied with red tape, and others lying in seemingly random piles. 'I'm sorry to turn up without an appointment, but I had to see you.'

'Please take a seat.' He rose from his chair, gazing around the room with a puzzled frown. 'There is a spare chair, only I can't seem to place it at the moment.' He hurried round the desk, leaping over the scattered documents like a child playing hopscotch. 'I wasn't expecting any clients today, Miss Pocket. You'll have to excuse the untidy state of my office.' He peered into a particularly dark corner. 'There it is.' Delving beneath a pile of coats and hats, he picked up a chair and taking care where he trod placed it in front of his desk. Producing a crumpled handkerchief from his pocket, he dusted the seat. 'Please sit down.' He fluttered back to his seat and perched on it, gazing at her with his head on one side. 'Would you like to tell me what I can do for you?'

'I need your services, Mr Goldspink, but I have to find the money to pay for them.'

He blinked several times and cleared his throat. 'May I enquire as to the exact nature of your request? Are you in some kind of trouble, Miss Pocket?'

'I've only recently discovered that my grandmother is in Chelmsford prison. I believe she's innocent of the charges brought against her, or at the very least she was an unwilling party to the crime.'

He leaned his elbows on the desk, peering at her through his steel-rimmed spectacles. 'What was the nature of the offence?'

'She was involved with a man who was notorious amongst the street gangs and dealt with stolen goods. He escaped capture, but she was caught on the premises where some of the items were found.'

'You talk about this villainous person in the past tense. Do I take it that he is deceased?'

'Murdered, Mr Goldspink. But that was long after my grandmother was incarcerated in the jail. There's no question that she was involved.'

He frowned, drumming his fingers on the desk. 'I see.'

'Can you help me? I'll pay you anything you ask, but first I need to raise the money, either from my annuity or perhaps I could take out a mortgage on the property in Leman Street.'

'Have you thought about asking Mr Daubenay for help? He's a comparatively wealthy man, and I doubt if he has managed to gamble away his assets in such a short space of time.'

'Linus wouldn't give me a penny. Anyway, I believe he is going to be married, so he will be even less likely to help.'

'The young lady broke off the engagement,' Mr

Goldspink said with a glimmer of a smile. 'I have it on good authority that a little bird told her things about her fiancé which brought about a change in her feelings towards him.'

'You told her, Mr Goldspink?'

He shook his head. 'Never admit to anything, Miss Pocket. That's my motto.' He tapped the side of his nose. 'The young lady in question will bestow her hand on someone more worthy.'

'I'm glad for her sake, but it won't help me. Linus would see me in hell before he'd help me financially.'

'Then we must find another way.'

'You'll take the case?'

'I will,' he said firmly. 'The first thing I must do is travel to Chelmsford and introduce myself to the lady in question, but I have a few ends to tie up first. It will take me a couple of days and then I'm at your disposal.'

Lucy rose from her seat and was about to leave, but she hesitated. 'There's just one more thing, Mr Goldspink. You have connections and you know a lot of people. If you ever get any news of my mother, Christelle Marriott, I'd be very grateful if you would tell me. She left when I was a baby and I believe she went abroad to seek her fortune on the stage.'

He nodded slowly. 'I'll give the matter some thought.'

Light-headed with relief that Mr Goldspink had chosen to accept the case, Lucy left the building and made her way to the Strand. She took a cab to Jermyn Street, alighting outside the

Northams' town house. Her down-at-heel appearance had caused the cabby to give her an old-fashioned look, and the Northams' butler regarded her with equal suspicion. She wished now that she had taken the time to return to Leman Street to change into something more appropriate, but she was eager to see Dora. 'Miss Lucy Pocket,' she announced firmly. 'Is Miss Theodora at home?'

'Wait here, if you please, miss.' The butler allowed her into the vestibule, walking away with a measured tread and returning moments later with a look of disapproval etched on his stern features. 'Miss Theodora is in the morning room. Come this way, miss.'

She knew the way well enough but she followed in his wake, acknowledging him with a brief nod of her head as he ushered her into the room.

Dora hurried to greet her with a beaming smile, but it faded as she took in Lucy's bedraggled appearance. 'Oh, my goodness. What's happened to you, Lucy?'

'That's a fine welcome,' Lucy said, laughing. 'Aren't you pleased to see me?'

Theodora made a move to hug her but held back, staring at Lucy's splinted arm. 'What have you done to yourself?'

'I was thrown from a horse. It's a hazard that we circus riders face every day.'

'Circus riders?' Dora sank down on the nearest chair, fanning herself with her hand. 'You're joking, of course.'

'I can explain.' Lucy made herself comfortable on the sofa. 'It's good to be back in London. I've missed you, Dora.'

'You've been away for nearly a month without so much as a word. Hester said you'd gone to find Froniga and that she'd joined a circus, but I'd no idea that you had too. We were all so worried, and now you return looking as though you've been dragged through a hedge backwards. You must tell me everything.'

Making her account as brief as possible, Lucy related the events of the past few weeks. Eventually her voice began to crack and she broke off with an apologetic smile. 'Dora, I love you, but I'm dying for a cup of tea and something to eat. I was in too much of a hurry to bother with breakfast, and I've just risked life and limb to visit my solicitor in Pickett Street.'

'Of course, how silly of me.' Theodora stood up and went to tug at the embroidered bell pull. 'You look half starved, and that outfit does nothing for you.' She stared at Lucy, shaking her head. 'I don't know Pickett Street, but if you have to dress like that to go there it must be even rougher than where you live now.'

'It doesn't matter; none of this matters. The good news is that I've found Granny, but there's a problem.'

Eyes wide with anticipation, Dora clutched her hands to her bosom. 'You've found her? This is like a story in a penny dreadful.'

'She's in prison.'

'Oh, dear! It gets worse and worse.' Dora sat down beside her, taking Lucy's hand in hers. 'I am so sorry. What was her crime?'

'She fell in love with a bad man. It happens to

the nicest women, Dora.' Lucy had a sudden vision of Monty dressed in the black tailcoat he wore in the ring. Quite why he came to mind was a puzzle. She liked him well enough, but that was all. Stella might think otherwise, but she was wrong.

'Don't stop there.' Dora gave her hand a squeeze. 'Go on.' She looked up at the sound of someone knocking on the door. 'Enter.'

A maidservant scuttled into the room. 'You rang, Miss Theodora?'

'Tea for two, Bessie. Ask Cook if there's any of the delicious chocolate cake left.'

'Yes, miss.'

Dora waited until the door closed. 'Now, start at the beginning and tell me everything. This is so exciting, and I was feeling particularly bored and out of sorts this morning. Now I'm agog to hear your adventures.'

'I'll give you a full account, but first I want to know about Sid and Essie. Hester told me you'd found them a home with a respectable family.'

'I was sorry for the poor mites and I knew that you must be struggling to provide for them as well as your young cousins. Then, to make matters worse, young Sid was caught stealing, and I had to work really hard to persuade the constable not to arrest him.'

'It was good of you to go to all that trouble.'

'Bram helped me.' Theodora's cheeks flushed a delicate shade of pink and her eyes shone. 'When I told him what I had in mind he went out of his way to make sure that the Coopers' household was suitable. He was so good with young Sid, who was being very difficult after you left.'

'That sounds like Bram. He was always wonderful with his sister's children.' The memory of her first encounter with him and his young niece and nephew brought a smile to her lips. 'I'm glad you took them under your wing, Dora, but I'd like to visit them myself and see how they're getting on. I feel responsible for those two little urchins.'

'We'll go together. Bram said he might call this morning. He wanted to make sure that the children were happily settled.' Dora's blush deepened. 'We got on so well, even though it was a brief acquaintance, and I have the feeling I'll be seeing a lot more of him.'

'The trouble with military men is that they can be posted almost anywhere in the world at a moment's notice, leaving a trail of broken hearts behind them.' Lucy had not meant to speak so sharply, but Dora must have mistaken Bram's natural charm and courtesy for something more.

'It's not like that, and even if it were it has nothing to do with you, Lucy.'

Her friend's sharp tone came as a shock. Dora was usually compliant and sweet-natured. They had rarely argued, and even when they disagreed it had been about trivial matters, but it was obvious that she was not going to be put off easily. Lucy was suddenly ashamed of her outburst. Bram was free to choose whomsoever he fancied and it was nothing to do with her. She managed a wobbly smile. 'I'm sorry, Dora. I spoke out of turn.'

'Yes, you did. And anyway, Bram's sold his

commission. He's leaving the army very soon. I thought you'd know that.'

It was a double blow. She had been aware of his plans, but he had not thought to tell her that he had carried them out. He had confided in Dora first, leaving her to find out at second hand. Lucy could only assume that he must be as smitten with Dora as she was with him. It had happened in the wink of an eye, and now they would both be lost to her. Bram would enter Dora's world while she, Lucy Pocket, struggled to earn a living in the East End, or risked her life in the complex world of circus folk. She struggled to think of a reply but was saved by the arrival of Bessie carrying a tray.

'Tea and cake; just what we need.' Dora smiled, seemingly oblivious to the turmoil raging in Lucy's breast. 'That will be all for now, Bessie.' She dismissed her with a careless wave of her hand. 'You must try some cake, Lucy. It's quite delicious. And then I want to hear all about the circus. This is turning out to be the best day ever.' She poured the tea and handed a cup to Lucy.

Lucy's appetite had deserted her but she sipped the tea, answering Dora's questions about her time with the circus as best she could. She omitted to tell her about Stella's attempts at scaring her into leaving, and was just coming to the end of her narrative when the door opened and Piers strode into the morning room.

He came to a sudden halt when he saw Lucy. 'Lucy, my dear girl. This is wonderful. I didn't expect to find you here.'

'We've had such a lovely long chat,' Dora said

enthusiastically. 'Lucy's been telling me of her exciting time in the wilds of Essex. You'll never guess what she's been doing.'

'Dora, please. You're making my head spin.' He took a seat opposite them. 'You're looking peaky, Lucy, my dear. How did you come by that injury?'

Lucy put her cup and saucer back on the tray. 'It's a long story, Piers, and to tell the truth my arm hurts and I'm a bit weary.'

'I'll send for the carriage and see you safely home.' He reached for the bell pull. 'You can tell me everything on the way.'

'Thank you, Piers, but a cab will do,' Lucy said hastily. 'There's no need for you to come with me.'

His disappointment was mirrored in his eyes. 'We parted on bad terms. I'd like to put matters straight. We can at least be friends.'

'Of course you can,' Dora said eagerly. 'We can go back to how we were.'

'I don't think so.' Lucy rose to her feet. 'Look at me, Piers. I don't normally dress like this, but even so I'm leading a different life now. I'm not in your set.'

'She's joined the circus.' Dora clapped her hands. 'Isn't that just the most remarkable thing you've ever heard?'

'I should go.' Lucy made for the door, but Piers stood up, moving swiftly to bar her way.

'Don't rush off on my account. I do want us to be friends, Lucy. I've never got over you and I realise now what a fool I was to break off our engagement.'

Lucy drew herself up to her full height, looking

him in the eye. 'We were never officially engaged. We've had this conversation before, Piers, and my answer is still the same.'

'We had an understanding and I let you down.' He held her at arm's length. 'Even as you are now I still have feelings for you, Lucy. Can we start again?'

'No, Piers. You might feel the same but I've changed, and when you know my circumstances you'll agree with me that we should leave things as they are.'

'I don't understand.'

'I've discovered my grandmother's whereabouts, and she's in prison. Do you want to be associated with such a family?'

'In prison?' He released her, turning his head away.

'I'm dressed like a pauper because I've just been to Pickett Street to see my solicitor. I'm going to do everything in my power to secure Granny's release and then I'm going to look after her, as well as Linus Daubenay's three children. They're my cousins, even if we were all born on the wrong side of the blanket. Do you understand now?'

Piers met her angry gaze with a reluctant smile. 'Say what you like, Lucy. It doesn't change how I feel. Seeing you again has brought back all the emotions I thought I'd conquered. I still love you, my dear.' He clasped her hand in his. 'Let me help you. I only have a modest income but I do have considerable influence in high places, which I could put to good use on your account. Will you at least give me another chance?'

Dora leapt to her feet, knocking her cup and

saucer off the table in her haste. 'Say yes, Lucy. Please say yes. I'd love to have you as my sister-in-law.'

Lucy shook her head. 'I'm sorry, Dora, but that can never be.' She turned to Piers with an attempt at a smile. 'I did love you once, or at least I thought it was love, but everything has changed. My feelings...' She broke off as the door opened and Bram entered the room.

The butler hovered behind him, making apologetic noises. 'It's all right, old chap,' Bram said, dismissing him with a wave of his hand. 'I can announce myself.' He came to a sudden halt. 'I wasn't expecting to find you here today, Lucy.' His smile faded. 'You're hurt. What have you done to yourself?'

'How dare you barge in on us unannounced, sir?' Piers snapped angrily.

Dora clasped her hands to her pink cheeks. 'Bram is a friend. Don't speak to him like that.'

'He's no friend of mine, and he's over-familiar as far as Lucy is concerned.' Piers took a step towards Bram, fisting his hands at his sides. 'What is your business here?'

'There's no need to be rude, Piers.' Dora stepped in between them. 'Bram is here at my invitation.' She tucked her hand in the crook of Bram's arm, looking up at him with an adoring smile. 'We have a mission to accomplish, haven't we?'

'We did, but perhaps we should leave it until another day. I think I ought to take Lucy home.'

Lucy glanced from one to the other with a growing sense of frustration. Had they been small boys she would have been tempted to bang their heads together in an attempt to make them see sense. Dora's eyes were brimming with tears of disappointment and her bottom lip was trembling ominously as she clung to Bram. 'You can't leave now. You've only just arrived.'

He removed her hand gently, but his attention was focused on Lucy. 'I'm sorry, Dora, but you must see that Lucy is not herself.'

'I do, of course, but my brother has offered to escort her home.'

'I have indeed. Lucy and I have important matters to discuss,' Piers said firmly. 'Very important personal matters.'

'We've said all we have to say.' Lucy's patience was almost exhausted and her temper at breaking point. 'I'm not a child. I don't need anyone to take me home.'

'I was going to Leman Street to see the children anyway,' Bram said, grinning. 'I'm sure Dora will excuse me this once.'

Dora reached for her hanky. 'Don't worry about me.'

'I don't want to spoil your plans.' Lucy could see that Piers was not going to back down, and she needed to speak to Bram, who seemed oblivious to the fact that he was about to break Dora's heart.

'Not at all,' Bram said casually. 'Dora wanted to make sure that the nippers had settled in, but we can do that any time. It's more important to see that you're taken care of. Isn't that so, Dora?'

She turned away, burying her face in her hanky. 'Of course,' she said in a muffled voice.

'I call it downright dishonourable to break a promise to a young lady.' Piers made a move towards the door. 'I was about to escort Lucy home. I think you ought to remain here and apologise to Dora for upsetting her plans.'

Lucy threw up her hands, exasperated beyond measure. 'I've had enough of this. I'll get a cab.' She left the room, hoping that Bram would make his peace with Dora, and that once and for all Piers would accept the fact that she had no intention of rekindling their relationship. She crossed the entrance hall, resisting the temptation to run. The footman, who had been staring idly into space, jumped to attention and rushed to open the door.

Despite her efforts, Piers caught up with her as she was about to step outside onto the pavement. 'Please reconsider, Lucy. I meant what I said.'

She turned to face him. 'And so did I, Piers. Thank you for offering to help, but I can manage on my own.' She was about to walk away when he caught her by the wrist.

'You don't mean that, Lucy.'

'I can assure you she does.' Bram tapped him on the shoulder. 'Let her go, my friend, or I'll be forced to take action.'

'You're both acting like schoolboys,' Lucy said crossly. 'Leave me alone, Piers. And you, Bram, should put Dora out of her misery. You seem to have given her the impression that you're courting her, and she needs to be told the truth.'

His eyes widened and he shook his head. 'I didn't say or do anything that might have given her that idea.'

'If you've been toying with my sister's affections you'll have me to answer to.' Piers squared up to him. 'I'd call you out if duelling weren't illegal these days.'

'I won't dignify that with an answer, Northam. Your sister is a lovely girl and I'm proud to have made her acquaintance. I'm equally sorry if she mistook my intentions, but I can assure you that it was the last thing on my mind.'

'Goodbye, Piers,' Lucy said, moderating her tone. 'I'm sorry we have to part like this yet again, but perhaps you'll believe me now. There is and never will be a future for us together.'

He muttered something beneath his breath and retreated into the house.

'Well, that told him,' Bram said, grinning. 'Anyway, he's not good enough for you, Lucy.' He took her by the hand, giving it a gentle squeeze. 'You're well rid of him.'

She managed a weary smile. 'I think we'll stand a better chance of hailing a cab in Piccadilly.'

'And on the way home you can tell me what's been going on while you were in Essex. How did you injure yourself, and why are you wearing those rags and that dreadful bonnet?'

'I'll tell you everything, but I must know one thing first.'

'What is it?'

'Were you flirting with Dora? And why did you tell her you'd sold your commission before you told me?'

He threw back his head and laughed. 'That's two questions, and I wasn't flirting with Dora. I simply tried to help her find a place for the moppets, because I knew that's what you'd want.'

'All right, I accept that, but you must be more careful. She's a delicate creature and she's taken a fancy to you. Let her down easily, Bram.'

'I never thought of myself as a heartbreaker, but of course I'll make things right with her. As to the commission, I could hardly tell you when I didn't know where you were. Pearl said you'd gone off on some wild goose chase to Essex and something about a circus, but it wasn't much to go on. As far as I was concerned you'd vanished into thin air, and now you've got some explaining to do.'

'There's a cab. Flag him down, Bram. You've got two good arms and I've only got one.' She smiled up at him as he raised his hand to attract the cabby's attention. After the nervous weeks she had spent with the circus people it was wonderful to feel at ease in his company, and safe. There was nothing she could not tell him, although it might be best not to make too much of Stella's threats, which in hindsight were over-dramatic and too theatrical to be taken seriously. She was jolted out of her reverie as the cab drew to a halt and a man sprang down to the pavement. She recognised him instantly. 'Quick,' she whispered. 'Walk on, Bram. I don't want him to see us.'

Chapter Nineteen

It was too late: Linus had spotted them. He crossed the street, brandishing his silver-topped cane in a gesture of defiance as cabbies, coachmen and carters shouted and swore at him for scaring their horses, and by some miracle he reached the pavement unscathed.

'I've spent the morning looking for you, Bramwell.' His angry gaze rested for a second on Lucy. 'And I have a bone to pick with you too, Miss Pocket.'

'I've nothing to say to you, Linus,' Bram said calmly. 'And I doubt if Lucy wants to speak to you either.'

'You owe me money, Southwood.' Linus barred their way. 'In fact you are both in debt to me.'

'If anything you owe me.' Lucy faced him with a defiant lift of her chin. 'The money you gave me to support your children won't keep them fed and clothed forever.'

Linus shook his cane at a couple of flower sellers who had stopped to stare at them. 'I suggest we go somewhere more private to continue this conversation.'

'This is nonsense and you know it.' Bram placed a protective arm around Lucy's shoulders. 'Let us pass.'

'I heard that you'd sold your commission, and I expect to be repaid in full.' Linus struck a pose, leaning on his cane, an insolent smile hovering on his lips. 'And you, miss. You've turned my little girls into slaveys.'

'I don't know what you're talking about,' Lucy said angrily.

'I visited that hovel you call home and found them scrubbing floors and cleaning windows. No doubt you offer their services as well as your own to your lodgers.'

Bram fisted his hands. 'Say another word and I'll floor you, Linus. You've gone too far this time.'

'I haven't even begun. I can make it impossible for you to find gainful employment in this city and I won't hesitate to expose your sister as a slut.' Linus turned to Lucy. 'And I want the sixty guineas back or I'll report you to the authorities for running a bawdy house.'

'You bastard.' With a neatly judged right upper cut Bram sent him sprawling onto the pavement, much to the amusement of the growing crowd of onlookers.

'Hit him again, guv.' The cabby who had dropped Linus off was one of those who had cursed him for striding across a busy thoroughfare and had stopped to watch.

Bram leaned over and dragged a purple-faced Linus to his feet. 'Threaten Lucy again and I won't be responsible for my actions.'

Clutching his cheek, Linus turned to the crowd. 'You saw that. This man attacked me. Someone call a constable.'

'Never saw nothing, guv.' A burly drayman flicked the reins, urging his horse to a trot, and as if by magic the crowd dispersed.

'You are an evil man.' Lucy's voice shook with emotion. 'How dare you say such wicked things about me? Your children are loved and well cared for and they're happy where they are.'

'It was a gift,' Bram muttered. 'It wasn't a loan. You bought the commission to please Meg. You hoped I'd be killed so that you could mistreat my poor sister and abandon her when it suited you.'

'Your sister was a whore.' Linus backed away. 'And I want my money back. I'll bankrupt you if necessary, but I'll have my due.' He flicked a malicious glance at Lucy. 'As for you, you'd better pay up or I'll blacken your name so that no decent man will look at you.' He crossed the street, waving to the cabby. 'Half Moon Street.'

'Can't oblige, guv.' The cabby flicked his whip and drove off, leaving Linus standing on the pavement.

'He won't go through with it, will he?' Lucy asked anxiously.

'Just let him try.' Bram lifted his hand to hail an oncoming cab. 'I was going to repay him in full, but I've changed my mind. I'll use that money to set me up in a nice little cottage somewhere in the country, with a bit of land to grow vegetables and room to keep a pig and some hens.'

'I doubt if he'd take you to court; it would be too costly.'

'If it was anyone else I'd pay up and be done with it, but Linus drove my sister to an early grave and abandoned his children. I'll see him in hell before I give him a penny piece.' He helped Lucy into the cab which had just pulled up at the kerb. 'Leman Street, please, cabby.' He climbed in and sat down beside her.

'Do you really mean to keep the money? It sounds as if he's been gambling again and he won't give up easily.'

'Let me worry about that.' Bram took her hand and held it in a warm clasp. 'Can you put me out of my misery and tell me where you've been these past weeks?'

'I've told this story so many times that I'm beginning to think I imagined it all.'

'A broken arm seems evidence that you haven't been sitting in your parlour with your embroidery.'

She met his earnest gaze with a reluctant smile. 'You won't believe half of what I'm going to tell you, but it's all true.' She started haltingly, but Bram was a good listener, and she told him everything, coming to an end as the cab reached Leman Street.

'That settles it,' he said firmly. 'I'll put the money to good use. We'll get Eva released from jail.'

She stared at him with a mixture of gratitude and dismay. 'I can't let you do that, Bram. She's my granny and I'm responsible for her. You must spend the money as you intended.'

'My mind's made up, Lucy. After everything you've done for Meg's nippers it's the least I can do. I'll go and see your solicitor and tell him to take whatever action is necessary to free Eva from prison, and I'll foot the bill.'

'Thank you, Bram. You're wonderful.' She flung her arms around his neck and kissed him, then drew away, regretting her impulsive action. 'I'm sorry. I shouldn't have done that.'

'I don't know why not,' he said, chuckling. 'You can kiss me whenever you want to.'

'I got carried away.' She knew she was blushing furiously and she alighted from the cab without waiting for his help. Leaving him to pay the cabby, she crossed the pavement and was about to mount the steps when the front door opened and Vicky emerged, closely followed by Maggie. They ran to meet Bram, clinging to him like burrs.

He met Lucy's amused gaze with a smile. 'I am a lucky fellow. It seems that all the young ladies are pleased with me today.'

'It's the uniform, Bram. It turns all the girls' heads, so you'd best enjoy it while you can,' she said, laughing and at ease again.

He picked Maggie up and flung her over his shoulder, taking Vicky by the hand. 'I'll be a free man at the end of the week.'

The next couple of days passed in a frenzy of activity. Lucy visited the house in Chelsea and was delighted to find that both Sid and Essie had settled happily in their new surroundings. The couple who had taken them in were middle-aged, childless and had obviously formed a strong bond with Essie, who was being treated like a much-loved daughter. Lucy took to them instantly and was satisfied that both Sid and Essie were assured of a much better future than she would have been able to provide. She left with a promise to visit as often as she could.

It was still early afternoon and she decided to

stop off at Jermyn Street on the chance of finding Dora at home. She arrived just as Dora was preparing to go out.

'You must come with me,' Dora said eagerly. 'I hate shopping on my own and I have a fancy for tea at Gunter's. It's not far to Berkeley Square and it's a lovely day. I'd enjoy the walk.'

Lucy had not intended to stay long, but she could see that Dora was in need of company as well as cream cakes. 'That sounds lovely. But I really can't afford it, Dora.'

'Well, it's fortunate that I can, and you'd be doing me a favour because it wouldn't be proper for me to go there alone. I'm in a spending mood, so we can go on to Oxford Street and see what the department stores have to offer.'

Lucy had not the heart to refuse. She could not afford to treat herself, but if Dora wanted to go shopping she was happy to accompany her, and it would take her mind off her own problems. She had tried to forget Linus and his dire threats, but the memory lingered on.

After a delicious tea and a greedy indulgence in their selection of cakes and pastries, Lucy insisted on walking to the Marshall and Snelgrove department store in Oxford Street. She had a fancy to see what Debenham and Freebody had to offer, which entailed a detour to Wigmore Street, and by this time Lucy was beginning to feel exhausted. Her injured arm was aching painfully but Dora seemed to be tireless, insisting that she was in desperate need of a new pair of gloves and they simply must visit Penberthy's. They retraced their steps to Oxford Street, and having tried on and discarded several pairs of lace gloves Dora decided that the one she liked best was the first pair she had seen. 'I find shopping cheers me up no end,' she said as they emerged into Oxford Street. 'I know it was silly of me to think that Bram was interested in me, but I'm determined to be more sensible from now on.'

'It wasn't silly at all. He's a very attractive man and he obviously likes you a lot, and who wouldn't?'

'You're sweet to say so, but I'm afraid I made rather a fool of myself.'

'You'd have to be made of stone to resist Bram. He doesn't realise how charming he can be, and he was mortified to think he'd upset you.'

'Was he really? Well, I'm just glad that Mama and Papa are out of the country. Piers suggested that I might join them in Paris, and I'm thinking about it.'

'I'm sure you'd have a wonderful time at the embassy. I expect they have parties and balls and you'd meet all sorts of interesting people.'

'And maybe catch a rich husband.' Dora was suddenly alert and waving madly. 'There's a cab. I'm not walking another step.'

'Perhaps I'll take an omnibus.'

'Nonsense. I insist you take the cab all the way home, and don't worry about the cost. I think Piers was feeling guilty for causing a scene and he gave me a generous amount to spend as I please, so it's only right that I give you the fare. Anyway, darling, you look a bit peaky. Is your arm hurting?'

'A little, and these parcels are quite heavy.'

The cab pulled up at the kerb. 'Jermyn Street, please, and then on to Whitechapel.' She tossed her packages onto the seat and climbed in. 'Can you manage one-handed, Lucy?'

'I'm getting used to it.'

Lucy arrived home to find Linus waiting for her in the parlour.

'Shall I come in with you?' Hester asked nervously. 'I know what a devil he can be when he's roused and he doesn't look too happy.'

'I don't think I've ever seen him laugh,' Lucy said with a wry smile. 'I'll be all right, just keep the children out of the way.' She entered the room, head held high and ready for battle. 'Good afternoon, Linus.'

He had been staring out of the window, hands clasped tightly behind his back, but he turned slowly, facing her with a hard stare. 'I've come for my money.'

'I haven't got it. Most of it went on buying beds for your children and necessities like food, and new shoes for Maggie, and a–'

He held up his hand. 'Enough. I'm not interested in your finances. You owe me sixty guineas and I want it now.'

'And I told you that I haven't got sixty guineas.'

'You can afford to travel in a cab, and you're wearing clothes that cost a pretty penny, so don't cry poverty to me. It won't wash.'

'Not that it's any of your business, but a friend paid my fare, and these clothes were bought for me by my grandfather. Sir William was your uncle, which makes us family, Linus, whether you like it or not.'

He crossed the floor in two angry strides, catching her good arm in a vicious grip. 'You are my cousin's bastard and I refuse to acknowledge you as a member of the family.'

She faced him, anger wiping away fear. 'Sir William made me his heir. You cheated me out of my inheritance, Linus Daubenay. Sixty guineas is a mere trifle compared to what you took from me.'

'You can't or won't pay? Then I'll take my children away from this house of ill repute.'

'This is a perfectly respectable lodging house.' She twisted free from him, backing towards the doorway. 'I won't let you do this.'

'They're my flesh and blood. I have every right to do as I please with them.' He pushed past her, wrenching the door open. 'Hester,' he shouted. 'Hester Gant, come here this instant.'

Lucy ran to him, catching him by the sleeve. 'Don't do this, Linus. Please, I'm begging you, don't take the children.'

He brushed her off as if she were an irritating insect. 'Shut up. You have no say in the matter.'

Hester rushed into the room, looking from one to the other with a worried frown. 'Why all the shouting? What's the matter?'

'Mind your own business, you old hag.' Linus towered over her, his thin lips quivering with rage. 'Fetch the children. I'm taking them away from here.'

'Don't do it,' Lucy cried passionately. 'Tell them to run and hide.'

Linus swung his arm, catching her a savage

blow on the side of her head. She stumbled and fell to the ground. Hester made a move towards her but Linus took her by the shoulders and propelled her out of the room. 'Get them,' he said through clenched teeth. 'If you refuse I'll call a constable. The law is on my side.'

Lucy struggled to her feet, clutching her injured arm. 'You are so brave when it comes to mistreating women and children, aren't you, Linus? You wouldn't dare behave like this if Bram were here.'

'I'll deal with him in my own way.'

'I suppose you've gambled away Grandfather's money. Even if I had sixty guineas to give you it wouldn't go far. You probably lose more than that every night at the gaming tables.'

'You can say what you like, but I'm taking the children and I'll send the bailiffs in to collect goods to the value of the money owed.' He glanced round at the shabby second-hand furniture. 'Although I doubt if this rubbish will raise five shillings, let alone the amount you owe me. I'll have you out on the street before the end of the week.'

'Papa?'

The sound of Vicky's tremulous voice from the doorway made Lucy bite back an angry retort and she slipped past Linus to put her arms around the frightened child. 'It's all right, poppet.'

'Why was Papa shouting at you?' Vicky asked anxiously. 'What's going on, Lucy?'

'Don't ask stupid questions.' Linus stared at her with cold indifference. 'I'm taking you home with me, child. Go and fetch your brother and sister.'

'Maggie wouldn't come upstairs,' Vicky whispered, clutching Lucy's hand. 'And Bertie hasn't come home from work yet.'

'Work? My son is labouring to keep you in style?'

'No, Linus,' Lucy said coldly. 'Bertie is doing an honest day's work and bringing home a wage to help support his family. It's the way most people exist.'

Ignoring this barb Linus turned to glare at Vicky. 'Fetch your sister and bring her to me. I'm taking you to my home in Albemarle Street. I've had to sack most of the servants so you'll be very useful. Fetch her now.' His voice rose to a roar and Vicky fled from the room.

'You're a cold-hearted bully.' Lucy spat the words at him. 'I've never hated anyone in my life, but I loathe you.'

'The feeling is mutual. You're a thorn in my flesh; a bug to be crushed beneath my boot. I haven't done with you yet, Lucy Pocket.'

'I don't care what you do to me, but if you've got a shred of human kindness you'll leave the children here where they're safe and happy.'

'I'll wait for the boy to return and then we're leaving. Think yourself lucky that I don't call a constable and have you arrested for abducting my children.'

'They won't believe your lies.'

'Will they not?' He leaned over so that his face was close to hers. 'I'm still a person of some note and you're a nobody.'

'Say what you like but don't do this, Linus.'

Taking her by the shoulders he forced her down

onto the nearest chair. 'Stay there and don't move. I'll tell Hester to let you out after we've gone.' He left the room and she heard the key turn in the lock.

Rising shakily to her feet she ran to the door and rattled the handle, calling for help, even though she knew it was useless. Linus would take the children and she was powerless to stop him. She leaned against the wooden panels, fighting back tears. Then the silence was broken by shouts and screams. She pounded on the door with her fist. 'What's happening? Let me out!'

The key grated in the lock and the door burst open. Hester shoved the girls into the room, handing the key to Lucy. 'Lock yourself in,' she said brusquely.

Lucy caught sight of Bedwin and Pearl struggling with Linus, and she thrust the key into Vicky's small hand. 'Lock the door and don't open it until I say so.' Consumed with anger she rushed into the hall, snatching an umbrella from the stand and bringing it down on Linus's back with all the force she could muster.

He turned on her with a howl of rage and would have struck her down if Pearl and Bedwin had not grabbed him from behind. With a roar like an angry bull Linus shook them off and seized Lucy by the throat. She dropped the umbrella, raising her good arm in an attempt to fend him off, but his fingers closed around her neck making it impossible to breathe. She was sinking into unconsciousness when she was released so suddenly that she fell to her knees.

'Are you all right, love?' Hester's voice seemed

far away.

'Y-yes, I think so.'

Hester helped her to her feet and as air filled her lungs Lucy's world began to right itself. She focused her eyes with difficulty and was amazed to see Linus being frogmarched across the hall by two of her lodgers, Cyril and Gilbert. Bedwin was pale and obviously shaken but he hurried to open the front door, standing aside as Linus was pitched out onto the street.

'Good riddance,' Pearl shouted. 'Come here again and you'll get more of the same.'

Lucy hurried to her side in time to see Linus as he picked himself up, scowling and shaking his fist. 'You'll get what you deserve, Lucy Pocket.'

'The children stay with me, Linus. You're not a fit parent.'

'I'll have the law on you, you bitch.'

'And I'll report you for attacking me in my own home. I've got plenty of witnesses.' She slammed the door.

'That got rid of him,' Gilbert said, rubbing his hands together. 'I don't know who the chap is but I enjoyed throwing him out.'

'Me too.' Cyril's cheeks were flushed with excitement as he ran his hand through his curly locks, making them stand on end even more than usual. 'I wish I'd punched him on the nose and drawn his cork.'

In spite of everything this made Lucy laugh. 'Cyril Aitken, that's not a very Christian thing to say.'

'No, miss, but it's true. I couldn't stand by and watch. He might have killed you if we hadn't stepped in.'

Gilbert slapped him on the back. 'I'm proud of you, boy.' He saluted Bedwin. 'And you, sir, are a man to be reckoned with. I'd like to buy you a pint if you feel inclined to accompany me to the pub this evening.'

'What about me, cully?' Pearl asked with a coquettish smile. 'I enjoy good company and a drop of tiddley.'

'Of course, Miss Pearl. It would be my pleasure.'

The sound of shrieks coming from the parlour made Lucy hurry to the door. 'Open up, Vicky. He's gone. You're safe now.'

Hester groaned softly. 'Not for long. I know Linus only too well. He'll not let this rest, Lucy.'

The door opened and the girls rushed out, throwing themselves into Lucy's arms. 'Why is Pa being so mean?' Maggie's bottom lip trembled and her eyes filled with tears. 'Why did he hurt Lucy?'

'Pa is a devil.' Vicky choked on a sob. 'You always said so, Hester, and sometimes Ma agreed with you.'

'Has he got horns?' Maggie's eyes brightened. 'And a tail?'

Lucy gave her a hug. 'Of course not. He doesn't know how lucky he is to have two such lovely daughters.'

'And Bertie too,' Maggie added solemnly. 'He didn't see Bertie today.'

Hester took her by the hand. 'Just as well, if you ask me. Come downstairs; it's time for your tea. I think we've had enough excitement for one day.'

Gilbert cleared his throat. 'You was a hero, Mr Bedwin. The offer of a drink still stands.'

Bedwin straightened his tie. 'Thank you, Mr Harker. I'm not a drinking man, but I used to enjoy a glass of Madeira occasionally.'

'We aren't all killjoys,' Pearl said, pouting.

'I think we should get a bottle of that stuff,' Cyril said, puffing out his chest. 'We could have a glass after supper tonight.'

'You're too young, my lad.' Gilbert headed for the stairs. 'I'm going to my room, but I'll be down in time to eat, Miss Gant. The food you prepare is nectar for the gods.'

Hester blushed and giggled. 'Oh, Mr Harker, you do talk nonsense sometimes.'

'I think he has a soft spot for you, miss,' Cyril said, grinning. 'But you do cook lovely meals. I never had nothing like it in the orphanage. I live like a king compared to how it was before I come here.'

Lucy patted him on the shoulder. 'I'm glad you're happy with us, Cyril.'

'It wasn't true what the gent said, was it?' His smile faded. 'About throwing us all out on the street?'

'No, I hope not. I'll do my best to see it doesn't happen. This is my home as well as yours.'

'Ta, miss. That means a lot to me.'

'Never mind the chitchat, Cyril,' Hester said with mock severity. 'Go upstairs and wash some of that dirt off your face and hands.'

He grinned at her and blew her a kiss as he bounded up the stairs, taking two at a time. Hester shooed the girls towards the stairs leading down to the kitchen. 'Come along, Mr Bedwin. I'll make a fresh brew and add a drop or two of brandy to your cup. You look as though you need it.'

'Thank you, Mrs Gant. It would be most welcome.'

Pearl sighed heavily. 'And I thought we might have a jolly time at the pub. I'll have to hope that Carlos is in the Black Horse when I finish at the vicarage.' She reached for her bonnet and put it on. 'I'm off then to cook the vicar's supper. He's a real gent, and if I play my cards right I think he'll ask me to live in as his housekeeper.' She nudged Lucy in the ribs. 'Can you imagine it? Me, Pearl Sykes, going respectable and living with a holy man.'

'Of course I can,' Lucy said, smiling. 'You'd brighten anyone's life, and he'd be lucky to have you.'

Pearl's face flushed bright pink and she giggled like a girl. 'Oh, you are a one, Lucy Pocket.' She opened the front door and left with a cheerful wave.

Lucy watched her walk away with a sigh of relief. It was good to see the old Pearl emerging from the shell of the drug-addicted woman they had found in Limehouse. That battle had been won but now she had a new fight on her hands. She knew Linus well enough to believe he meant what he said.

Her fears were confirmed later that evening when a police sergeant from the station further along Leman Street called at the house. 'You're accused of the abduction of three minors, Miss

Pocket, but the person in question is prepared to drop the charges if the children are returned to their rightful home by noon tomorrow.'

Chapter Twenty

Shattered by the news and yet unsurprised, Lucy tried not to panic. She had expected Linus to retaliate but she had not thought it would happen so quickly. After supper when the children had gone to bed Lucy, Hester and Bedwin sat round the kitchen table. 'He knows I can't raise the money in such a short time,' Lucy said with a sigh. 'And the law is on his side.'

Bedwin cleared his throat, a sure sign that he was about to say something momentous. 'Mr Northam is a wealthy gentleman, Miss Lucy. It was said in the servants' hall that you and he would marry.'

'That was a long time ago. I can't ask him for money.'

'You went shopping with his sister,' Hester said gently. 'She seems to be a wealthy young lady. Wouldn't she help you?'

'Dora spends her allowance the moment she gets it. Linus will bankrupt me if I can't repay him. He'll take this house and sell it to pay off his gambling debts and he'll go on and on until he's lost everything.'

Bedwin nodded wisely. 'It's like a disease. I've seen it happen before, Miss Lucy. I was with a gentleman many years ago who went the same way. Put a bullet in his head and ended it all when he'd run through his fortune.'

Hester reached for the brandy bottle and took a nip. 'I don't normally touch the stuff,' she said apologetically. 'That man has driven me to drink. What will we do?'

Bedwin took the bottle from her and poured a generous amount in his tea. 'We need to fortify ourselves, Miss Gant. Let battle commence.' He raised his cup in a toast.

'I have to take the children somewhere Linus won't find them.' Lucy rose to her feet and paced the floor. 'I promised to return to the circus, but I can't work until my arm heals and I couldn't expect Froniga to feed the four of us.' She came to a halt, frowning thoughtfully. 'I need a safe place to go, just for a few weeks until I can start earning again. Maybe I could find work for Bertie in the big top, but the girls are too young, and they really ought to be in school.'

Bedwin drained his cup, his face flushed and his eyes shining. 'I have the perfect solution, Miss Lucy. Marriott Park hasn't been occupied for years. Sir William closed it up after your grandmother died, leaving a caretaker in sole charge.'

'But it belongs to Linus now,' Lucy said impatiently. 'I can't go there.'

'It's the last place he'd think of looking for you, miss. I remember him coming there when he was a boy and he was nothing but trouble. He hated the countryside and he made himself so objectionable that Lady Marriott sent him home to his mother. On his last day he swore he'd never put a foot in the place again, and to the best of my knowledge he never has.'

'Are you certain of that, Bedwin?'

'As certain as I can be of anything, Miss Lucy.'

'But the caretaker would tell Linus.'

'I know Ron Lugg well. He was head gardener years ago and he had more reason than most to dislike Master Linus.'

'It might be the answer,' Hester murmured. 'Bram would sort Linus out if he knew what was going on.'

'We don't want Bram to get into trouble because of Linus, and I've only got until midday tomorrow.' Lucy stared at the clock on the mantelshelf as if seeking inspiration. 'We'll do it, but I can't just turn up at Marriott Park. You must come with us, Bedwin, so that you can explain things to Lugg.'

'Yes, Miss Lucy. But how will we travel?'

'I don't know yet. I'll have to visit Mr Goldspink tomorrow morning to tell him what's happened, and maybe he can advance me the money for the train fares. Whatever happens, we have to leave London.'

Lucy was waiting outside the office door when Goldspink arrived at eight o'clock. She knew that he was a punctual man who kept long office hours and she was not disappointed. His jaw dropped when he saw her. 'Miss Pocket. You're an early bird.'

'I'm in dire trouble, Mr Goldspink. I need your help.'

'Come inside, dear lady.' He produced a large iron key and unlocked the door, ushering her into the stuffy room. 'Forgive the untidiness,' he murmured apologetically. 'I was rather busy yesterday.'

The state of the office seemed exactly the same as she remembered it from her last visit, but she made no comment as she waited for him to find the chair beneath a pile of books and ledgers. Sweating profusely, he dusted the seat and motioned her to sit down. 'Now then, Miss Pocket, how has your situation changed?'

'I have to leave London before noon or the police will arrest me for abducting the children. Linus made the charges because I couldn't repay the sixty guineas he gave me for their keep.'

'I see.' Goldspink perched on his chair, eyeing her curiously. 'A trumped-up charge?'

'He's determined to ruin me, sir. He only wants his offspring because he can't afford to pay servants, and I'm afraid he'll treat them abominably. I accepted the money in good faith and I spent most of it making a home for the children.'

He rested his elbow on the desk, peering at her intently. 'Quite so. It was a reasonable expenditure, and something that was foisted upon you by Mr Daubenay. Why would he behave in such a manner towards you?'

'I think he's desperate for money, and he intends to bankrupt me and take my only asset, which is the house in Leman Street.'

'And I suppose you cannot contact Lieutenant Southwood – or should I say Mr Southwood?'

'That's correct. I think that Bram will be moving his things out of the barracks tomorrow, but that will be too late. Linus has made certain of that.'

'So what do you intend to do?'

'I thought perhaps you might give me a small loan.'

'Dear lady, I would if I could.' Goldspink opened a drawer and pulled out a cash box. 'It's not even locked.' He lifted the lid and tipped it upside down. 'Empty. Not a penny piece.'

'Then I'll have to do as I planned and leave London for the country. And there again I'm hampered by lack of funds. I'll have to find the money for our train fares.'

'Dear me.' He shook his head. 'You are in a pretty pickle and no mistake. Is there no one to whom you can turn?'

'There is one person. I suppose I could ask Piers, but it would put me in an embarrassing position.'

Goldspink angled his head. 'More embarrassing than being arrested?'

'Well, no.' Lucy stood up. 'You're right, Mr Goldspink. This isn't the time to be proud. I'll go to Jermyn Street and ask for his help.' She was about to leave, but she hesitated. 'I've no doubt Bram will contact you soon. Would you be kind enough to give him a message from me?'

'Most certainly.'

'Tell him that Hester knows where we've gone.'

'I'll do that, of course, but first I have some good news for you regarding your grandmother.' He stood up and walked round the desk, beaming at her. 'I've been in touch with the court where her case was heard and she has only a few months of her sentence left. I took it upon myself to petition the local magistrate for her early release on the grounds of ill health. Whether or not it will be granted is another matter, but there is always hope.'

She shook his hand. 'Thank you. That's wonderful. I'm truly grateful.'

'It hasn't happened yet, but I'll keep Mr Southwood informed and he can pass the information on to you. I'd prefer not to know where you are until the matter with Mr Daubenay is settled.'

'I understand.' She leaned over and kissed him on the cheek. 'Thank you again. It's good to know I have at least one friend in London.'

His dark skin flushed scarlet. 'You'd better hurry, if you're going to Jermyn Street, or you won't get home in time.'

'I'll run all the way.'

Arriving breathless and dishevelled, Lucy faced the footman with an imperious toss of her head. 'Please inform Mr Northam that Miss Pocket wishes to see him on urgent business.'

'Wait here, please. I'll see if the master is at home.'

'He must be,' Lucy cried in desperation. 'Assure him that it is of the utmost urgency.' She stepped into the vestibule, patting her tumbled hair into place. Her bonnet had come off as she raced along the Strand, and she had not stopped to put it on. She glanced at her reflection in one of the gilt-framed mirrors and wiped a smut from the tip of her nose. It seemed as if time had stood still while she waited for the footman to return, but eventually he reappeared and showed her to the morning parlour. Moments later Piers entered the room. He took in her appearance with raised eyebrows.

'What's brought you here so early, and in such a state of disarray?'

'I had to see you, Piers. I need your help or I wouldn't have presumed on your good nature.'

He stared at her, unsmiling. 'You didn't seem to think much of my good nature at our last meeting. You led me to think I was the last man on earth you wanted to associate with.'

'That's not true. I refused your offer of marriage, but that doesn't mean I have no regard for you.'

'Sit down and tell me what you want. I haven't time to play games.'

She sank down on a chair by the fireplace. 'This isn't a game. I need to borrow some money for train fares. The children and I have to leave London before midday or Linus will have me arrested for their abduction.'

'Abduction? What nonsense.'

'Yes, of course it is. You and I both know that, but Linus is determined to ruin me.'

'Then let him have his children. If he is their father then he is their legal guardian, not you.'

'I can't allow that, Piers. He'll treat them abominably.'

'The law is on his side, Lucy.'

'He's desperate for money because of his gambling. He'll take my home from me to pay his debts, and then he'll lose the house in Albemarle Street and Marriott Park. There'll be nothing left.'

Piers gave her a long look. 'What do you want me to do?'

'I need money to get us away from London. I'll repay you as soon as possible. It's just a loan, only

I didn't know who else to turn to.'

'What about your friend Lieutenant Southwood? I thought you two were close.'

'Bram is an old friend, that's all.'

'Dora will be pleased to hear that. She was quite smitten by his charms.'

Lucy leapt to her feet. 'Are you prepared to help me or not?'

He stood up slowly, reaching out to brush back a lock of her hair that had fallen across her forehead. 'I'll do more than that. I'll take you all in my carriage, but on one condition.'

'Anything, Piers. Name your price.'

'That you agree to become my wife. I've fought against it, heaven knows, but my feelings for you haven't changed, and if this is the only way to win your hand in marriage, so be it.'

She stared at him, shocked by his proposal, which could not have come easily to a proud man like Piers. 'But I don't love you.'

'You did once.'

'I thought I did, but I was mistaken.' She stood up. 'I'm sorry, but it wouldn't work. We'd end up hating each other.'

He moved to the door and opened it. 'Then I can't help you.'

She walked out of the room. There was nothing left between them, not even friendship. Dry-eyed and saddened, she was about to leave the house when she heard Dora calling her. She stopped and turned to see her friend hurrying across the entrance hall. 'Wait. Please wait, Lucy.'

'I can't stop, Dora. I have to leave London by midday.'

'But why? I don't understand what's going on. Piers looks like thunder and now you tell me you're going away.'

'It's Linus. He's the cause of it. You'll have to ask Piers because I must go.'

Dora caught her by the sleeve. 'Why did you come here if it wasn't to see me?'

'I'm not proud of myself. I came to borrow money from your brother because he's the only person I could think of to ask. I have to take the children to a place of safety and I can't raise the train fare.'

Dora's eyes widened and her pretty mouth formed a circle of surprise. 'You're running away?'

'I haven't got time for this. I have to go, Dora.'

'Wait.' Dora put her hand in her pocket. 'I have a guinea. It's the last of my allowance and I was going to spend it on a new bonnet, but your need is greater than mine.' She pressed it into Lucy's hand. 'I don't know how far it will get you, but it's all I have.'

Lucy kissed her on the cheek. 'Thank you. I'll pay you back as soon as I can, and now I really must go.'

'Good luck,' Dora called after her.

Lucy arrived in Leman Street with little time to spare. She had walked to Charing Cross and caught the Bow omnibus which dropped her off in Whitechapel. It had been an extravagance, but the minutes were flying by and she needed to get home quickly. Bedwin was waiting for her in the hall with the children. Bertie met her with a frown. 'Why do I have to go? I've lost my job because of this, and I was getting on well in the bakery.'

Breathless from running, Lucy met his surly gaze with a straight look. 'Perhaps you'd rather go and live with your pa. I'm sure he'd have plenty of work for you to do.'

Maggie began to cry and Vicky put her arm around her sister's shoulder. 'It's an adventure, Mags. We're going back to the country. You remember our little cottage in the forest? It will be just like that.'

Hester appeared from the depths of the house carrying a wicker basket. 'I've brought food for the journey and something for your supper. You'd best make haste or the coppers will be here and it will be too late.'

'Hold on a moment.' Pearl came racing down the stairs preceded by a cloud of cigarette smoke. 'I've got three bob you can have, Lucy.' She thrust her hand in her pocket and produced the coins.

Bedwin picked up the largest of the cases. 'Mr Rossman contributed five shillings towards our fares.'

'And Gilbert added a half-crown,' Hester said, blushing rosily. 'He's taking me to the music hall on Saturday.'

Lucy gave her a hug. 'Take care of everything while I'm away. I don't know when we'll return but I hope it won't be too long. You will tell Bram where we've gone, won't you?'

'Of course I will, and he'll sort everything out. You can rely on Bramwell.'

Bedwin stepped outside. 'Best be quick, Miss Lucy. I can see a blue uniform heading this way.'

It was late afternoon by the time they arrived at Marriott Park. The children were subdued, the excitement at travelling on a train for the first time having worn off after waiting over an hour for a connection, and suffering the discomfort of travelling third class on a branch line where the train stopped at every station. They had walked the mile or so from the station in the blistering heat and were now hot, tired and crotchety.

'Where are we?' demanded Bertie, running his finger round the inside of his stiff white collar. 'Why have we stopped here, Mr Bedwin? It's the middle of nowhere.'

Bedwin dumped the cases on the ground, took off his top hat and mopped his brow. 'We've reached our destination. Or I should say we're close to the gatehouse where Lugg lives.'

'Slug,' Maggie said, giggling. 'It's a good name for a gardener.'

Lucy smiled and gave her a hug. 'Don't let him hear you calling him that, darling. We're going to depend on Mr Lugg to keep us safe, and he might refuse to take us in. After all, he depends on Linus for his livelihood.'

'What's a livelihood?' Maggie asked, puzzled.

'Don't be silly, Mags.' Vicky took off her bonnet and dangled it by its strings. 'I'm tired, Lucy. Is it much further?'

Lucy sent a questioning look to Bedwin. 'Is it far?'

He picked up the cases. 'See that gap in the hedgerow? The gates are set back from the lane. You could ride past and not know they were there. Come along, it's just a step or two now.'

They followed him, the children dragging their feet and Lucy trying to put a brave face on things, although she was close to exhaustion herself. Each time the train pulled into a station she had peered out of the window, half expecting to see policemen waiting to board and make an arrest. Even now she was still anxious. Their safety depended upon Lugg, and if he took against the idea of sheltering them they would have nowhere to go.

She came to a halt behind Bedwin and was surprised to see tall wrought-iron gates with the family crest worked into the ornate design. Through the metal scrolls she could just make out the house itself, although it seemed far distant at the end of a tree-lined avenue. The copper beeches were at their most magnificent and if she had been a visitor to Marriott Park she would have been impressed, but as it was all she could think about was Lugg and his reaction when Bedwin explained why they had come. He rang the bell and they waited. Eventually a man emerged from the gatehouse, shrugging on his jacket. He peered at Bedwin, squinting in the sunlight, his bushy grey eyebrows meeting over the bridge of his bulbous nose. Lucy was forcibly reminded of the stone gargoyles at Westminster Abbey, but she managed to keep a straight face.

'Don't you recognise me, Ron? Frank Bedwin.'

Bertie sniggered and Vicky giggled, receiving a warning look from Lucy. 'Hush. Remember your manners.'

'Frank,' Maggie murmured. 'I didn't know Bedwin had another name.'

'Shh.' Lucy laid a hand on her shoulder. 'Be polite.'

'Frank, is it really you?' Lugg opened the gates and they trooped into the grounds. He stared at Lucy and the children. 'Is this your wife and nippers, Frank?'

Bedwin took him by the arm and marched him into the gatehouse, leaving the others standing outside.

'I call that rude,' Vicky said crossly. 'I'm thirsty and I want a drink of water.'

'A glass of ale would go down better,' Bertie said loudly.

'When have you had beer to drink?' Lucy demanded.

'We have a pint at the end of the day. It's hot work.'

Lucy was saved from replying by the re-emergence of Bedwin and his friend, who seemed to be on the best of terms. Bedwin was smiling, which happened so infrequently that it made Lucy look again to make sure it was not a grimace of pain or indigestion. 'Well?' she said urgently. 'What's happening?'

'Ron says you're welcome to stay as long as you like, provided you don't bother him.'

'Aye,' Lugg said, nodding. 'I don't hold with kids and I ain't no housekeeper, but as long as you look after yourselves it don't matter to me. The house needs airing and you can earn your keep by doing a bit of spring cleaning. It'll save me getting a woman in to do the work.'

'You might lose your job if Mr Daubenay finds out you gave us shelter.' Lucy felt compelled to warn him, although he seemed oblivious of the risk he was taking.

He shrugged. 'I ain't gonna tell him, and he never shows his face here. Just keep to yourselves and don't go wandering down to the village, because they're a pack of busybodies.'

Bedwin retrieved the cases he had left on the path. 'Come along then, everyone. Lugg has given me the key. Let's see what state the old place is in.'

It must, Lucy thought, be a good half a mile from the gates to the main entrance, but the trees created welcome shade and they walked on with renewed energy. The parkland surrounding the house was overgrown and ablaze with buttercups and dandelions. The long grass was studded with the cool white faces of moon daisies and brightly painted butterflies floated above them like scraps of coloured tissue paper. Wild deer grazed beneath splendid old oak trees and the air was filled with birdsong. Lucy fell in love with the house at first sight. The starkly elegant lines of Palladian architecture pleased her eye, and the tall windows reflected the sunlight, making the house seem warm and welcoming.

Bedwin unlocked the door and let them into the vast entrance hall. It was cool inside but a musty smell lingered and dust motes danced in the sunbeams that filtered through the grimy windowpanes. Their footsteps echoed off the high ceilings and their subdued voices came back to them in eerie whispers, as though the spirits of past occupants were hovering above them. Seemingly oblivious to anything supernatural, Bedwin marched on, opening doors which led into large rooms with furniture shrouded in dustsheets. 'Where are we going?' Maggie asked plaintively. 'My feet hurt and I'm thirsty.'

'Me too,' Vicky added.

'The kitchen and butler's pantry are at the back of the house,' Bedwin announced like a tour guide. 'We need to get a fire going in the range and hope the chimney isn't blocked by birds' nests and the like.'

'It's too hot for a fire,' Vicky said in a low voice.

'We need hot water and I'm dying for a cup of tea,' Lucy said, trying to make light of their situation. She felt at home in the house but she could quite understand why the children found the old building a little daunting. The long corridors were dark and cold after the heat outside and the house felt sad and unloved. She longed to bring it back to life and allow the ghosts of the past to rest in peace. She had never known Grandmother Marriott, but she could feel her presence in every room. She quickened her pace in order to catch up with Bedwin.

The kitchen was huge, with one wall taken up by the ingle nook beneath which was an ancient but serviceable cast-iron range. Bedwin shook his head. 'We'll get a fire going and hope for the best.' He beckoned to Bertie. 'Come outside and I'll show you where they used to keep the coal and kindling; there might be some left.' He opened a door which led into a scullery. Bertie followed him, grumbling.

'There's a bread oven,' Vicky said excitedly. 'Bertie's a baker now. He can make fresh bread every day.'

Maggie ran round opening cupboard doors. 'There's nothing to eat.'

'If there was I think it would be very mouldy by now,' Lucy said, chuckling. She placed the wicker basket containing the remains of their food on the scrubbed pine table. 'Let's see what we've got.'

Bertie rushed into the room with an armful of kindling and Bedwin followed more slowly with a bucket of coal. Between them they managed to get the fire going in the range and the tired old kitchen came to life. Vicky and Maggie found the china cupboard and drawers filled with cutlery, exclaiming with delight at each new find. Lucy smiled to herself as she filled the kettle and placed it on the range. She had become adept at managing with one hand, although it was frustrating to be hampered by having her arm in a sling. She sighed. At least they were safe for the time being, and what possible harm could come to them in the country?

After a simple supper of bread and cheese, Lucy and Bedwin sat drinking tea while the children went outside to explore the grounds.

'Listen to them,' Lucy said, cocking her head on one side. 'They sound as though they're having a wonderful time. I'd almost forgotten that they were brought up in the country; this must seem like coming home to them.'

Bedwin sipped his tea. 'Lugg said he'd get supplies for you and I gave him what was left of the money, but it won't last more than a few days.'

'I know,' Lucy said, frowning. 'I was trying not to think about that. I was hoping that Bram would join us soon.'

'I'll have to return to London in the morning. That'll be one mouth less to feed.'

'You're leaving us here?'

Bedwin's expression remained stony. 'You don't need me, Miss Lucy. But you can't expect Mrs Gant to manage the housekeeping and look after the gentlemen lodgers on her own. You can't count Pearl because she's either asleep or at the vicarage or in the pub with that Carlos.'

'I'm sorry you're going, but you mustn't worry about us,' Lucy said, trying hard to sound convincing. 'You're right. Hester needs you.'

'When Mr Daubenay finds out that you've taken the children away he'll try to make her tell him where you've gone, and I don't think she'd be able to stand up to him alone.'

'Poor Hester. I hadn't thought of that.'

'I'm not afraid of Mr Daubenay. He won't get anything out of me.'

'Of course you must return to London. We'll be fine here,' Lucy said, with more conviction than she was feeling.

Chapter Twenty-One

Every day Lucy awakened in the elegantly furnished but now faded glory of the bedchamber that had once belonged to her grandmother. Everything, from the damask curtains on the four-poster bed to the silver-backed hairbrush and hand mirror on the burr-walnut dressing table, had been left untouched since Lady Marriott's passing. The perfume in the cut-glass bottles had long since evaporated but the scents lingered, as if the lady herself had just left the room. Her gowns remained in the clothes press, with sachets of dried lavender laid between the folds. Lucy had been tempted to try them on, but to do so had felt wrong, as if she were disrespecting her grandmother's memory. She fell asleep at night, trying to picture the face of the woman who had held her in her arms when she was a baby, and in her dreams she conjured up an image of the woman whose gentle smile told her that she had indeed come home. In the days and weeks that followed the first night when Bedwin had shown her to the room, telling her that she was mistress of Marriott Park no matter what Mr Daubenay thought or said, Lucy felt she had come to know her grandmother. Now, a month later, they existed from day to day by foraging in the countryside for anything that was remotely edible. Lugg had taken Bertie under his wing and had taught him how to snare rabbits and prepare them for the pot. He showed him what wild plants and fungi could be eaten and how to distinguish those that would do them harm. Lugg was not a particularly sociable man, but he was generous with the produce he grew in the kitchen garden, and always willing to lend a hand with tasks that were too heavy for Bertie to manage on his own.

The money had run out after a few days and Bram had not put in an appearance. Lucy had not worried at first, but after a couple of weeks she had begun to feel anxious and now she was frantic for news. It was growing harder to conceal her fears from the young ones, and Bertie was hardly a child now. With Lugg as his mentor he seemed to have grown from a boy to a man in a surprisingly short space of time. He loved nothing better than to go out hunting and was becoming adept at fishing in the river that ran through the estate. Their diet of rabbit stew was supplemented by freshly caught trout and salmon, and utilising Bertie's newly acquired baking skills Lugg supplied the flour for bread making on condition that he was kept supplied with loaves.

The children were tanned and healthy, roaming the grounds and surrounding countryside while taking care to avoid being seen in the village. It might be an idyllic existence for them, but Lucy was going out of her mind with worry. Something might have happened to Bram, she thought one night when she woke in the early hours and sleep evaded her. She lay in the four-poster bed, staring up at the faded tester with unseeing eyes. Anything could have happened in her absence, but there must be some good reason why he had seemingly abandoned them. Perhaps he had fallen for Dora's charms, or maybe his fellow officer had reneged on his promise to purchase Bram's commission. She was growing more and more frustrated by her inability to contact those at home, especially Mr Goldspink. She could, of course, send a telegram, but that would mean going into the village, which was out of the question. It was a nail-biting situation and one that she could not discuss with the children. The only good thing to come out of this enforced rustication was that her arm was virtually healed.

Wide awake now, she knew that she would not sleep another wink and she rose from her comfortable feather bed. She had not bothered to draw the curtains and a shaft of moonlight created a silver path on the worn Persian carpet, leading her to the open window. The sweet scent of the climbing roses and honeysuckle wafted in on a gentle breeze and towards the east a faint glow in the sky showed the promise of dawn. It would be another fine summer day, hot and sunny and filled with hope at the start, but how would it end? She leaned her arms on the windowsill, cupping her chin in her hands. The avenue of copper beeches was just emerging from the darkness and the trees seemed to float on a cloud of morning mist. The view was romantic and yet hauntingly sad. Her father would have roamed the grounds as a boy, just as Bertie did now. This was the closest she would ever be to the parent she had never known, and she had given up hope of being reunited with her mother. She sighed, and was about to turn away when she heard the sound of a horse's hooves on the gravel drive.

She was suddenly alert. Dreams banished and imagination put in its place, she clutched the windowsill for support. Her heart was racing, and she was about to run and warn the children that their hiding place had been discovered, when the rider came closer. He drew the animal to a halt on the carriage sweep and looked up. 'Bram.' She uttered his name on a sigh of relief and raced from the room, pausing to snatch up her wrap, shrugging it on as she went. She reached the front entrance and wrenched the door open before he had a chance to knock. 'Bram, thank God it's you.'

'Lucy, are you all right?' He stepped over the threshold and enveloped her in a warm embrace. 'I'm sorry I couldn't get here sooner.'

She wrapped her arms around his waist, hugging him. His clothes were damp and imbued with the smell of horse, leather and his own personal scent that was both familiar and comforting. In a confusion of emotions she pushed him away, anger momentarily overcoming relief and the joy of seeing him again. 'Where have you been all this time? I was expecting you weeks ago.'

'Your arm must have healed,' he said, grinning. 'I see you've got your strength back.'

It was impossible to be angry with him for long and a gurgle of laughter escaped her lips. 'You say the nicest things, but I forgive you for being boorish because I'm so pleased to see you. Come through to the kitchen and I'll get the fire going. We'll have a cup of tea and you can tell me your news. I've been going mad stuck here with no idea of what's going on.'

'If you'll stop gabbling for a moment, I'll tell you everything,' he said, chuckling. 'But first I need to stable the old nag I bought for twice his worth because the gypsy dealer could see that I was desperate.'

'I'll show you where to take him.'

He glanced down at her bare feet. 'I expect I can find the stables. Just point me in the right direction.'

'The coach house and stable block are at the back of the house. I'll go through and open the scullery door. Come in that way.'

He brushed her cheek with a kiss. 'I've missed you, Lucy.'

'You wretch. You always know the right thing to say.' She stopped to light a candle, holding it high so that she could see his face. 'You look tired. Have you ridden all night?'

'Not quite, but I'll explain later. Anyway, I'm used to keeping odd hours. It's part of being a soldier.' He opened the door and disappeared into the grey light of early dawn.

Lucy's relief was so great that she felt as if she was floating and her feet barely touched the cold flagstones as she hurried to the kitchen. She unbolted the scullery door and set about riddling the ashes in the range and laying a fire. She had just put a match to the kindling when Bram strolled into the room. She sat back on her haunches. 'Now you can tell me what's been happening at home.'

He pulled up a chair and sat down. 'I had to wait for the chap who wanted my commission to pay up, and he took his time. I didn't get away from camp until several days ago, but I went straight to Goldspink and settled up with him. After that I went to Leman Street and Bedwin told me where to find you.'

'How are they? Is Hester managing without me?'

'Hester could have taught the Iron Duke a few things about military strategy. She's coping well and so is Bedwin.'

'Thank goodness for that. I didn't like leaving them.' Lucy concentrated on getting the fire going. 'What about Pearl?'

'She's moved into the vicarage as housekeeper. She's a respected member of the community or so she'd have me believe, but Hester told me that she still slips out to the pub every now and then, and she goes into the back yard for a smoke when the parson isn't looking.'

'How like Pearl.' Lucy eyed him curiously. 'You managed to evade Linus, then?'

'He didn't dare take me on personally, the coward, but he'd been pestering them in Leman Street, trying to discover your whereabouts. They sent him off with a flea in his ear, but he's not one to give up easily, especially when he's desperate for money.'

'I've been so frustrated, but I couldn't do anything or go anywhere for fear of being seen. Linus would take great pleasure in evicting us if he discovered our whereabouts.' Lucy scrambled to her feet, brushing the ash from her skirt. 'Did Mr Goldspink give you any idea when Granny might be released? It must be soon.'

'I was coming to that, Lucy. His appeal was successful and she's a free woman.'

'That's wonderful, but where is she? Who's looking after her?'

'Don't panic, Lucy. Eva's with Froniga.'

Lucy sat down suddenly as her knees gave way beneath her. 'I don't understand.'

'Goldspink suggested that it might be best if he and I went to the prison to meet Eva. He said that in his experience newly released prisoners needed time to readjust to their changed circumstances.'

'But it should have been me,' Lucy said, shaking her head. 'I should have been there for her.'

'Goldspink warned me that she might be in a bad way, and of course I knew you'd want to look after her, but you have the children to care for. Then I thought of the gypsy woman who'd helped you find her, so I took the train to Chelmsford and discovered that the circus had moved on to Colchester. Anyway, to cut a long story short I found Froniga and explained the situation. She agreed to accompany us to the prison, and it's just as well she did because Eva was in a bit of a state.'

'At least she's free from that dreadful place.' Lucy's breath hitched on a sob of relief. 'Where did Froniga take her?'

'They're safe in Colchester. I didn't dare risk bringing her here because there was a chance that Linus might have tracked you down.'

Lucy jumped to her feet and flung her arms

around his neck. 'I can't believe you've done all this for me, Bram. I'll never be able to thank you enough.'

He held her close, smiling down at her. 'It was what anyone would do for a dear friend.'

'A dear friend, of course,' she said slowly. 'That's what you are to me, and I to you.' She curved her lips into a smile. This was not how she had imagined their reunion would be. Bram seemed distant, despite his outward show of cheerfulness, and there was a wary look in his eyes. Something had changed between them, but she was at a loss to know why.

The kettle was bubbling merrily on the hob and she moved away. 'I'll make some tea,' she said, avoiding his gaze. 'You must be hungry. There's bread in the crock. Bertie is very good at baking and I'm learning to cook, although it doesn't always turn out as I'd wish.' She was babbling and she knew it, but Bram was sitting at the table watching her in silence. 'I can boil an egg for you. Lugg gives us eggs and flour in return for some of Bertie's bread.'

'A cup of tea will be fine. I'll eat later.'

She filled two cups and placed one in front of him, taking a seat on the opposite side of the table. 'Was Granny very upset and confused?'

'Froniga thinks she'll recover in time.'

Lucy could stand it no longer. She looked him in the eye. 'What aren't you telling me, Bram?'

'I met some of your friends in the circus.'

'I had quite a lot of acquaintances. I wouldn't say they were all friends.'

'Monty wanted to know when you were going

to return.'

'I did say I'd go back when my arm healed, but I'm not a performer. It was just a way to earn some money. After all, I had to live, and I hoped to raise the money to pay Mr Goldspink.'

'He's paid in full.'

She was suddenly angry. 'What's the matter? Why are you looking at me like that?'

'I also met Stella. She told me all about your affair with Monty.'

'What?'

'She said that you and he were lovers. I can't put it any plainer.'

'And you believed her?' Lucy leapt to her feet. 'That woman tried to kill me. She caused my accident, and it wasn't the first time she'd tried to get rid of me.'

'She said you took her place in the ring as well as in his affections.'

'You only have to ask Froniga and she'll tell you what really happened. As to Monty, I liked him well enough, and he was good to me, but there was never anything romantic between us.'

'He's a good-looking fellow. I wouldn't blame you for taking the easy way out.'

'I should slap your silly face for saying that.' Lucy glared at him, clenching her fists at her sides. 'You are a stupid man, Bramwell Southwood. In fact, I think all men are equally idiotic.' She broke off as the door opened and Bertie strolled into the kitchen looking bleary-eyed and half asleep. He came to a halt, running his hand through his already tousled mop of hair as he stared at Bram in disbelief.

'I heard voices and I thought it was Lugg.'

Bram stood up, holding out his arms. 'It's me all right. Are you too grown-up to give your uncle a hug?'

Lucy moved away, choking back the tears that threatened to overcome her. It was not only the injustice of the accusations Stella had made against her; the fact that Bram had chosen to believe her was even more hurtful. She placed the kettle on the hob. 'I want to see Granny,' she said when she could trust herself to speak. 'As soon as the horse is rested I'll ride to Colchester.'

'It's a good ten miles,' Bram said sharply. 'You can't go alone.'

'I'm quite capable of riding that far, and I want to see Granny. You should have brought her here. Never mind Linus. I'm past caring about him.'

'You wouldn't say that if you'd seen him in a fit of temper,' Bertie said in a low voice. 'Let Bram go with you.'

'Someone must stay here with you children.' Lucy faced them angrily. 'And from what I saw of that poor old nag he'd collapse under the weight of two people. I'm going and that's that.'

Bram's brow creased into furrows and he shook his head. 'You can't go alone. I wouldn't put it past Linus to have had me followed. You wouldn't stand a chance of getting away on that poor creature.'

'Let Pa try to take me and the girls and he'll have a fight on his hands,' Bertie said, drawing himself up to his full height. 'I'm a man now and I'll look after my sisters.'

'Of course you will.' Lucy patted him on the

shoulder. 'And I'm proud of you, Bertie.' She turned to Bram. 'If you'd lend me the money to repay Linus the sixty guineas I could go home and take Granny and the children with me.'

He shook his head. 'Sit down, Lucy. I wanted to give you the good news first, that Eva is safe and in good hands, but the real reason I took so long to get here is that Linus sent the bailiffs into the house in Leman Street soon after you'd left. He's taking you to court in an attempt to bankrupt you so that he can seize your assets. I gave Goldspink the money to repay him but he rejected the offer.'

'You said that Hester and Bedwin were coping well. Why did you lie to me?' Lucy gazed at him in horror. 'But why would he do such a thing?'

'They are managing well, and they're still in residence, but they're fully aware of what Linus intends. As I understand it his debts are crippling. I heard that he's already lost the house in Albemarle Street, and this one will be next. He's a desperate man who'll stop at nothing. Even if I gave him the money I received from selling my commission it wouldn't make a scrap of difference. He's virtually bankrupt and he won't be happy until he ruins the pair of us.'

Lucy sank down on the nearest chair. 'I won't let him do this. Why should he take what's mine and rob you of the money that's rightfully yours?'

'I'll knock his block off,' Bertie muttered, dancing about like a prize fighter. 'I'll take him on man to man.'

'I know you would, dear,' she said gently. 'But it's gone beyond that. What did Mr Goldspink say, Bram?'

'He said he'll do what he can. I think you should allow him to do his work, Lucy. He didn't think it wise for you to return to London just yet, given the fact that Linus will use the law to take the children from you. But I think we should leave this house before Linus's spies tell him you're here.'

Dazed, Lucy considered all the facts that had been thrust upon her. 'What will happen to Hester and Bedwin and our lodgers? Surely they won't be evicted?'

'We have to leave it to Goldspink. He might be a funny little chap, but he knows what he's doing.' Bram reached out to take her hand in his. 'There's one place we can go where Linus will never think of looking.'

They left that night. Bram and Bertie had found an ancient dog cart in the coach house and with Lugg's help they had made it roadworthy. The horse had recovered and seemed accustomed to being put between the shafts, and with Lucy seated up front and the children huddled in the back of the vehicle, Bram climbed up on the driver's seat and they set off under cover of darkness.

It was a chilly, starlit night, but Lucy had taken coverlets from the beds so that the children would be warm and comfortable and they soon fell asleep. She herself was wide awake, struggling with the reality of Linus's fall from grace and his determination to take them with him on his spiralling descent into bankruptcy and disgrace.

'You mustn't worry,' Bram said as if reading her

thoughts. 'You can trust Goldspink. He's a good man.'

'But Linus isn't. He's cruel and he's devious, and for some reason he wants to ruin us all.'

'Let's hope his creditors get him before he can do any more harm. In the meantime you and the nippers will be safe with the circus folk. Froniga will see to that, and you can look after Eva.' He shot her a sideways glance. 'I'm sure Monty will be glad to have you back.'

'I'll ignore that last comment,' Lucy said with dignity. 'I didn't have much choice in the matter when I was with the circus, but I did enjoy the applause and the rush of excitement before the grand parade. Perhaps I take after my mother after all.'

'Goldspink said you'd asked him if he could find out anything about her.'

'She can't have disappeared without a trace. She must be somewhere.'

'How old were you when she left?'

'Two.'

'A lot can happen in nineteen years.'

'I know, but I can always hope.'

Their progress was slow and they had to stop several times to allow the horse to drink from a nearby pond or stream and rest his ageing bones. Lucy dozed a little, waking suddenly to find herself leaning against Bram's shoulder. He seemed tireless, but eventually as the sun rose in a cloudless sky they approached the field where the big top loomed above the caravans, tents and wagons. Already there were signs of life as wood smoke billowed upwards from newly lit camp fires. The animals were restive in their cages, waiting to be fed and watered, and sleepy-looking artistes, tenters and trainers were beginning to emerge and begin their daily routine.

Froniga's tent had been set up a short distance from the others: Lucy left Bram and the children to wait by the entrance as she hurried across the tussocky grass. She lifted the flap slowly. 'Froniga? Can I come in?'

Froniga was already up and dressed. She emerged to give Lucy a warm embrace. 'You've come. I knew you would.'

Lucy glanced anxiously over her shoulder. 'How is she?'

'Still sleeping. She sleeps a lot, but then that's to be expected. The poor soul is worn to the bone after her experiences in prison. She should never have been put there in the first place.'

'Is she ill?'

'Not in body, but the spirit seems to have gone from her. Perhaps seeing you will bring her back to her normal self. Have you come to take her home?'

'There might be a bit of a problem,' Lucy said softly. 'I'll tell you all about it, but first I want you to meet my young charges. They're tired because we've been travelling all night, but they're very excited to be here. I hope Monty doesn't mind.'

'Mind what?' Monty's voice behind her made Lucy spin round to face him.

'I didn't hear you coming.'

'I tread like a panther when I want to.' He held out his hand. 'Welcome home, Lucy. I see your arm is healed. Are you ready to perform again?'

She managed a weary smile. 'I don't think so, but I have a favour to ask.'

'Perhaps it would be better if you came to my caravan.' Monty glanced at Bram and the children. 'Bring your family with you.'

Seated on the grass outside the Charters' van, the children took in their new surroundings wide-eyed and silent, but Lucy suspected that at any moment their excitement might bubble over into a torrent of questions and requests. Bertram had welcomed them cordially and he sat in his chair like a king on his throne, ruling his small world with dignity and good humour. 'You are welcome to remain with us for as long as you like, but as Lucy knows, everyone has to pitch in and do their bit.'

Bram nodded enthusiastically. 'I've just left the hussars, sir. I'm more than happy to work with the horses and help in any way I can.'

Monty had been leaning against the side of the van but this last remark seemed to catch his attention. 'You'll be an excellent horseman, of course.'

'Tolerably so, sir.'

Monty turned to his father. 'We might have an addition to the act, Father. I have an idea that would suit both Bram and Lucy.'

Vicky raised her hand as if she were in the classroom. 'Please, sir. I'd like to wear a spangled dress and be in the circus too.'

'And me,' Maggie added eagerly.

'I could be a clown or a strong man,' Bertie volunteered. 'And I'm a good baker too.'

Bertram reached over to ruffle Bertie's hair. 'Well, my boy, we might make use of your talents, and there's always work to do.' He glanced at his son. 'They'll need a tent, Monty. Have we any spare?'

'I'm sure I can find something suitable, Father.' Monty beckoned to the children. 'Come with me. I'll show you round and you can give me a hand.' He turned to give Bram a cursory look. 'You too, soldier. Setting up a tent is man's work.'

'It won't be the first time I've done it,' Bram said grimly. 'I've spent most of my career living under canvas.'

Lucy found herself left alone with Bertram. 'I hope Stella doesn't get the wrong idea again,' she said in a low voice. 'I don't want to cause an upset.'

'Stella will do as she's told, my dear.' Bertram gave her a reassuring smile. 'And I hope you might be persuaded to perform again. Pretty girls in fancy costumes are always a hit with audiences, especially the men.'

Lucy stood up. 'Thank you, Mr Charter. I'll think about it.'

'And I can see that you're eager to be reunited with your grandmother. I hear that she's making steady progress, although it's early days yet.'

'You know about her?'

'My dear, I know everything that occurs in our tiny world.'

Lucy hurried back to the tent, arriving just as Froniga was helping Eva to get dressed. She hesitated. 'Granny, it's me, Lucy.'

Leaning on Froniga, Eva turned her head

slowly. Her eyes, which had once burned with the lust for life, were dull and expressionless, sunken and underlined with dark circles. Her once rosy cheeks were ashen and her fiery curls were streaked with grey. She stared at Lucy as if trying to place her.

'It's your granddaughter, Eva,' Froniga said gently.

Eva shook her head. 'Lucy is ten years old. She can't be my little girl.'

Lucy slipped her hand inside her blouse and pulled out the locket. Unfastening the chain, she held it up for Eva to see. 'I am still your little girl, but I've grown up now. You gave me this on my eleventh birthday, Granny. You left it for me at the house in Albemarle Street. Don't you remember?'

Chapter Twenty-Two

Eva snatched the locket and chain, clutching it in her hand. 'You stole it from the child. It's Lucy's.'

Froniga pressed her down on the pile of cushions. 'A nice cup of tea is what you need, my dear.' She sent Lucy a warning look. 'The kettle's boiling.'

'I'll see to it.' Lucy backed out of the tent, her dreams of a blissful reunion shattered. Somehow she managed to make a pot of tea without scalding herself, but her hand shook as she passed a cup to Eva. 'I remember how you like it, Granny.

Strong and sweet with two sugars.'

Eva snatched the cup, spilling some of the hot tea on the grass. 'Ta,' she muttered, taking a sip. 'It's better than the stuff they give you in clink.'

Froniga gave Lucy an encouraging smile. 'Why don't you sit with Eva for a while? She might feel like talking when she's had her drink. I'll go and see if Jenny has any bread to spare.'

'We had gruel for breakfast in jail,' Eva muttered. 'It was pigswill. I ain't going back there, not ever.'

'Of course not. I'll look after you now. You're safe.' Lucy struggled to control the tears that burned her eyes. Her throat ached, but she was determined not to cry. She must be strong or she would not be able to rescue this broken woman from the hell she still inhabited. She slipped her arm around Eva's shoulders. 'It's all right, Granny. I've come to take you home, but first we must get you better.'

Eva gulped her tea. 'I sold my girl for fifteen pounds. I deserve to be punished.' She tossed the tin cup out of the tent and threw herself back on the cushions in a storm of weeping. Lucy sat beside her, at a loss as to how to comfort her.

After what seemed like an eternity, Froniga returned bringing bread, butter and jam. She glanced at Eva, shaking her head. 'She's been like this ever since we brought her here. Leave her, Lucy. She'll quieten down in a while and then she'll sleep.'

Lucy rose from the floor and followed Froniga outside. The sun was warm on her face and the air was fresh and clean, in contrast to the stuffiness inside the tent. 'Will she get better? I can't bear seeing her like this.'

'I don't know, my duck. They say that time heals all so you'll have to wait and see. She needs rest, good food and quiet. This isn't perhaps the best place for her.' Froniga sat cross-legged on the ground, placing the bread on a small plank of wood and producing a knife as if from nowhere. She chuckled. 'It was in my pocket. I don't dare leave anything sharp in the tent in case Eva decides to go on the rampage.'

Lucy sat down beside her. 'She isn't violent.'

'I haven't found her so, but you never know. She's had to fight for every crumb of food and sip of water while she was inside. Who knows what she suffered.'

'Well, I'll look after her from now on. But, as I said earlier, there's a problem.'

Froniga put her head on one side, pausing with the knife poised. 'I don't need my crystal ball to tell me that the problem might be your cousin.'

'He mustn't find us or he'll take the children. He's trying to have me declared bankrupt so that my house is forfeit. He's already sold the one in Albemarle Street, and Marriott Park will be next, because he's lost everything at the gaming tables.'

Froniga buttered a slice of bread and handed it to her. 'Help yourself to jam. Jenny makes it herself and sells it. We'll save the rest for that man of yours and the nippers.'

'He's not my man,' Lucy said, spreading jam on her bread. 'Bram is just a friend.'

'Hmm.' Froniga took a bite of food, saying nothing.

In the end two smallish tents were found and erected: one for Bram and Bertie and the other for Lucy and the girls. It was decided that Eva was best left in Froniga's care and she herself was not in any state to have an opinion. Acting on an appeal by Bertram, the circus people rallied around to find palliasses and blankets, donating other small comforts which they thought might make the tents more homely.

Everyone seemed pleased to see Lucy, with the exception of Stella, who made it clear that nothing had changed. She caught up with her outside the big top where Bram was about to show Monty what he could do. 'I know what you're up to,' she hissed. 'Monty's mine, so hands off.'

'I see you haven't changed,' Lucy said coldly.

Stella's expression altered subtly as Bram approached, leading the horse that Monty had selected for him. She sidled up to him, fluttering her long lashes. 'Welcome to the circus, soldier. We were in desperate need of a strong handsome man like you.'

Bram acknowledged her with a nod of his head. 'How do you do, ma'am.'

'Oh, you are so polite.' Stella trilled with laughter. 'We have a gentleman in our midst. How refreshing. I'll see you later, soldier.' She sashayed away to join Dario, who was eyeing them with an ominous frown.

Bram met Lucy's amused gaze with a shrug of his shoulders.

'I thought you might fall for her,' she whispered. 'Most men do. Dario has his work cut out fending off her admirers.'

'He won't have any fending to do when it comes to me.' Bram tightened the girth and adjusted the stirrup leathers. 'I've no intention of being lured into her web of intrigue and romantic trysts. I can see what type of woman she is and she's poison. Keep away from her.'

'That's easy to say, but very hard to accomplish when you live and work so close together.'

He vaulted into the saddle. 'I'm not sure about this, Lucy. I'm a soldier, not a circus performer.'

'We have to pay our way,' she said, stroking the horse's neck. 'And we have to live somewhere until Linus gives up his rights to the children. I'm not afraid of being poor again, although I'd hate to lose my house in Leman Street.'

'We have to let Goldspink do his job. If Linus continues the way he is at present he'll bankrupt himself and he won't want to be saddled with three youngsters. At least, that's what I hope might happen.'

'I'm not sure he'll ever leave us alone, Bram. I don't know why he hates me so, but I don't think he'll stop until he sees me back in the gutter.'

'I'll worry about him later.' Bram glanced over his shoulder. 'This is where I go into the ring and show Monty a thing or two. I'd like to see him ride into battle.'

'Don't upset him, Bram. He's our bread and butter for the time being, and at least you don't have to wear a hideous pink velvet riding habit.' She looked round as Monty rode up to them, his horse snorting and prancing as if eager to be in the ring.

'Are you ready, Bram? Let's see you go through your paces.' He gave Lucy a searching look. 'Are you sure you're fit enough to join us?'

Out of the corner of her eye she caught sight of Stella, who was watching them intently, and her mind was made up. 'Yes, of course, Monty. I'll go and change.'

The children settled into circus life as if they had been born to it, and Bram adapted to the change in his circumstances with the fortitude of a man used to surviving in far harsher conditions than a field outside Colchester. It was Lucy who found things increasingly difficult. She had managed well enough before, but now she had her grandmother to think about as well as the children's well-being. She missed Marriott Park more than she had thought possible, and the weeks they had spent there seemed like halcyon days compared to the frenetic life of the circus people. The only consolation was that they were relatively safe, and Eva was beginning to show signs of improvement. As each day passed she grew physically stronger, and the confusion that had addled her brains had begun to recede. But she still clung to the belief that Lucy was ten years old, and refused to part with the locket.

Froniga was ever patient with her charge, putting up with the occasional tantrum and soothing her when the horrors of her past experiences came back to haunt her. Lucy was grateful but saddened by what she saw. The vivid memories of her childhood and her vivacious, fun-loving grandmother seemed like a distant dream. Eva was locked away in the world she had invented for herself when reality became too much for her to bear.

Even as one problem began to lessen, another and more dangerous situation arose. Monty was ever more attentive these days. It might, Lucy thought, be his competitive spirit that made him determined to win her from Bram, whom he obviously considered to be his rival. She avoided being alone with him, which was not difficult in the general run of things. Space and solitude were luxuries that most circus folk had to do without, and living in a close-knit community had advantages as well as disadvantages. Lucy knew only too well that every compliment Monty paid her and the small privileges he allowed her never went unseen. Stella was always there, lurking in the shadows, watching, and waiting her chance to pounce. At times Lucy felt like a sparrow being stalked by a particularly vicious cat. A momentary lack of concentration might prove to be her downfall. She did not think Stella would make the mistake of trying to kill her a second time, but a crippling accident might occur at any moment in the dangerous world of the circus ring. The sooner they could return to London, the better. Lucy sent a letter to Yorick Goldspink, informing him of their whereabouts and asking him to keep her informed of his progress. She also wrote, against Bram's advice, to Hester and Bedwin, giving them a progress report and ending with the fervent hope that she would be able to come home soon.

At the end of the month, just when everyone had settled into a comfortable routine, they had to uproot themselves, pack all their belongings and make ready to move on to the next location. This time they were heading for Braintree, some ten miles distant, which entailed a full day's travel, added to which was the exhausting business of dismantling the big top. It then had to be packed on several wagons together with the tents and other equipment, and all this done at night to ensure an early start next day.

After a gruelling few hours and very little sleep, it was finally time to leave. Bertie was to be allowed to drive the dog cart, taking Froniga, Eva, Vicky and Maggie, while Lucy and Bram rode the horses they used in their act. It was a slow procession, led by Monty on horseback and his father driving their caravan. The others fell into line behind them, with the elephants and their trainer bringing up the rear. It was cool at the start but it grew progressively hotter as the sun rose higher in the sky, and they had to stop many times to allow the animals to rest and slake their thirst.

Their presence caused huge interest in the villages they passed through, and almost the whole population turned out to wave and cheer them on their way. Leaflets were handed round and the performers put on wide smiles as they invited people to come and watch the show. It was late at night by the time they arrived at their new camp site, but somehow the weary entertainers found enough energy to put up their tents and unpack their bedding. When the animals had been fed and watered and settled for the night, everyone else turned in and Lucy was no exception. She took off her sweat-soaked riding habit and tumbled into bed in her shift. Vicky and Maggie were already asleep and their gentle breathing was barely audible. Lucy drifted off, hoping that the fliers she had posted to Leman Street and to Goldspink's office would arrive safely, letting them know that the show had moved on to another town.

Next morning, after only a few hours' rest, the men were up early to erect the big top. Flags were hoisted and banners placed over the entrance to the ten acre field. Lucy was an early riser and it was no hardship for her to get up and start the fire. They had bought provisions at one of the villages on the way and as a special treat she had bacon and eggs to fry for breakfast. Soon the kettle was hanging on a tripod over the flames and bacon was sizzling in the pan. She was engrossed in her task and didn't realise anyone was there until she looked up and saw Monty standing over her.

'I was lured by the smell of bacon and the sight of a beautiful woman cooking,' he said smoothly.

She shrugged and laughed. 'You have your own food, Monty. This is for Bram and the children.'

He squatted down at her side. 'Come on, Lucy. I'm sure you can spare a slice of bread and a rasher of bacon for your boss.'

'That sounds like blackmail.'

'Gentle persuasion is a term I prefer.' He reached out to brush a lock of her hair from her cheek. 'You should make those girls do the hard work. If you were my woman I wouldn't allow you to wear yourself out in such a way.'

She shot him a wary look. 'I'm not your woman, and I like cooking for my family.'

'They could be my family too.'

'It's too early in the morning for jokes,' she said sharply. 'Haven't you got any work to do, boss?'

'You're determined to put me in my place.' He stood up, moving with feline grace. 'Perhaps this isn't the right time, but I have more to say to you, Lucy Pocket, and you will listen to me then.' He strolled off without giving her a chance to respond.

She took the pan off the fire and sat back on her haunches, watching his tall figure as he disappeared into the big top. The trouble with Monty Charter was that she never quite knew if he was teasing her or if he was serious. She hoped he had been joking; any affection she might have felt for him had dissipated like morning mist the moment she saw Bram again. Bram himself might not be aware of her feelings, but she knew that she had fallen in love with him that summer's day at Strawberry Hill pond; it had not been a childish fancy and it had not faded with the passing of the years. She was about to call the girls for breakfast when she saw her grandmother walking across the grass towards her.

'Christelle, is that you?' Eva's voice was filled with wonder and she quickened her step, coming to a sudden halt as Lucy rose to her feet. Her mouth drooped at the corners. 'You're not Christelle.'

'No, Granny. I'm Lucy, her daughter. I'm your granddaughter.'

Eva stared at her, slowly nodding her head. 'You were only ten when I last saw you, but I remember you now. That lovely hair – mine used to be just like that, and your eyes are like your mother's. I thought for a moment you were my Christelle.'

Lucy hurried to her side. 'Come and sit down, Granny. I'm just about to make a pot of tea, and there's some nice crisp bacon in the pan.'

'A cup of tea will be fine, ta.' Eva sat down obediently. 'I've been ill, haven't I?'

Lucy hooked the kettle off the tripod. 'Yes, Granny.'

'But I'm better now.' Eva fingered the locket hanging round her neck. 'I think this must be yours.'

'You brought it to the house in Albemarle Street on my eleventh birthday. I'm twenty-one now.'

'Twenty-one,' Eva mused. 'Christelle would be thirty-six. She was born in August and it was very hot. I remember it as if it were yesterday. That's what happens when you get old, dear. I can't remember much that happened recently but I remember things from years ago.'

'It's best to forget the recent past.' Lucy made the tea and set the pot aside. 'I'll let that brew for a moment. I'm afraid we haven't any milk. It goes off too quickly in this weather, but I have some sugar.'

'I was beautiful once, like you,' Eva said dreamily. 'And Christelle was lovely too. She had such a wonderful singing voice, but then she got in with that toff and everything changed.'

'Don't think about it now, Granny.' Lucy filled a tin cup with tea, and added some sugar. 'Sip this and be careful. It's hot.'

Lucy was about to crack an egg into the pan when Bram and Bertie appeared, sniffing the air like hungry hounds. They were joined by Vicky and Maggie, clamouring for food. Lucy was fully occupied and did not realise that her grandmother had gone until she turned to ask her if she wanted the last rasher of bacon. She looked round anxiously and saw her walking slowly back towards Froniga's tent.

'She's recovering,' Bram said as if reading her thoughts. 'Don't try to rush her, Lucy.'

'At least she knows me now. She thought I was my mother when she saw me this morning, but then she realised her mistake. That's a good sign, isn't it?'

He nodded. 'A very good sign, I'd say. Does anyone want the last rasher?'

Vicky scrambled to her feet. 'You're a pig, Uncle Bram.' She giggled and ducked as he tossed a clod of earth at her. 'Missed.'

'There's a stream on the far side of the field,' Lucy said hastily. 'Fetch some water, Vicky, and you can help her, Mags.'

Maggie's dark eyebrows drew together in a scowl. 'Why can't Bertie do it? He's bigger than me.'

'Because I'm going back to help put up some of the sideshows,' Bertie said, wiping his mouth on his sleeve. 'It's men's work, nipper.' He advanced on her, grinning. 'I know your ticklish places, little moppet.'

Maggie uttered a shriek and ran off after her sister, who had collected two pails and was trudging across the grass towards the stream.

Bram sandwiched the bacon between two slices of bread before rising to his feet. 'Come on then, Bertie. We'd best get back to it before Monty comes looking for us.'

'All right. I'm going.' Bertie strolled off with his hands in his pockets, whistling tunelessly.

'He's a good boy. He'd make a good soldier.' Bram met Lucy's amused gaze with a grim smile. 'Monty's working us hard, but if he thinks he can break me, he's heading for disappointment. I was toughened up in a harder school than this.'

Lucy felt a cold shiver run down her spine. She leapt to her feet and clutched Bram's sleeve. 'Be careful. These people live by their own rules.'

He paused, his smile fading. 'What has he said to you?'

'Nothing. It's just a feeling I get.'

'Come on, Lucy. I know you better than that. What passed between you two? I saw him come over here while I was helping Johann secure one of the guy ropes.'

'It isn't important. He was just flirting; he treats all the women like that.'

'If he's bothering you just say the word and I'll sort him out.'

'I can handle Monty. You needn't worry about me.'

'But I do worry about you. The only reason I'm here is because of you – and the nippers, of course,' he added hastily.

Lucy gave him a searching look. 'What are you saying?'

'I've been thinking things over and I really should return to London. Linus has been allowed to get away with too much and he should be stopped. I can't do that if I remain here.'

'He'll take your money, or what's left of it.'

Bram shook his head. 'He can bully and bluster all he wants but he won't get a penny of it. I've nothing to lose, but you have. I know how much that house in Leman Street means to you, and I don't like leaving Hester to cope on her own.'

'You're leaving us?'

He grasped both her hands. 'This business with Linus needs settling once and for all.'

'Then you must go. I'll miss you, but I can look after the children.'

'But can you look after yourself?'

'If you think you can stop Linus from taking my home I can manage quite well on my own, but it's a lot to ask of you. You're not responsible for me, Bram.'

He raised her hand to his lips. 'I love you, Lucy. I think I've always loved you, from the very first day when you wandered off into the forest and I had to rescue you. I'll do anything I can to save you from more heartache, even if it means that I risk losing you to Charter.'

She held his hand to her cheek. 'That will never happen. There's only one man for me and it's you. It always has been.'

'What about Northam? You were almost engaged to him.'

'It was something my grandfather wanted for me, and my life was different then. I was a child when I last saw you, and I had no reason to think we'd ever see each other again.'

'I don't like leaving you, but I have to put an end to this cat and mouse game.'

'You needn't worry about me. I can cope with anything now.' She stood on tiptoe and brushed his lips with a kiss. 'You'd better go quickly before I change my mind and beg you to stay.'

He drew her into his arms and kissed her. For a brief moment she clung to him, dazed by a rush of desire and a maelstrom of emotions. Then she broke away, forcing her lips into a smile. 'How will you get to London? The poor old horse barely made it here.'

'I heard Johann saying he was going into town for supplies. I'll get him to take me to the station. I suppose I'd better go and tell Monty. He'll be angry because it upsets the act, but he'll be delighted to get rid of me. Keep him at arm's length, Lucy, and watch out for Stella. I've seen the way she looks at you.'

'Don't worry about me. I'm used to taking care of myself.'

'When this is settled you'll have me to look after you. I'll never let you go again, and that's a promise.' He strode off in the direction of Johann's caravan.

Vicky and Maggie came hurrying towards her, spilling water as they swung the buckets by the handles. 'Where's Bram going in such a hurry?' Vicky demanded.

'He looks cross,' Maggie added, dumping her

bucket on the ground beside Lucy. 'Why was he angry?'

Lucy put her arms around their shoulders. 'He had to go to London on business. He didn't want to leave us, but he'll be back very soon.'

Maggie's bottom lip trembled. 'I don't want Bram to go away again.'

'Don't be such a baby, Mags.' Vicky eyed the dirty plates, frowning. 'I suppose I'll have to do the washing up, as usual.'

Lucy straightened up with a sigh. 'I'll do it. Why don't you go to Jenny's van and see if she's made any cakes on that little stove of hers. I don't know how she does it, but she's a wonderful cook, and very generous. You could offer to mind her babies in return.'

Maggie brightened instantly, tugging at her sister's hand. 'I love Jenny and the little ones. Let's go.'

Vicky rolled her eyes. 'All right, if you insist.' She met Lucy's amused gaze with a sigh. 'I suppose I'd better keep an eye on her.'

Lucy tried not to laugh as they walked off hand in hand. Suddenly everything was back to normal. She had the children to look after as well as Granny, and Bram loved her. She could hardly believe he had uttered those magic words, but it made it even harder to part and she wished with all her heart that she could go with him. She looked round at the sound of footsteps on the sun-baked ground. Froniga hurried up to her. 'It's a miracle,' she said breathlessly. 'Eva spoke to me quite sensibly just now. She knows that you're her granddaughter.'

'I know. It happened quite suddenly. One moment she thought I was my mother and then everything seemed to fall into place. It's such a relief.'

Froniga gave her a searching look. 'He's gone, hasn't he? I can tell by your face.'

'He thought someone ought to be in London to put a stop to the game Linus is playing.'

'And you want to go with him?'

'Of course I do, but I can't leave the children, and Granny is my responsibility, not yours. You've been marvellous, Froniga. I don't know what I'd have done if you hadn't been there to help.'

'I can look after the youngsters, and Eva can help me. It would give her something to think about other than herself.'

'I can't just walk out on Monty. He's been good enough to take us in. It would be very ungrateful.'

Froniga stood arms akimbo, a determined look on her face. 'And why do you think he's been so good to you? Do you imagine that Stella is jealous for nothing? Use your head, girl. Stop worrying about other people for once and follow your inclinations.'

'Do you think I should go with Bram?'

'That's something only you can decide, my duck. But I know what I would do if I was in love with the fellow.'

Chapter Twenty-Three

Bedwin's rheumy eyes opened wide and his jaw dropped. 'Miss Lucy. You've come home at last.'

Forgetting that she was mistress of the house, Lucy flung her arms around him and kissed his papery cheek. 'I couldn't stay away a day longer. I've been so worried about you and Hester.' She bent down to make a fuss of Peckham, who had seemingly forgotten his aged bones and had come to greet her, wagging his stumpy tail.

'Him and me are growing old together,' Bedwin observed with a hint of a smile.

'I love you both,' Lucy said, giving the dog an extra pat. 'It's good to see you.'

Bram dumped their hastily packed valises on the floor. 'How are things, Bedwin? Has Mr Daubenay been troubling you?'

'Not in person, sir.' Bedwin stood to attention. A touch of colour had sprung to his cheeks and he was suddenly alert. 'I wouldn't have admitted him if he had. This is Miss Lucy's house.'

Lucy breathed a sigh of relief. 'Thank you, Bedwin. I knew I could rely on you.'

'You're a good man.' Bram slapped him on the shoulder. 'I'll take these cases up to our rooms.'

'That's my job, sir.'

Bedwin made a move to pick up Lucy's valise, but Bram shook his head. 'I'll do it. I need to stretch my legs.'

Lucy flashed him a grateful smile. 'And I must see Hester and find out what's been happening while I've been away.' She made her way downstairs to the kitchen, where she found Hester preparing vegetables for the evening meal.

'Lucy.' Hester dropped the knife and hurried round the table to give her a hug. 'Thank God you've come home. Linus came to the house yesterday while Bedwin was out. I didn't tell the poor old chap because he gets all of a flutter.'

Surprised by this unexpected outward show of emotion, Lucy returned the embrace. 'Are you all right, Hester? I hope Linus didn't say anything to upset you.'

'He tried to make me tell him where you were, but he doesn't frighten me. I told him to go to hell.' Hester's cheeks flushed rosily and her generous bosom heaved. 'I've seen him at his worst and for two pins I'd have knocked him down with my rolling pin.'

'Hester, you're a marvel.' Lucy took off her bonnet and tossed it onto one of the pegs behind the door. 'It's good to be home. Bram has come with me and he's determined to put an end to Linus's threats and bullying.'

'Where are the little ones?' Hester asked anxiously. 'Are they safe and well? Linus mustn't be allowed to get his hands on them. He might be their father but he's no more feeling for them than a codfish.'

'Don't worry about them. They're thriving and they love everything about the circus. I left Froniga in charge and she won't stand for any nonsense.'

Hester put her head on one side. 'And what about Eva?'

'She was in a bad way at first, but she's recovering slowly.'

'I'm glad to hear it, even if I'll never understand how the woman could sell her own flesh and blood. Anyway, I'd better put the kettle on. You must be hungry and thirsty after your journey.'

'Has it been very difficult here on your own? I mean, have you been able to manage with just the money from the lodgers?'

'I got used to making do on a pittance when I was with Meg, but we were a bit short of the reddies so I took in someone else to help make ends meet.'

Lucy pulled up a chair and sat down. 'Another gentleman?'

'No, as a matter of fact it's a lady. Well, I suppose you could call her a lady.' Hester pursed her lips. 'A theatrical person. She's appearing at Wilton's music hall.' She lowered her voice. 'She sings bawdy songs, or so I've been told. Gilbert and Leonard took the boy there to see her perform. They asked me to accompany them but I said I didn't like that sort of vulgarity.'

'Even so, it's quite exciting.' Momentarily forgetting her problems, Lucy leaned forward, resting her elbows on the table. 'Is she here now?'

'Sleeping.' Hester moved the kettle onto the hob. 'Sleeps all day and gets up in time to go to the theatre. Eats like a bird and is always asking for hot water. I never knew anyone who washed themselves as much as she does. I know cleanliness is next to godliness, but she carries it a bit too far.'

Hester lowered her voice. 'And she smokes little black cigars.'

'I'm looking forward to meeting her,' Lucy said, suppressing a giggle. She had never seen Hester shocked by anything before, which made the mystery lady even more interesting. She glanced over her shoulder as Bram entered the room. 'I expect you're ready for some refreshment.'

'I am indeed.' Bram pulled up a chair and sat down beside her. 'Who were you talking about?'

'Hester's just told me that we've got an interesting new lodger – a lady who performs on stage in Wilton's music hall. Perhaps we could go and see her, Bram. It would be lovely to do something together.'

Hester turned to stare at them. 'What's going on between you two?'

'Nothing,' Lucy said hastily. 'We're good friends, as always.'

'Seems like there's more to it than that, but it's none of my business.' Hester sniffed and stood on tiptoe to take the tea caddy from the mantelshelf. 'I'll need some money if I'm to feed both of you as well as the lodgers.'

Bram reached for Lucy's hand beneath the table and gave it a gentle squeeze. 'Don't worry, Hester my love. I've got funds, and I've no intention of letting Linus get his hands on what's left of my money.'

Lucy returned the pressure on his fingers. 'What next? Will you go and see Mr Goldspink?'

He nodded. 'Yes. I need to find out if there are any developments, and then I think I'll pay a call on Linus.'

'Is that wise?'

'I'm not afraid of him, Lucy. The nippers are safe with Froniga and you're here with Hester and Bedwin. What can he do, that he hasn't done already? I'll pay him back the money he says you owe him and have done with it.'

'There's no need for that.' A silvery voice from the doorway made them all turn to look at the woman who leaned against the door jamb, striking a dramatic pose. She paused for a moment, allowing them time to observe the elegant cut of her purple silk gown, which accentuated her voluptuous bosom and an impossibly small waist. 'Since Miss Gant seems to have lost her tongue I'll have to introduce myself.' She walked slowly towards them, gliding swan-like over the flagstones. 'My name is Christelle Arnaud.'

Lucy stared at her with a strange stirring in her breast. The intriguing newcomer was not in the first flush of youth, and the blush on her cheeks might have been created by a skilful application of rouge, but she was a remarkably handsome woman. There was something achingly familiar about her sparkling green eyes and guinea-gold curls which convinced Lucy that they had met before, and slowly the truth dawned upon her. She rose unsteadily to her feet, hardly able to breathe. Her pulses were racing so fast that the blood drummed in her ears, and for a moment she thought she might faint. 'Mama?'

Christelle frowned. 'Don't call me that. I'm too young to have a grown-up daughter.'

'But you are my mother, aren't you?'

'I gave birth to you, my dear, but I am not the

maternal kind. I'd much prefer it if you would call me Christelle. Besides which, my husband isn't aware of your existence, and I would rather he didn't find out until I'm ready to break the news to him.'

Bram pushed his chair back and stood up to place a protective arm around Lucy's shoulders. 'You should think yourself lucky to have such a wonderful daughter.'

'You're more than fortunate,' Hester said angrily. 'I wouldn't have taken you in if I'd known you were the one who abandoned your child. Shame on you, woman.'

Christelle shrugged her delicate shoulders. 'Sticks and stones. I'm inured to bad press, so nothing you can say will make any difference. I'm an artiste, and as such I lead a different life from the dull day to day routine of people like you.'

Hester opened her mouth to retaliate but Lucy held up her hand. 'This is getting us nowhere.' She turned to her mother, trembling but in full control of her emotions. 'You're right, Christelle. You don't know me nor I you, so why did you come here? It couldn't have been by chance.'

'Why don't we all sit down and talk this over like civilised people?' Bram said, pulling up a chair.

Christelle sank down gracefully, arranging her skirts with well-manicured hands. 'I would like a cup of tea, if you please, Miss Gant, or something stronger if you have it.'

'And what if I don't please?' Hester muttered.

Lucy shot her a warning look, but Hester merely shrugged and rose from the table to take a cup and saucer from the dresser. If Christelle had heard she chose to ignore Hester's remark. 'A tot of brandy would go down nicely,' she said, sighing. 'I dislike emotional reunions of any sort.'

'Why did you come here?' Lucy repeated the question, scarcely able to believe that this beautiful but seemingly self-obsessed woman was the mother she had longed to find.

Hester slapped a cup of tea down on the table in front of Christelle. 'There are no spirits in the house. You'll have to go to the pub if you want to get drunk.'

Christelle gave her a brittle smile. 'You're too kind.'

'Did you come here knowing that this was my home?' Lucy asked urgently. 'I don't understand why you've gone to the bother if you're not interested in me.'

Christelle sipped her tea, eyeing Lucy over the rim of the cup. 'If I tell you the truth you'll be shocked.'

'I don't think there's much that would shock me,' Lucy said with a wry smile. 'You left Granny and me to cope on our own. We survived the best way we could.'

Christelle flicked a glance at her, and looked away. 'I knew you were well cared for. Your grandfather wouldn't have anything to do with me, but you were his only grandchild and I was certain he would look after you. As to Ma, I knew she would protect you like a tigress.'

'You know nothing of my life.' Lucy stood before her mother, gazing down at her in a mixture of disbelief and anger. 'Granny and I lived on the streets for years, stealing sometimes just to put food in our mouths, while you were travelling the world and living in luxury.'

'Answer that if you can.' Hester clutched the teapot as if she would like to bring it crashing down on Christelle's coronet of golden curls.

'So why have you come back now, Christelle? And why come here if you're not interested in your daughter's well-being?' Bram moderated his tone although Lucy could feel the tension in his fingers as they rested on her shoulder.

'My being here should prove something to you, young man.' Christelle looked him up and down. 'You're a handsome, well set up fellow. Are you two lovers?'

'Are you always this rude to people you barely know?' Lucy demanded. 'Or do you want to humiliate me further?'

'My dear girl, I returned to London with only one thought in mind.' Christelle's eyes narrowed to cat-like slits. 'I intended to put a bullet through Linus Daubenay's wicked heart.'

There was a stunned silence. Lucy was the first to speak. 'You wanted to kill Linus? Why?'

'He murdered my husband. I've waited for eighteen years to wreak my revenge on that despicable man.'

'Murder? I was told that my father died in a duel.'

'Julius died at the hands of his cousin, Linus Daubenay. He was a much better swordsman than my poor husband. It was cold-blooded murder.'

'But it was a duel,' Bram said slowly. 'Why did they fight?'

'I think you'd better tell us everything,' Lucy murmured, sinking down onto her chair.

Christelle produced a gold case from her reticule and took out a cigarillo. She eyed Bram with a seductive flutter of her eyelashes. 'Have you a match?'

'I don't hold with smoking in my kitchen,' Hester said primly.

'I'm beginning to dislike you, Miss Gant.' Christelle bared her teeth in a smile which did not reach her eyes. She sat back in her chair, folding her white hands over the gold case with a sigh. 'Linus was my lover before I met Julius. I was very young, little more than a child, with dreams of becoming a music hall star. He was rich and handsome and he turned my head with his compliments and promises to make me famous, but then I met your father. It was love at first sight for both of us.'

'Trollop,' Hester said loudly.

'Julius asked me to marry him but Sir William forbade him to have anything to do with me, so we ran away. We lived in a hovel south of the river and that's where you were born.'

'And then you got married,' Lucy said breathlessly.

'No. That's not true. We were married in secret before you were born. I can show you my marriage certificate if you don't believe me.'

'But Linus had a copy of it which proves that I'm a bastard.'

'The only bastard in this case is Linus himself.'

'But why have you come looking for me now, after all these years?' Lucy demanded.

'I've had to wait a long time before I had enough money saved to return to London. My husband handles my financial affairs and he's a generous man when it comes to buying me clothes and jewels, but had he known my intentions he would have tried to stop me.'

'As any man would,' Bram said, frowning.

Christelle's slender fingers tightened around the gold case and her knuckles whitened. 'I knew where Linus lived and I went to his house, determined to make him grovel before I put an end to his worthless life, but when I saw him in his drunken debauched state I knew that he had been the architect of his own downfall. There was no need for me to commit murder.'

Lucy uttered a sigh of relief. Despite her mother's indifference she could not bear the thought of her ending her life at the end of a hangman's noose. 'What did he tell you?'

'When he realised that I couldn't go through with my plan he reverted to his old arrogant, boastful self. He told me how he'd cheated you out of your inheritance by obtaining a copy of my marriage certificate and that he'd altered the date so it looked as though you were born out of wedlock.'

'I can't believe that even he would stoop so low,' Lucy said slowly.

'There's nothing that man wouldn't do. He never forgave me for leaving him for Julius, and he was determined to destroy my happiness. He seems to have carried his vendetta on to the next generation, namely you, my dear girl.'

'He ruined my sister's life,' Bram said angrily.

'She was the sweetest person you can imagine, but he used her and then abandoned her. I think she died of a broken heart.'

'That sounds so like him.' Christelle took a cigarillo out of the case and stood up. 'I'm sorry, Miss Gant. I must have a smoke.' She moved gracefully to the range and lit a spill.

'Pity you didn't pull the trigger,' Hester said with a grim smile. 'If anyone deserved to be shot it's that bastard, if you'll excuse my language.'

Lucy stared at her mother, trying to understand what had motivated her to consider such a desperate action. 'But what did he do to make you hate him so much? He's a despicable person but there must be something you're not telling us.'

'This isn't easy for me.' Christelle inhaled smoke and exhaled with a sigh of satisfaction. 'I don't like talking about it, but you were a baby at the time and we were living in dire poverty, even though Julius had found himself a job in a counting house. His meagre wages only just kept us from starvation. Then one day Linus turned up on the doorstep. He said that he had come with a message from Sir William. I was young and naïve and I let him in, and he forced himself on me. He took me on the floor like an animal while my baby lay sleeping in her cradle. When Julius came home he found me in a terrible state. It was all I could do to prevent him going after Linus there and then.'

'That's awful,' Lucy said slowly. 'But you were in London. The duel was in Paris.'

'I thought Julius had left for work as usual next

morning, but I discovered later that he had gone to Half Moon Street, intent on having it out with Linus. The servants told him that debt collectors had been hammering at the door and Linus had fled to Paris. When Julius returned home he told me what had happened, but he couldn't look at me, let alone touch me. Later that evening he walked out of the house and I never saw him again.'

Lucy sensed her mother's deep distress and she longed to comfort her, but she was at a loss to know how. 'That must have been terrible,' she whispered. 'I'm so sorry.'

Christelle tossed the butt of the cigarillo into the fire and sank down on her chair. 'It was the worst time in my life. I had no money and no way of finding out what had happened to my husband. If it hadn't been for Ma I think we would have starved to death. Then one day Sir William came to tell me that Julius had followed his cousin to Paris, and they had fought the fatal duel.' She fixed her lambent gaze on her daughter. 'Can you imagine how I felt? I was just sixteen and a widow. He offered to take you and bring you up as his own, but I refused. A decision I came to regret.'

'That's quite a story,' Bram said warily. 'It's so far-fetched it could be true; either that or you're an accomplished actress, Miss Arnaud.'

Christelle inclined her head. 'Thank you, but I can assure you that every word is true. And it's Madame Arnaud.'

'Did you go to France when you left us?' Lucy asked dazedly. She was shocked but somehow unsurprised by the things she had just heard. It was not difficult to believe that Linus had behaved in such a despicable fashion.

'I couldn't afford the rent, small as it was. We moved north of the river and took a room in Whitechapel, not far from here. Ma did her best to earn money selling second-hand clothes in Rosemary Lane, but it wasn't the life I wanted for myself and I couldn't convince myself that Julius was dead. I was desperate to find his grave if only to say a last goodbye.' She lit another cigarillo. 'I earned a little money by singing in the local pubs, and then I met a French sailor who promised to take me to Paris. He smuggled me onto his ship, but having got what he wanted he abandoned me in Calais. I'm not proud of myself for being such a young fool. I was still only sixteen and didn't speak a word of French. I had no money and I was stranded.'

'Serves you right, if you ask me,' Hester muttered. 'Women of easy virtue usually get what they deserve.'

'Hester!' Lucy turned on her, scowling. 'That's enough. Can't you see it hurts Mama to speak of such things?'

Hester shrugged her shoulders. 'I've got to get on with supper or you'll all starve.'

'I've told you everything,' Christelle said, rising to her feet and tossing the half-smoked cigarillo into the fire. 'I confess that I didn't come to London to find you, Lucy. But suddenly, and to my surprise, I felt the need to see my girl and find out what sort of woman she had become. I asked Linus if he knew your whereabouts but he swore that he had no idea where you were living. He told me to go and see your friend Theodora Northam, although I don't think his intention was to be helpful; he simply saw a way to get rid of me. I still had the gun and he was probably afraid I might carry out my threat. I wish now that I had.'

'So you went to see Dora.' Lucy stood up, facing her mother with a perplexed frown. 'But she wouldn't have known where I was. I've been away.'

'Performing in the circus,' Christelle said, chuckling. 'My dear, you're more like me than you realise. She directed me to your man Goldspink and he told me everything. You've had quite an adventure, Lucy.'

Bram moved to Lucy's side. 'What do you want from her, Christelle? If you didn't come to make amends for abandoning her, why are you here?'

She was silent for a moment. 'I really don't know. Perhaps I do have some maternal feelings after all, or maybe it was just curiosity.'

'And now you have satisfied your curiosity I suppose you'll be heading back to France.' Bram reached out to take Lucy's hand in his. 'Do you really think it was the right thing to come here and rake up all the hurt from the past?'

'I don't suppose I gave it any thought at all.' Christelle's laughter was shrill and mirthless. 'That's the sort of woman I am, but Theodora told me how much Lucy has suffered and how she's handled all the bad things that have happened to her, and it makes me proud to have borne such a child.'

Lucy looked her mother in the eye with an unflinching stare. 'But I'm no longer a child. Are you going to run away again and leave me?'

'I have another two performances at Wilton's,' Christelle said evasively. 'I have to honour my agreement with the manager, and then I should return to France.' She opened her reticule, turning her head to give Hester a whimsical smile. 'No, I'm not going to smoke again. This is something much more important.' She handed a folded document to Lucy. 'This is the genuine marriage certificate. I was going to give it to Goldspink, but I wanted you to see it first. He's already started proceedings to reclaim your estate, or what's left of it, from Linus, but he'll need this to take to court.'

Lucy took it from her and unfolded the sheet of paper. Her eyes filled with tears. 'Thank you. I don't know what else to say.'

'I suppose I should be grateful that you speak to me at all,' Christelle said with a sudden flash of humour. 'Now I really must go and rest before my performance. Will you come and watch the show tonight? I could leave tickets for you at the box office.'

Lucy nodded her head. 'We'll come, of course. I wouldn't miss it for anything.'

On stage Christelle was undoubtedly the star of the show. The audience clapped, cheered, stamped and whistled their approval, calling for encore after encore. Lucy sat with Bram in the gallery overlooking the stage and her heart swelled with pride. For all her faults, Christelle was her mother and she had eventually come to find her. She could have returned to France when she had done with Linus, but she had chosen to take work locally and await her daughter's return. Lucy knew now that the mother–daughter bond was there, even if it was tenuous, and if she had her way it would never again be broken. They might not have the close relationship she would have wished for, but she had a growing admiration for her mother's brave stand against a critical world and her determination to succeed. She turned her head to meet Bram's steady gaze. He smiled. 'She's a star in her own right, Lucy.'

'Yes, she's wonderful. I'm proud of her.'

He leaned forward to kiss her cheek. 'Then you must tell her so. I think it took a lot of courage for her to come here and relive the past. I thought at first it was an act, but then I realised how important it was to her that you understood and accepted her for what she is.'

'I do,' Lucy whispered. 'I couldn't leave my own child, but Ma is different from the rest of us. I suppose that comes with a great talent like hers.'

Bram leaned back in his seat. 'She's a popular lady. Perhaps now she'll return to London more often and make a name for herself here.'

'That would be perfect,' Lucy said, leaning her head against his shoulder. 'And tomorrow I'll take the marriage certificate to Mr Goldspink and hear what he has to say.'

Goldspink looked up from a sheaf of papers on his desk. The office was in its usual state of chaos, with open law books abandoned on the floor and parchment scrolls tied with red tape tossed seemingly at random into the corners of the room. Lucy perched on the edge of the chair with Bram standing at her side. 'Now we have proof of your legitimacy it's a foregone conclusion that you will be able to claim your inheritance.' Goldspink peered at her over the top of his spectacles. 'Or what's left of it, Miss Pocket. I'm sorry to say that the house in Albemarle Street has already been sold to pay off the majority of Mr Daubenay's creditors.'

'I suspected as much,' Lucy said calmly. 'Do you think he'll carry out his threat to bankrupt me? The money in question was for the upkeep of his children, but Bram is prepared to repay it if necessary.'

'If anyone is going to be bankrupted it will be Mr Daubenay. You need not worry about the money you accepted in good faith and no doubt spent for the purpose for which it was intended.'

'Yes, of course, and the children are safe and well.'

Goldspink took off his glasses and huffed on the lenses, wiping them on a grubby handkerchief. 'Where are they now, Miss Pocket? I only ask because it might be better if you removed them from their present abode to a place of safety.'

Lucy's hand flew to her mouth and her stomach jolted as if she had missed a step on the stairs. 'Why? What's happened?'

Chapter Twenty-Four

Goldspink replaced his spectacles, hooking them over his tiny ears, having had to search beneath tufts of grey hair to find them. 'I'd say that Linus Daubenay is now an extremely desperate man. He'll do anything to save himself from the disgrace of bankruptcy, and from what you've told me he knows that his lies have been exposed. The children would seem to me to be his only asset. If he should discover their whereabouts who knows what action he might take?'

Lucy glanced up at Bram. 'We must stop him at all costs.'

He laid his hand on her shoulder. 'Don't worry, my love. He doesn't know where they are and has no way of finding out.'

'I hope you're right, but I won't be happy until I have them safe and sound.' Lucy rose to her feet. 'Am I correct in thinking that Marriott Park will be mine again when everything is settled?'

Goldspink nodded his head, beaming. 'Yes, that is so. Mr Daubenay seems to have run through most of your late grandfather's assets, but you should be left with the estate in Essex, which has a substantial acreage of good farmland and an income from several small tenants.'

Lucy slipped her hand through the crook of Bram's arm. 'It's a bit bigger than a country cottage, but it will make a wonderful home for us and our children.'

His lips twitched. 'Hold on, Miss Pocket. As far as I know it's not a leap year. When the time is right, I'll do the proposing.'

Lucy tossed her head. 'Why would I need to marry at all? I'm an heiress now, Bram. I'm an independent woman.' She turned to smile at Goldspink, who was watching them open-mouthed. 'Thank you for all you've done for me, Mr Goldspink. I understand what you're saying, but the children are in a very safe place. Linus would never find them where they are now.'

They arrived home to find a carriage and pair waiting at the kerb outside the house. Lucy recognised it instantly. 'It must be Dora,' she said excitedly. 'I doubt if Piers would pay a visit after our last meeting.'

'If that fellow is still bothering you I'll put a stop to his game.' Bram stopped to pay the cabby, leaving Lucy free to hurry up the front steps.

Bedwin let her in, but she could tell from his expression that all was not well. 'What's the matter?' she demanded anxiously. 'Is everything all right?'

'Miss Northam is in the front parlour, miss. I think you'd best go in and hear what she has to say, although I couldn't make head or tail of it myself.'

Lucy burst into the room to find Dora seated by the window. She jumped to her feet. 'I've done a terrible thing. I'm so sorry but he made me tell him, and I didn't know what to do. I came straight here in the hope of finding you, although I was afraid you might still be with the circus and if that was the case I would have been quite desperate.'

'What are you talking about?' Lucy asked, pressing her down on the sofa. 'Sit down and tell me what's happened.'

'It's so dreadful. He came to our house and forced his way in. Piers wasn't there and I had to deal with him on my own.'

'You're not making any sense, Dora dear. Slow down and catch your breath. Who came to your house?'

'Can't you guess?' Dora dabbed her streaming eyes with a scrap of lace that served as a handkerchief. 'Linus, of course. He demanded to know where you were, and he kept on and on until finally I gave in and told him about the circus. He was so angry and wild-looking that I was terrified of him. Have I done the wrong thing? Please say you understand and you're not angry with me.'

Lucy shook her head. 'Of course not. You weren't to blame in any way. I know what Linus is like, but he must be stopped. Mr Goldspink warned me that he might try to snatch the children, and I'm sure that must be his intention.'

'But why? I don't understand.'

'It's a bit complicated, Dora. But I have to stop him. How long ago did this happen?'

'An hour ago, or maybe two – I'm not sure. I came here as soon as I'd found the right bonnet to go with my dress. I couldn't wear an ugly straw hat with this peach tussore gown; it simply wouldn't go and I'd have looked a positive fright.'

'I must speak to Bram. Stay there and try to calm yourself, Dora. I'll ask Bedwin to bring you a glass of water.' Lucy ran from the room and was met in the doorway by Bram.

'What's the matter?' he demanded, glancing over her shoulder at Dora, who was sobbing quietly into her hanky.

'Linus forced her to tell him where the children were. He'll have gone to get them, Bram. I know that's what he'll do. He's a desperate man and we have to stop him.'

'Calm yourself, sweetheart. I'll go right away.'

'I'm coming too.'

'All right. I'll go and look for a cab.'

'My carriage is outside,' Dora said, stifling a sob. 'I can take you to the station. Perhaps I ought to come too as it's my fault Linus knows where to find the children.'

'Taking us to the station would be a big help, but there's no need for you to come with us. If you really want to do something for me you could send a message to Mr Goldspink and let him know what's happened.' Lucy knew there was little point in telling her solicitor, but it would give Dora something to do and hopefully make her feel less guilty.

'What on earth is going on?' Christelle appeared in the doorway, blinking sleepily. 'My room is directly above this one and I could hear raised voices and someone crying.' She stared at Dora. 'I know the weeping person. Why is she here?'

'Yes, Mama – I mean, Christelle – you've already met my friend Dora Northam. She came with some disturbing news.'

Dora looked up, her tears drying on her cheeks. 'You're the famous singer Madame Arnaud,' she said shyly. 'You didn't tell me that when you came to call, but I saw an article about you in the newspaper and an engraved portrait, which, if I may say so, didn't do you justice.'

Christelle smiled graciously. 'Thank you, my dear. You're too kind.'

'My parents have seen you perform,' Dora added, warming to the subject. 'They're in Paris, you know. Papa has a position in the British Embassy and I'm thinking of joining them.'

'You'll love it, my dear. Paris is heaven on earth and I've always wanted to see inside the embassy.'

'I'm sure Papa could arrange it.'

'Really, Dora? That would be delightful.'

Bram held the door open. 'You were on your way to speak to your coachman, Dora.'

'So I was. I am a silly scatterbrain sometimes.' Dora picked up her peach tussore skirts and hurried from the room with Bram close on her heels.

'Charming girl,' Christelle said airily. 'The embassy balls are legendary in Paris. An invitation to attend one would be a plume in my bonnet, let alone a feather in my cap.' She turned her attention to Lucy. 'Where are you going in such a hurry?'

'I haven't time to go into details, but Linus made Dora tell him where the children are. He's gone to look for them.'

'They're his brats, aren't they?'

'He didn't want anything to do with them when their mother died. He left them in my care because he thought he'd hooked a rich heiress, and now he wants them because he thinks he might be able to wriggle out of trouble using them as hostages. He has no feeling for them at all.'

'That sounds like the Linus I know and hate. Give me a moment and I'll be ready to accompany you.' Christelle made for the door. 'Don't go without me. I want to make sure that worm gets his just desserts.'

Lucy followed her into the hall. 'Wouldn't it be better if you stayed here? You've got a show tonight.'

'I've waited for years to see Linus humiliated and reduced to nothing. I'm not missing this for the world.' Christelle disappeared into the gloom at the top of the staircase, leaving Lucy staring after her.

It was late afternoon by the time they arrived at their destination. Christelle had entertained them on the train journey with accounts of her many successes on the stages of Europe and far beyond, but Lucy's attention had wandered. She could only hope that they would reach the circus before Linus descended upon the children, wielding his rights as their father.

They clambered down from the farm cart which had been the only means of transport available when they arrived at the station. The farmer had just dropped off several crates of chickens and the cart itself was less than clean. To Lucy's surprise Christelle had taken it all in her stride. She had bundled up her silk skirts and perched on the wooden seat, ignoring the fact that her dainty shoes were resting on a bed of straw and animal droppings.

Lucy left her mother with Bram as she hurried off in search of the children, but she was waylaid by one of the white-faced clowns, who asked if she was going to perform in the show that evening. She had hoped to avoid Monty, but he was standing outside the Starrs' caravan talking to Obadiah, and he spotted her before she had a chance to hurry past. 'Lucy. You're back.' He walked towards her, beaming. 'Have you come to stay this time?'

'I'm looking for the children, Monty. I can't explain now, but I must find them.'

His smile faded. 'And I thought you were eager to see me.'

'This is serious. I must know they're safe.'

'I saw them not ten minutes ago. Bertie was with the horses, as usual, and the two girls were helping Froniga fetch water from the stream.' He caught her by the arm as she was about to walk away. 'What's the matter? Why are you so worried about them? Don't you trust us to take care of our own?'

She glanced down at his strong, suntanned fingers as they closed in a vice-like grip around her arm. 'Let me go, please, Monty. I'm seriously worried about their safety, and it has nothing to do with the circus people.'

He loosened his hold and his handsome features relaxed. 'They are perfectly all right, but you are obviously upset and I want to know why. Don't you think you owe me an explanation?'

'It's very complicated.'

'You obviously need my help.' He glanced over Lucy's shoulder. 'I see Bram coming towards us with an elegant lady. You need to tell me everything.'

As briefly and succinctly as possible she did her best to satisfy his curiosity, ending as Bram managed to guide Christelle over the rutted, sun-baked field to her side. 'So this is your mother, Lucy,' Monty said, bowing to Christelle. 'I'm honoured to welcome the famous Madame Arnaud.'

She extended a gloved hand. 'I'm surprised that my fame has spread this far.'

'The good people of Essex have yet to be treated to your talents, Madame, but we have travelled Europe with our circus and I've had the privilege of seeing you perform.'

'I'm flattered and delighted,' Christelle murmured coyly. 'I really must consider doing a tour of my native land, especially now that I've been reunited with my beautiful daughter.'

'You must allow me to show you round my small empire, Madame.'

'Please do.' Christelle gave him a coquettish smile. 'I've always wanted to see a real circus.' She sniffed the air. 'We must be near the animals' cages. This is real indeed.'

Lucy started to edge away. 'I must find the children. Monty assures me that they're safe and well but I need to make sure.' She turned to Bram. 'Will you come with me? I'm afraid that Linus might show up suddenly and take us all by surprise.'

'Of course I will.' Bram took her by the hand. 'We'll leave this evening and take the children with us, Charter. You'll be glad to see the back of us, no doubt.'

'Not at all. In fact I was going to suggest that you stayed to see the show. I'm sure I can find reasonably comfortable accommodation for Madame Arnaud, and you are both quite used to sleeping under canvas.'

'That would be delightful,' Christelle said before anyone had a chance to speak. 'I myself would find it highly diverting. I might even be persuaded to do a number.'

'But you have a performance at Wilton's tonight,' Lucy said hastily. 'Had you forgotten?'

'No matter. We wouldn't be back in time anyway, and I'm sure they will manage without me.'

'That's settled then,' Bram said firmly. 'We'll find the children and make sure they stay with us.'

Lucy shot him a grateful smile. 'Thank you,' she whispered as they walked away without giving Monty a chance to argue. 'Mama has a new audience to charm and it will take her mind off Linus. The only trouble is that she has yet to meet Granny. I think there might be sparks flying when those two get together.'

'Don't worry about that, sweetheart. Let's find those nippers and make sure we don't lose sight of them. The two older ladies can fight it out in private.'

Lucy tugged at his hand as they approached the area where the horses were being prepared for the evening show. 'There's Bertie. You'd better tell him what's happened and I'll go and find the girls.'

She found them outside Froniga's tent preparing

a meal under Eva's supervision. They shrieked with delight the moment they saw her and abandoned their culinary duties to race across the grass and hurl themselves at Lucy. 'I've missed you,' Vicky said, hugging her. 'But you're back now.'

'I've missed you too.' Maggie's eyes filled with tears. 'You won't leave us again, will you, Lucy?'

'No I won't, and that's a promise.' Lucy could have cried too, but it was with relief on finding the children safe and oblivious to the danger they faced. 'Now put me down and let me go and give Granny a hug.'

Eva walked slowly towards them. She was still a shadow of her former self, but there was a smile on her face and a spring in her step. 'Welcome back, my duck.' She embraced Lucy and for a moment they clung together, united by blood and a love that had never died.

'I have a surprise for you, Granny,' Lucy said when they were settled round the fire, drinking tea laced with a tot of Froniga's medicinal brandy, which she had produced to celebrate Lucy's return.

'A surprise?' Eva and Froniga exchanged knowing glances.

'My crystal ball tells me that there might be a wedding soon,' Froniga said, smiling.

Lucy knew she was blushing but she shook her head. 'It's not that. I think your crystal ball must be fogged up or you might have foreseen her arrival.'

'Don't mock my powers, young lady,' Froniga said, wagging a finger.

'And don't keep us in suspense.' Eva leaned towards Maggie, patting her on the shoulder. 'Be careful when you turn that bread. Those stones are red hot from the fire and you'll burn your fingers.'

'Don't worry, Granny,' Vicky said calmly. 'I'll keep an eye on her. Anyway, the bread is almost done and the stew is ready. I'm blooming starving.'

'We'll eat in a minute.' Eva turned to Lucy. 'Well, what is this surprise?'

Lucy scrambled to her feet. 'I can see her coming. I was going to break it gently but she's beaten me to it.'

Eva shielded her eyes as she peered into the glow of the setting sun. Silhouetted against the fiery crimson, orange and purple-streaked sky, Christelle walked slowly towards them. She came to a halt, staring at her mother with raised eyebrows. 'You look as though you've been in the wars, Ma.'

'Christelle?' Eva struggled to her feet and they faced each other, neither moving, their expressions stony.

Lucy looked from one to the other. 'Say something, please. Aren't you pleased to see each other?'

'Well, you're a sight for sore eyes and no mistake,' Eva said, breaking the silence. She patted Christelle on the shoulder. 'You look as though you done well for yourself, girl.'

'Ma, you old fright, what's happened to you?' Christelle held her at arm's length, shaking her head. 'I can see I'll have to take you in hand.

Where did you get those awful clothes? You look like a rag-bag.'

'Leave her alone,' Lucy said angrily. 'Granny's suffered enough without you making it worse, Mama.'

Christelle shot her a sideways glance. 'Don't call me that. I'm Christelle to you, young lady.' She tempered her words with a crooked smile. 'Ma understands, don't you, old girl?'

'I see that nothing's changed. You're still the same stubborn, wayward girl you always were, Christelle Pocket, but I still love you and that will never change. A mother's love is forever.'

Christelle stared at her for a moment and then, to Lucy's astonishment, her face seemed to crumble beneath the layer of powder and rouge. Tears rolled down her cheeks and she wrapped Eva in an embrace that swept her off her feet. 'Ma, I'm sorry,' she sobbed. 'I've been a bad daughter and an even worse mother.'

'What's up with her?' Maggie demanded, staring at them in amazement. 'Why is the painted lady crying?'

Vicky grabbed her sister by the hand. 'We need another bowl. We'd better see if we can borrow one from Jenny.'

Froniga rose slowly to her feet. 'This is a family matter. I'll go for a walk.'

'No, don't go.' Lucy caught her by the sleeve of her flowing gown. 'You're as much part of our family as I am, Froniga. None of this would have been possible without you.'

Froniga's eyes filled with tears. 'It's so long since I had a real family I've almost forgotten what it feels like to belong.'

Lucy hooked her arm around her shoulders. 'I don't know what magic you worked, if any, but it's brought us all together. I never thought I'd see my real mother and yet here she is.'

Christelle released Eva with a smacking kiss on her lined cheek. 'That's for all the kisses I should have given you when I was a girl, but I'm a woman now and a rich one too. The first thing I'm going to do is buy you a new gown, Ma. I can't afford to be seen with a mother who looks like a scarecrow.'

'Cheeky mare,' Eva said, mopping her streaming eyes. 'I ain't in me dotage yet, Christelle. I can look after myself, given half a chance.'

'You're coming back to France with me, Ma.' Christelle produced her cigarillo case and offered it round. 'I need a dresser when I'm on tour. You'll have the time of your life.'

Eva shook her head. 'No, ta. But I could do with a tot of brandy to keep the cold out.'

'Maybe we ought to eat first,' Lucy suggested, having spotted the girls racing across the grass towards them. 'We're not out of trouble yet. There's a lot to tell and I'd like to do it with a clear head.'

'It's Linus, isn't it?' Froniga said slowly. 'I had a feeling something bad was going to happen tonight.'

'You and your feelings.' Eva picked up a ladle. 'Let's have some of this delicious stew that Vicky and Maggie helped to make.'

'And the hot bread.' Maggie handed her the enamel bowls. 'It's a bit burnt but it will taste nice.'

Lucy sat down on the grass beside Vicky. 'I've come to take you home.'

'To Leman Street?' Vicky's bottom lip trembled. 'I like it here, Lucy. I don't want to go back to the city.'

Lucy cleared her throat, tapping her spoon against the tin plate to attract everyone's attention. 'The good news is that Marriott Park is mine, or very nearly. It's big enough for all of us to live there, including you, Froniga, if you could bear to give up your travelling life.'

'At my age it's getting harder and harder,' Froniga said, smiling. 'I think I might enjoy staying put for a change.'

Eva had been about to start serving the stew but she paused, looking Lucy in the eye. 'That is good news, but I can tell by your face that there's something else.'

Lucy was about to answer when Maggie uttered a cry of fright. 'Pa. It's Pa.' She pointed in the direction of the big top. 'He's coming to get us. Don't let him take us away.'

Chapter Twenty-Five

Lucy leapt to her feet, ready to fly at Linus if he came close enough to threaten the children, but he was already being challenged by Bram and Monty. They were too far away for her to hear what passed between them, but she could tell by their actions that it was not a friendly conversation. She put her arms around the girls as they too had stood up and were clinging to her. 'It's all right. Bram won't let him take you away from us. We're all here to protect you.'

'Pa is a bad man,' Maggie sobbed. 'He hit Ma and made her cry.'

'I'm not going anywhere with him,' Vicky added fiercely. 'He used to beat Bertie if he made him angry, and I was always afraid he was going to hit me too.'

Lucy watched Linus being ushered none too gently towards the exit and she breathed a sigh of relief. 'He's gone. The circus people will make sure he's not allowed in again, but you two must stay close to us this evening. We'll leave first thing in the morning.'

Christelle held her bowl out to Eva. 'That's that, then. I'm hungry and the stew smells delicious. Can we eat now? I need to keep my strength up if I'm to entertain the good people of Essex tonight.'

Lucy kept the girls at her side all evening. They were given front row seats to watch the show, which thrilled Vicky and Maggie even though they had seen the performance many times, but Bertie chose to stay with Bram to help with the horses. Lucy knew they were safe but somehow she could not relax, despite being surrounded by crowds of ordinary people who were simply out to enjoy themselves. She had already had a brush with Stella who, once again, had made it clear that she was not welcome. Lucy had tried to be friendly but nothing she said seemed to have any effect. Stella, she realised, was an implacable enemy, but they would be leaving in the morning and it was unlikely they would ever meet again. The future looked brighter now and she was reunited with her mother; she must concentrate on the good things in her life and try to put the past behind her.

She came back to the present with a start as a trumpet fanfare introduced Monty, who entered the ring on his black stallion, closely followed by Bram on the roan he had ridden in previous shows. Lucy sat on the edge of the seat as they went through their old routine but without her. In her impossibly pretty pink riding habit she had acted as a perfect foil for the two daring horsemen. She had been the object of their rivalry, much to the delight of the audiences who had alternately booed and cheered as the two young men vied for her hand. Now they were riding at speed, picking up hoops on the points of swords, before enacting a mock duel on horseback. Vicky and Maggie clapped and cheered with the rest of the spectators, shouting the loudest when Bram performed feats of horsemanship that only a well-trained hussar could accomplish. Lucy had never been so proud of him, and when they took a bow it was to her that he doffed his hat. Not to be outdone, Monty attempted to follow with a similar routine, but it was obvious that he was more of a showman than an expert equestrian.

The rest of the acts followed in swift succession, Dario and Stella entering the ring just as Johann finished his eye-watering performance as the world's strongest man. Stella paraded round the ring, demonstrating the sharpness of the knives by throwing up an apple and slicing it into quarters before it fell to the ground. She moved closer to Lucy, running her finger across the blade so that a tiny spurt of blood showed scarlet against her pale skin. The menace in her expression was obvious to all, but the audience seemed to think it was part of the show; only Lucy knew better and a chill ran down her spine.

Finally, with an introduction delivered by Monty in the most glowing terms, Christelle walked into the ring and with only a fiddler to accompany her sang a selection of popular songs, ending with a rendition of 'Home Sweet Home'. The applause was deafening, with loud stamping, whistling and cries for more. Christelle performed an encore but it seemed that the crowd would never let her go, and in the end Monty had to come to her rescue. She left the ring waving and blowing kisses to the delighted audience.

Lucy ushered the girls outside the big top to find her mother surrounded by admirers. Froniga and Eva were hovering close by, and judging by the expression on her grandmother's face Lucy could see that she was revelling in Christelle's success. The reunion with her long lost daughter had completed Eva's transformation from a bewildered, sickly shadow of her former self to something like the woman she had once been.

Monty made his way through the crowd, forging a path towards Christelle, who was in danger of being swamped by all the attention. 'Ladies and gentlemen, stand back please. Make way for the star of our show.' He reached Christelle, holding his hand out to her. 'Come, Madame, allow me to escort you to your caravan.'

'Star of the show indeed.'

The sound of Stella's voice made Lucy turn to see her emerge from the shadows, glowering at them. 'Leave us alone, Stella,' she said softly.

'Why did you come back?' Stella hissed. 'Why can't you stay away from my man?'

'That's not why I'm here. Anyway, we're all leaving in the morning. You won't see us again.'

'I don't believe you. He hasn't been the same since you came on the scene. He loves me and only me, but you've got the witch to cast a spell on him.' Stella pointed a shaking finger at Froniga. 'She brought you here and she made him want you and not me.'

'You're mad,' Lucy said in disbelief. 'Froniga may have second sight but she's not a witch. They only exist in storybooks.'

Stella's eyes narrowed and her lips twisted into a snarl. 'You beguiled him with your fancy words and ladylike ways.'

Lucy could see that Stella was working herself up into a rage and it was useless to try to reason with her. 'I'm not interested in Monty. I–' She broke off as someone shouted a warning. She turned to see Linus forcing his way through the crowd, but Bram had seen him first and tackled him, bringing him to the ground.

'Froniga, take the girls away. Keep them safe.' Lucy's voice cracked with fear. She was too far away to do anything, but Eva had already seen the danger and she made a grab for the girls, who were standing frozen to the spot as they witnessed the ugly scene.

Bertie emerged from the crowd, shouting at his father to leave them alone, but Linus was like a man possessed. He broke free from Bram's hold and lunged at Froniga, who had placed herself between him and the children. Monty abandoned Christelle to join Bram and they advanced on Linus, moving slowly like hunters stalking their prey. The crowd drew back, forming a circle around the protagonists, once again seeming to think that this was part of the show. Lucy made a move towards her grandmother, intent on protecting the girls, but Stella seized her by the arm. 'Let them fight it out,' she said in a voice that throbbed with anger. 'Let the stupid bastards kill each other and be done with the lot of them.'

Lucy snatched her arm free. 'Don't be ridiculous.' She was about to rush forward when she saw the flash of a steel blade. Linus had a knife in his hand, but as he raised his arm, seemingly intent on stabbing Bram, the sound of a pistol shot rang out, stunning everyone into silence. The percussive echo boomed like thunder in the darkening sky and Christelle stepped forward, holding the smoking gun in her right hand. For a moment Lucy thought that someone must have been shot dead, but it seemed that her mother had fired above their heads. 'I planned to kill you, Linus Daubenay,' she said in a loud voice. 'But a quick death is too good for you.'

Linus pointed the knife at her. 'Fetch my children or I'll take pleasure in slitting your throat, you Jezebel. I should have done it years ago instead of killing my own flesh and blood.'

Lucy could stand it no longer. She pushed her

way through the crowd to stand a few feet away from Linus. 'Haven't you done enough harm to my family? You killed my father and tried to take everything from me.'

A ripple of interest ran through the onlookers, who moved forward a few inches, craning their neck to get a better view. Linus brandished the knife. 'Don't try to stop me. I want the brats, all three of them.' He glared at his son, who was standing at Lucy's side. 'Get over here, boy, and bring your sisters. We're leaving, and I'll kill anyone who tries to stop us.'

Bram moved a step closer. 'You can't get away with it, Daubenay. Put the knife down and leave now. You're not taking the nippers anywhere.'

Linus spun round to face him. 'Another word from you and I'll take great pleasure in slitting your throat. You always were a damned nuisance.' He beckoned to his son. 'Come here, Bertie. I won't harm you or your sisters. I'm your pa. You have to do as I say.'

'I'll come with you,' Bertie said in a shaking voice. 'But only if you promise to leave the girls here with Lucy.'

'Of course, son. I've been a good father to you, haven't I?' Linus stretched his lips in a smile, but his eyes were like dark holes in his pale face, and his hand shook.

Forgetting everything but the need to protect the children, Lucy pushed Bertie aside and walked slowly towards Linus with hands outheld. 'Leave them all with us, please. Don't do this to them, Linus. They're just children, not pawns in your game.'

'You're ruined, Daubenay,' Bram added, inching closer. 'Give up now before you do something you'll regret for the rest of your life.'

Monty also took a step forward, but Linus had spotted him and he sprang at Lucy, gripping her round the neck and pressing the knife to her throat. 'Give me the children and let us leave here now. Lucy is coming with me to make sure we're not followed.'

'No! You can't do that. I won't let you.' Bram lunged at him, but Linus twisted Lucy round so that she was acting like a shield.

'One more step and I'll slit her throat instead of yours. If she dies the estate will revert to me as the only living relative.'

Lucy struggled and tried to kick out with her feet, but Linus was stronger than he looked and he had his arm around her throat, pressing on her windpipe. He increased the pressure and she had to fight for every breath until she felt herself slipping into a state where she was barely conscious. Dimly she heard Bram's voice, and Monty was shouting, but she could not make out the words. She went limp and Linus relaxed his hold just enough to allow her to gasp for air.

'You fool,' Christelle said icily. 'If you kill my girl the only thing you'll get is the hangman's noose.' She pushed Monty aside, advancing on Linus with the gun still clutched in her hand. 'Let her go or I'll shoot. Don't think I won't, Linus Daubenay. You killed my husband – I won't allow you to take my only child from me.'

'Let him finish her off.' Stella rushed at Christelle, taking her by surprise as she snatched the pistol from her hand. She pointed it at Lucy. 'Kill her, mister. I don't know what she's done to you but she's taken my man from me. If you don't kill her, I will.'

Lucy felt Linus stiffen and his grip loosened. The red mist that had blurred her vision cleared and she met Stella's malevolent stare with a defiant look, but it was obvious that Stella meant business.

'Put the bloody gun down, you mad bitch.' Linus took a step backwards, dragging Lucy with him, but in his eagerness to get away from Stella he did not see Bram, who grabbed him from behind.

Quite what happened then Lucy could never remember. There was a moment of complete chaos and then a shot rang out and Linus fell to the ground, taking her with him. Winded and struggling to fill her lungs with air, Lucy felt herself being lifted to her feet. 'You're all right, my darling. You're safe now.'

As she regained control of her breathing she was aware of people rushing round, shouting, and Monty's voice calling for calm.

'Are you all right, Lucy?'

She could smell her mother's heady perfume and she opened her eyes to see Christelle's concerned face hovering above her. She managed a weak smile. 'I was winded, that's all. What happened?'

Bram helped her to her feet. 'Stella tried to shoot you and got Linus instead.'

'Is he badly hurt?'

'The crazy woman did what I'd planned to do,'

Christelle said with a grim smile. 'Linus won't be harming anyone ever again.'

'The children. Where are they?'

'Eva and Froniga are looking after them,' Bram said gently. 'This is a matter for the police now. I think we might have to stay here for a while longer.'

The police came and arrested Stella, who was taken to Chelmsford prison to await trial. A sense of shock numbed everyone, young and old. Bertie had witnessed the whole thing and he was shaken but seemingly unmoved by the death of his father. Lucy went with Bram to break the news to the girls. Their stoical acceptance of the fact was more upsetting to Lucy than floods of tears. Linus had never shown affection to any of his offspring and to them he was little more than a stranger, and a violent one at that.

Lucy remained in her tent next morning, unsure of her reception if she went outside. She was afraid that people might blame her for Stella's actions. Vicky and Maggie had risen at daybreak and gone to Froniga's tent for breakfast, but Lucy had no appetite. She might have stayed inside all day if Jenny had not paid her a visit. 'You mustn't blame yourself, Lucy. We all knew what she was like,' she said gently. 'Stella was one of us, but most people were a bit scared of her if the truth be told.'

'But I do feel responsible for her actions, at least in part. Perhaps I could have done more to convince her that I wasn't interested in Monty.'

Jenny laid her tiny hand on Lucy's arm, her large grey eyes filled with compassion. 'It wouldn't have made any difference, love. It was obvious to everyone that Monty fancied you, and to be fair to him he'd made it plain to Stella that their little fling was over long before you arrived. She just wouldn't accept it.'

'Thanks, Jenny. I told the police that Linus was a madman and that Stella probably saved my life, but they wouldn't listen.'

'We're all going to put some money towards paying a lawyer to stand up for her in court,' Jenny said softly. 'Maybe if you told him that he'd be able to save her from the noose.'

Lucy patted her hand. 'I will, and what's more I know a good solicitor. If you haven't found one already I'll ask Mr Goldspink to take her case.'

Jenny scrambled to her feet. 'Goldspink? That's a country name for a goldfinch. I like the sound of him. Bertram is organising everything so I'll put it to him, but I expect he'll be more than grateful to have the matter taken out of his hands. Bad news travels fast and a murder at the circus might put people off coming, or attract a lot of rowdies who are out for trouble.' She lifted the tent flap. 'I'll let you know what he says.'

Lucy put on her boots and prepared to go outside.

The circus people were in deep shock. Dario was inconsolable and Monty went round with the look of a man haunted by his past. Bertram took it upon himself to try to keep spirits up, but performances were cancelled until the police had had time to interview all those concerned. It took several days for them to ascertain the facts and interview everyone who was present that evening, which included most of the village. Bertram had hoped to keep the events of that fateful night from the wider public, but the news leaked out and the local newspaper sent a reporter. The sensationalised article attracted the attention of Fleet Street and soon they were besieged by reporters, clamouring for interviews with the famous Madame Arnaud who had heroically tried to save her daughter from being murdered by a madman. Stella's part in Linus's sudden death seemed to have been forgotten and Christelle had become the heroine of the hour. Lucy was content to sit back and let her mother deal with the press, and Monty, now apparently recovered, took every opportunity to publicise his show.

Days later, when everything was slowly getting back to normal, Lucy had left the children helping with the horses and was about to go in search of Froniga to tell her of their plans to return to London next day when she saw Monty approaching on horseback. He reined in beside her and dismounted, handing the reins to one of the roustabouts. 'I've just come from the magistrate's court. Stella is pleading insanity.'

Lucy met his intense gaze with a puzzled frown. 'She was mad with jealousy, but I don't think she was out of her mind.'

'None the less, that's what she's been advised to plead. Juries can be quite sympathetic to women who claim to be insane. She'll probably be sent to a lunatic asylum instead of the gallows.'

Lucy shuddered. 'That might be a worse fate. If she's not crazy when she goes in, the odds are that she soon will be.'

Monty laid his hand on her shoulder. 'She tried to kill you and she took someone else's life instead. She can't walk away from a crime like that.'

'She loved you, Monty. She was obsessed by love for you. Isn't some of it your fault for encouraging her?'

He recoiled as if she had slapped his face. 'That's a cruel thing to say.'

'But you were lovers. She told me that.'

'That was a long time ago, and it was over before you joined us.'

'Not in her mind. She thought you wanted me.'

His hand slid down her shoulder to caress the exposed skin on her forearm. 'She was right. I fell in love with you the first moment I saw you, Lucy. But I honestly didn't know that she still felt anything for me, if she ever did. I don't think love came into it where Stella was concerned. It was more about power and possession.'

Lucy flicked his hand off. 'I don't believe you. She tried to kill me before and yet you treated it more or less as a joke. Did it flatter you to have a woman so desperate for your attention that she would commit murder?'

'No,' he said fiercely. 'How can you think that of me? I'm used to temperamental people. We're none of us like ordinary folk, that's how we come to be in this profession, but I had no idea what was going on in Stella's head.'

'You can't wriggle out of it like that.' Lucy was angry now. Stella had been driven mad by lust for a man who had used her. 'You're no better than

Linus. You take what you want from women and then you abandon them. That's exactly what he did to Bram's sister. I'm going to ask my solicitor to take Stella's case and I'm afraid it won't look good for you.'

He dropped his hand to his side. 'You're still upset. It's understandable after all you've been through.'

'We're leaving in the morning,' Lucy said, averting her gaze. She was shaken by his declaration of love but she was determined not to let it show. 'I suppose I should thank you for taking us in, but I see now that you had an ulterior motive.'

He grasped her by the shoulders, giving her a gentle shake. 'How can you think that of me? I love you, Lucy Pocket. You're all that I ever wanted in a woman. Won't you stay with me? We can build an act that will bring audiences from far and wide. We could travel the world and make a life for ourselves.'

She wriggled free from his grasp, shaking her head. 'You only have one true love and that's your circus. Everything you do or say is connected to it in one way or the other. I admire your dedication but I couldn't live with an obsession like that.' She held up her hand as he opened his mouth to respond. 'And more to the point, I don't love you.'

His brows snapped together in an angry frown. 'Then you were leading me on. What did all those coy looks and sweet smiles signify if you didn't have feelings for me?'

'I admit I was attracted to you at first and I was grateful to you for giving us shelter, but that's all it ever was. I'm sorry if you got the wrong impression, but my heart belongs to someone else.'

'I should have allowed my sword to slip while we were rehearsing. You might feel differently if your soldier hero was no longer with us.'

'I have a mind of my own, Monty. I know who I love, and I'm sorry but it could never be you. The one person who was totally devoted to you is now in prison. She's paid a terrible price for loving you.' Lucy turned on her heel and walked away. She could hear him calling her name but she did not look back.

They arrived back in London to find the house surrounded by newspaper men who had somehow got wind of their arrival. It was clear to Lucy as she stepped onto the pavement that it was her famous mother who was the object of interest, and she left Bram to help Christelle alight. Reporters swarmed around them, shouting questions and vying with one another to get the best position possible. Lucy managed to dodge them and ran up the steps to knock on the door. Bedwin opened it just as a hackney carriage pulled up and the children spilled out, followed more slowly by Eva and Froniga. Lucy beckoned to them and they hurried into the house before the men from the press realised that they might have missed another angle to their stories.

She closed the door. 'Don't worry about Christelle,' she said when Eva gave her a questioning look. 'Bram will see that she doesn't get trampled to death in the crush, and she revels in all the attention.'

'That is so like her.' A small, mustachioed gentleman wearing an expensively cut pinstripe suit emerged from the front parlour.

'We have a visitor, Miss Lucy,' Bedwin said apologetically.

'I am Pascal Arnaud.' The dapper gentleman bowed to Lucy. 'I have come to London to find my wife.'

Lucy stared at him in amazement. So this was her stepfather: she was about to introduce herself when Eva stepped in between them. 'Cor blimey,' she said, staring at him curiously. 'You're my son-in-law, mister.' She turned to Fromiga with a triumphant grin. 'You never saw that one coming did you?'

Froniga shook her head but her reply was drowned by someone hammering on the door. Bedwin hurried to open it and Christelle breezed in followed by Bram, who slammed the door and leaned against it. 'Those fellows are harder to get rid of than a swarm of bees.'

'Pascal.' Christelle stared at her husband in disbelief. 'What are you doing here?'

He embraced her, kissing her on both cheeks. 'That is not much of a welcome, chérie. I've travelled all the way from Grasse to find you.'

She peeled off her gloves, handing them to Vicky, who was staring from one to the other with great interest. 'I left you a note, Pascal. I told you that I had unfinished business in London and that I would be home as soon as it was completed.'

Lucy cleared her throat nervously. 'Er, aren't you going to introduce us, Mama?'

'Mama?' Pascal twirled his moustache with agitated fingers, his dark eyes taking in every detail of Lucy's appearance. 'You must be mistaken, mademoiselle.'

'This is my daughter, Pascal.' Christelle indicated Lucy with a casual wave of her hand. 'I might have forgotten to mention that I had a child. It was such a long time ago and I was very, very young when she was born.'

'I am speechless.' Pascal looked from one to the other. 'Such an admission to make after all the years we've spent together.'

'You always was a poor liar, Christelle,' Eva said, wagging her finger. 'You chose to forget you was a mother. You should think yourself lucky to have such a beautiful daughter.'

'It's all right, Granny,' Lucy said hastily. She held her hand out to Pascal. 'I'm very pleased to meet you, sir. Welcome to my home.'

Pascal raised her hand to his lips. 'Thank you, mademoiselle. I too am happy to make your acquaintance.' He cast a darkling look at his wife. 'But a little warning would not have come amiss, chérie.'

Bedwin coughed politely. 'Might I suggest you adjourn to the parlour, ma'am? You might like some refreshments after your long journey.'

'What a good idea. I'm sure you two have a lot to discuss.' Lucy shooed the children towards the basement stairs. 'Hester will be longing to see you. Go and surprise her.'

'I smell baking,' Bertie said, grinning. 'Hester must have known we were coming.' He followed his sisters, urging them on in his hurry to reach the kitchen.

'Shall I bring tea and cake, Miss Lucy?' Bedwin

lowered his voice to a whisper. 'We don't have any coffee, which is what the gentleman seems to prefer.'

'I'll go and get some,' Bram said in a low voice. 'And I'll go out the back way or I'll have to face the reporters again. Apparently our story is still headline news.' He followed the children downstairs.

Eva marched into the parlour. 'I need to sit down.'

'Me too. I'm exhausted.' Froniga followed her.

Left in the entrance hall with her mother and stepfather, who were eyeing each other like gladiators about to enter the arena, Lucy looked from one to the other. 'Please don't argue. It's wonderful for me to have a family after all these years of being orphaned. We're complete now.'

Christelle put her arm around her daughter's waist. 'I think motherhood suits me, don't you, Pascal?'

'It has been a shock, of course, but I am a man of the world.'

'Of course you are, my love.' Christelle treated him to a beaming smile, but he responded with an ominous frown.

'You should have told me before, but I am content to have a delightful stepdaughter. Even so, there is a problem, Christelle, as you are well aware.'

'What are you talking about, Pascal?'

'The shooting to death of that man in the circus, chérie. You were involved, and the publicity will do your career no good. We must return to France immediately. Anyway, I have a concert booked for you in Paris, next week, and after that Madrid and then Rome. You cannot afford to have scandal attached to your name.'

'Paris.' Christelle closed her eyes. 'That child, Lucy, your friend whose parents live in Paris. What was her name?'

'You mean Dora Northam.'

'Yes, dear Dora. She promised me an introduction to the British Embassy. I've always dreamed of being asked to perform at one of their balls.' Christelle glided into the parlour and subsided onto a chair by the fireplace.

Lucy hurried after her, followed by Pascal. 'But you can't go yet, Mama. You've received offers to tour England. You said you wanted to come home. Please don't leave me so soon.'

Chapter Twenty-Six

Christelle sighed, smoothing her crumpled skirts. 'So tempting. I don't know what to do.'

'You could start behaving like a mother, my girl,' Eva said crossly. 'You abandoned your child in order to follow your dreams, and now you've got a chance to make amends. I'm not going to be here forever.'

Christelle shot her a withering look. 'You'll outlive us all, Ma.'

'Look out of the window,' Froniga suggested, pointing to the faces pressed against the windowpanes. 'That's your public, Christelle. Are you going to disappoint them by running off to France?'

'Pardon, madame.' Pascal's moustache quivered with suppressed emotion. 'Is it any of your business?'

'Don't speak to her like that.' Eva rose majestically to her feet. 'Christelle, are you going to let your man insult our friend?'

Lucy heard the rattle of teacups on their saucers and she hurried to open the door for Bedwin. 'I'm sure we'd all feel better for some refreshment,' she said brightly.

Bedwin placed the tray on a side table. 'We've got the coffee but Hester said she's forgotten how to make it.'

'Oh, mon Dieu,' Pascal said, throwing up his hands. 'This is an uncivilised country. I can't wait to go home. We're leaving right away, Christelle.'

She regarded him calmly. 'You may go, but I've decided to stay and accept the offers I've received.'

He puffed out his chest. 'I am your husband. I'm ordering you to obey me.'

'I'll return to France when it suits me, Pascal. In the meantime I want you to instruct my maid to pack my costumes and bring them to England. Give her this address.' She turned to Lucy. 'If it's all right with you, my dear girl.'

'Of course it is, but only if you're sure. I mean, perhaps you ought to listen to your husband.'

'Christelle's never listened to anyone in her whole life,' Eva said with a knowing wink.

'I will remain in England as long as it suits me.' Christelle glared at her husband as if daring him to argue. 'Don't try to bully me, Pascal.'

Lucy had been about to pour the tea but she handed the pot to Bedwin, who was hovering at her side. 'Do the honours, please, Bedwin. I'm going to get Mama's room ready.' She shot a sideways glance at Pascal. 'Do I take it that you won't be staying? You'd be most welcome, and it would give us time to get to know each other.'

'Thank you, Lucy. Your kindness is much appreciated, but...' His moustache quivered and drooped and the bravado seemed to desert him, leaving him helpless in the face of an apparently overwhelming burst of emotion. He grasped Christelle's hand and pressed it to his lips. 'I am sorry, chérie. I meant none of the things I said. I am bereft without you. Please come home.'

Christelle's cheeks reddened and her full lips trembled. 'You're just saying these things, Pascal. It is a ploy to make me do as you wish.'

'No, chérie. On my honour, I swear it is true. I love you and I need you. My life is nothing without you.'

'Men will say anything to make you do what they want,' Eva muttered, frowning. 'I was never fool enough to let a man put a ring on my finger. I loved Abe, but he never owned me.'

'That's enough, Ma,' Christelle said sharply. She leaned forward to brush her husband's lips with a kiss. 'You silly old fool, Pascal. You know I'll come home when it suits me, but for the time being I want to stay in London and get to know my daughter.'

He bowed his head. 'I can't live without you, ma belle.'

Lucy looked from one to the other, torn by the desire to beg her mother to stay with her forever and pity for the man whose devotion was beyond doubt. 'I think we ought to leave you to talk this over,' she said softly.

Froniga stood up. 'Lucy's right. I'd like to go to my room anyway. Come along, Eva.'

For a moment Lucy thought that her grandmother was going to argue, but Eva rose slowly to her feet. 'You was always a fool when it came to men, Christelle.'

Lucy found Bram in the kitchen helping Hester to make coffee. He looked up as she entered the room and greeted her with a sunny smile. 'This is how we made it in camp,' he said, stirring the ground coffee into a pan of boiling water. 'I don't suppose it's the way they do it in coffee houses, but it works after a fashion.'

'All this fuss for a foreigner,' Hester said, crossly. 'A good strong cup of tea would do him the world of good.'

Maggie looked up from her plate, munching a mouthful of cake. She gulped and swallowed. 'That funny little man with a curly moustache makes me laugh.'

'I didn't like him,' Bertie said, reaching for another slice of seed cake and receiving a reproving look from Hester. 'Just one more small piece, Hester, darling. I'm a growing boy.'

'You'll have to earn your keep, young man.' Hester shook the wooden spoon at him. 'You can bake the bread tomorrow. What's the use of having a baker's apprentice in the house if he doesn't help in the kitchen?'

'Quite right.' Bram abandoned his attempt to make coffee and pulled up a chair for Lucy. 'I'm a tea man myself. Can't abide coffee.' He sat down beside her. 'What next? We need to have a long talk.'

'The first thing I'll do is get the room ready for my mother. Even if she only stays for a short time it will give me time to get to know her properly, and then I must see Mr Goldspink.'

He frowned. 'Are you still going to ask him to represent Stella in court?'

'You're mad.' Hester slapped a lid on the saucepan. 'That woman tried to kill you according to what Vicky just told me.'

'It's true,' Vicky said earnestly. 'We saw it all, didn't we, Maggie?'

Maggie nodded, rendered speechless by a mouthful of cake.

Hester made a move towards the table. 'You've all had enough to eat. Bertie, you can go and fetch some coal for the range and you girls can help Lucy. Your days of idling with the circus people are over. You're home now.'

Grumbling, the children left the table and drifted off to do Hester's bidding. Lucy sipped her tea and smiled. 'You've got them well trained.'

'Years of practice,' Hester said, taking a seat at the table. 'Now, while they're out of the room you can tell me exactly what's been going on in the wilds of Essex.'

Even though Lucy was eager to be alone with Bram, a suitable opportunity never seemed to arise. The house was buzzing with activity after Pascal left, apparently on the best of terms with his wife. Christelle admitted with a wry smile that she had promised to return to France when her prospective tour of the English music halls came to an end. 'Love is a complicated emotion, Lucy,' she said, sighing. 'Alas, I am the sort of woman who cannot live without a man, but he does not get things his own way.' She winked and tapped the side of her nose with an impish grin. 'You have to know how to handle them, my dear. Now where is my room? I wish to change out of these travel-stained garments.'

As soon as they had snatched a quick breakfast next morning, Lucy and Bram set off for Goldspink's office. He did not seem surprised to see them. 'I read the newspapers,' he said by way of explanation. 'I knew you would arrive sooner or later.'

'How do I stand regarding Marriott Park?' she asked anxiously. 'Is it really mine?'

'It's yours, as is the house in Leman Street. Had Linus's life not been terminated he would have faced criminal charges for his attempt to defraud you of your inheritance, and he still had outstanding gambling debts. He must have been a desperate man.' He rested his elbows on the desk, looking from one to the other with a wry smile. 'We have a satisfactory outcome, and that concludes our present business.'

'Not quite,' Lucy said hastily. 'I'd like you to consider taking on Stella's case.'

His eyes widened, magnified by the pebble

lenses of his spectacles. 'The young woman who shot Linus? Surely there's no question as to her guilt?'

'She was driven mad by jealousy. At the very least she'll plead insanity, and in actual fact she saved my life. Linus clearly intended to harm me and I think he would have killed me there and then if she hadn't intervened.'

'I'm very glad she did.' Bram grasped Lucy's hand and gave it a comforting squeeze. 'But I can't say that I agree, because that woman was intent on harming you, Lucy.'

'But she's not right in the head,' Lucy protested. 'I thought you understood that, Bram.'

'I suppose I do, in a way. But that doesn't alter the fact that she was prepared to go to any lengths to get rid of you. She was responsible for you breaking your arm, and you might easily have broken your neck when you were thrown from that horse. Or had you forgotten?'

'No,' Lucy said angrily, 'of course not. I knew that Stella wanted me out of the way, but Monty was partly to blame. He used her and then he abandoned her. I still say Linus might have killed me if she hadn't intervened.'

Bram frowned, shaking his head. 'I can see that we're never going to agree on this, and yet you expect me to pay for her defence.'

She snatched her hand free. 'How could you bring this down to money? I thought we had an understanding, and we both felt the same about everything, but obviously I was wrong.' She rose to her feet, leaning her hands on the edge of the desk. 'Mr Goldspink, I want you to represent

Stella Smith. I'll be responsible for the costs.' She shot a sideways glance at Bram. 'After all, I'm a woman of property now.'

Goldspink reached for a pad of paper and a pen. 'Give me the details, Miss Marriott, and I'll see what I can do.'

'We'll discuss it later, Mr Goldspink. I have to go now.'

'Lucy, for God's sake be reasonable.' Bram leapt to his feet, but Lucy had reached the door and she wrenched it open.

'I can find my own way home.' She raced down the stairs, blinded by tears of humiliation and hurt pride. She would have entrusted her life to Bram, and she had never imagined that they would disagree so fundamentally about something that was so important to her. Stella was a spiteful, calculating woman, but it was her obsession with Monty that had turned her into a murderer, and the least she deserved was for her side of the story to be heard in court. It was not a question of forgiveness; it was a matter of fairness.

'Lucy, stop. Please.' Bram caught up with her as she reached the foot of the stairs. 'I didn't mean to upset you.'

'I thought you were on my side,' she said angrily.

'I am, of course I am.'

'You brought everything down to money – your money. You sounded just like Pascal when Mama said she wasn't going to do as he wished. You men are all the same.' She headed for the main entrance, but Bram caught up with her in two strides.

'This is ridiculous. You mistook my meaning.'

She turned to face him. 'I think it was perfectly clear. You didn't want to spend your money on paying for Stella's defence.'

'The woman tried to kill you. Why would I want to save her from the law?'

'Because I asked it of you.'

'You're being unreasonable.'

'If you really loved me you'd understand how I feel.'

'I do love you, Lucy. I've always loved you. What's mine is yours, little though it may be.'

'That's not what you said in Goldspink's office.' She opened the door and stepped outside into the crowded street, covering her nose with her hand as the stench of unwashed bodies, horse dung and overfull sewers took her breath away. 'Leave me alone, Bram.'

'I'm not leaving you on your own. You'd be set upon and robbed for your hanky let alone your purse by this rabble.'

'You're forgetting that I was once one of this rabble, as you call them.' She tossed her head. 'I can look after myself. I've been doing it all my life and I don't see the need to change now.' She marched off, head held high. She knew he was following her but she did not look back.

'Let me hail a cab. I'll see you safely home.'

'I'm going to see Dora. It's not far and I'll walk, on my own.'

'You are the most stubborn woman I've ever met.'

She quickened her pace and did not look back until she reached the Strand. Bram was nowhere in sight.

'Lucy. You're safe.' Dora dropped her embroidery hoop and leapt to her feet, holding out her arms. 'I've read all about it in the newspapers, but I didn't know when you were returning to London.'

Lucy embraced her but drew away quickly. 'Sorry, I'm a bit out of breath. It's hot and I walked from Pickett Street.'

'You shouldn't go there on your own. You know what a rough area it is.' Dora moved swiftly to tug at the bell pull. 'Sit down and I'll send for some lemonade, or tea if you'd rather.' She resumed her seat, staring at Lucy with a worried frown. 'What's happened to upset you? It's not because of what happened to Linus, is it? I mean, he deserved what he got. I know I shouldn't say it, but it's true.'

Lucy sank down on the sofa. 'Everything is in a muddle. I don't know what I'm going to do.'

'But you've found your mother. She's rich and famous, and now Linus is no more you'll get what's rightfully yours. You're an heiress and very eligible.'

'Yes, I suppose so. I have the house in Leman Street, and Marriott Park, but...' She broke off, unable to continue.

'But what?' Dora angled her head. 'It's Bramwell, isn't it? What's he done to upset you?'

'I thought he supported me in everything, Dora.'

'Darling, you're bound to disagree about something now and then. Life would be very boring if you didn't.'

'It's more than that, but it would sound like something and nothing if I went into details. I just feel he's let me down.'

Dora moved from her chair by the window to sit at Lucy's side. 'But you love him, and I'm sure he loves you. It's a lovers' tiff, that's all. You're exhausted after all you've been through and you need a rest.'

Lucy gave her a watery smile. 'When did you get to be so wise, Dora?'

'I may not be very clever, but I know what's in people's hearts. I think you ought to go to the country and spend some time away from everyone who takes so much from you.'

'But I love my family, Dora. Are you suggesting I leave them all in London?'

Dora smiled and her dimples deepened. 'Who would you least like to leave behind?'

'The children, I suppose, and perhaps Bedwin. He's as solid as a rock and I know I can depend on him, and Hester too. But she's needed to run the lodging house.'

'What about your grandmother and Froniga?'

'I think they'd rather stay in London, and Mama will be making arrangements to tour the music halls.'

'Then you have your answer. Take your little household with you and leave the others, including Bramwell, to sort themselves out. You can't be responsible for everyone's happiness, Lucy. Sometimes you have to be a bit selfish and do things just for you.'

A tap on the door preceded the maid who bobbed a curtsey. 'You rang, Miss Dora?'

'We'd like tea and lemonade, and perhaps some of Cook's shortbread.'

'Yes, miss.' The maid retreated, closing the door softly.

'I'm going to do something just for me as well,' Dora confided. 'I'm joining Mama and Papa in Paris. Piers will have to find someone else to act as hostess for his boring dinner parties. It's high time he married, but I can't seem to find a woman who's prepared to take him on. I love him dearly, but he's a bit of a bore.'

As if on cue Piers strolled into the room. He stopped, staring at Lucy in overt astonishment. 'Lucy. So you've returned to London none the worse for your adventure.'

'I wouldn't call it an adventure, Piers.' She stood up. 'I'm back, but only for a day or two.' She glanced down at Dora. 'I'm thinking of going to Marriott Park for the rest of the summer.'

'To recover, I should think. You and your family have been headline news for days. I've had people accosting me in the House of Commons, asking about you. I've told them, of course, that we are no longer affianced.'

'We never were, Piers. And perhaps it's just as well considering the scandal I would have brought to your door.'

He smiled and nodded. 'It would have been an embarrassment, but I hope I'm a big enough man to overcome such prejudice.'

'Well, you won't have to since we're just friends.' Lucy treated him to a smile as she made her way to the door. 'I have to go now, but I hope I'll see you before you leave for Paris, Dora.'

Dora rose gracefully from the sofa. 'I'm leaving tomorrow, but this is au revoir and not adieu. You see, I'm speaking the language already. Do tell Christelle to contact me if and when she comes to Paris. I'm sure she'd be more than welcome at the Embassy.'

'My little sister has developed a mind of her own at last.' Piers moved to open the door for Lucy. 'Are you returning to Leman Street?'

'I am.'

'I'm going that way as it happens. I have business in the city and my carriage is waiting outside. I'll take you home.' He held up his hand as she was about to argue. 'Indulge me, Lucy. We've not always seen eye to eye, but I want us to remain friends, and if ever you're in need you know where to come.'

'Thank you, Piers.' She turned to give Dora a fond hug. 'I'll miss you, but we won't lose touch. We'll always be good friends.'

'The best,' Dora said, wiping tears from her eyes.

The carriage drew up outside the house in Leman Street and Piers stepped out to help Lucy alight. To her consternation she saw Bram striding along the pavement towards them. Of all people she did not want him to get the wrong impression. 'Thank you, Piers,' she said hastily. 'I mustn't keep you.'

He bowed over her hand. 'Remember what I said, Lucy. I've never found another woman who could match up to you and I doubt if I ever will.'

'I hope that's not true.' She withdrew her hand, glancing over her shoulder at Bram, whose grim expression said more than words.

He came to a halt, scowling at Piers. 'Is he a

part of this, Lucy?'

'What on earth are you talking about?' Piers drew himself up to his full height, but he was still half a head shorter than Bram.

Lucy marched up the steps to knock on the door, leaving them to posture like prizefighters about to go into the ring. Bedwin let her in and she went straight to the kitchen where she knew she would find Hester. 'I've come to a decision,' she said, taking off her bonnet. 'I'm going to open up Marriott House and take the children away from London for the rest of the summer. Will you come with us, Hester?'

Hester stopped kneading bread dough to stare at her. 'What about your granny and Froniga?'

'I think they'd prefer to stay here, but of course I'll speak to them. If they choose to remain they can look after the lodgers.'

Hester put her head on one side. 'And Bram?'

Lucy could hear his footsteps on the stairs. 'I think he has plans of his own,' she said tersely.

Hester took one look at Bram's face when he strode into the kitchen and slapped the dough into a bowl. 'I've got water to fetch.' She left them facing each other across the kitchen table.

'What was going on with you and Northam?' Bram demanded suspiciously.

'I'm not talking to you while you're in this mood, and it's none of your business anyway.'

'Of course it's my business. I thought we had an understanding.'

'I thought we had too, but it seems that it's based entirely on what you want. You don't seem to think that my opinions count. You assume that

I'll do anything you say and agree with every word you utter. Well, I'm sorry but it's not so.'

'It's not like that.'

'I'm going to Marriott Park for the rest of the summer and I'm taking the children with me. They can run wild and have the freedom they won't get if we stay here.'

'Don't I have a say in it?'

'Not unless you can offer them a better home and a more settled way of life. Can you?'

'I always assumed that we'd look after them together.'

'Then perhaps you should have spoken to me about it first. When I mentioned a home and children you told me to wait for the romantic moment when you would propose. I'm not waiting for any man. I learned that lesson years ago when I thought that Piers and I had an understanding. He backed out at the first sign of trouble.'

Bram ran his finger round the inside of his starched white collar. 'You're being unfair, Lucy. Haven't I stood by you and tried to help?'

'Yes, and you were kind enough to remind me that it was your money I was reliant on. Well, I'll have my own income when I get matters straight and I won't ever have to depend on another person, male or female.'

'Monty Charter wouldn't have anything to do with this change of heart, would he?'

'Why do men always assume they have a rival? I haven't had a change of heart, Bram. But I don't want to make a mistake that will ruin the rest of my life. If I marry anyone it has to be as equals or not at all.' She left the room.

The grounds of Marriott Park were ablaze with colour but the once well kept herbaceous borders were in danger of being strangled by weeds. Dog roses and convolvulus vied with lupins, hollyhocks and delphiniums in their efforts to reach the light. The lawns were knee high in buttercups and daisies and the gravel carriage sweep was pockmarked with scarlet pimpernel and clumps of yellow fumitory. The house itself lay beneath a blanket of dust and a curtain of spider's webs, but Hester and Lucy set about cleaning it with the help of Vicky and half-hearted efforts from Maggie, who had found the library and was more often than not curled up on the window seat with a book. Lucy was prepared to be lenient. 'It's good for her education,' she said when Hester complained.

Bertie roamed the grounds, fishing in the river for trout and helping Ron Lugg snare rabbits for the pot. Lugg was teaching him to shoot and soon pheasant was added to the menu. Peckham was enjoying a new lease of life and hunting rabbits had brought out the terrier in his nature. He followed Bertie everywhere and came home each day dirty and exhausted, wagging his stumpy tail furiously when he rushed up to Lucy and falling asleep on the foot of her bed at night.

Bedwin put himself in charge of the butler's pantry and spent days cleaning the silver which they found locked in a cupboard. Not that they would be entertaining the local gentry in any style, but Bedwin was insistent that they must keep up appearances. Lucy had inherited a country house and an estate and was now a personage of some note in the community. She kept her opinions to herself and concentrated on keeping busy, which was the only way she could stop her thoughts from wandering to what might have been. But she could not control her dreams and it was Bram who haunted them, causing her to wake up with a pillow soaked with tears and suspiciously swollen and reddened eyes. If Hester noticed she was wise enough not to comment.

Lugg put Lucy in touch with Septimus Copper, Sir William's erstwhile land agent, who had apparently been scrupulous in collecting the rent from tenants, paying them into an account at the local bank. Lucy discovered that she had what to her was a small fortune, but as Copper explained, most of that money was needed to make long-needed improvements to the cottages and outbuildings. She spent many mornings sitting with him in the kitchen discussing what needed doing first, and found the business of running a large estate both absorbing and fascinating. They had left the aged carthorse with the circus as well as the cart, and Lucy attended a horse sale with Copper where she purchased a grey mare for herself and three ponies for the children. She also bought three goats, two nannies and a billy, and half a dozen hens. Copper dissuaded her from buying a cow, suggesting that she ought to wait a while before investing in more livestock, and reluctantly she agreed.

Riding her little mare, Lucy accompanied Copper on his visits to the tenant farmers and became acquainted with them and their families. She listened to their problems and made notes as to their requirements, promising to do what she could for them.

The fields were now heavy with golden corn ready for the harvest and the fruit trees were groaning beneath the weight of apples and pears in the orchards. The children were tanned and healthy and, more important, they were happy. Hester was queen of the kitchen and delighted to be away from the stews of London. Bedwin was ruler of the butler's pantry and he laid down the laws of etiquette for the children to obey without question. 'You won't always be little heathens running wild,' he told them solemnly. 'No one likes a man or a woman who eats like a pig and doesn't know how to behave in company.' Lucy smiled to herself, sending a warning glance to Bertie, who looked as if he might argue.

Eva arrived at the beginning of September, having left Froniga in charge of the lodging house. 'Two women in a kitchen is one too many,' she said, dumping her carpet bag on the polished wooden floorboards in the entrance hall. 'Besides which, I may be a Londoner but I wanted to be with my girl again. We was apart for too long, Lucy.'

'I've got your room all ready for you, Granny.' Lucy kissed her fondly. 'I'm glad you feel you can live here with us, and you can visit London whenever you feel the need.' She was about to close the door but Eva held up her hand.

'You've got a visitor, darling girl. Be nice to him.' She sniffed the air. 'I'm starving; I think I can find the kitchen on my own.' She hurried off without giving Lucy a chance to argue.

She went to the door, which had been left ajar, and opened it wide. Her heart lurched against her ribcage when she saw Bram standing on the step, half hidden behind a huge bouquet of red roses. From what she could see of him he was dressed in a well-cut tweed suit. He took off his hat and tossed it over his shoulder. 'I'm done with city life, Lucy. I've come as a humble admirer to beg your pardon for my behaviour. I was being boorish and I promise on my honour it will never happen again. Will you forgive me?'

She was quick to hear the note of uncertainty in his voice, and his expression was that of a shy boy. The sun shone on his hair, and he was once more her golden boy. His smile went straight to her heart, and the look in his eyes sent pleasurable shivers down her spine. She held her hands out for the flowers. 'Of course I will, Bram. Why have you left it so long?'

His reply was to take her in his arms, crushing the roses as he claimed her lips in a kiss that was tender yet demanding, passionate and filled with longing. 'I love you,' he whispered into her hair, holding her close regardless of the shower of red petals that fluttered to the ground at their feet. 'I've always loved you, but I was a pompous fool and I took you for granted.' He released her just enough to look deeply into her eyes. 'Say something. Am I forgiven?'

She answered him with a kiss, winding her arms around his neck and pressing her body against his. She could feel him hard against her and she was dizzy with desire. Her heart and her body were speaking for her, and she mouthed the words against his cheek. 'I love you too, Bram.' She leaned back, holding his gaze. 'And you are forgiven.'

He lifted her in his arms and carried her over the threshold on a carpet of red rose petals.

The publishers hope that this book has given you enjoyable reading. Large Print Books are especially designed to be as easy to see and hold as possible. If you wish a complete list of our books please ask at your local library or write directly to:

Magna Large Print Books
Magna House, Long Preston,
Skipton, North Yorkshire.
BD23 4ND